THE
TRAITOR
QUEEN

THE
TRAITOR
QUEEN

BY *USA TODAY* BESTSELLING AUTHOR
DANIELLE L. JENSEN

Cover Artwork Illustration: Richard Anderson
Cover Design: Silver Wing Press, LLC
Interior Formatting: Silver Wing Press, LLC
Based on *The Traitor Queen*, by Danielle L. Jensen, an Audible Original

Map designed by Damien Mammoliti

Published by: Context Literary Agency, LLC
125R Cedarhurst Avenue, Suite B
Cedarhurst, NY 11516

Ebook: 978-1-7330903-3-9
Bae Crate Hardcover: 978-1-7330903-4-6
Hardcover: 978-1-7330903-5-3
Paperback: 978-1-7330903-6-0

Also by

USA TODAY BESTSELLING AUTHOR
DANIELLE L. JENSEN

THE MALEDICTION TRILOGY
Stolen Songbird
Hidden Huntress
Warrior Witch
The Broken Ones (Prequel)

THE DARK SHORES SERIES
Dark Shores
Dark Skies

THE BRIDGE KINGDOM SERIES
The Bridge Kingdom
The Traitor Queen

https://danielleljensen.com/

For my dearest friend and confidant,
Elise Kova

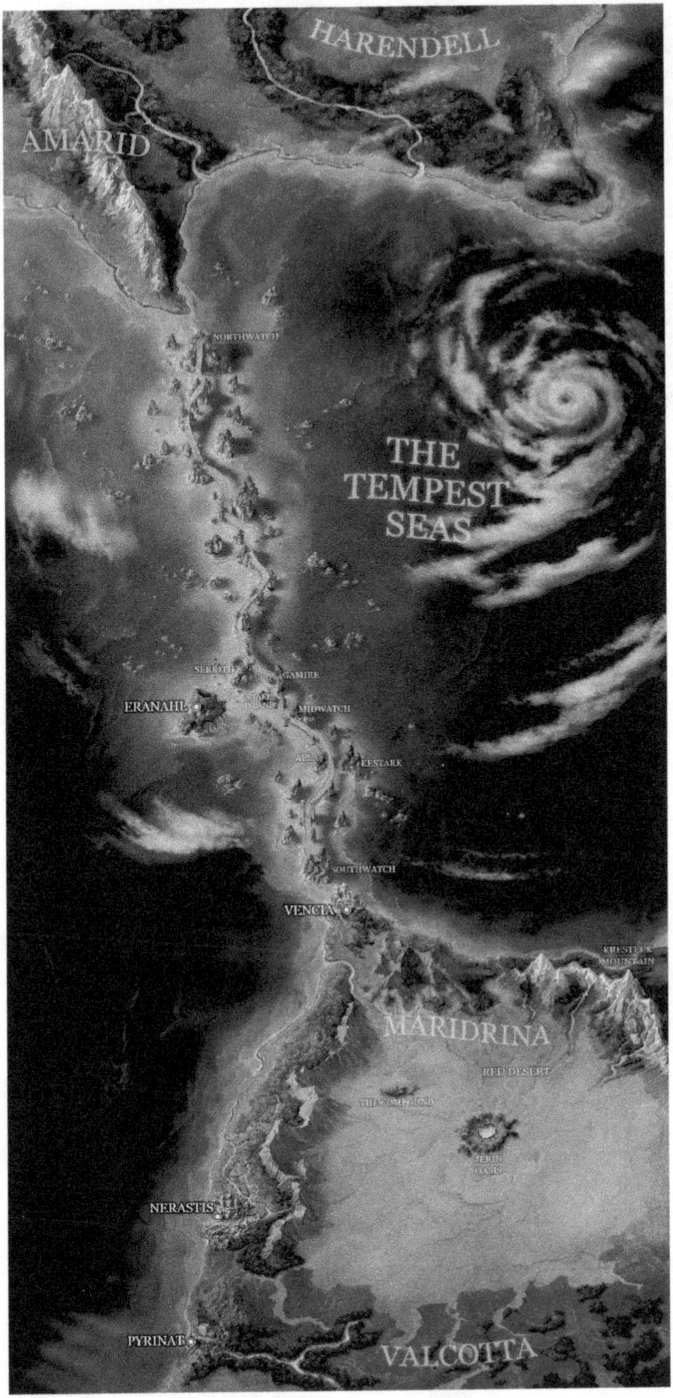
HARENDELL
AMARID
NORTHWATCH
THE TEMPEST SEAS
SERRITH
GAMIRE
ERANAHL
MIDWATCH
KESTARK
SOUTHWATCH
VENCIA
KRESTECK MOUNTAIN
MARIDRINA
RED DESERT
THE COMPOUND
JERIN OASIS
NERASTIS
PYRINAT
VALCOTTA

1
AREN

H<small>E'D BEEN BLINDFOLDED</small> for thirteen days.

Shackled too, and occasionally gagged, but despite the persistent burn of the ropes sloughing the skin of his wrists and the foul taste of the fabric shoved in his mouth, it was the endless shadow of the blindfold that was driving Aren, the former King of Ithicana, to the brink of madness.

For while pain was an old friend, and discomfort almost a way of life, to be confined to what sights his own mind could conjure was the worst sort of torture. Because despite his most fervent wish it were otherwise, all his mind wanted to show him were visions of *her.*

Lara.

His wife.

The Traitor Queen of Ithicana.

Aren had more pressing matters to consider, the foremost how the *bloody hell* he was going to escape the Maridrinians. Yet the practicalities of that need faded as he examined every moment with *her,* trying and failing to decipher truth from lie, reality from the act— though to what end he could not say. What did knowing if any of it had been real *matter* when the bridge was lost, his people were dead and dying, his kingdom was on the brink of defeat, and all of it the result of him trusting in—*loving*—his enemy.

I love you. Her voice and face filled his thoughts, honey hair tangled, her azure eyes bright with tears that carved their way through the mud smearing her cheeks.

Truth or lie?

Aren wasn't sure which answer would be a balm to the wound and which would tear it wide open again. A wise man would leave it alone, but God knew he had no claim to that particular attribute, so around he circled, her face, her voice, her touch consuming him as the Maridrinians dragged him, kicking and fighting, from his fallen kingdom. Only once he was off the seas and beneath the heat of the Maridrinian skies did he get his wish: the blindfold removed.

Wishes were the dreams of fools.

L ARA HADN'T KNOWN Eranahl had a dungeon.

But there was no other word for the dark cell built into caverns beneath the island city, the stone walls slick with mildew and the air stagnant. The steel bars were devoid of even a hint of rust, because this was Ithicana, and even the things that were barely used were well maintained.

Lara lay on her back on the narrow cot, the thin blanket she'd been given doing little to ward off the damp chill, her stomach tight with hunger because she was subjected to the same rations as everyone else on the island.

This wasn't how she'd hoped things would go.

Rather than convincing Ahnna of her plan to rescue Aren from her father's clutches, all her display of martial skill in the council chamber had done was see her slapped in irons, dragged through the city streets, and tossed in this cell. Those who brought her food and fresh water refused to speak to her, ignoring her pleas to see Ahnna.

And every day that passed was another day that Aren remained prisoner in Maridrina, subjected to God-knew-what sort of treatment.

If he was even still alive.

The thought made her want to curl in on herself. Made her want to scream with frustration. Made her want to break free of this place and try to free Aren herself.

Except she knew that would be folly.

She *needed* Ithicana.

If only she could make them realize that they needed her, too.

"GOOD MORNING, YOUR MAJESTY," a voice said as the blindfold was removed from Aren's face.

Aren blinked rapidly, tears streaming down his cheeks as the sun seared into his eyes, blinding him as surely as the sweat-stained fabric ever had. Gradually, the burning white receded to reveal a manicured rose garden. A table. And a man with silvered hair, sun-darkened skin, and eyes the color of the Tempest Seas.

The King of Maridrina.

Lara's father.

His enemy.

Aren lunged across the table, not caring that he was unarmed or that his wrists were bound. Knowing only that he needed to hurt this man who had destroyed everything he held dear.

His fingers inches from their mark, Aren found himself snapped back against his chair, a chain belted to his waist holding him in place like a dog to a post.

"Now, now. Let's not be uncivilized."

"Fuck. You."

The Maridrinian king's upper lip curled with disdain, as though Aren had barked rather than spoken. "You are as your kingdom was, Your Majesty. Feral."

Was.

The sneer turned into a smile. "Yes, Your Majesty. *Was.* For I'm afraid Ithicana is no longer, and your title now a courtesy you will have to do without." He leaned back in his chair. "What shall we call you? Master Kertell? Or perhaps, given we are family of sorts, a certain amount of familiarity is appropriate, *Aren.*"

"I don't give a shit what you call me, *Silas.* As to your other point, the bridge is not Ithicana. *I* am not Ithicana. My—"

"—people are Ithicana," Silas finished, his gaze gleaming with amusement. "Pretty words, boy. And perhaps there is truth to them. Ithicana stands . . . for as long as Eranahl does."

Aren's stomach twisted, the name of his city on his enemy's lips both unfamiliar and unwelcome.

"Such a secret to keep." King Silas Veliant shook his head. "Yet a secret no longer."

"If you mean to use me to negotiate Eranahl's surrender, you're wasting your time."

"I don't waste my time. And I don't negotiate." Silas rubbed his chin. "Nearly all your people gathered on one island, cut off from supplies and with no hope of salvation. How long will they last? How long until Eranahl is not a fortress, but a tomb? No, Aren, I don't need *you* to see the destruction of Ithicana through to completion."

It wouldn't come to that. Whoever was in command of Eranahl would begin smuggling civilians out of Ithicana under the cover of the storms. North and south. Scattered to the winds.

But alive.

And as long as they were alive . . . "If I'm so useless, why am I here?"

Silas steepled his fingers together, silent. Aren's heart sped, thundering against his chest, each beat more violent than the last.

"Where is Lara?"

An unexpected question, given that Aren had expected her to be *here*. Back in Maridrina. Back at her father's side. That she wasn't . . . That her father didn't know where she was . . .

I love you.

Aren shook his head sharply, a bead of sweat running down his cheek. She'd stabbed him in the back, lied to him from the beginning. *Nothing* she'd said mattered now. "I have no idea."

"Is she alive?"

Unease prickled across his skin, Lara's voice echoing through his thoughts: *I thought I'd destroyed all the copies. This is . . . this is a mistake.* The tears in her eyes had glinted like jewels. "Your guess is as good as mine."

"Did you let her go? Or did she escape?"

Please don't do this. I can fight. I can help you. I can—

"Allowing a traitor to go free seems an ill-advised choice." Yet it had been the one he'd made. Why? Why hadn't he killed her when he'd had the chance?

The other man's head cocked. Then he reached into the pocket of his gleaming white coat and extracted a ragged and stained piece of paper, the gilt long worn off its edges. "This was found on your person when you were searched. Such an interesting document."

Silas laid it flat on the table. Aren's writing was barely visible through the watermarks and bloodstains. "On one side, she betrays me. On the other"—he flipped it over—"she betrays you. A puzzle. I must say, we were uncertain what to make of it, especially in conjunction with your visit to my fair city. Tell me, where do you believe Lara's loyalties lie?"

Aren's shirt glued itself to his back, the stink of sweat filling his nose. "Given our present circumstances, I'd say the answer is obvious."

"On the surface, perhaps." The Maridrinian king's fingers grazed over the damning piece of paper. "If I might ask, who killed Marylyn?"

"I did." The lie slipped out before Aren could question why he felt the deception necessary.

"No," Silas mused. "No, I don't think you did."

"Believe what you want. It makes no difference."

Folding the paper, Lara's father leaned over to tuck it into the neck of Aren's shirt. "Let me tell you a story. A story about a girl raised in the desert with her beloved sisters. A girl who, upon hearing that her own father intended to kill her and ten of her sisters, chose not to save herself but to *risk* herself to save their lives. Chose not to flee into a certain future but to condemn herself to a dark fate. All to save those precious lives."

"I've heard this story." Pieces of it. From Lara. And from the sister she'd murdered.

"Heard it, perhaps. But did you understand it? For within every good story, there is something to be learned."

"By all means, enlighten me." Aren lifted his bound wrists. "I'm a captive audience."

Silas chuckled, then asked, "Why, given the girl was so damned and determined to protect her sisters' lives, would she take one of them herself?"

"Marylyn threatened the others."

"The others were not there. She had time. Yet instead of using it, she snapped her sister's neck. Which leads me, Aren, to believe that something she valued greatly was in more immediate jeopardy."

Images flashed across Aren's vision. Lara's face when her eyes had landed upon him on his knees, her sister's knife at his throat. The way she'd searched the room, not for a means of escape, but for a way through an impossible situation. There had only been one choice: his life or Marylyn's.

Silas Veliant leaned across the table, not seeming to care that he was well within reach of Aren's hands. "I made my daughter a promise, *Your Majesty*"—his voice was full of mockery—"I promised that if she ever betrayed me, I'd have her killed in the worst of ways. And I always keep my promises."

Maridrinian bastard blue. That was the color of this man's eyes. And Lara's. But whereas hers had been full of depth and life, staring into her father's eyes was like meeting the gaze of a snake. Cold. Dispassionate. Cruel. "She didn't betray you. You have what you wanted."

A slow smile revealed teeth that had seen too much tobacco. "Even now, after all she's cost Ithicana, you lie for her. You love her."

That was a lie. Lara had cost Ithicana its bridge. Its people their lives. Aren his throne. He *hated* her. "I care nothing for her."

Silas chuckled, then murmured, "We shall see. For of a surety, she knows I have you here. And with even greater surety, she will come for you. And when she does, I will cut her down."

"I'll hand you the sword."

His chuckle turned to a wild, jarring laugh. "We'll see if you're singing the same tune when your wife is on her knees begging for your life. Or when she starts to scream for her own."

Without another word, the King of Maridrina rose, leaving Aren alone and chained in the garden. And though for days all Aren had wanted was *sight* to wipe away the vision of her face, now he closed his eyes to see it. *Run, Lara. And don't ever look back.*

4
LARA

THE SOUND OF footfalls invaded her dreams, and Lara jerked upright, blinking blurrily in the darkness.

How many days had she been down here? Without the sun, the only way to tell was the daily arrival of her singular meal. *Six? Seven?* She shook her head to try to clear the fog, then focused on the light that accompanied the footsteps.

The Princess of Ithicana, Commander of Southwatch Island, and Aren's twin sister appeared before her cell door. Ahnna gave her a once-over. "You look like shit."

"I wasn't expecting company."

And Lara wasn't the only one looking the worse for wear. Ahnna was dressed in the typical tunic, trousers, and boots worn by most everyone in Ithicana, her dark hair pulled into a tail at the back of her head. But shadows darkened the skin beneath her eyes, and her mouth was drawn into a thin line of exhaustion. The wound Ahnna had received fighting the Maridrinian invaders was still a livid red line stretching from forehead to cheekbone, and as Lara watched, she touched it once, as though reminding herself it was still there.

Though she was terrified to ask, Lara said, "Is there news of Aren?"

Ahnna shook her head. "There's been a bad storm sitting above us for close to a week, so we're cut off."

"Then why are you here?"

Taking hold of the bars to the cell with both hands, Ahnna leaned against them. "The whole city is demanding I execute you. Do you know how we deal with traitors in Ithicana?" She didn't wait for Lara to answer. "We dangle them about hip-deep in the sea and then chum the waters. If you're lucky, a big one will come along and finish the job quick, but that's not often how it goes."

Lara stared at the princess. "Do you intend to accede to their request?"

Ahnna was silent for a long moment, before saying, "I'm going to give you the opportunity to convince me otherwise. I think the best place to start is the truth."

The truth.

Aren was the only person she'd ever trusted with it, and even still, there'd been much she'd held back. Lara wouldn't hold back now.

Ahnna listened silently as Lara told her about being taken with her sisters to the compound in the Red Desert. About the ordeal that was their training with Serin, the Magpie. How they'd been brainwashed to believe Ithicana the villain, never once suspecting the true evil was their own father. About the dinner where she'd saved her sisters' lives by sacrificing herself, and then everything that had come after, sparing no detail.

By the time she finished, Ahnna was sitting on the ground, elbows resting on her knees. "Aren told Jor that you escaped. But I knew as soon as I heard that he'd let you go. Bloody sentimental idiot."

"He told me he'd kill me if I ever came back."

"And yet here you are." Ahnna touched the wound on her face, her eyes distant. Then she focused on Lara. "You said you had a plan? A way to get Aren free?"

Triumph raced through Lara's core, but she kept her face in check.

"To get Aren free, yes. But also to liberate Ithicana from my father."

Ahnna's eyes narrowed. "How? The Maridrinians hold all of our garrisons, including Northwatch and Southwatch. They're protected by all the defenses we put into place, and we don't have the manpower to break through them. Believe me, we've tried. That's how Aren got caught in the first place."

"Which is why you need allies."

Snorting, Ahnna looked away. "You sound like Aren. And that's the sort of thinking that got us in this position in the first place."

"Hear me out." Rising to her feet, Lara paced back and forth across the floor of her cell. "After I fled Ithicana, I went to Harendell. They aren't happy about Maridrina holding the bridge, because my father's alliance with the Amaridian queen means Amarid gets preferential treatment at Northwatch and on the bridge. Harendell is losing money hand over fist, and you *know* how they feel about that."

Ahnna nodded.

"The Harendellians don't want Maridrina holding the bridge, nor do they want it for themselves. If we go to their king, I believe we can convince him to aid Ithicana in this fight."

"He's not going to agree to risk his navy just because we ask him nicely, Lara. Harendell might be losing money in trade, but they stand to lose more if they go to war."

"He will if you hold him to his word." Grasping the bars to her cell, Lara met Ahnna's gaze. "The alliance of the Fifteen Year Treaty might be broken with Maridrina, but it still stands with Harendell. Or it will if—"

"If I marry their crown prince."

Squeezing the bars, Lara nodded. "Yes."

In one rapid motion, Ahnna turned away, crossing the corridor to rest her forehead against the opposite cell. Finally, she said, "I've never left Ithicana, you know. Not once."

Most Ithicanians hadn't, only the select few trained as spies, but given who Ahnna was, the information was surprising.

"The moment my mother allowed it, Aren was off like a loosed arrow. North and south, he went everywhere. And there were years where it felt like he spent more time pretending to be someone else in another kingdom than he did being my brother home in Ithicana." Ahnna was quiet for a moment. "I never understood it. Never understood why he would want to be anywhere but *here*."

"Because," Lara answered softly, "he knew there'd come a time when he wouldn't be allowed to leave. Just like you knew there would come a time when you wouldn't be allowed back."

Ahnna's shoulders trembled, and Lara heard the other woman draw in a ragged breath before turning. Digging in her pocket, she extracted a key, which she inserted into the lock on Lara's cell. "What's the rest of the plan?"

I T DIDN'T TAKE him long to determine that they were keeping him in the inner sanctum of the palace in Vencia—a place reserved for the King of Maridrina, his wives, and his numerable progeny. *Why* he was being kept in this place rather than in a cell in one of Maridrina's innumerable prisons was less clear.

Probably because it made it more convenient for Silas to gloat, Aren thought.

As much time as Aren had spent in Maridrina, the palace was a place he'd never been inside. What might be gained from the venture was not worth testing the layers of security Silas kept upon it. Especially for someone of Aren's importance. The only Ithicanian spy to make it inside had been his own grandmother. Nana had arranged to be recruited into the previous king's harem, where she'd lived for over a year before faking her own death to escape. And that had been fifty years ago.

Only now was Aren cursing his lack of knowledge of this place, because it put him at a gross disadvantage when it came to trying to break out of it.

The interior wall was thirty feet high, with guard posts on each of the four corners and soldiers patrolling the top. There was only one gate for entry, which was always kept shut and guarded, both inside and out. Within the inner walls there were two curved buildings, between which stood the tower with its bronze roof that could be seen for miles around. And amidst it all were the gardens, servant women spending their days cultivating the lawns and hedges and flowers, while others swept the stone paths and cleaned the fountains of the debris scattered by the storms, all their efforts to ensure the comfort of Silas and his wives.

There were fifty wives in the harem, the women taking advantage of the breaks in the weather to come outside, all of them draped in the finest of silks, fingers and ears glittering with gemstones. Some were older, but most were young enough to be Silas's daughters, which made Aren cringe. He'd been ordered not to speak to them, though in truth, the women kept far enough away from the stone table at which he was chained that there was never any opportunity.

And then there were the children.

He'd counted sixteen, all under the age of ten, and while not all of them had inherited their father's eye color, several of them had. Each time one of them fixed him with azure eyes twin to Lara's, Aren felt like he'd been punched in the gut.

Where was she?

Where had she gone?

Was she even still alive?

And worst of all: the question of whether she'd take Silas's bait and come for him. *Of course she won't,* he told himself. *She doesn't give a shit about you. It was all lies.*

But if they were lies, why was Silas hunting her?

Why, if she'd given him everything his heart desired, did he want her dead?

The thoughts drove Aren to madness, and chained to a bench in the gardens, he had nothing to distract him, nothing to temper the anxiety that grew in his guts with every day that passed.

A female scream cut the air, snapping Aren from his reverie. Over and over the woman screamed, and Aren watched as the wives who'd been in the gardens fled inside, the servants herding the children with them.

The screams came closer, the guards at the gate moving to open it, revealing a hooded old man who slowly strode between the buildings in Aren's direction.

The Magpie.

"So lovely to see you again, Your Grace." Serin inclined his head. Then he made a face. "Excuse me, I grow forgetful in my old age. You're no longer king, so we are to be familiar, aren't we, *Aren*?"

Aren didn't answer, the spymaster's demeanor wholly at odds with the screaming coming from just outside the open gate. Sweat rolled in fat beads down his spine, his pulse roaring in his ears.

"It happens that you have a visitor," Serin said, and with one hand, he motioned to the guards.

Two soldiers appeared at the gate to the courtyard, dragging a struggling figure between them. Aren tried to stand, but his chains jerked him back down onto the bench.

The woman wore a Maridrinian-style dress, but her face was concealed by a sack. Her clothing was stained with blood, and each time she tried to jerk out of the soldiers' grip, droplets splattered against the pale paving stones.

Was it Lara? He couldn't tell. She was the right height. The right build.

"It was only a matter of time, wasn't it?" Serin purred, extracting a knife from the folds of his robe. "I must say, she was easier to catch than I anticipated. Emotion makes for sloppy execution, even for one with her training."

Aren couldn't breathe. Couldn't think.

"Lara and her sisters are used to pain, Aren. More used to it than you could possibly imagine."

Serin held the knife blade over a brazier one of the soldiers had brought, watching the metal heat. "It was what I used to temper their minds. It's fascinating how despite it being me who burned them—me who cut them, me who buried them alive—that by whispering the right words in their ears, they blamed *you* for their tears. Children are such malleable things. Remove one of her shoes, please."

The soldiers jerked up one of Lara's legs, pulling off her shoe, and without hesitation, Serin pressed the hot blade against the bottom of her foot.

She screamed, and it was the worst sound Aren had ever heard.

He lunged toward her, the stone bench skidding against the ground, the manacles slicing into his wrists, blood running down his hands. "Let her go!" he screamed. "Lara!"

Serin smiled. "And here I'd heard that you cared nothing for our errant princess. That if her father chose to cut off her head, you'd hand him the sword."

"I'm going to kill you for this!"

"I'm sure you'd like to." The Magpie held the knife back above the brazier. "How much do you think she can take? As I recall, Lara was *quite* resilient. Remarkably so."

"Please." Aren dragged the bench, inch by inch, toward her, but the guards only retreated back a pace.

"What was that?" Serin pressed the blade to Lara's other foot, her shrill screams echoing through the courtyard. "Age has done nothing for my hearing, I'm afraid."

"Please! Please don't hurt her."

"Ah." Serin lowered the knife. "Well, in that case, perhaps we might come to an agreement. You tell us how to breach Eranahl's defenses, and all this will be over."

No.

Serin snapped his fingers, and a guard appeared, carrying a leather roll of tools, which the spymaster carefully unrolled. "I've made something of an art of this over the years."

"There is no way to break inside Eranahl." The words croaked from Aren's throat. "The shipbreakers will destroy any ship that gets close."

"What if one had a rather large fleet at their disposal?"

"Try it. See how it goes."

Serin extracted one of the tools. "It's your city. You surely know its weaknesses."

"There are none."

"Shame." Serin turned to Lara, glittering metal in his hand, and a heartbeat later, she shrieked wordlessly.

"Stop! Let her go! Please!" A garbled mix of words spilled from his throat, his body shuddering from the effort of dragging the bench closer. He had to help her. Had to save her.

"How do we get into Eranahl?" Serin turned to look at him. "No? Let's see how she holds up to losing her fingers."

"Pull out the damned gate!" Desperate, Aren screamed the words. It was the truth, except it would do them no good. But if it saved Lara . . .

"How do we manage that?" Serin picked up another tool, and Aren fell to his knees, saying, "Please."

"A strategy, Aren. Give us a strategy, and this will all be over."

At that moment, Lara twisted. Jerking free from the grip of the guards holding her, she threw herself toward Aren, tumbling into him. And before the guards could fall upon them, she reached up with her bound wrists and pulled the sack from her head.

Emra, the young commander of Kestark garrison, stared up at him, her eyes full of agony and desperation. Blood oozed from her mouth, explaining why she hadn't spoken. Her eyes were blackened and swollen.

"Idiots," Serin hissed at the guards. "Get her back."

The men moved closer, their eyes wary, and Aren pulled the young woman against him even though he knew he wouldn't be able to hold them off for long. And once they had her, Serin would torture her until she was dead or Aren gave him what he wanted.

Emra made a noise, the word barely distinguishable. But the plea was clear.

Aren took a deep breath.

"Stop him!" Serin shrieked, but Aren was faster, the crack of Emra's neck breaking stopping both soldiers in their tracks.

Slowly, he lowered the young woman to the ground, not bothering to fight as the men dragged her out of his reach.

"Hang her up," Serin said, and Aren clenched his teeth, forcing himself to watch as the men dragged her over to the wall. One of the soldiers above dropped a rope, which they fastened around her neck, the trio hauling her up until she hung, out of reach, from one of the cornices, the blood dripping from her foot splattering against the green of the lawn.

"Is this how it's to be, Serin?" Aren forced his voice to steady. "You mining Ithicana for young women to masquerade as Lara?"

The Magpie rubbed his chin. "Mining . . . You see, Aren, mining isn't the correct word. That would imply we sought this little bird out, when in reality, she flew to us."

Aren's blood chilled.

"Your people seem unwilling to let you go," Serin said. "And while this was only the first attempt to rescue you, I highly doubt it will be the last." Then he gestured to the waiting soldiers. "Bring out the other two prisoners."

But before they could move, a voice cut through the air. "Good God, Serin! Don't you have holes and dark places where you conduct this sort of business? What's next? Beheadings at the dinner table?"

Aren turned his head to see a slender man dressed in Maridrinian finery watching from a dozen paces away, his arms crossed and his lip curled up with disgust. He picked his way toward them, carefully avoiding the splatters of blood on the path. Behind him, two Maridrinian soldiers escorted a Valcottan woman, her wrists bound. She was tall and slender, her curly dark hair cut short, her brown eyes wide and framed with an abundance of lashes. Beautiful, but her brown skin bore faded bruises and her bottom lip was scabbed where it had been split.

"Your Highness." Serin gave a cursory bow. "You are supposed to be in Nerastis."

"Yes, well, we captured ourselves quite a prize. It seemed prudent that I ensure she arrive in one piece. Broken things make for less valuable leverage."

Eyeing the captive, Serin arched an eyebrow. "General Zarrah Anaphora, the Empress's niece. You've outdone yourself, Highness. You'll be in your father's favor."

"I doubt that."

Serin made a noncommittal noise. "Now that you've delivered her, I assume you'll be returning to Nerastis immediately."

Not a question, but a statement. Whichever one of Silas's sons this was, the Magpie clearly did not care to have him in Vencia.

The prince pushed a lock of his dark blond hair behind one ear, blue eyes regarding Aren with interest. "Is this the Ithicanian king, then? I must say, he's less terrifying than I anticipated. I'm rather disappointed to see that he does not, in fact, have horns."

"The *former* king. Ithicana no longer exists."

The prince's gaze flicked to where Emra hung from the wall, then back to Aren. "My mistake. Do carry on."

Stepping past Aren, he started in the direction of the tower, the soldiers escorting General Anaphora following.

But as they passed, she wrenched out of their grip, falling to her knees in front of Aren. "I am sorry, Your Grace." Her eyes latched on his, and he saw they glistened with tears. "For all that you have lost. And for the part I played in that coming to pass. I pray one day to have the opportunity to atone."

Before Aren could answer, one of the soldiers dragged her back up, snarling, "The only thing you should be praying for is that His Majesty chooses not to spike your head on Vencia's gate, you Valcottan wretch!"

Zarrah spat in the man's face, and he lifted his hand to strike her, but then the prince's voice cut the air, his tone frigid. "Have you forgotten the fate of the last man who struck my prize?"

The soldier blanched and lowered his hand, muttering, "Move along."

The party carried on, but before they disappeared from sight, the prince called back over his shoulder. "Make sure you clean up your mess, Magpie."

"Get the other two prisoners," Serin said between clenched teeth. "Time to see what else his Grace has to offer."

"HOW YOU MADE IT to Harendell and back again without drowning in a sea of your own vomit is a bloody mystery to me, girl."

Lara lifted her face from the sand and wiped a hand across her mouth, pissed off that after three days stuck on rough seas the *ground* now intended to sway and buck beneath her as some personal form of punishment. "It's not an experience I care to repeat." She climbed slowly to her feet before brushing the sand from her skirts.

Only she and Jor stood on the beach, the other Ithicanians—the few survivors of Aren's honor guard—all remaining in the boat, their faces as dark as the skies behind them.

"We don't have time to waste on this errand," Jor said, the politest version of the refrain she'd heard continually since they'd left Eranahl.

"Maybe not." Bending to retrieve her bag, Lara slung it over her shoulder, eyeing the steep hills she'd need to climb. Best to get that done before the sun was fully up. "But given our circumstances, I don't see how we have much choice."

"We could strike now. Your bastard of a father has had Aren for *weeks*, Lara. God knows what has been done to him."

"My father won't have harmed him. Not while he thinks there's still a chance Ahnna will surrender Eranahl in exchange for Aren's return."

Lara had been present when the Ithicanian princess had received the letter from her father. Had read it herself while Ahnna was doubled over with grief, the words dancing across her thoughts now.

To Her Royal Highness, Princess Ahnna Kertell of Ithicana,

It is time this war came to an end. In a gesture of goodwill, your brother, Aren Kertell, will be delivered to you upon the surrender of Eranahl Island to the naval forces surrounding it. Assuming they are peaceable, your people will be brought to Maridrina and, after a suitable length of time, will be gifted lands in the interior where they may settle. We hope you will employ more empathy and foresight toward the future of your people than your brother.

Our most sincere of regards,
Silas Veliant, King of Maridrina and Master of the Bridge

"He's lying," she said to Ahnna. "If you open the gates, he'll slaughter everyone."

"I'm aware," Ahnna answered, lifting her face. "But if I refuse, he might decide that Aren has outlived his usefulness."

"He knows that I'll come for Aren. He won't give up the chance at seeing me dead."

The princess met her gaze. "He knows you'll come to rescue Aren. But he knows you're equally likely to come for revenge."

Jor coughed, pulling Lara back into the moment. "Your father knows Ahnna isn't going to take that deal."

"Maybe. But one can't leverage the dead, and it costs him nothing to keep Aren prisoner. He'll keep Aren alive at least until the war is won."

"You mean until Eranahl falls."

Lara grunted an affirmative. *That* was the clock they were running against. The city was at capacity, and even with rationing in place, the stores were running down at an alarming pace. The fishermen were out in force whenever there was a break in the storms, but they didn't dare venture far. Not with her father paying the Amaridians to risk violent seas to keep watch over the island fortress. Eranahl had enough to last them until the beginning of next storm season, but not a day longer. If they reached that point, Ithicana was well and truly lost.

Jor glared at her. "And with that much at stake, you want us to sit and wait while you attempt to organize a family reunion?"

"That would be ideal." Lara frowned at the dawn sky. "But I expect you'll continue to throw away the lives of our best men and women in an attempt to infiltrate my father's palace. Which will make this rescue even more difficult when the time comes. We need to work together if there is any chance of freeing Aren. And if that's not enough for you, remember that Ahnna agreed to this plan. And last I checked, *she* was the one in command."

Jor exhaled an aggrieved breath, and Lara eyed him warily. This was hard for the old soldier. He'd been with the group skirmishing with the Maridrinians when Aren had been captured, and she knew he blamed himself, though it was no fault of his. Lara had managed to extract the details from Aren's bodyguard, Lia, and had learned that Aren's risk-taking had finally caught up with him. He'd gotten in too deep, and when the Maridrinians realized the prize they had, they'd retreated, allowing Jor and the rest no chance to retake him. "It's not your fault."

"You're right," he snapped. "It's *yours*. And there is no *we*. There is *us* and there is *you*, so don't think to lay any sort of claim to the men and women who've fought and died trying to undo your . . . *mistakes*."

Despite nearly every Ithicanian she crossed paths with having spit some variation of those words in her face, Lara flinched. She deserved their ire, their distrust, their hate because it *was* her fault that Ithicana had fallen. That it had been a mistake compounded by her own cowardice only made things worse. "I know, Jor. Which is why I'm doing everything in my power to undo the damage that's been done."

"Can't bring back the dead."

"Best you hope otherwise," she replied, remembering how her sisters had sprawled across the dinner table, chests still and eyes unmoving. "Or we're well and truly screwed."

Jor spit into the sand. "You can have your weapons back." He reached for the sack at his feet, then swore when the fabric swung limply as he lifted it.

Smiling, Lara pulled up the hem of her skirt, revealing one of the blades she'd stolen back hours ago.

"We thought Maridrina had sent us a sheep," he said, shaking his head. "But the whole time we had a wolf dining at our table, deceiving us all."

"Aren knew." *And had loved her, in spite of it.*

"Aye. And look where it got him."

Aren's face, stricken with the anguish of betrayal, filled her vision, but Lara shoved the memory away. She could not change the past, but she damn well intended to shape the future.

"I'll be back in a few weeks. If I'm not, it means I'm dead." Lara turned her eyes back on Maridrina. If what Marylyn had said was true, her sisters were out there, alive and well.

And it was time Lara called in her due.

"TELL US HOW TO take Eranahl."

Serin whispered the words, the feel of the man's breath against Aren's ear cutting through his exhaustion and sending waves of revulsion down his spine. For days, he'd been locked in the tiny, barren room and subjected to the spymaster's questions, all of which he'd refused to answer.

"There's nothing to tell," Aren growled around the piece of wood they'd fixed between his teeth, lest he get any ideas about biting off his tongue. "It's impenetrable."

"What about up the cliffs?" The tone of Serin's voice never changed, no matter what Aren said. No matter how hard he tried to bait him. "Could a single soldier make it inside the volcano crater undetected?"

"Why don't you try?" Aren attempted to shift his head enough that he could see the spymaster, but the motion sent his whole body rotating on the chains he dangled from, his vision fuzzy from the blood pooling in his head. "Though I expect you already have. Did my sister use the shipbreakers to throw the corpses at your ships? Ahnna has *very* good aim." If she were even there. If she were even still alive.

"Describe the interior of the crater to me." Serin walked with Aren as he rotated. "What does it look like? What materials are the buildings made of?"

"Use your imagination," Aren hissed, but he was having trouble keeping his focus, his consciousness blurring and fading.

Undeterred, Serin kept asking questions. "The gate . . . Is it the same design as the portcullis at Southwatch?"

"Kiss my ass."

"How many soldiers are guarding it?"

Aren gritted his teeth, wishing he'd pass out but knowing they'd only wake him up with a bucket of water to the face. And then it would be more questions. Endless questions. That much Aren knew. After days of this torment, Aren *knew.*

"How many vessels do you keep inside that cavern?"

"How many civilians live on the island?"

"How many children are there?"

All Aren wanted to do was sleep. Anything, anything to sleep. But Serin wouldn't allow him more than a few minutes before tearing him awake in the worst sorts of ways. Ways that made his heart want to explode out of his chest from the panic.

"What sort of supplies does the city have?"

"Where do you keep them?"

"What is their source of water?"

"Rain, obviously!" The words exploded from Aren's lips, his whole body trembling and shaking. Hot and then cold. Why the hell was the man asking such stupid questions?

Abruptly, Aren was lowered to the damp floor of his chamber. Two guards caught him under the arms, then dragged him to his cot, where he was unceremoniously dumped, one of them unfastening the piece of wood from between his teeth and then handing him a cup of water. Aren guzzled it down, and the guard refilled it without comment.

Slumping onto the cot, Aren curled around his chained wrists. *There's no harm in giving him answers to useless questions,* he told himself, barely noticing as the guard tossed a blanket over him. But his anxiety followed him into sleep.

He dreamed of Midwatch.

Of the hot springs in the courtyard.

Of Lara.

Of teaching her to float on her back, her naked body suspended on his hands, her hair swirling on the eddies from the current. She arched her back, full breasts rising above the water, her nipples peaking as cold raindrops struck them. His eyes trailed down the flat plains of her stomach to linger where the froth from the waterfall revealed and then concealed the apex of her thighs, igniting a desire that never truly ebbed when he was in her presence. "Relax," he murmured, not certain whether he was instructing her or himself. "Let the water carry you."

"If you let go of me," she answered, "I shall not be pleased."

"It's only waist-deep."

She opened her eyes to regard him, steam beading on her lashes. "That's not the point."

Smiling, he bent and kissed her lips, tasting her thoroughly before whispering, "I'll never let you go."

But instead of answering, Lara screamed.

Aren's eyes snapped open and he tried to sit, but he was bound to the cot beneath him. The room was cast in total blackness, and Lara was screaming, her voice full of pain and terror.

"Lara!" he shouted, fighting against his restraints. "Lara!"

Then the screams cut off, his ears filled instead by the patter of fleeing footsteps. A door opened and shut, then a lamp flared, burning his eyes and revealing Serin's hooded face. "Good morning, Aren."

It hadn't been Lara screaming. Just another of Serin's mind games. Marshaling his composure, Aren said, "I've had better mornings."

The Magpie smiled. "Two more of your people were caught last night in the sewers beneath the palace—apparently they were unaware of our recently installed security. Care to join me while I give them a *proper* Maridrinian welcome?"

LARA

LARA SHIELDED HER eyes from the blinding glare of the mountain lake, carefully picking out the details of the town built among the trees on its western shore. Over the past week, she'd visited a dozen just like it, cautiously asking questions about a beautiful woman with black hair and ocean-blue eyes.

Sarhina. Her favorite sister. Her closest sister. The sister in whose pocket Lara had deposited her note of explanation moments before she'd poisoned her and the rest.

How certain she'd been in that moment that they'd understand her deception. That they'd wake from their near-dead stupor, find the note, and realize that she'd bought them a chance at life and freedom. That they might not thank her for it, precisely, but would at least realize that it had been the only way for them all to survive.

Marylyn's fury had shaken that belief to the core.

She'd had the most cause to be angry. Marylyn was the chosen sister—the one intended to be the Queen of Ithicana—and Lara had robbed her of that honor. *Or rather the rewards that their father had promised would come with it,* she reminded herself, remembering the manic brightness in Marylyn's eyes when she'd revealed her true motivations.

But perhaps her other sisters had equal cause to hate Lara for what she'd done. Their lives had been spent vying for one position—a position which Marylyn had earned and which Lara had stolen using subterfuge. She'd lied to them all. Poisoned them all. Left them to fight their way out of the Red Desert without camels or supplies. For all she knew, they would take one look at her and slit her throat as punishment.

Sarhina alone was the sister she was certain would forgive her actions.

The brightest of Lara's sisters, Sarhina was a brutal fighter, grim strategist, and natural-born leader. Yet time and again, she'd score in the middle of the pack when by all rights she should've been on top. Average by design, Lara had come to believe, but if any of their masters had suspected her sister's tactics, they'd never been able to prove it. Sarhina hadn't been foolish enough to admit that she was sabotaging her own chances at becoming queen, but fears were revealing, as Lara had come to realize.

"They say Ithicana is shrouded in mists so thick one can't see more than a dozen paces in either direction," Sarhina had whispered to her in the dark nights in their shared bedroom. "That the jungles are so dense one must carve through them with a blade, and the unwary find themselves caught in branches like a fly in a spiderweb. That once you are on the islands, you never see the sky."

"Sounds wonderful," she mumbled. "I could use some respite from the sun."

"Sounds like a tomb," Sarhina replied.

Sarhina's concerns had mattered little at the time, but as Serin had intensified the sisters' training, making them complicit in one another's torture, Lara had come to understand Sarhina's fear. Had watched her sister break down in the pit while the others had rained shovel after shovel of sand on her head, burying her alive. Watched her plead and offer any information in order to extract herself from the situation.

Serin had only thrown his hands up in disgust, screaming at Sarhina that the Ithicanians would bury her alive in truth if she confessed, then ordered her tossed back in the pit to repeat the exercise. Time and again until Sarhina learned to master her terror. To hide it. To compensate for it.

But never to defeat it.

Which was why Lara stood at the highest point in Maridrina: the Kresteck Mountains. The range ran down the eastern coast, craggy and wild, filled with glittering lakes, rushing streams, and the crisp scent of pine. It was thinly populated, mostly hunters and trappers living in isolation in their rough cabins, the few hamlets tucked in valleys and on lakeshores rarely home to more than a hundred people. The range was dangerous to traverse, prone to rockslides, flooding, and in the winter, avalanches, all of which was made worse by the highwaymen who haunted the few established routes running north and south.

A dreadful place in Lara's opinion, cold and unwelcoming. But the peaks reached up to the sky, the view wide and open for miles and miles around, and in her heart, Lara knew this was where Sarhina had gone.

Tracking her, however, would be quite another matter. In the days before that fateful dinner in the desert oasis, there'd been no opportunity to consider how she might reunite with her sisters in the future—not without revealing her plan. Which was why she was dependent on Sarhina finding *her*. The other girls knew their father wanted them dead. Quite possibly they knew that the cover Lara had given them had been compromised by Marylyn. Either way, they'd be prepared for pursuit. And would be equally prepared to deal with anyone who came looking for them. Like Lara, all the Veliant sisters were hunters; she needed only spring one of their traps.

And given she'd been tipped off in the last town that there might be a young woman of Sarhina's description in this place, Lara was certain that she'd finally done just that.

Dismounting, Lara tethered her mountain pony far enough away from the path that he wouldn't be seen, then started toward the hamlet. Smoke rose from the chimneys of the houses, and she spotted two men stretching hides over frames to dry, the fur destined to travel through the bridge and eventually be sold to line the cloaks and gloves of Harendellian or Amaridian nobles. Another man, fine of form and stripped to the waist, chopped wood to add to a formidable pile. An old woman crouched near a fire, basting the meat turning on a spit, and behind her, a gaggle of children raced through buildings, their laughter drifting through the trees to reach Lara's ears.

She circled the town, marking each individual and the weapons they wore as well as the best routes for escape if the situation escalated. The mountainfolk were peaceful enough, but necessity made them both wary of strangers and capable fighters. No one had troubled her yet, but that could change in a heartbeat. And the last thing she needed was word of a woman of her description reaching Serin in Vencia, especially if it was paired with the information that she was searching for women fitting the description of a Veliant princess.

Satisfied she had the lay of the land, Lara took a step toward the town, the story of her search for a lost sister sitting on the tip of her tongue, when the door to one of the homes opened and Sarhina stepped out, a basket under one arm.

Lara froze mid-step as she watched her sister stroll across the common area to the man chopping wood. He paused in his task, wiping sweat from his brow before bending to whisper something in her ear. Sarhina's laugh spilled through the air and she leaned back, her cloak parting to reveal two marriage knives belted above a swollen belly.

Lara could not breathe.

Casting a flirtatious wink over her shoulder at the smiling man, Sarhina continued down the path toward the forest, cloak flowing out behind her.

Lara didn't move, the slow realization that things had changed seeping into her mind. For reasons she couldn't explain, she'd envisioned finding her sisters as they had been: warrior princesses vying for the right to defend their country. As though they'd existed in some sort of stasis. Except it had been over a year and half since she'd left them at the oasis, and Sarhina, at least, had moved on.

Had gotten married.

Was pregnant.

Had made a life for herself.

Just as Lara had hoped her sister would. How could she disrupt that now? How could she risk everything that Sarhina had built for herself, the lives of the people she clearly loved, for the sake of rectifying Lara's mistakes? For the sake of saving one man?

Lara's eyes closed, tears seeping out to fall on the scarf around her neck. She knew that she needed to walk away. To leave her sister in the peace she'd bought for her. To try to find one of the others . . . Cresta. Maybe Bronwyn.

Or maybe none of them.

Maybe this was something she needed to do herself.

Then a blade pressed against her throat, and a familiar voice said, "If you thought to catch us unaware, Marylyn, you're even crazier than we gave you credit for."

"**M**ARYLYN'S DEAD."

The woman holding the knife gave a sharp intake of breath, but the blade remained against Lara's throat even as her hood was jerked back to reveal her face.

"*Lara?* We thought *you* were dead."

"The little cockroach is hard to kill." She turned her head, able to see her taller, brunette sister out of the corner of her eye. "You mind moving the knife, Bron?"

"Not until you explain what you're doing here."

"Drop the bloody weapon, Bronwyn." Sarhina's voice cut through the cool air. "If Lara wanted you dead, that knife of yours wouldn't stop her."

"Doesn't mean I have to make it easy for her."

"Relax, Bron," Lara said. "I'm not here to make trouble."

"All you do is make trouble."

Not an inaccurate statement. Sighing, Lara snapped her arm up, catching hold of Bronwyn's knife hand, which she jerked down against her chest even as she rotated under her sister's arm. But instead of using her momentum to shove the blade between the other woman's ribs, Lara let go and backed away. Across the clearing, Sarhina made her way toward them, an amused Cresta dogging her heels.

"Should've listened to me, Bron." Sarhina rested one hand on her hip, basket still hanging from her elbow. "Spared yourself that bit of embarrassment."

"Noted." Bronwyn rubbed her wrist, glowering.

"Is that real?" Lara gestured to her sister's swollen belly, unable to take her eyes from it.

"Better be," Cresta said, a smirk rising to her lips. "No other explanation for the quantity of wind she's been passing."

Sarhina rolled her eyes. "You've got another three months of it."

"Is that man in town chopping wood the father?" Lara asked.

"The father and my husband." Sarhina pushed her silky black hair behind her ear. "But we have more important matters to discuss than my love life."

None of them spoke, the four sisters facing each other in taciturn silence, the only sound the wind blowing through the pines. She was an outsider now, Lara realized. No longer one of them, not really. Was it because of what she'd done? Or was it because the past year and a half had changed them as much as it had changed her?

Unsurprisingly, Sarhina broke the silence. "You said Marylyn is dead. Was it Father who killed her?"

A sour taste filled Lara's mouth, and she swallowed hard. "No. I killed her."

The tension between the four of them mounted, Cresta and Bronwyn shifting uneasily, hands drifting to their weapons, then away again. Only Sarhina stood unmoved. "Why?"

"Father sent her to kill me the night he took Ithicana. She threatened my hus—the Ithicanian king. And she threatened the rest of you." Her pulse roared in her ears, each word needing to be ripped from her throat. "The way she was acting . . . the things she said . . . It had to be done."

Sarhina's eyes narrowed, a crease forming between her brows. "Why would Father want you dead? Surely your . . . *successes* outweighed that bit of duplicity you pulled back at the oasis?"

"Probably wants her dead *because* of her successes." Cresta's fingers played over the hilt of her sword. "He didn't need her anymore, and we *all* know how fond he is of tying up loose ends." Lifting her hand, she drew one finger across her throat.

"It was because I betrayed him."

Three sets of blue eyes latched on to her, all of them filled with disbelief.

"Betrayed him how?" Sarhina asked. "You did *exactly* what you—what *we*—were trained to do. You infiltrated Ithicana's defenses and created a strategy to defeat them. A strategy that was clearly effective, given that Ithicana is broken, its king a prisoner, and our father wholly in control of the bridge."

Lara's heart beat an uneven staccato in her chest, her breath coming in fast little gasps that didn't seem to fill her lungs. There was no pride in Sarhina's voice over what Lara had done, but rather condemnation.

They knew.

Knew that they'd been fed lies most of their lives—that Ithicana was no more the power-hungry oppressor than Maridrina was the starving victim. Knew that Lara was no hero for having saved her nation, but rather a bloodstained conqueror who'd captured a war prize.

"Lara?"

The words she'd prepared to explain what had happened between her and Aren disappeared from her head, leaving her opening and closing her mouth like a fool.

But Sarhina had always been able to tell what she was thinking. "You fell in love with him, didn't you? The Ithicanian king? Told him what you were sent to do and tried to undo the damage you'd done, and Father found out? Something like that?"

"Something like that." Lara sat on the damp ground, trying and failing to quell the nausea twisting in her guts, even as a hot tear trickled down her face. "I screwed up."

"Not entirely surprising. You manage your emotions about as well as Bronwyn executes a rear knife attack. Like shit." Sarhina eased herself down onto the ground in front of Lara. "You screwed up, and now Father has both your kingdom and your husband in his clutches."

"That's the sum of it."

Sarhina gave her a knowing look, then shook her head. "And let me guess, you're here because you need our help getting them back."

ARHINA AND HER husband, Ensel, lived in one of the small cabins that made up Renhallow. Their home was made of felled logs that had been cunningly fitted together like pieces of a puzzle, effectively warding off the chill of the air. It smelled of woodsmoke and pine, all the furniture handcrafted by Ensel and made comfortable by blankets woven by his mother, who lived in the neighboring home. The clean wooden floors were covered with rugs in dark greens and blues, and the main room was dominated by a heavy wooden table, its surface nicked and scarred but polished to a high shine.

It felt oddly comfortable for a place she'd never been, but Lara swiftly determined that the comfort came from the fact it was her sister's house, Sarhina's touch visible in countless ways. Jars in perfect rows, pots hung just so, and boots with their heels all lined up as if by a ruler. Sarhina took comfort from order, and Lara took comfort from her sister, so it felt right to settle at the kitchen table across from her.

She and Sarhina watched while Bronwyn set a kettle on to boil, the firelight turning her brown hair to bronze. Cresta appeared from outside with an armload of wood, kneeling next to Bronwyn as she stoked the flames, her red hair hanging in a thick braid down her back. The pair were close in the same way Lara and Sarhina were, though they couldn't be more different. Bronwyn was tall, brash with her words and open with her feelings, whereas Cresta was tiny, sparing with her words and only readable when she wanted to be.

"Where do you two stay?"

"With Ensel's mother," Bronwyn answered. "She needs the help and we need the roof, so it's a perfect arrangement."

"Where are the others?"

"No idea. Seemed best that we didn't all know where each other were, in case Serin caught any of us."

"Wise. I assume you have ways of reaching each other?"

"Maybe we do, maybe we don't." Bron turned to warm her skinny backside against the fire.

Cresta's brow furrowed as she leaned against the wall, and though she said nothing, Lara felt the distrust radiating off her sister, and she suspected she knew the cause.

"When did you realize that Marylyn wasn't on our side?" Lara asked, accepting a steaming cup from Ensel. "Was she angry from the moment she woke from the drugs?"

"We were *all* angry at you from the moment we woke up, Lara. Or at least after we determined you weren't among the dead," Cresta said. "Do you have any idea what it was like, waking up surrounded by smoke and flame and *corpses?* I still have nightmares more nights than not."

"You were gone." Sarhina stared at the wooden table between them, eyes distant. "I woke with the worst headache of my life, so sick with nausea I could barely stand, but all I could think was that you were gone. That you had died fighting."

Lara's stomach hollowed. "But the note—"

"Looking in my pocket for a note was *not* the first thing I thought of doing." Sarhina lifted her head to meet Lara's gaze. "The first thing we did was dig through the bodies, trying to find you." She turned her hands upward, revealing palms marred by pink scars. Scars from burns. "We all have them. Even Marylyn."

"I'm sorry." Guilt flooded her. "It was the only way I could think of to get you all out of the situation alive."

"I don't suppose you considered telling us Father's plan?" Bronwyn asked from where she stood next to the fireplace. "That would've been a good place to start. Then at least we would've woken knowing what was what."

"Obviously I thought of that. But when have us twelve ever agreed about anything without fighting over it for days?" Lara took a mouthful of her tea, wincing when she burned her tongue. "We would have fought over what to do. Then fought over who should go to Ithicana. Then gone back to fighting over what we should do again. There wasn't time for it, so I made the call."

"And we're all alive because of it," Sarhina said, shutting down the argument the way she always did. "But to answer your question, Marylyn didn't say much on the subject until we were out of the Red Desert. Then she said nothing at all, only disappeared in the night. Our first clue that she'd betrayed us was when Father's soldiers started hunting us." She spit across the room into the fireplace. "Traitorous bitch."

"She wasn't who we believed she was." Though Lara still felt sick whenever she thought of her sister's death. Still felt the snap of Marylyn's neck reverberating up her arms. Still saw the light go out of her sister's eyes.

"She was Father's creation," Cresta murmured. "More than any of us."

They were all silent for a time, the only sound the crackle of the fireplace and the soft noises Ensel made as he prepared dinner, calloused hands methodically chopping carrots for stew. He was deaf, she'd been told, but Sarhina had been quick to add that he could read lips on a moonless night, and Lara felt his gaze on them as she asked, "How have you remained hidden from Father's men?"

Sarhina shrugged. "The people of this region are no friends of his—or of Serin's. When an outsider arrives asking questions, we get a warning. If they get too close, we deal with them. But it's not sustainable. Serin knows we are in these mountains, and it's only a matter of time until one of us gets caught."

"I assume you have a plan for that?"

"We planned to part ways for good come the end of the storm season. Take ships north and south to places away from Serin's reach."

Lara glanced at Ensel, then Sarhina. "Even you?"

"Not me. This is my home now."

A home that would be under constant threat, because all of them knew their father would never stop hunting.

Needing to ease the tension that had built in the room, Lara asked, "How did you two meet?"

A soft smile formed on Sarhina's face as she looked to her husband, who was watching her lips move. "After we stripped the compound of what we needed, we headed east out of the desert. Once Marylyn left, we decided it was safer if we split into smaller groups, so Bron, Cresta, and I went deeper into the mountains.

"We didn't have money, so we were hunting what we could and stealing the rest. Mostly from travelers on the road who looked like they could spare it, but sometimes we had to take from the hamlets. Or go hungry."

Lara's guilt flared anew knowing that her sisters had gone hungry while she'd eaten her fill on the finest food to be had. That they'd slept in the rain and the cold and the dirt while she'd soaked in Midwatch's hot spring.

"We had been sneaking into Renhallow on and off for about a week," Sarhina continued. "Picking vegetables from the gardens. Lifting the occasional chicken."

"Four chickens, love." Ensel murmured, then returned his gaze back to vegetables in front of him. "You lasses know a hundred ways to kill a man, but not how to snare a rabbit."

Sarhina's cheeks colored. "At any rate, I was about to make it five, but Ensel had rigged a trap outside the coop, and I stepped in it. Found myself dangling upside down with an arrow pointed at my face."

Ensel smiled. "I thought I'd caught myself a wraith. Little did I know that I'd caught myself something far more dangerous." Stepping away from the stove, he bent his head to kiss Sarhina, who said, "He won me over with his charming compliments, and I decided to stay."

And now Lara was here to take her away. To risk her sister and the life of her unborn child in order to rectify her own mistakes. "I shouldn't have come here," she said, rising to her feet. "It's not right for me to ask you to help. You've moved on with your lives."

"Have we?" Sarhina's gaze was unblinking. "Who are you to be the judge of that? And even if we have moved on, that doesn't mean we've forgotten what Father and Serin and the rest did to us. No amount of time or distance will allow us to forget it."

Both Cresta and Bronwyn nodded in agreement.

"Father needs to pay," Sarhina said. "And I for one would take great satisfaction if he were made to pay with what he trained us to take in the first place. Because knowing you as I do, your plotting isn't limited to rescuing Ithicana's king."

Lara gave her wry smile, then shook her head. "But he is key. For Ithicana's sake, I have to get him free." And for her own sake. "But it will be dangerous. He's locked up in Father's palace in Vencia, surrounded by guards at all times. The Ithicanians have tried multiple times to get him back, but everyone they've sent so far has been captured or killed." Seeing the cocky glint in Bronwyn's eyes, she added, "They're good fighters and even better spies, Bron. That they haven't succeeded means it might be impossible."

If anything, the glint in her sister's eyes only grew. "We were trained to do the impossible. And for better or worse, what you accomplished proved we are more than capable."

"Father and Serin know I'm coming for Aren. And Serin, especially, knows everything I'm trained to do. How I think. Ithicana didn't have that advantage."

Bronwyn tilted her head sideways. "Did you come here to convince us to help or dissuade us? Because it's sounding distinctly like the latter."

Out of the corner of her eye, Lara could see Ensel watching them intently, reading their lips. So she turned to look at him directly. "Your lives aren't worth less than Aren's. And neither is the life of that baby in your belly, Sarhina."

Ensel's jaw tightened, his gaze shifting to his wife, the pair exchanging wordless conversation. Then he exhaled and gave a short nod.

"Some things need to be done," her sister said, "no matter the risk. I don't want my child growing up with this legacy, Lara. I want them to be proud of their mother. And their aunties."

Chewing on the inside of her cheeks, Lara considered arguing further, but instead said, "You need to stay out of the fighting. I want your word on that."

Abruptly, Lara found herself flat on her back, her chair having been yanked out from under her with a quick jerk of her sister's foot under the table.

"You are such a bitch," Lara muttered, rubbing the back of her head while Cresta and Bronwyn laughed.

Sarhina circled the table, then bent down so that they were nose to nose. "I'm in charge, Your Majesty. Understood?"

Lara glowered at her, then smiled. "Understood."

"You two," Sarhina said to Cresta and Bronwyn, "eat your fill, then pack your things and hit the road. It's time the Veliant sisters had a little reunion."

11
AREN

THE WIND GUSTED through the garden, rustling the manicured rosebushes and sculpted hedges before whistling away through the cornices adorning the wall, leaving behind the *creak creak* of the ropes from which the corpses swayed. There were eighteen of them now. Eighteen Ithicanians dead in the attempt to rescue their king. In the attempt to rescue *him*.

He didn't deserve it. Didn't deserve their lives. Not when all that had befallen Ithicana was the result of the choices *he'd* made. Lara might have been the one who wrote the letter with all its damning details, but if he hadn't trusted her, if he hadn't *loved* her, she'd never have had the power to harm his people.

Yet still the bodies swayed, a new man or woman added to their ranks every few days. Sometimes a longer stretch would go by, and Aren would foolishly hope that his people had given up. Then Serin would arrive with another struggling form in tow, and Aren would retreat into himself, the only way he could stand to sit through the things Serin subjected his people to without giving up every secret

Ithicana ever had.

Emra's corpse was little more than a skeleton picked dry by the crows, unidentifiable except by his memory. But the fresher bodies watched him with empty eye sockets, familiar faces blackening and bloating with each passing day he was chained to the stone table in this garden of hell.

From which there was no escape.

Though God knew, he'd tried. A dozen of the guards bore black eyes, broken noses, and one a necklace of bruises courtesy of the chain linking Aren's wrists. He'd killed another after managing to take his sword but had been immediately overpowered by a dozen more. All it had netted him were bruised ribs, an aching head, and more security surrounding him day and night with never a moment of privacy. He was regularly searched for anything he might use to pick the locks of his manacles, forced to sleep bound to a cot under a brilliant lamplight so there was no opportunity to free himself using the cover of darkness. The only piece of cutlery he was allowed was a goddamned wooden spoon.

He'd exhausted every trick that he knew in desperate attempts to escape, when the logical strategy would've been to bide his time. But logic meant little when every day that passed saw more Ithicanians tortured and killed in their attempts to free him.

Which left Aren with only one alternative: to take himself out of the equation.

He stared at the stone of the table, gathering his will, feeling his heart thunder in his chest. Sweat ran in a torrent down his back, the fine linen they'd dressed him in saturated. *Do it,* he silently commanded. *Get it done. Don't be a damned coward about it. If you're dead, Ithicana will have to move on without you.* He leaned back as far as his chains would allow, and took a deep breath—

"The wives are starting to complain about the smell. Can't say that I blame them."

The voice startled Aren enough that he jerked, his chains rattling as he took in the blond prince he'd met the day Emra had died, a worn book tucked under the young man's arm.

"It's a terrible practice," the prince said, squinting up at the bodies lining the walls, their putrefying flesh crawling with insects. "Never mind the smell; it invites flies and other vermin. Spreads disease." His attention shifted back to Aren. "Though I expect it's far worse for you given that you know them, Your Grace. Especially given they died trying to break you free."

This was the last topic of conversation Aren wished to discuss, the sight and smell and *knowledge* bad enough without idle words to go along with it. "You are . . . ?"

"Keris."

The prince sat across the table from Aren with surprising boldness, given what Aren was capable of, and yet the gleam in this man's eyes suggested he was no fool. This was the philosopher prince whom Aren had given permission to travel through the bridge to Harendell, where he'd supposedly planned to attend university. The escort accompanying him had really been soldiers in disguise, a key part of the Maridrinian invasion. If Aren could've reached across the table, he'd have gladly snapped the prince's neck. "Ah. The *inadequate* heir."

Keris shrugged one shoulder, setting his book, which appeared to be about ornithology, on the table. A philosopher *and* a bird-watcher. No wonder Silas wanted nothing to do with him.

The prince said, "Eight older brothers who fit the mold, all dead, and now my father is stuck trying to weasel his way out of naming me heir without breaking one of his own laws. I'd wish him luck in the endeavor if not for the fact that his and Serin's weaseling is likely to see me in a grave next to my siblings."

Aren leaned back in his chair, manacles rattling. "No desire to rule?"

"It's a thankless burden."

"True. But when you have the crown, you can change the décor." Aren gestured at the corpses lining the garden walls.

The laugh that exited the prince's mouth was eerily familiar, the hairs on Aren's arms rising as though he'd been touched by a ghost.

"To rule is a burden, but perhaps especially so for a king who enters his reign desirous of change, for he will spend his life wading against the current. But you understand that, don't you, Your Grace?"

It was the second time the prince had used Aren's title—something

Silas had expressly forbidden. "You're the philosopher. Or was that, too, part of the deception?"

A wry smile formed on the prince's face, and he shook his head. "I think Serin took particular glee in using my dreams in such a perverse fashion. It is one of the only instances in which he has successfully pulled the wool over my eyes, the shock of being trussed up and stuffed in a corner while my *escort* invaded Ithicana not one I'll soon forget. Even still, I might have forgiven the duplicity if my father had allowed me to carry on to Harendell in pursuit of my studies, but as you can see"—he stretched his arms wide—"here I am."

"My condolences."

Keris inclined his head to Aren's sarcasm, but said, "Imagine a world where people spent as much time philosophizing as they did learning to swing weapons."

"I can't," Aren lied. "The only thing I know well is war, which doesn't say much given that I'm on the losing side of this one."

"Losing, perhaps," he murmured. "But not yet lost. Not while Eranahl stands, and not while you still live. Why else would my father insist on these theatrics?"

"Bait for his errant daughter, I'm told."

"Your wife."

Aren didn't answer.

"Lara." Keris rubbed his chin. "She's my sister, you know."

"If you meant that to be a great revelation, I'm afraid I have to disappoint you."

A soft chuckle, but Aren didn't miss how the prince's eyes swiftly scanned the garden, the first crack in his façade of amused indifference. "Not my half sister. We have the same mother, too."

Despite himself, Aren straightened, the memory of that brutal game of truth he'd played with Lara coming to the forefront of his thoughts. Her worst memory, she'd told him, was of being separated from her mother and being brought to the compound where she was raised. Her fear that she wouldn't recognize her mother now, wouldn't know her. Logic told him that it had been nothing but a story intended to manipulate his sympathies, but his gut told him otherwise. "What of it?"

Keris ran his tongue across his lips, eyes distant for a heartbeat before they focused on Aren. "I was nine when my father's soldiers took my sister—young enough to still be living in the harem, but old enough to remember the moment well. To remember how my mother fought them. To remember how she attempted to sneak out of the palace to go after my sister, knowing in her heart that my father intended her for some fell purpose. To remember how, when she was caught and dragged back, my father strangled her himself in front of us all. As punishment. And warning."

Lara's mother was dead.

A twinge of pain filled Aren's chest. This truth would hurt Lara enormously, especially given that her mother had died in her defense.

He abruptly shoved the thought away. What did he care if she wept? She'd lied to him. Betrayed him. Destroyed everything that mattered to him. She was his enemy. Just like this man sitting before him.

But if what Keris said was true, he was an enemy who might be turned into an ally. The prince had cause to both hate and fear his father, which meant he, like Aren, had a vested interest in seeing Silas dead. "What game are you playing, Keris?"

"A long one, and you are but a singular piece on the board, albeit one of some significance." The prince watched him, unblinking. "I sense that you're considering removing yourself from the game. I ask that you might reconsider."

"As long as I'm alive, they'll keep trying to save me. And keep dying in the attempt. I can't allow that."

Keris's eyes went over Aren's shoulder, a flash of hate rolling across them at whatever he saw. "Keep playing the game, Aren. Your life isn't as worthless as you think."

Before Aren could answer, an irritatingly familiar voice spoke. "A questionable choice of company, Your Highness."

Keris shrugged. "I've always been a victim of my own curiosity, Serin. You know that."

"*Curiosity.*"

"Indeed. Aren is a man of myth. Former king of the misty isles of Ithicana, legendary fighter, and husband to one of my mysterious warrior sisters. How could I resist plying him for details of his escapades? Sadly, he hasn't been particularly forthcoming."

"You were supposed to have returned to Nerastis," Serin replied, naming the much-beleaguered city near the contested border between Maridrina and Valcotta. "You need to study with your father's generals."

"My father's generals are boring."

"Boring or not, it's a necessary part of your training."

"*Mag, mag, mag!*" Keris reproduced a shockingly realistic magpie call. "No wonder the harem wives christened you so, Serin. Your voice truly does grate on the nerves." He rose to his feet. "Was a pleasure meeting you, Aren. But you'll have to excuse me, the smell is making me quite nauseous."

Without another word, Prince Keris sauntered across the courtyard, leaving Aren alone with the Magpie.

"His Majesty desires your presence at dinner this evening."

"No." The last thing Aren wanted was to make small talk with Silas and his wives.

Serin sighed. "As you like. I'll leave you in the company of your countrymen. I believe another has come to join your party." He snapped his fingers, and a moment later, several guards appeared dragging a still form wrapped in a bloodstained sheet.

"Sadly, this one took his life when he realized he was caught." Serin shook his head. "Such loyalty." Then he strolled in the direction Keris had gone.

Aren watched as the soldiers heaved the corpse up the wall, fixing it in place to one of the cornices. *Gorrick.* His friend since childhood and one of the few remaining of Aren's bodyguards.

His shoulders curled in on themselves, and Aren clenched his teeth, trying to hold back the sob of anguish rising in his chest, to keep down the nausea rising in his stomach. *Why?* Why did they keep coming for him? Why couldn't they let him go? He didn't deserve their loyalty. Didn't deserve their sacrifice.

He had to make it stop.

Eyes burning, Aren blinked furiously, fixing his gaze on the smooth stone of the tabletop, steeling himself. Then he hesitated.

Keris had left his bird book.

Magpie.

Manacles rattling, Aren reached for the book, slowly flipping the pages until he found the chapter on Corvidae, scanning the text until he found a drawing of the bird common to the eastern coast of Maridrina. He read the description, pausing when he reached the bird's feeding habits. *Opportunistic, the magpie will kill and eat the chicks of songbirds . . .*

Aren closed the book and pushed it away. Keris said the harem wives had christened Serin with his moniker. But not, Aren thought, because of the rankling nature of the spymaster's voice. The wives knew it was Serin, on the orders of the king, who had taken Lara and her sisters. And they had not, he suspected, forgiven the Magpie for his crimes.

His dead countrymen watched him. They'd died trying to win him freedom, and until this moment, Aren had been intent on taking his own life before allowing another to perish on his behalf. But if the wives were willing to help him, perhaps he could get word to his people to stop their attempts to rescue him. And maybe with that respite Aren could, as Keris put it, play the game.

The trouble was: Aren was forbidden contact with the wives. And any attempt he made would rain scrutiny down upon the woman in question. Unless . . .

Aren turned to one of the guards standing at the entrance, barking, "You! Get over here."

Face sour, the man came before him. "What do you want?"

"I've changed my mind," Aren said. "Tell your king that I'd be delighted to join him for dinner tonight."

"**Y**OU SURE THIS IS it?" Sarhina asked, tugging on the reins and drawing the cart they rode to a halt.

"It's where Jor told me to come." It was the only specific detail he'd been willing to give her, still not trusting Lara enough to compromise the Ithicanian presence on Maridrinian soil. "He gave me a code to provide the barkeep, who will know how to get in contact with them."

"Then I suppose we better go order a drink."

Despite her large belly, Sarhina swung down from the cart with a nimbleness that still stunned Lara, even having been on the road with her sister for over a week. For much of that time, Ensel had accompanied them, partially to help dissuade anyone from attacking them along the journey, but mostly to reduce any questions people might have about two Maridrinian women traveling alone. He'd started back this morning, and the swelling around her sister's eyes from the resultant tears had only just faded, the good-byes they'd exchanged sounding permanent enough that Lara had considered trussing Sarhina up and sending her back home.

After tying the mule to a hitching post, Lara led the way into the common room of the inn, the scent of spilled beer and spicy food washing over her as her eyes adjusted to the dim light. It was a rough establishment suited to the small fishing village, the ground covered with sawdust and the furniture showing signs it had endured more than a handful of brawls. Two old men sat at a table in the corner, both more engaged with their bowls of soup than with each other. Otherwise the only other person in the establishment was the barkeep, who stood behind the counter polishing a glass.

Lara gave a long sigh. "We're in the right place."

Marisol's hands paused in their polishing, her eyes fixing on the pair of them. Gone were the expensive embroidered gowns she'd worn when Lara had met her—her dress a drab homespun and her golden hair woven into a single braid down her back. She set down the glass as Lara approached, Sarhina following at her heels. "Look what the cat dragged in."

"Hello, Marisol." Taking a seat on one of the stools, she rested her elbows on the bar. "Far cry from the Songbird."

"Your visit compromised my cover. It seemed prudent to lay low for a time."

"Wise."

Marisol stared at her, and Lara didn't miss the look in her eyes, the muscles of her jaw tightening visibly, her hands trembling with repressed fury. So it was no surprise when the woman swung her hand, palm cracking against Lara's face. "They should've killed you. *I* should kill you."

Rubbing her stinging cheek, Lara shook her head at Sarhina, who looked ready to go across the bar. "Fortunately for me, those in power decided I was more useful to them alive than dead."

"You are a repugnant, disgusting creature," she hissed. "A traitor. How they can trust you is beyond me."

"They don't trust me." Seeing that the other woman was readying to slap her again, Lara added, "You got your piece. Try it again and I'll break your wrist."

Marisol's eyes grew wary, suggesting that she'd been warned of Lara's skills, but the anger in them didn't diminish. "You're just like your father."

"Watch yourself." Sarhina's voice was frigid, the tone of it drawing Marisol's attention to her for the first time.

"I was told to come here," Lara said before the situation could devolve further. "That you could get me back in contact with my associates. Perhaps we might save the catching up for later given that time is of the essence."

Marisol glared at her, but gave a short nod, then retrieved a green scarf from beneath the counter and headed to the front door.

"Who is she?" Sarhina asked under her breath. "Looks Maridrinian, not Ithicanian. Sounds like it, too."

"Because you're so familiar with what Ithicanians look and sound like?" Lara muttered back.

"Just answer the question."

"She's Maridrinian, but she spies for the Ithicanians." Lara hesitated, then added, "Aren used to frequent Vencia in disguise. She was his lover."

"That much was obvious."

Their conversation was cut short by Marisol's return. "Do you want something to eat while you wait?"

Lara shook her head, but Sarhina said, "Yes. And a pint of milk, if you have it. Get my sister here something stronger."

Marisol's jaw dropped, then she peered through the dim light at Sarhina's eyes, which were twin to Lara's. She shook her head, then growled, "I hope one of you princesses has coin to pay."

"Put it on our associates' tab," Sarhina replied, then pulled Lara over to one of the tables. "You look nervous. Should we be worried?"

"The only thing I'm worried about is whether I will be able to deliver on *my* promises." They'd heard nothing from Bronwyn or Cresta about whether they'd been successful in recruiting the rest of their sisters, and at this point, Lara was concerned that she'd wasted weeks on a fool's errand that would have been better used in Vencia trying to free Aren.

Sarhina made a noncommittal noise, seemingly more interested in the food Marisol was bringing in their direction. The woman slammed the tray down on the table. "Enjoy." Then she retreated to the bar and her glassware.

Pulling one of the bowls in front of her, Sarhina began eating with gusto. "It's not bad. You should eat."

Probably true, but the thought of putting anything in her stomach made Lara nauseous. Picking up her glass instead, she sipped the amber liquid, recognized the taste, and lifted it in toast to Marisol. The other woman only gave her a flat glare.

"They're here." Sarhina paused in her eating, watching the two old men in the corner abandon their food and leave the common room.

Only moments after, the door opened again and Jor came inside, Lia at his heels. Both were disguised in Maridrinian clothes, their only weapons the marriage knives Lia wore at her waist, though Lara knew they'd have others.

"Not the slightest bit demonic," Sarhina said between mouthfuls of soup. "I'm disappointed."

Lara shot her a warning look, then sat back in her chair, meeting Jor's dark gaze.

"Well now," he said, taking a seat. "Weeks of waiting for you to bring us reinforcements and you deliver us"—he looked Sarhina up and down—"a pregnant girl with a healthy appetite."

"Spoons are remarkably formidable weapons when wielded by adept hands." Sarhina slurped soup off her spoon and gave him a bright smile before digging back into her food.

Jor ignored her, fixing Lara with a glare. "Well?"

"It's taking longer to gather my sisters than I anticipated. They weren't all in one place." Never mind that she wasn't sure if they were coming at all.

"Always an excuse." Lia pulled out one of her knives and set it on the table, the edge razor-sharp. Sarhina picked it up and used it to slice her roll in half, though Lia snatched it back when she started using it to butter the bread.

Lara had known this would be a contest of wills, but she hadn't expected it to start so soon. "The delay can't be helped." Leaning forward, she asked, "Is there any news? Has anyone seen him? Do you know if he's all right?"

"We know he's alive."

Alive. Lara exhaled a long breath, tension seeping out of her shoulders. *Alive* she could work with. *Alive* meant he could be saved. "And Eranahl?"

Jor gave the slightest shake of his head. "Storms have been violent. No breaks. No updates."

And no chance for boats to get on the water to catch fish, which meant the city would be running on provisions alone. Lara gritted her teeth, but there was nothing she could do about that problem.

"Gorrick's dead."

Lia's voice was bitter and cutting, and Lara flinched. The two had been lovers as long as she'd known them, and Aren had often speculated that it was only a matter of time until they wed. Not every casualty of war was a corpse. "I'm sorry."

"I'm not interested in your apologies. The only reason I haven't cut your throat is that the honor belongs to Ahnna."

Sarhina shifted, and Lara knew she was reaching for a weapon. She stomped on her sister's toe.

"He and Aren grew up together, you know." Lia's voice sounded strange. Stifled. "Gorrick couldn't stand the fact that Aren was imprisoned while he was free. Got tired of waiting on you and decided to go it alone." Her jaw trembled. "If I'd known waiting for you would be such a waste of time, I'd have gone with him. And maybe he'd still be alive."

"More likely the Rat King would have had two corpses to taunt Aren with," Jor snapped. "If you can't handle this, step outside."

"I'm fine."

Lara barely heard the woman's retort, her eyes fixing on a gouge in the wooden table, blood roaring in her ears. Aren was inured to the casualties of battle, but this? Having his people's corpses shoved in his face and knowing they'd died trying to save him? The guilt would destroy him. "I told you to stop with the rescue attempts. You're going to push him over the edge."

"Better for us to do nothing, is it?" Lia snapped. "Or is that all part of your plan, *Your Grace*? To distract us with promises until it's too late to do anything at all?"

Lara's skull throbbed, and she rubbed her temples, attempting to drive away the visions flowing through her mind of Aren taking his own life in a desperate attempt to keep any more of his people from dying. He was no coward. If he thought there was no other way, he'd do it. "We need to get him out."

"Where are your sisters?" Jor demanded. "How much longer until they get here?"

"I don't know." She should've tried to get him out herself. *Alive* wasn't good enough. To save Ithicana, Aren needed to be strong. Unbroken. "They'll come."

They had to come.

"This is a waste of time. I'm going." Lia rose, turning as she did.

Only to find herself face-to-face with Athena.

Known to her sisters as *the wraith,* Athena had hair the color of ash, her ghostly white skin courtesy of a mother from somewhere north of Harendell. She could move through an open space in full daylight without the sun noticing her enough to cast a shadow. As she had just proven.

"Where the hell did you come from?" Jor demanded, rising to his feet. Only to find Cresta and Shae flanking him, hands resting casually on their hips. Behind them, Brenna and Tabitha were sitting on the bar, smiles plastered on their faces. "What sort of devilry is this?"

"No devilry." Sarhina pushed back her empty bowl even as Katrine, Cierra, Maddy, and Bronwyn strolled into the common room. "Just good planning. Now how about we all sit down and figure out a strategy for kicking our father where it counts."

"What matters is rescuing Aren," Jor said. "You must put him ahead of your desire for revenge or this isn't going to work."

"Two birds," Sarhina replied. "One stone."

And if there was one thing Lara knew for certain, it was this: the Veliant sisters had very good aim.

AREN

REN'S GUARDS LED him into a dining room that was heavy with incense. The chains between his ankles rattled noisily despite the plush carpets lining the room. He'd been polished within an inch of his life, a dozen armed men watching apprehensively as the king's own barber had shaved him. The man's hand had trembled so hard that Aren had held his breath as the razor scraped over his jugular, wondering if Silas intended to get rid of him and claim it an accident. But he'd made it through unscathed and, dressed in a green coat, black trousers, and ridiculous shoes because the manacles wouldn't fit around boots, Aren was finally deemed fit to dine with the King of Maridrina.

Pushing him down into a seat, the guards fastened his chains to the legs of the table so that Aren could reach no farther than his own wine glass, which one of them eyed for a moment, then removed, ordering a passing servant to retrieve the child-size tin cup that was all they'd allow him.

There were several Maridrinians seated at the table, all of whom were watching him out of the corner of their eyes while they attempted to maintain conversation. At the far end, Prince Keris, nose in a book, sat next to Zarrah, both of them studiously ignoring each other. Zarrah rose to her feet and pressed her hand to her heart in acknowledgment of Aren. Keris only turned a page in his book, frowning at whatever he read.

The room itself was dimly lit with no visible windows, although they could be lurking behind the dark folds of velvet concealing the walls and draping the ceiling. Everything but the table was plush and padded, the air thick and warm, giving Aren a faint sense of claustrophobia.

"It's rather like being stuffed back inside the womb, isn't it?"

Aren blinked, turning to regard the plump woman who had sat at his right. She was perhaps Nana's age, although considerably less weathered. Her golden-brown hair was laced with gray, her shoulders slightly stooped, and wrinkles creased the skin to either side of her green eyes. She wore a gown of red brocade that was stiff with golden embroidery, her wrists were heavy with bracelets, and a ruby the size of a pigeon egg decorated one of her fingers. A woman of wealth or rank. Probably both. "A poetic way of describing it."

She chuckled. "My nephew is always trying to foist his poetic nonsense on me. What's the term? Metaphor?"

"Simile, I believe."

"An educated man! And here I'd been told that you were nothing more than a vicious beast prone to fits of violence."

"Contrary to the beliefs of some, they are not mutually exclusive characteristics."

She chuckled. "My nephew would argue with you, but then again, he argues with just about everyone, though he doesn't call it such."

"Debate."

"Indeed. As though the semantics change the nature of the thing. Passing wind smells just as bad as a fart."

Despite himself, Aren laughed, her remark reminding him again of Nana. But his laughter faded at the thought of his grandmother. He had no idea if she was alive. She and her students hadn't been in Eranahl when the bridge fell, and Lara's letter had included details of how to access Gamire Island using the pier. That same letter sat in his pocket now, never away from him, and he touched it, using the paper to reignite his fury. To remember his purpose. "You know who I am, but I'm afraid I can't claim the same of you, Lady . . . ?"

"Coralyn Veliant," she supplied, the answer lifting both of Aren's eyebrows. She was one of Silas's wives—the first he'd seen who wasn't at least twenty years the man's junior. The woman's mouth quirked at his reaction. "One of his father's. He inherited me, much to his chagrin."

The prior king's harem . . . Nana had spent a year in that harem as a spy before making her escape. Did they know one another? The thought teetered around Aren's mind, tempting him with the possibilities. "An . . . *interesting* custom." So caught up was he in the chance there might be a link he could exploit that the sarcasm slipped out before he could curb it.

Lady Veliant twisted in her seat, resting one elbow on the arm of her chair in order to lean back and look up at him. "A *law* that keeps men from tossing the old out into the street. So, please contain your derision toward that which you don't understand."

Aren considered her words. "My apologies, Lady Veliant. I was raised to respect the matriarchs of my people. The idea of doing otherwise is beyond my understanding because understanding implies a degree of sympathy for a behavior I find reprehensible. So my derision, I'm afraid, remains intact."

"A smartass with a backbone is a terrible thing," she muttered. "Truth be told, I was only twenty-three when the old bastard died, and I'd have been happy to make my own way in the world, if not for the children."

"You have many?"

"I've lost count at this point."

Aren blinked and she smiled. "That's the nature of the harem, *Master Kertell.*" Her voice dripped with sarcasm, as though to call him such was the epitome of ridiculousness. "Every son or daughter born to the harem is family to every woman within it. So while I have no child of my own blood, I have countless children of my heart, and I'd protect each with my life."

And there was no greater enemy to the harem's children than the man who'd fathered them all.

The conversation was cut short as two men sat at the table. The shorter one settled in the chair to Coralyn's right and the tall skinny one to Aren's left, the latter shifting his chair as far from Aren as he could without climbing into the neighboring seat.

Coralyn laughed. "Clearly he's up on the gossip and not wanting to find that chain between your wrists around his neck."

"What? This?" Lifting his hands, Aren set his manacled wrists on the table, taking a sort of wry amusement from the way the reedy man recoiled.

"Don't bother learning their names," she said. "They're nothing more than my husband's sycophants sent to spy on your every word, the risk of you breaking their necks worth the favor they might gain by delivering valuable information. Not much you can do about that, but at least you need not trouble yourself making small talk with them. Or with trying to take them hostage."

The two men glowered but made no retort.

"What of you, my lady?" Aren asked, taking in the rest of the individuals filling the table. All Maridrinian nobility, with the lone exceptions of a red-haired man with pale skin, whom he suspected was the Amaridian ambassador, and a blond man with an enormous nose who'd be from Harendell. They sat at opposite sides of the table, both of them glowering at each other with undisguised disdain. The blood between the two nations was nearly as bad as between Maridrina and Valcotta, though they tended toward trade embargoes, political posturing, and the occasional assassination rather than outright war.

Aren turned back to Coralyn. "Were you also seated here to spy?"

"I was seated here because protocol demanded you be given female conversation, but Silas wasn't willing to risk one of his favorites. He'd shed no tears if you did me in, lest you get any ideas about putting that chain around *my* neck. He's been trying for years to find a way to shut me up that won't turn his bed into a dangerous place. You'd be doing him a favor."

Doing Silas a favor and also costing Aren any chance of gaining assistance from the harem. "I'll have to suffice myself with verbal sparring."

A soft chiming filled the room, and everyone rose. Aren only leaned back in his chair, watching as Silas entered the room, flanked by his bodyguards and six of his wives. Each of the women were dressed in gauzy silk and adorned with jewels, all young and strikingly beautiful.

Silas took his seat at the head of the table, his wives gliding into the empty chairs between emissaries and viziers, all of whom remained standing. His eyes fixed on Aren's lounging form, his face expressionless as he likely considered whether to have his guards force Aren to stand.

Aren suspected his presence here tonight was to demonstrate to all the kingdoms, north and south, that Ithicana had been cowed. But every one of them knew Ithicana was not yet broken—not with Eranahl still autonomous. Forcing Aren to stand would only draw attention to Ithicana's defiance. But saying nothing would make Silas look weak. No fool, the Maridrinian King said, "Do we need to find you a lighter set of chains, Aren? Perhaps we could have one of the jewelers fashion you something less burdensome?"

The heavy links joining his manacles clunked and rattled ominously against the wood of the table as Aren reached for his tiny tin cup of wine, drinking it without waiting for one of the tasters to check it for poison. Then he shrugged. "A lighter chain would make a fine garrote, but there is something more . . . *satisfying* about choking a man to death. I'd ask you if you agreed, Silas, but everyone here knows you prefer to stab men in the back."

Silas frowned. "You see, kind sirs? All the Ithicanians know are insults and violence. How much better now that we no longer have to deal with their ilk when conducting trade through the bridge."

The Amaridian ambassador thumped his hand against the table in agreement, but the ambassador from Harendell only frowned and rubbed his chin, though whether it was because he disagreed with Silas or was loath to be seen agreeing with the Amaridian, Aren couldn't be certain.

"I'm afraid Valcotta does not concur with your sentiment, Your Grace," Zarrah said. "And until Maridrina withdraws from Ithicana and you release its king, Valcottan merchants will continue to bypass the bridge in favor of shipping routes."

"Then your aunt best get used to losing ships to the Tempest Seas," Silas snapped. "And you would do well to remember your place and curb your tongue, girl. Your presence is only a courtesy. You should be thanking me for sparing your life, not testing my patience with your prattle. Your head would look rather nice spiked on Vencia's gates."

The young Valcottan woman lifted one brown shoulder in a graceful shrug, but next to her, Keris's knuckles whitened around the stem of his wineglass, seeming to take issue with Zarrah's life being threatened. Which was rather interesting, given that they were supposed to be mortal enemies.

Sipping from his own cup, Aren said, "As one intimately acquainted with this issue, Silas, allow me to let you in on a little secret: An empty bridge earns no gold."

Zarrah and the Harendellian smirked behind their hands, but it was the Amaridian ambassador's reaction that Aren watched, a faint rush of excitement filling him when the man frowned and cast a sideways glance at Silas. It seemed someone was late on paying his dues to the Amaridian queen for the continued use of her navy.

Whether by some silent cue or the innate sense of well-trained servants, young men bearing plates of fancifully sculpted greens chose that moment to enter the room, cutting the tension. One of them gingerly set a plate in front of Aren, next to the wooden spoon that was all he was ever given.

Something fell into his lap, and he glanced down to see a silver fork. "Pardon me," Coralyn said. "My fingers aren't quite as nimble as they once were." Then she snapped those very fingers loudly, a servant scuttling forward to provide her a replacement.

"Are you mad, woman?" the short man to her right demanded. "Guards, he's got a—"

"Oh, shut your mouth, you cowardly twit. It's a fork. Just what do you think he's going to do with it?"

Aren could put those silver tines through a jugular in short order, but instead he took a mouthful of salad, barely tasting the vinegar and spices of the dressing as he chewed. One of the guards started in his direction, but a sharp glance from Silas had him retreating. An individual who was supposed to be in a position of power did not quibble over forks.

It was, however, too much for the skinny man on Aren's left, who muttered something that implied he needed to relieve himself, then scuttled out the door. The young wife who was seated one over continued to eat, but Aren didn't miss how her eyes flicked to Coralyn, or the faintest nod she gave to the older woman.

From behind one of the curtains, the first trills of music began to play, and the girl set down her fork. Rising to her feet, she inclined her head once in Silas's direction, then began to dance, a slow and seductive set of movements that seemed more appropriate for a bedroom than a dining room, but hardly anyone at the table paid her any notice. Except for the short man to Coralyn's right, who watched the young woman with undisguised lust.

Clever.

"This nonsense of a salad looks like a garden topiary," Coralyn said, knocking the architectural feat of lettuce and cucumber over with a violent blow of her fork. "Do you have gardens in Ithicana?"

"We do." Aren swallowed a mouthful, thinking of the courtyard in his house at Midwatch. Even if he had the fortune to return, he'd raze that place to the ground before ever sleeping in the bed he'd shared with *her.* "But not cultivated like your gardens here. One must let the plants grow as they will or the typhoons destroy them. Wild things better off untamed. More beautiful because of it."

"Sounds like a child I once knew."

Aren's teeth clenched, and he watched the dancing girl sway past, her blonde hair grazing the spy's shoulder. The music was loud enough to drown out conversation from the other end of the table, and while Silas didn't turn his attention away from the ambassadors, Aren could see the muscles in the man's jaw were tense with irritation.

"She was a determined child. I'm not surprised she succeeded at what she was set to do."

Discussion of Lara was inevitable. Any chance of the harem helping him was predicated upon their resentment of Silas for taking their daughters, of which Lara was one, and for Aren to reveal how deeply he loathed his wife would do more harm than good. "She's not fool enough to come here and fall into his trap, if that's what you fear."

"Are you so certain?"

No. "Yes."

Coralyn exhaled softly. "What of our other flowers?" Despite how well she played the game, Aren detected the anticipation in her voice. And the fear.

"One was clipped," he said, pausing as a servant took the plate from in front of him, along with his damnable fork. "The gardener has his sights on the others."

"The gardener." She hesitated. "We've another name for him."

"So your nephew tells me."

"Somewhat less vigor," Silas snapped at the musicians. "I can barely hear myself think!"

Coralyn's hand stilled on the stem of her wineglass, moving only when another servant brought out the soup. At least for this, Aren could use his spoon. Except his throat was dry and the thought of eating made him sick.

Giving up this information would mean risking his people, but if it worked, it would mean stopping them from throwing away their lives in a futile attempt to rescue him.

He had to take the chance.

The music was fading, the dance nearly finished, and from across the room, the skinny man had reentered. Aren said, "I understand you aren't fond of the scent of the flowers that have recently been planted in your garden."

"No," Coralyn replied, picking up her soupspoon. "I am not."

"Perhaps you might consider asking the supplier to desist in sending them."

She was silent, but Aren didn't dare look at her. Didn't dare draw any attention to this conversation that could turn the tide of his imprisonment.

"That's an idea. Sadly, I'm not certain where to find the man."

"Woman," he corrected, his chest tightening. What if he was wrong about Coralyn? What if this was all just a ruse to capture more of his people? What if he was playing into Silas's hands?

Countless uncertainties, but there was no doubt in Aren's mind what would happen if he didn't take this chance.

"Do you visit the Sapphire Market on the east side?" he asked, knowing the answer.

"Obviously." She lifted one jeweled wrist. The Sapphire Market catered to the elite of Vencia, its streets lined with shops full of jewels, fine fabrics, and other costly merchandise, exotic flowers included.

"The florist you seek is on the corner of Gret and Amot," Aren said, giving the address. Not a florist, but a jeweler—the same who'd crafted his mother's necklace, which he'd last seen hanging around Lara's cursed neck. The woman was an Ithicanian spy, and she'd contact her handler, whom he prayed knew where to find whichever of his commanders was ordering these rescue attempts.

"The flowers are being sent for the king," she said. "There would be consequences if it were discovered I canceled the order. Seems a great deal of risk to take over a smell. Why should I bother?"

The skinny man was circling the table. It would only be seconds before he was in earshot, and there was no time left for this roundabout conversation. "Revenge."

"Won't bring our flowers back. Nor will it do anything to keep them safe from the elements that threaten them."

Aren had nothing else to offer. This wasn't a woman who could be bought, and he was in no position to offer protection to Lara's sisters, which was the only thing that might have tempted her. All he had was a chance that Coralyn's loyalty to the wives of the harem and their children would extend to the only woman who'd escaped its clutches. To the spy who'd returned to Ithicana and remarried. Who'd had a son who wed a queen, who'd given birth to a king.

"Enough!" Silas shouted at the dancing wife. "Sit down!"

Aren said, "Visit the florist, my lady, and tell her Amelie Yamure's grandson sent you."

THE SISTERS WERE staying in small groups throughout Vencia to avoid attention, but their meeting place was the workshop in the rear of a jewelry merchant's store, the Maridrinian proprietor also a spy for Ithicana.

They slowly filtered in out of the rain, dressed in their various costumes, some pretending to be highborn patrons, some fellow merchants, and others servants or suppliers. The room was soon full, damp cloaks draped over the backs of chairs and the wooden floorboards tracked with mud and water. Once everyone was seated around the table, including Jor and Lia, Sarhina raised her hand, calling for silence.

Which meant they all heard the door to the shop slam open and an old woman snap, "Anyone could walk in here, Beth. At least lock the goddamned door when you have a meeting with the most wanted women in Maridrina going on under your roof."

"Shit," Lara muttered, her eyes flicking to Jor's in accusation.

He only shrugged.

"Where is that traitorous little bitch we call a queen? I saw ten blue-eyed princesses waltz their way inside, but not her. Has fate delivered me some luck and killed her off?"

Sarhina's shoulder bumped against Lara's. "Whoever she is, she doesn't appear to be your greatest admirer."

Swallowing hard, Lara turned to the doorway to the front of the shop, watching as Nana appeared, resting age-spotted hands on her hips, water dripping from her clothes to pool at her feet.

"You didn't honestly believe I was going to let you handle this job without supervision, did you, you conniving little twit?" The old healer pulled off her cloak and tossed it at Jor. "Not given your prior history of botching things up."

From behind Lara, there was the scrape of chairs pushing back, blades hissing out of sheaths as her sisters rose. Sarhina stepped between Lara and Nana. "Mind your tongue when you're speaking to my sister, old woman, or you'll soon find yourself without one."

A scowl on her face, Lia moved to Nana's side, hand on her weapon. But Aren's grandmother only scoffed. "Quite the army you've assembled, Lara. A pack of pretty faces and a pregnant woman."

Sarhina pantomimed a sorrowful pout. "One night of passion and I've been evicted from the pretty-face pack? It's so unfair. Is it the belly? Or the spots? I'm told they'll both disappear when the baby comes."

Nana was not amused. "You'll be next to useless for this task, girl. Get yourself home and concern yourself about what's growing in your belly."

"*I* decide what to concern myself with, woman," Sarhina answered, her voice light and unconcerned. "And at the moment, it's the pimple on my cheek and *you.*"

Sarhina's words were more intimidating than the arsenal standing behind them. But none of this, none of the bickering and threats, would do *anything* to see Aren freed. Lara rested a hand on her sister's arm, drawing her back. "This is . . . Amelie. She's Aren's grandmother."

The grandmother who hadn't forgiven Lara for her mistakes and likely never would.

If it had been up to Nana, Lara would've been executed within the hour of arriving in Eranahl, probably by way of being fed to the sharks the Ithicanians held so dear.

"His grandmother and the only person in this room who's familiar with the layout and security within the inner walls of that palace," Nana replied.

"We were all born there," Bronwyn said. "Spent the first five years of our lives there."

"Childhood memories!" Nana stomped through the room to take a seat at the head of the table. "I spent a year in that harem spying for Ithicana."

"A year *a hundred years ago*?" Bronwyn looked Nana up and down. "Which gives you an octogenarian's memory of the place."

"Watch your mouth!" Lia jerked her knife out, eyes bright with anger.

Bronwyn tapped her own knife against her chin, smiling devilishly. "Who are you again?"

Lara met Jor's eyes and he gave a clipped nod, seemingly the only person present as frustrated as she was. "Enough," she said. "Everyone here wants the same thing, and that's Aren freed. We are at a disadvantage regarding the layout and security of our father's inner sanctum, but perhaps our collective knowledge of the place will be enough. If we work together."

"A big maybe." Sarhina said. "At this point, we'll be going in blind. Not only are we unfamiliar with the guard patterns and defenses, we have no idea where they are keeping Aren or his patterns during the day. The only way this works is if enough of us go in to overwhelm his guards, which will be no easy feat. And a group of strange women wandering around the inner sanctum checking behind every locked door is not the path to success. We need someone on the inside."

"We've tried buying servants." Jor took a sip from the flask he'd extracted from his pocket. "For one, they're difficult to reach. Only a handful are allowed free passage in and out of the palace, and those are either too loyal or too afraid of Silas to be turned. We thought we had one, but he gave us garbage information that got two of my best killed."

"What about the guards?"

"Silas's cadre members are loyal to the core."

"Then we need to infiltrate the palace ourselves," Sarhina said. "One of us hired as a servant, perhaps."

"Servants work for the king for years before they're allowed to take duties within the inner sanctum," Nana interrupted. "And years we do not have."

"What about as a servant to someone in the nobility?" Lara suggested. "They seem to come and go as they please."

"Personal servants are only allowed within the outer walls." Nana rested her elbows on the table, eyeing the rough schematics Bronwyn had drawn sitting on the top of a hill with a spyglass. "And the viziers have no freedom within the inner walls. They are brought where their presence is required, then escorted out."

"Unless they're blindfolded, they'll still see things," Sarhina said. "Can any of them be bought?"

"Not with the funds we have at our disposal," Jor replied. "Silas cleaned out the coffers at Northwatch and Southwatch, along with those at Midwatch. Risking a trip back to Eranahl poses its own set of risks."

"What about the ambassador from Harendell?"

Jor snorted. "Impossible. They don't even allow him to piss in private."

Pushing away the schematics, Nana leaned back in her chair. "Did you think this would be easy, girls? I didn't whore myself to your smelly old grandfather because I was charmed by him. It was the *only* way in. And the only reason I was able to get out was that I had somewhere to go that I knew would be safe. We no longer have that." She glared at Lara, her resentment palpable.

Lara had known this wouldn't be easy, but now, faced with a ticking clock and so many seemingly insurmountable hurdles, the impossibility of the task hollowed out her stomach. Strategy after strategy circled through her mind, considered, then cast away. The Ithicanians were excellent with explosives, but the palace was full of women and children, never mind that they might accidentally kill Aren in the blasts. They could bring in reinforcements from Ithicana, but the death toll would be astronomical with no assurances of success. She and her sisters could try to infiltrate the palace blind, but that was likely to get more than a few of them killed, and the fact was, she wasn't willing to risk them on a flimsy plan. Casualties every which way she looked, bodies to stack upon the bodies of all those who'd already died because of her mistakes.

"Suggestions?" she asked.

Everyone stared silently at the schematic until the sound of loud knocking saved them from having to answer.

"Beth has the 'closed' sign up," Jor said. "Whoever it is will have to wait."

Another loud knock, and the faint sound of a voice from outside demanding to be let into the shop.

"Damnable Maridrinians," Nana muttered. "Never take no for an answer."

"Beth will have to—" Jor was interrupted by the click of a latch and a soft chiming as the front door was opened.

"You said this woman was loyal to Ithicana," Sarhina hissed at Jor, who gave a panicked nod even as he inched over to the doorway. Easing the curtain open a crack, he peeked out, while Bronwyn and Cresta went to the rear of the building, checking for any sign that the meeting had been compromised.

From out front, the jeweler said loudly, "It is an honor to have one of His Majesty's wives in my establishment, my lady. How might I assist you this fine morning?"

Shit. Beth hadn't had a choice. Not opening the doors for one of the harem wives would've drawn all sorts of trouble down upon them, but it was still a fine bit of bad luck.

"You lot wait outside," an unfamiliar voice said, the timbre that of an older woman. "I don't need you peering over my shoulder so you can spy on how much of Silas's money I spend."

"My lady—" a man started to respond, but was cut off with a fierce "Out!"

The door slammed shut. Cresta reappeared from the rear, whispering, "Six-guard escort. Seems like an unfortunate coincidence."

Which meant they had no choice but to wait it out.

"I was led to believe this was a flower shop," the harem wife said.

"And that *you* were a florist, not a jeweler."

Jor's hand went to the knife at his waist and Lia drew hers, both their expressions grim.

"That's her code name," Lia said softly. "We've been made. Time to go."

Bronwyn returned, shaking her head. "Two guards came around back to smoke. Can't get past without killing them."

"I specialize in jewelry set in the shape of flowers," Beth responded. "Perhaps that was the cause for the miscommunication."

"It wasn't a miscommunication," the wife said. "It was a misdirection. There's a difference, you see."

The two guards were likely decoys meant to appear as easy marks. There'd be others waiting. Dread pooled in Lara's gut. She'd brought her sisters here, had risked them all for the sake of saving Aren. *Another mistake. She'd made another mistake.*

"Of course. I see." There was a faint shake to the jeweler's voice. "Might I show you some of my work, or do you wish for me to direct you to a reputable florist nearby?"

"Neither."

"My lady?"

"We have a mutual acquaintance, I'm told. He suggested you might be able to do something about the flowers that keep arriving in the palace garden. Neither of us is particularly fond of the smell, and he suggested you might be in a position to see any future orders cancelled."

"There's something familiar about her voice . . ." Sarhina said, scowling as Nana pushed her aside to step up next to Jor, trying to peer over his shoulder at the women beyond.

"How peculiar," Beth said. "Unfortunately, I don't see how I can help you. My business is gemstones, not flowers, and I have no commissions with the crown."

"Not with the Maridrinian crown, you mean. But perhaps another."

Bronwyn dragged at Lara's arm, pointing up to the ceiling, where a hatch was already open, rain falling through to splatter the table. "You and Sarhina go," she hissed. "We'll distract them while you take the rooftops."

"No." Lara pulled her arm out of her sister's grip. "It's me Father wants most, and I'm sure he wants me alive. I'll provide the distraction, the rest of you go."

Sarhina had turned back around. "Don't be a fool, Lara. Once Father has you, he has less reason to keep Aren alive. And if he dies, so does any chance of Ithicana enduring. This is about more than just you."

The jeweler was blathering on about works she'd done for foreign royals, trying to keep the wife's attention long enough for the group to flee.

"We need to go." Sarhina climbed onto the chair Bronwyn had placed on the table, reaching up to the trap door leading to the attic.

"You too, Nana. Aren will never forgive me if I let you get caught." Jor hauled on the old woman, trying to pull her back from the door, but she shooed him away.

And from the front, the harem wife's voice carved through the noise of marching soldiers. "Enough with your babbling, woman. I only have so much time. Now tell whatever Ithicanians you're harboring that Amelie Yamure's grandson sent me."

15
LARA

T HE JEWELER, BETH, continued to ramble, trying to buy them
time to escape, but no one in the room moved.

"Let her in." For the first time since she'd met Nana, Lara
heard a slight shake in the old woman's voice. A hint of nerves.

"Enough of this." There was a clack of heels against the wooden
floor, and an elderly woman draped in expensive velvet and even more
expensive jewels appeared in the doorway.

Where she stopped dead, her eyes growing wide as saucers at the
sight of them. "My God—can it be?"

Sarhina stepped forward, her brow furrowed. "Auntie?"

The woman's gaze fixed on her. "Little Sarhina?" In two strides,
she closed the distance, wrapping her arms around Sarhina's shoulders
and pulling her close even as she took in the rest of them. "This is not
what I expected to find. How did he know?" Then she shook her head.
"No, of course he doesn't know. Would never have agreed to it, if it
meant . . ." Her voice turned sharp. "Which one of you is Lara?"

Lara stepped forward, wishing she was dressed in finer attire.
Clothes had always been armor for her, tools to wield. And right now,

she felt woefully unequipped. "I am."

The old woman stared at her for a long moment, then dropped into a curtsy. "Your Majesty."

"Please don't." Lara's voice croaked. "It's not a title I deserve."

"Most people with titles don't deserve them."

"Least of all her," Nana said. "It's been a long time, Coralyn. You look like you've been living soft."

"And you look like you've been left out in the sun to bake for the past fifty years."

No one in the room breathed while the two matriarchs glared each other down.

"So you remember me," Nana finally said.

"It's my body that's gone soft, not my head." The old woman—Coralyn—sniffed. "You're the only one to have ever disappeared without explanation." Her jaw tightened. "We thought you were dead."

"Nah," Nana said. "Just had what I needed. Goodbyes would've put all that I'd worked for at risk."

Lightning fast, Coralyn moved, her hand cracking against Nana's face. "That's for the lies. And for abandoning the harem."

"I suppose I deserved that." Nana rubbed her cheek with one hand, then, to Lara's shock, closed the distance and hugged the other woman tightly. "You've seen my grandson, then?"

"Oh, yes. Quite the pretty thing Aren is—he inherited your good looks."

Sarhina guffawed, but both women ignored her. And Lara lost her patience.

"Is he all right? Has Father hurt him?"

Exhaling, Coralyn shook her head. "The Magpie isn't fool enough to harm him in any visible way—not while Silas is still attempting to negotiate the surrender of Eranahl in exchange for Aren's life, and certainly not with the Harendellians grumbling over his imprisonment in the first place. But as for Aren's mind . . ." She trailed off, giving a slow shake of her head. "Guilt is nearly getting the better of him, and it is compounded every time you lot send another person to be caught and killed. Serin has them tortured and then strung up in the gardens, and then ensures your boy spends a healthy amount of time out there with nothing to do but watch them rot. It's only a matter of time until the Magpie's tactics break him."

Lia gasped, and Jor's face tightened with grief. But all Lara felt was icy resolve filling her core. "I'm going to kill him. I'm going to cut out his goddamned heart."

"And he fully expects you to try," Coralyn answered. "He's ready for you, Lara. If he catches you, he'll kill you in the worst of ways."

"Prepared for me, but not for all of us together."

"And imagine how pleased he will be that you've made his desire to have every one of you dead that much easier to achieve." The old woman shook her head, the heavy earrings she wore swaying back and forth. "You girls need to go. Need to run as far away from Maridrina as you can get."

"No." Lara growled the word, and she heard her sisters shift forward, not one of them backing down. "If you care so much for our well-being, then help. Give us the information we need to get Aren out."

"There is nothing I could tell you that would make a difference. You'd need an army to get him out, which you don't have. And I'll not help you with anything that puts the lives of the harem and its children in danger."

"You can tell us where he's kept. Give us information about the layout of the place and where the guards are stationed. You can help us find a way in."

Coralyn's jaw tightened and she sharply shook her head. "In? In is the easy part, girl. It's trying to get out, especially with Aren in tow, that will get you all killed. The palace was built to contain. It's nothing more than a beautiful prison."

"She's right." Nana's voice was rough. "I never intended to spend an entire year inside the harem, but once I was in . . ." She exhaled a long breath. "Getting out was impossible. My only choice was to work to earn enough of the king's trust that he'd allow me to leave the palace under escort. Even then, it took multiple attempts before I was able to escape. And I wasn't under near the scrutiny that Aren will be."

A dull roar filled Lara's ears. *It's impossible. Impossible.*

"But you can get us *in*." Sarhina's voice cut through the noise filling Lara's head. "You said that was easy, although we've not found that to be the case."

"Easy is relative."

"Please answer the question, Aunt," Sarhina said. "We *will* do this, with or without your help."

Silence.

"What sort of training were you given in the desert?" Coralyn finally asked, giving them all an appraising look. "Not the warrior spy nonsense. Your other skills." She held up a hand before Lara could answer. "A different question—*Who* did your father have training you to be wives?"

Lara gave Sarhina a quick glance, then said, "Mistress Mezat."

Coralyn's face darkened, but she nodded. "I may have a way, but I'll need some of the younger wives to help."

"Do you think they'll agree?" Lara asked, dubious that women who were closer in age to her and her sisters would care about decisions her father had made over sixteen years ago, much less be willing to risk everything to punish him for them.

Coralyn nodded. "You girls weren't the only children Silas allowed the Magpie to spirit away. And you certainly aren't the only ones whose lives are in danger from him."

"Excellent," Sarhina said. "Now we just need to figure a way out of a place we haven't seen in over sixteen years."

What they needed were eyes on the inside. And not just any eyes.

Biting her thumbnail, Lara considered the problem. Coralyn would be able to provide them descriptions of the interior, but she lacked the training to spot the details that might be useful for an escape. For that, they needed someone who knew everything there was about defense, and therefore every possible way to get around it. "I have an idea."

A STORM HAD descended the day after the dinner party, a monstrosity that plunked itself overhead and showed no inclination to move for the better part of a week. Vencia was subjected to a steady deluge of rain, which meant Aren was kept inside the majority of the time, mostly confined to his small room. Not for his comfort, he suspected, but rather because Silas's soldiers had no interest in standing outside in the downpour.

Being so confined would have normally grated on Aren's nerves, but instead he found himself lost in thought as he considered how he might use an alliance with the harem to his advantage.

The first step would be whether Coralyn succeeded in meeting with his people and delivering his orders to desist in their rescue attempts. Aren couldn't think with the bodies stacking up, with faces he knew and loved slowly filling the walls of Silas's awful garden. He'd rather be dead than endure that.

But if his people stopped dying . . .

While he did pull-ups hanging from the doorframe to the bathing chamber, Aren considered precisely what it was he might hope to achieve by remaining alive. Escape was an obvious, albeit a selfish, goal. Locked in this palace, he felt helpless to do anything to aid his kingdom. The only information he had about Ithicana was what select pieces Silas or Serin chose to give, all of which were to be taken with a grain of salt. He had no idea how much of his army had survived, where they were hiding, or whether they were in any condition to fight. Without that knowledge, it was impossible to strategize—like trying to fight in the dark. But if he could just get out . . .

On the heels of that thought always came the self-doubt that even if he *were* free, it would do nothing to change the tides. After all, what good had he done before he'd been captured? Fighting day in and day out, but always being pushed back by the Maridrinians and Amaridians, who had more manpower, more resources, more of everything. His presence wouldn't change that, and Ahnna or any of the other watch commanders were just as capable of commanding Ithicana's army as he was.

You're worthless.

He tried to shove away the thought, which reared up again and again, despite his best efforts. *He'd* caused all this by trusting Lara. All of it was his fault. Which meant, perhaps, that Ithicana was better off without him.

Growling in irritation, he dropped to the floor and started doing sit-ups, the chains around his ankles and wrists clinking.

"Don't know why you bother," one of his guards said from where he stood leaning against the wall. "Seems like a waste of effort."

"Maybe," Aren said between sit-ups. "I just don't want to start looking like you."

The guard's face reddened, and he cast a sideways glance at his comrade, who smirked. "I suppose it's important to look your best on the way to the executioner's block."

Aren's brow furrowed. Not because the threat particularly concerned him, but because he was beginning to question *why* Silas was keeping him alive. To bait Lara was the reason he'd been given, but a great deal of time had passed since his capture, and if anyone had heard a whisper of the Queen of Ithicana's whereabouts, it hadn't been repeated to him.

Maybe she's dead.

The thought sent a flurry of emotion through him, and in one violent movement, he stood and went to the barred window, looking out into the courtyard.

It was possible she hadn't escaped Ithicana. Storm season had begun when Maridrina had attacked, and Lara was no sailor. Nor had she any practical knowledge of Ithicana's geography beyond what lay in and around Midwatch. There was a very good chance she'd died within a day of her wild sprint away from him, one of the many dangers lurking on Ithicana's shores or in its seas having gotten the better of her.

Except his instincts told him that she wasn't dead. That, however impossibly, she'd survived. Which meant her silence was by choice.

She's not coming.

Aren wasn't certain whether he felt regret or relief about that fact, only that she refused to leave his thoughts, her face taunting him.

I love you, Lara's voice whispered in his head.

"Liar," he muttered back at her. As he did, his eyes fixed on a lean figure moving into the courtyard, a book in one hand. Turning to his guards, he said, "I want to go outside."

Keris sat at the same table where they had first spoken. Surrounding him were his youngest half sisters, the little princesses clothed in vibrant dresses that were miniature versions of that worn by the wife presiding over them. Judging from the musicians sitting to the side, the girls were about to receive some form of dancing instruction. Despite being in the center of the twirling group of girls, Keris paid them not an ounce of interest, his gaze fixed on the book he held in one hand.

Aren sat across from him, chains clanking as his guards fastened them to the bench. Only when they stepped back did the prince lower his book and fix his azure gaze on Aren. "Good morning, Your Grace. Come to enjoy the brief respite from the storm?"

"Rain doesn't bother me."

"No, I suppose it wouldn't." Keris set his book on a spot on the table that had dried in the sun, attention going to the guards who lingered. "Is there something you need?"

Both men shifted uncomfortably. "He's dangerous, Your Highness," one of them finally answered. "It's best we remain close in case he needs to be restrained. He's very quick."

Keris's brow furrowed, then he bent to look under the table at Aren's legs, his voice slightly muffled as he said, "He's chained to a stone bench." Sitting upright, he demanded, "Just how feeble do you believe I am that I can't outpace a man chained to a bench?"

"His Majesty—"

"Is not here," Keris interrupted. "You two are close enough to be part of the conversation, and from this brief exchange, I can already tell that I've no interest in further discourse with either of you. Plus, you are in the way of my little sisters' practice. Move."

The guards' faces darkened, yet they retreated a respectable distance. But one looked over his shoulder as they went and said, "Scream if he causes you trouble, Highness. It's what the wives have been told to do."

"Noted," Keris replied, and though his expression didn't deviate in its exercise of boredom, Aren saw the flash of darkness in the other man's eyes. The way the defined muscles in his forearms flexed like he was of a mind to reach for a knife. A wolf in sheep's clothing, much like his sister. Aren wondered if Silas knew.

Noting his scrutiny, Keris pulled the sleeves of his coat down, despite the heat burning through the clouds. "Now, how might I be of assistance, Your Grace? More reading material, perhaps?"

"As enlightening as your bird book was, I'll pass."

"As you like."

The young girls began to twirl in circles, clapping their hands at measured intervals, the harem wife calling out the occasional instruction.

But Keris paid them little mind, instead watching Aren intently, as if waiting for him to speak.

"You risk a knife in the back with the way you treat your father's men."

"That risk is there regardless of what I say or do." The prince rested his elbows on the table. "Like my father, they took my lack of interest in soldiering as a personal insult, and short of turning myself into something I am not, there is no path to redemption with either. My bed is made."

Aren rubbed his chin, considering the prince's words, none of which, he thought, were said without purpose. Silas did not favor Keris, that was known. That he'd have his heir murdered to make way for younger brothers whom Silas considered more suitable for the throne seemed inevitable, but for all his words, Aren didn't believe for an instant that Lara's brother had resigned himself to death. "There are ways to popularity other than swinging a sword."

"Like feeding a starving nation?" Keris held a hand to his ear. "Listen. Do you hear them?"

Vencia was always loud, especially in comparison to Ithicana, the voices of thousands of people out on the streets a dull drone. But today, shouts rose above the noise, the anger in them clear even if the words were not. Dozens of people, he thought. Perhaps hundreds. And for him to hear them, they must be just outside the palace walls.

"A rumor is swirling that you are being tortured for information about how my father might defeat Eranahl," Keris said. "Such dreadful ideas the masses come up with while cooped up during storms. Idle hands may do the devil's work, but idle minds . . ."

Achieved a prince's ends.

Though what those ends were, Aren wasn't certain. "I'm surprised they care."

"Are you?" Keris's nose wrinkled with disdain. "My aunt believes you to be cleverer than you look, but I'm beginning to question her judgment."

"Did you just call me *stupid?*"

"If the shoe fits . . ."

God, but there was no mistaking him as anything other than Lara's flesh and blood.

Listening to the growing shouts, which were sounding distinctly more mob-like, Aren narrowed his gaze. It had been Lara's plan to use Ithicana's resources to feed Maridrina, thereby undercutting her father's scheme to blame Ithicana for Maridrina's woes. All through War Tides, Aren had believed her plan had worked—the Maridrinians had been singing his name in the streets, declaring to all who'd listen that the alliance with Ithicana was their salvation. There'd seemed little chance that Silas would follow through on his intentions to take the bridge, but of course Aren had been proven painfully wrong in that. So wrong that he'd presumed Lara's plan had been a deception intended to cause him to lower Ithicana's guard. But now . . .

"Allow me to help you along," Keris said. "Would you say that understanding the nature of the Ithicanian people was key to you ruling them successfully?"

"I didn't rule them successfully."

Keris rolled his eyes. "Don't be morose."

Obnoxious Veliant shit. Aren glowered at him. "Obviously it was key."

"Extrapolate. I'll know from the expression on your face when you come to an understanding."

Closing his eyes and taking a deep breath to curb his irritation, Aren considered the question, which had nothing to do with him and Ithicana, but everything to do with Silas and Maridrina.

The Maridrinians were angry about Aren's captivity because he'd earned their loyalty, and their friendship. And unlike their king, they didn't take kindly to those who stabbed friends in the back. Aren had seen the behavior on countless occasions during his times in Maridrina—the unwillingness to profit from a friend's hardship. They'd starve before taking a mouthful of ill-gotten bread. Understanding abruptly dawned on him, and Aren's stomach flipped.

"Finally!" Keris clapped his hands, and as if on cue, the musicians began to accompany the dancing children, who leapt and shook bells, their high-pitched voices filling the air. "I thought I might have to wait all morning."

Aren ignored the mockery. "The Maridrinian people don't want the bridge."

"That they do not. They've gained nothing from it, but it has cost them a great deal."

Aren had been so focused on his own people that he'd not stopped to think about the Maridrinians. Had not stopped to consider what possessing the bridge meant for them.

The bridge was as much a burden as it was an asset, demanding that its master shake hands with the same people who'd raid given the opportunity. Demanding impartiality when dealing with nations despite one being friend and the other foe. Demanding the blood of good men and women to protect it from those who'd take it, and then, and only then, would it provide. But Silas was denying the Valcottans. Favoring the Amaridians over the Harendellians. The only thing he was giving it was Maridrinian blood, but it wasn't enough.

Trade had dried up.

The bridge was empty.

"I imagine this is how parents feel when their child learns to speak," Keris said. "It's tremendously satisfying to see this display of intelligence from you, Your Grace."

"Be quiet," Aren replied absently, considering the complex twist of politics in play, though it was difficult with the noise the children were making.

How long would the Maridrinians accept paying in blood for something they didn't want? Something that yielded them nothing? How long until they pulled Silas from his throne and replaced him with someone more aligned with their way of thinking?

Someone like the prince sitting in front of him.

"When will the money run out?" Aren asked, knowing the Amaridian queen wouldn't allow the continued use of her navy if she wasn't being paid. Especially if tensions were rising between Amarid and Harendell.

Keris smiled at a pair of his little sisters as they twirled past him. "The coffers, I'm afraid to say, are completely dry."

"You seem remarkably pleased to be heir to a nearly bankrupt kingdom."

"Better that than a grave."

Aren made a noncommittal noise, tracing a crack in the table with one fingertip as he thought. But for once, Keris seemed too impatient to wait.

"If Eranahl surrenders, my father won't need the Amaridian navy any longer," the prince said. "And given he's unlikely to be merciful to those surrendering, Ithicana will no longer be a threat to Maridrina's control of the bridge. My father's position will be the most powerful it has ever been. So you see, Your Grace, a great deal is dependent on the continued survival of your little island fortress."

"First and foremost, your ability to take the Maridrinian crown from your father by way of a coup."

Keris didn't so much as blink. "First and foremost, my *life*. The coup and crown are merely a means to an end."

"You're risking a great deal telling me any of this," Aren said. "And I fail to see to what end. My involvement changes nothing. If anything, my death will serve to turn your people further against your father. But I also know we wouldn't be having this conversation if there wasn't something you wanted from me."

Keris was silent. And despite the fact that the entire conversation had been circling in on this precise topic, he could feel the reluctance the prince felt to give voice to his request. No . . . not reluctance. Unease. Maybe even fear. "Zarrah."

Keris gave the slightest of nods.

"You want me to arrange for her escape."

Another nod.

"Why do you believe I'd risk my own people to save her when I'm not even willing to risk them to save my own skin?"

"Because," he answered, "if you do it, she's promised Eranahl will be supplied with enough food to outlast my father's siege."

It was an offer better than Aren could've dreamed of. Especially given he'd burned Ithicana's relationship with Valcotta to the ground when he'd broken their blockade around Southwatch. "I can't see the Empress agreeing to that."

"Zarrah's a powerful woman, and the deal is with her, not the Empress. Take it or leave it."

"Allying with your kingdom's greatest enemy to win the crown." Aren gave a low whistle. "If your people discover that bit of information, it will cost you."

"Agreed. Which is why it's much better for both of us if it's perceived that you and yours were responsible for liberating her."

It was a gamble. One that could potentially cost dozens of his people their lives if the rescue attempt went sour. But Zarrah was under much less intense scrutiny than Aren was. And if his people managed to get her free, it would mean potentially saving everyone in Eranahl.

But there was still one thing that troubled him. "You've access to my people now. You don't need me for this."

Keris grimaced. "Serin doesn't trust me, so I'm under near-constant surveillance when I leave the palace, which means I can't contact your people directly. I need the harem to facilitate communication. But here's the rub: They despise Valcottans as much as any Maridrinian, so there isn't a chance of them agreeing to this plan of mine."

"And your solution to this rub?" Aren asked, seeing exactly where the prince was going.

"The harem won't help me free Zarrah. But they will help free *you*." Keris smiled, his eyes gleaming. "Which is why you're going to use them to help orchestrate your own escape, and when you run, you're going to take Zarrah with you."

17
AREN

FOR DAYS SINCE his conversation with Keris, Aren had spent every waking minute studying the palace's defenses, swiftly recognizing what he already knew: There was no way out. At least, not for someone as well guarded as him.

Eight men always within a few paces of his person. Another dozen watched over any route that accessed him. Countless more were waiting to reinforce them if needed. And for Aren, only the very best soldiers were employed. There wasn't a chance of his people silencing them all without an alarm being raised, and the moment those bells began to ring, the true defenses of Silas's inner sanctum fell into place.

Gates barred and locked from both inside and out.

Dozens of men deployed to the top of the inner wall.

Countless more soldiers sent to patrol the base.

The list of contingencies seemed endless, much to Aren's frustration, because every single day, he'd tried a different route of escape. Not because he had any chance of succeeding on his own, but because the only way to reveal all of the inner sanctum's defenses was to trigger them.

Test after test after test, all of which left him battered and bleeding, but nothing he tried yielded anything other than the truth: Escape was impossible.

For all of his adult life, he'd been part of making Ithicana impenetrable, putting himself into the mind of his kingdom's enemies to try to understand how and where they'd attack. How best to repel them. And most of all, how to identify weaknesses in Ithicana's defenses. But no matter how much time he spent trying to put himself in Silas's shoes, Aren couldn't come up with a solution.

But that didn't mean he had any intention of giving up.

His guards walked him through one of the covered walkways linking the palace buildings, two gripping his arms, the rest ahead and behind. Rain misted down from the sky, yet the wives were still out in the gardens, six of them working on some sort of dance while Silas looked on.

Predictably, Aren's guards were watching the women dance— or rather the way the mist caused their dresses to cling to their lithe bodies—and Aren saw his window.

Throwing his greater bodyweight sideways, Aren smashed the guard on his left into the railing even as he caught hold of the man's arm and lifted.

The soldier screamed as he went over the side, but Aren didn't let go, using the man's weight to pull him free from the other soldier's grip.

They plunged down, Aren pulling himself against the soldier so that the other man's body took the impact as they hit the ground.

It still hurt.

But this was the first time he'd gotten so far away from his guards, and Aren intended to capitalize upon it.

Ignoring the screaming wives in the distance, he clambered to his feet, moving as quickly as the chain strung between his ankles would allow as he shuffled in the direction of the open sewer grate to one side of the garden.

Alarm bells rang, the air filling with shouts as the Maridrinians fell into action, Aren taking in every move they made as he dodged around potted plants and statuary.

Ahead, he could see the grate sitting to one side of the opening. If he could just get inside, then—

Someone hit him hard in the back, knocking him down, then more piled on top of him until Aren could scarcely breathe.

"You just can't give up, can you?" Silas's voice drifted into Aren's ears. "I'm beginning to wonder if you're more trouble than you're worth, Master Kertell. If I wasn't a man of honor, I'd have your head spiked on Vencia's gates this afternoon."

"I've met rats with more honor than you," Aren spit out, elbowing one of the guards in the face, his efforts rewarded with a groan of pain. "And you're wasting your time—Lara's not going to risk her own neck to save mine. It's not in her nature."

"Are you so sure?" Silas bent low, his face only inches from Aren's. "How long will you keep your sanity when we skin her alive and then hang her on the wall to watch you?"

He was being crushed beneath the weight of the soldiers, but still Aren clawed at them, caring about nothing more than killing the man before him.

"Like a feral dog trying to escape its cage," Silas said to the wives waiting behind him. "Willing to break its own bones on the bars despite the futility of its efforts. It's the nature of his people, my dears. They aren't anything like us."

Furious, Aren bared his teeth, and several of the young women leapt back in alarm.

"Have no fear, darlings," Silas chuckled, then pulled one of them, whose belly had the curve of early pregnancy, toward him. "This dog has been muzzled."

The soldiers waited until Silas and his wives had departed, then slowly disentangled themselves. As they dragged him to his feet, Aren's gaze fixed on the tower above him, rising high into the sky, and an idea formed in his mind.

Silas was right: Aren was nothing like him. And it was time Aren remembered how to think like an Ithicanian.

L ARA STOOD AT the counter of a confectioner, Bronwyn at her elbow, both of them sampling sweets.

"Where is she?" Bron muttered, shoving another salted caramel into her mouth.

"She'll be here." The message requesting Lara's presence had come to Beth at her shop this morning, and Lara's guts had been twisting with a combination of nerves and anxiety ever since.

The door opened. "Wait outside," a familiar voice barked. "I don't need you dripping water on me while I shop."

The other patrons turned, so Lara did as well, watching as her Aunt Coralyn strolled across the room, clothing dry and shoes miraculously free of mud.

The confectioner was scrambling to put together a tray of samples, setting it on the counter right as Coralyn stepped next to Lara. Reaching out, the old woman plucked up a chocolate, examined it for a heartbeat, then popped it in her mouth. As she chewed, she murmured, "Your husband delivered."

"Pardon, my lady?" The confectioner leaned forward.

"I said I'll take a hundred of these."

The man's eyes brightened, and he turned to retrieve an order form. As he did, Coralyn slipped a piece of paper into Lara's hand. "It's time."

IT HAD TO be at dinner. It was the only time when he and Zarrah were in the same room together, and while there might be more opportune times and places for his people to rescue *him*, the necessity of getting the Valcottan general free trumped the increased danger. So, dinner it would be.

Coralyn intended to sneak six of his soldiers inside the walls, but beyond that, Aren knew nothing more of his people's plans. It had been hard enough getting the information to her. He'd been forced to scribble the details on a piece of paper hidden in the toilet during the minute of privacy he received, the process requiring him to fake digestive distress for several days in order to get all the information down.

Even then, it was only half of the plan, the rest dependent on those who were coming for him.

Keris's little rumor had gained a life of its own, and there was a veritable mob outside the palace gates, day and night, the shouts demanding Aren's release permeating the thick stone walls. The protest had grown violent of late, Silas's soldiers resorting to force to drive the people back so that the nobility could come and go without harassment. Nobility who were in turn instructed to tell the mobs that Aren was being treated with the utmost courtesy and respect.

All it did was fuel the fires of the rumors, the Maridrinian people distrustful of the nobility at the best of times. And this wasn't the best of times.

The guards led him through the corridors of the palace and into the dim confines of the dining room, where the majority of the guests were already gathered, conversing among themselves. Wearing a blue Maridrinian gown that bared her arms and most of her back, Zarrah sat at the far end of the table, her face devoid of expression as she listened to the chatter, but Keris was nowhere in sight. Knowing what he knew, the little shit was probably hiding somewhere.

But perhaps that was just as well. In the long run, Aren needed the prince alive, and accidents happened during a battle.

Taking his usual seat at the end of the table, Aren nodded at Coralyn while his chains were fastened to the table legs. "Good evening, my lady."

"It is a lovely evening, isn't it? Not a cloud in sight." She beamed at him, then her face grew serious, her wrinkled hand pressing down against his. "Do take care."

His heart skipped, and it took every ounce of control to keep the twist of excitement and fear rolling through his guts from showing on his face.

Silas entered the room, for once not flanked by his favorite wives. "Where are they?" he barked at Coralyn. "If you begin shirking your duties, your days of extravagance in the Sapphire Market will come to an end."

Coralyn inclined her head. "The harem's girls will be along shortly, *husband.* They've prepared a performance for you. Given the effort they've put into making it memorable, you might consider giving them your full attention when they arrive."

Silas's expression tightened, but he gave a short nod before turning to the ambassador from Amarid, clearly having no intention of following the directive of his *least* favorite wife.

Servants stepped inside bearing the salad course, and Aren ate mechanically, his ears tuned for sounds of fighting in the corridor. For the pounding of boots. For shouts or screams or any other sign that his people were on their way.

But there was nothing.

Sweat trickled down Aren's spine, the salad in his mouth tasting like sawdust. But next to him, Coralyn ate enthusiastically, seeming not to have a care in the world.

The servants returned to clear the plates, though Aren's was barely touched.

Where were they?

The main door flung open, and Aren lurched, his chains rattling. But instead of Ithicanian warriors, two men entered the room pounding vigorously on drums, followed by another two shaking cymbals, taking up positions on opposite sides of the room. They kept up the furious beat, then with a resounding thunder, went silent.

Aren's pulse replaced the sound, roaring in his ears with the same rhythm as the drums. Then Silas's wives entered the room, and his stomach dropped.

It had been a trick.

All a trick because there was no chance Coralyn would risk the harem to violence. Either his people were captured, or they weren't coming. Either way, all of it had been for nothing.

With dull eyes, Aren watched, which was more than he could say Silas was doing, the bastard still deep in conversation with the Amaridian.

All six of the women were dressed in gossamer silks and veils that concealed their faces, bells attached to both their ankles and wrists, feet bare. A rainbow of color, they encircled the table, their strides a seductive sway of the hips that made the silks shimmer in the lamplight.

There was an energy—a purpose—to their step that Aren hadn't seen before, and though he wasn't entirely certain why, his focus narrowed in on them as they took their positions.

"You're such a dear." Coralyn reached over to pat his cheek. "And in truth, they'll perform better for you than the smelly old wretch at the other end of the table."

A lithe woman with honey-blonde hair began to dance, the tiny shakes of her wrists making the bells decorating them jingle softly. She swayed through an elaborate set of steps, hips moving from side to side seductively. Then the others joined, replicating her motions in perfect unison, the musicians joining in.

The women circled the table, bare feet rapidly striking the floor in a complicated series of steps that filled the air with music. They spun, long locks swinging out behind them before falling to brush against their naked lower backs.

The drumbeat intensified, the women rounding the dining table, hips moving in suggestive circles that had some of the men breaking off the pretense they weren't gaping openly, but Silas fixedly ignored them.

A young woman with long brown hair brushed past Aren, the silk of her transparent sleeve grazing his cheek, and he turned to look at her. Like the others, her face was concealed by a veil, only her eyes visible. Azure eyes. She gave him a wink before spinning away.

None of the wives had eyes that color. None of them. But as his attention leapt from woman to woman, each of them with eyes of Maridrinian bastard blue, Aren's skin began to prickle.

"Talented, aren't they?" Coralyn murmured.

"Yes." He had to drag the word out of his throat as he marked the muscled tone of the women, which was entirely uncharacteristic of Silas's pampered wives. His eyes picked up the faint lines of scars that had been mostly concealed by cosmetics. There was a fire to the performance, a spirit that he'd never seen in any of the harem wives, who knew they were entertainment to be ignored.

These weren't harem wives.

These women were something else. What had Coralyn called them? *The harem's girls.*

The harem's daughters.

With his heart in his chest, Aren moved his attention to the honey blonde, whom he'd been both consciously and unconsciously ignoring each time she passed, the silk of her clothing drifting and moving to reveal a body he knew better than his own.

Lara twisted and danced, studiously avoiding his gaze until she rounded behind her father. Then her head turned and their eyes locked. Aren's heart gave a violent thump in his chest.

She had betrayed him. Stolen away his kingdom and caused the death of his people. Been the reason Silas had kept him locked up. Aren *hated* her like none other, yet in that moment, it was memories of tangling his fingers in her hair that assaulted his thoughts. The feel of her hands on his body, her legs wrapped around his waist, lips pressed against his. The smell of her filling his nostrils and the sound of her voice in his ears.

It was all lies, he silently screamed at himself as she circled the table. *She is your damnation.*

Yet there was no denying that she'd come here for him.

The drums took on a frenzied pace, finishing the piece with a rattling crash of cymbals as each of the women struck a final pose.

"Well done!" Coralyn cried out, clapping her hands. "Beautifully performed, my lovely girls. Weren't they stupendous, Silas?"

The King of Maridrina gave her a sour smile. "Wonderful, if somewhat overloud." Then he waved a dismissive hand, and the young women backed into the shadows of the walls, heads lowered.

All, that is, but one.

Lara took three quick steps and jumped, landing on the center of the table like a cat and rattling the glassware.

"What are you doing, woman?" Silas demanded. "Get down and get out before I have you whipped."

"Now, now, Father," Lara purred, walking down the table and kicking over glasses of wine with every step, nobleman and ambassadors pulling back in alarm. "Is that any way to greet your most *favored* of children?"

Silas's eyes widened as she pulled away the veil concealing her face, allowing it to flutter down onto a plate. Gasps filled the air, but no one spoke. No one dared.

"You little fool." Silas rose to his feet and pulled out his sword. "Just what did you think to accomplish by coming here tonight?"

"I intend to take back what's mine."

I am not yours, Aren wanted to scream at her, but Coralyn pressed

a hand against his arm.

Lara stopped in her tracks, one hip jutting out as she tapped a slender finger against her lips. "You lied to me. Manipulated me. Used me—not for the benefit of our people, but for your own benefit. To satisfy your own greed. For that, I think punishment is in order."

Silas pointed the tip of his sword at her. "I admire your confidence that you can accomplish such a feat on your own, Daughter."

Laughing, Lara tipped back her head. "Do you really think that I'm such a fool as to come alone?"

The air was split by distinct gurgles, bodies thudding to the ground.

Aren's attention jerked from Lara to the five other dancers, all of whom now held weapons glistening with the blood of the guards they'd just dispatched. As one, they removed their veils and smiled as they said, "Hello, Father."

The room erupted into chaos.

Guests screamed as they tried to scramble to safety, colliding with Silas's guards as they rushed the dancers. But the young women only picked up the weapons of their victims and slaughtered the soldiers with ease.

"Never mind *them*—get *her!*" Silas shrieked, and two soldiers charged toward the table, naked blades in hand and their eyes on Lara. Who was unarmed.

Aren jerked upright, but his wrists and ankles were bound to the table, rendering him helpless to do anything but watch as the soldiers moved in for the kill.

But Lara didn't need his help. Or anyone else's.

Snatching up a glass, she threw it in one guard's face, using the distraction to kick him in the wrist, sending his blade flying.

The other guard swung his weapon, but she leapt, the blade whistling under her, one leg striking out and catching the man in the face. He fell back, clutching a shattered nose.

The first guard recovered, snatching hold of her ankles. Before he could jerk her legs out from under her, Lara dived onto him, both of them falling out of sight behind the table.

Aren heard the snap of a breaking neck, then Lara appeared, sword in hand. With a ruthless slice, she cut the throat of the guard with the broken nose, then whirled to engage another, parrying the large man's blows, her shoulders shuddering from the impact of the weapons.

Once, twice, she blocked his blows, but on the third, the force knocked the sword from her hand.

"No!" Aren tried to lunge forward, fighting against his restraints, but the table barely shifted.

With a guttural roar, the man swung at her neck.

Lara ducked under the blow while catching hold of a broken wine glass, which she stabbed into his shoulder as she rotated, heel flying out to shatter the man's kneecap.

"I suppose we should take care of those chains, shouldn't we." Coralyn rose from where she'd sat serenely watching the carnage. Extracting a key, she unlocked the manacles on Aren's wrists before bending to do the same to his ankles. From across the room, shielded by eight of his guards, Silas saw her do it.

"Kill him!" the king shouted. "Kill the Ithicanian!"

A guard broke away, running in Aren's direction, but Aren whipped one of his chains, the links wrapping around the man's sword. A hard jerk sent the blade flying. The man stumbled, reaching for another weapon, but Coralyn freed Aren's ankles in time for him to lunge, tackling the soldier to the ground.

They grappled, rolling between the legs of panicked guests. The man pulled a knife, but Aren blocked the blow, catching hold of the man's wrist. Grinding his teeth with effort, he slowly forced the blade down, the man screaming, then choking as it pierced his throat.

Clambering to his feet, Aren punched a guard in the face, then used the knife to gut another, his ears filling with the sound of hammering.

The doors.

They were jammed shut.

Just as he requested they'd be in the plan he gave to Coralyn. Who'd subsequently given it to *Lara*, which meant he'd been unwittingly working with his wife this entire time. But now was not the time to dwell on how he'd been manipulated.

Whirling, Aren searched the chaos for Zarrah, finding the Valcottan general fighting, armed with a broken piece of a chair. She caved in the head of one man, about to move on another when Aren caught hold of her, barely avoiding being cracked in the skull as she switched targets.

"All this is for nothing if you get killed," he hissed, dragging her toward one of the curtains and shoving her behind it.

Leave. A voice whispered inside his head. *The rest of the plan is yours—you don't need them. All that matters is getting Zarrah out.*

But instead of listening, he searched for Lara's familiar form, finding her fighting two soldiers, a sword in one hand and a knife in the other.

The men were skilled. Head and shoulders taller than her. But the speed with which she moved . . .

He'd never seen her fight, only seen the results she'd left behind on Serrith. But now . . . Now he understood why the body count had been so high.

Aren stared, captivated, as Lara dodged and ducked. She twisted around a guard right as his comrade swung his sword, the blade sinking deep into the man's chest even as Lara flitted forward to gut the other, both men falling to the ground at her feet.

She turned, eyes widening. In one swift motion, she moved, the knife in her hand flying past Aren's ear. Twisting, he found a soldier behind him, sword lifted to strike even as he toppled backward, Lara's knife embedded in his left eye.

"You aren't going to escape." Silas's voice cut through the din.

The King of Maridrina was backed into a corner, the shield of soldiers standing in front of him showing no interest in attacking the young women who'd slaughtered their comrades.

"I knew you would come." Silas's laughter was wild. "This trap was for you, and you fell for it. All the better that you brought your sisters with you."

"It's not a very good trap." Lara reached down to slit the throat of the soldier gasping at her feet. "You're losing your touch."

Silas's grin was murderous. "There is no way out. Serin trained you—do you think he hasn't guessed every possible move you might make? He knows exactly how you think!"

"I'm counting on it." Lara flung the knife in her hand at Silas's head.

One of his soldiers threw himself in the way, the blade striking him with a meaty *thunk,* but Lara was already across the room, sword raised, cutting down another.

Then a loud crack split the air. Aren's eyes jerked to the main door. A large split had formed in the wood, the soldiers on the other side trying to force their way through. They had minutes to escape.

Maybe less.

He saw Lara turn to the door. Watched her lips form an angry curse, and then she was retreating, her sisters following suit, all of them so drenched with blood and gore that they looked more demon than woman.

"You need to come with us, Auntie," Lara said, pulling on Coralyn's arm, but the old woman only shook her head, moving to stand between them and Silas's guards.

"Even if I wasn't too old to run, I'd never abandon my family." Then she raised her voice. "Did you think we'd let you get away with it, Silas? Let you get away with stealing our children? With murdering our children? Did you think there wouldn't be a price to pay for your greed?"

"I'm going to gut you for this, you old bitch!"

"By all means, Silas, please do!" Coralyn laughed. "It will entertain me in the afterlife to watch how well you sleep knowing that every wife you have and every wife you ever take will be watching and waiting for a moment to take revenge for what you've done. The harem protects its own, and you've proven yourself our *enemy.* I think you'll not drop those trousers of yours so easily knowing that all the pretty mouths you surround yourself with have teeth. So by all means, Silas. Martyr me. All it means is that I'll have an exceptional vantage point to watch you pay for your crimes."

The split in the main door widened. They only had seconds.

"We have to go," said one of Lara's sisters. "There's no more time."

Aren caught hold of Coralyn's arm, but, knowing what sort of woman she was, he didn't ask her to run. "Thank you."

"Forgive her. She loves you."

He dropped the old woman's arm, feeling Lara's gaze on him. Knowing she was listening. "She doesn't know what love is."

"That's *why* you should forgive her."

Before Aren could answer, Coralyn extracted a glass jar from the folds of her dress and threw it to the ground, thick, choking smoke filling the room.

They needed to get out. Now.

Lara and her sisters had already taken action, pulling the heavy table over to use as a shield. Racing to the curtains, Aren caught hold of Zarrah's arm. "Get behind the table and cover your ears!"

Eyes burning from the smoke, he found the bottles the harem had left sitting on the window frame. Tucking two in his pockets, he used the others to set up the explosive, then activated the fuse. Throwing himself sideways, Aren covered his ears.

A deafening boom split the air, the window and the metal barring it exploding outward to rain down on the gardens. Scrambling back to his feet, Aren raced to the opening, retrieving the bottles from his pockets and throwing them into the fountains and pools below.

A hazy mist rose from the water, making it impossible to see more than a foot ahead of him.

"Who is she?" Lara had Zarrah by the arm, both of them coughing.

"Later," he hissed. "Climb!"

The sisters leapt nimbly onto the blackened ruin of the window frame, disappearing upward into the mist. Ripping the skirt of her dress so that her legs were free, Zarrah climbed after them.

Aren clambered onto the frame, the coughing of those trapped in the room covering the sound of his motion. He climbed the wall of the palace, his fingers finding handholds where the mortar had crumbled, his thin shoes nearly as good as bare feet. Below him, Lara followed, a knife clenched between her teeth.

Reaching the balcony, Aren used the wrought iron railings to pull himself over. One of the sisters stood on the balcony throwing the bells they'd worn into the courtyard, but the rest were waiting inside.

He muttered, "This way."

The alarm bells were ringing, the noise making Aren's ears ache, but it covered any sound they made as they moved into the empty hallway, the regularly spaced lamps lighting their passage. From behind the doors, Aren could hear the alarmed chatter of women. A crying baby. A child shouting something about a missing toy.

"They'll stay locked in their rooms until the alarm ceases and they are instructed the palace is secure," Lara murmured from where she walked on his left. "But Coralyn said we would only have a few minutes before the guards come to check that everyone is accounted for."

It was strange to hear her voice, and yet . . . *not.* She'd consumed his thoughts. Consumed his dreams. So it felt almost like they'd never been apart.

His eyes moved to his wife, drinking in the sight of her. The blood covering Lara did more than the ruined dancing costume to conceal her body. The torn silk she wore hung loose to reveal the inner curve of her right breast, her muscled abdomen completely exposed. In one hand she held a knife, and in the other a sword, the knuckles on both split from fighting. What he wanted to feel was repulsed, but instead desire burned hot in his veins.

Annoyed, he stepped ahead to where Zarrah strode, silent on her bare feet. "How much did he tell you?" Keris alone seemed to know all the parts of this plan. All the players.

"Only to follow your lead."

"Do you trust him?"

Dark eyes looked up at him. "With my life."

Boots thundering up the stairs put an end to further questions.

They ran down the hall, carpets muffling their footfalls. Rounding a bend led them to a door, which Aren eased open, revealing one of the covered bridges over the gardens. The interior was dark, but the smell of recently extinguished lamps still hung thick on the air. Outside, dense, smoking mist rose from the fountains, the jars the wives had placed in them having dissolved, the chemicals inside reacting with the water. It created a fog as murky as any in Ithicana, and it did an equally good job disorienting the hunting Maridrinian soldiers.

"The harem delivers again," Lara said, and they hurried across, keeping low despite there being little chance of them being seen.

Reaching the far side, they crept into the tower, and Aren gestured to the staircase. "Up."

Lara and her sisters took the stairs two at a time, none of them appearing even winded. But a cramp formed in Aren's side, the long sedentary days he'd spent as a prisoner catching up with him. Up and up, they bypassed each door leading to another level of the tower.

Then the door to Aren's right swung open, a figure stepping into the stairwell.

Lara shoved Aren sideways, blade rising as she moved to engage the individual. Just before she swung, Aren recognized Keris's face. Reaching out, he caught hold of Lara's slender wrist, hauling her backward.

"Who is he?" she demanded.

"It's been a long time, little sisters," Keris said, inclining his head to the Veliant women. "I wish we could've reunited under better circumstances."

Lara stared at him, then her eyes widened. "*Keris?*"

The prince nodded, a smile rising to his face, though he vanquished it a heartbeat later.

"You're helping us?"

"I'm helping myself," Keris answered. "But tonight, our interests are aligned." He shifted his attention to Zarrah, who stepped past Aren.

Keris reached up to touch a bruise darkening the Valcottan woman's cheek. "Are you all right?"

"It's nothing."

Nodding, the prince turned his attention to Aren. "This is where you part ways with the general."

"I don't think so. Zarrah's coming with us. I intend to make sure she delivers on her end of the deal."

Keris stepped between him and the Valcottan woman, ignoring Lara and her sisters when they lifted their weapons. "There's too much chance of you being caught or killed. And her life is more important than yours. While everyone is pursuing you, I'll get her out."

Aren scowled. "I'm just your goddamned decoy?"

"Precisely. But given my plan is more likely to achieve that which you desire, perhaps you'll refrain from whining. Time is short." Keris gently pushed Zarrah toward the open door, but Aren caught her arm.

Her dark eyes met his. "On my word, if I get out alive, I'll have supplies delivered to drop points in Ithicana where your people can reach them." Then she touched her hand to her heart. "Good luck, Your Grace."

Without another word, she disappeared into the room.

"Time for you to carry on," Keris said. "But before you go, I need you to make it look like I at least *tried* to stop you."

"Gladly." Aren swung, his fist connecting hard with Keris's cheekbone.

The prince stumbled into the doorframe, wincing as he touched his already swelling face. "You have ten minutes until I start down to alert the guards. Make them count."

They raced to the top of the tower, reaching a glassed-in room encircled by a wide balcony. The view of the city was incredible, but there was no time to appreciate it. "Where is it?" he demanded.

One of the sisters went to a wall and pulled down a framed piece of artwork. It was pieces of wood and metal laid out in a random pattern, but as the woman pulled apart the frame and dumped the contents at his feet, Aren realized what he was looking at.

"Jor tells me that you should be able to put this together," she said.

"He's alive?"

"Was the last time I saw him. He said that if you can't build this, then perhaps you deserve your fate. I'm Bronwyn, by the way."

Not answering, Aren dropped to his knees, sorting through pieces while the women pulled on the Maridrinian uniforms that had been hidden in one of the chests.

Lara set clothes and boots next to him. "Move quickly," she said. "It's already been five minutes."

As if he needed more pressure. Sweat beaded on his brow as he fitted together the pieces of the weapon, using the small tools to twist screws and tap parts into place. Seconds rolled by. Then minutes.

"Hurry," one of the sisters muttered, but Aren ignored her, focusing on the task at hand.

"There."

Lifting the large crossbow, he tested the mechanism twice to ensure it worked, then picked up the single bolt that had been part of the artwork. While he'd been building, the tall brunette called Bronwyn had taken apart the hollow frame that had encased the artwork, revealing a line of rope, which she handed over.

"You sure this is long enough?" he asked as he pulled on the clothing, shoving his feet into the boots.

She only lifted one eyebrow, then nodded to the balcony. "Time to live up to your reputation, Your Majesty."

"You just don't want to miss the shot."

She smirked. "Pretty *and* clever. I should've fought harder to be the one to marry you."

"Enough, Bronwyn," Lara muttered. "Save it for when we are free of this place."

Shaking his head, Aren eased open the door to the balcony, keeping low as he crept out to peer through the wrought iron railing. Below, the courtyard was completely concealed with mist, which had risen high enough to float around the boots of the soldiers swarming the inner wall. The exterior wall was also well manned, but their focus was on the enormous mob surrounding the palace, the civilians screaming Aren's name and demanding his liberty.

Lara dropped to her knees next to him, face shadowed by the hood of her coat. But even over the smell of blood, there was no mistaking the sweet scent of her filling his nose, her presence too familiar to be any of the other women.

He shifted away, focusing on the domed roof of the guard post on the corner of the inner wall. This was potentially the fatal flaw in his plan. A few of them might be able to get down the zipline before the guards noticed, but not all of them. And the second the soldiers saw them, they'd have a fight on their hands.

"It won't work." Lara said quietly. "You need to get us all the way to the exterior wall."

He looked to where her finger pointed: the exterior wall guard tower, the structure made of stone and nothing else, never mind that it was a good fifty feet farther than his intended target. "Impossible."

"Jor said it's not."

"There's nothing for me to hit. That guard tower is made of solid stone—the bolt will bounce right off."

"You just need to shoot it through that window," she said. "My sisters should have taken the guard tower by now. They'll signal as soon—" She broke off as two quick flashes of light shone through the narrow slit of the window.

"It's a long shot." And he'd have to make it the first time. There'd be no dragging the bolt back across the palace grounds for a second shot. "There is no chance the soldiers on the wall won't notice us flying over them, Lara. We'll be easy targets for their archers to pick off. It's a shitty plan. We're trapped."

"If you don't think you can make the shot," she said, "then give the damned thing to me. As for the rest, our people have arranged for a distraction."

"Our people?" It wasn't the time. It wasn't the place. But the months they'd been apart had done nothing to temper his fury over her betrayal. "Would those be the people who lost their homes? Their loved ones? Their lives? Because of *you*. They are *not* yours."

Lara jerked back the hood of her coat, turning on him. "Save the dramatics for once we're out of here. Ithicana has put nearly every resource it has left into this rescue, and it would be a shame to waste everyone's efforts because of semantics."

"Lara, they're ready." Bronwyn's voice cut through the tension, and in the distant hilltops, Aren caught sight of a light flashing again. Once. Twice. Three times.

"Can you make the shot or not?"

Aren lifted the crossbow, aiming at the guard tower. "I'll make it."

"Five. Four. Three," Bronwyn counted. "Two—" Her whisper was drowned out by an explosion in the city that sent the tower shuddering. Then another explosion and another. Blasts of brightness illuminated the dark sky, Aren's eardrums ringing from the noise.

"Now," Lara said, and he took a deep breath, focusing on the tiny opening. Then let the bolt fly.

It shot through the air, cable trailing out behind it, and as it flew, more explosions rattled the city. Beneath them, the soldiers were shouting, organization turning to chaos with the belief the city itself was under attack. But Aren barely heard them. Barely saw them. "Come on. Come on."

The bolt flew through the window.

Bronwyn reached over to pat him on the cheek. "Oh, you are magnificent."

Aren jerked away, glaring at her.

Two of the other sisters tied the cable off, tension rising as they waited for whoever was in the guard tower to do the same on their end. Then a light flashed.

Lara and her sisters all had hooks identical to those they used in Ithicana, and Lara held one out to him. "I'll go first. Then you." Her eyes flicked to her sisters. "Don't lose your nerve."

Taking a firm grip on the hook's handle, she placed it over the cable.

"Wait." Aren reached for her, having seen lines fail before. Having seen his soldiers fall, though usually it was into the water, which meant they survived. No one would survive a fall into the courtyards below. "Let me—"

Another explosion lit up the night sky, and Lara jumped.

Aren's stomach dropped. He gripped the railing, watching as Lara soared silently downward, picking up speed as she went. *Don't look up,* he prayed silently as she flew over the wall, only a dozen feet over the soldier's heads. *Don't look up.*

But luck or fate was with them, and the panicked soldiers kept their gaze on the misty gardens and courtyards below, where they assumed Aren to be hiding.

Nearing the guard tower, Lara reached up with a gloved hand to slow her progress. Her feet struck the stone, and she paused to ensure no one had noticed her presence. Then she pulled herself on top of the tower, where she perched, hidden in the shadows.

"Go!" Bronwyn gave him a gentle push between the shoulders and, glancing down to confirm no one was looking up, Aren jumped.

S HE COULDN'T BREATHE as he flew over the misty palace, black
clothing rendering him almost invisible in the moonless night.
More explosions rattled the earth, the air thick with smoke.
Outside the wall, the mob had turned to chaos, people screaming, but
she spared them no attention.

So far, everything had gone according to her plan, but that could
change in a heartbeat. Her *brother*—who had, unbeknownst to her,
been in on the planning—would be on his way to alert the guards that
they were in the tower. Those searching the grounds wouldn't be able
to see through the fog, but those on the inner wall would. And her
sisters would be sitting ducks.

But all she could think about was Aren's eyes when he'd
recognized her. When she'd seen them last on Midwatch, they'd been
red-rimmed and filled with anger and hurt. But now . . . they were
cold. As though she meant nothing to him and never had.

Aren's boots slapping against the guard tower dragged her back
to the moment. She reached down to help him, but he pushed her hand

away, pulling himself up in one easy motion.

He crouched next to her in the shadows, and Lara clenched her teeth, her chest aching to have him so close.

And yet so far.

"Don't think this changes anything," he whispered between explosions. "I don't value my own neck enough for your saving it to undo the damage you caused. The second we are away from your father, I want to see the back of you. Understood?"

There was no point arguing, given the plans she had in play, and she was spared having to do so as Athena climbed onto the tower to join them.

Four more to go.

Heart hammering, Lara split her attention between watching her sisters slide down the zip line and the guards milling below. Despite the chaos in the city, none appeared to be readying to leave the palace, their focus entirely on recapturing her and Aren.

Cierra clambered up top with them, followed by Cresta. Brenna was next, her face white as a sheet. "That was bloody awful," she muttered. "Never again."

Only Bronwyn was left. But the mist was dissipating on the wind of a coming storm. Lara clenched her teeth, watching her sister's shadowy figure ease on to the line, then start the slide downward. "Come on," she muttered. "Faster."

Bronwyn picked up speed, but as she flew over the inner wall, yells echoed out of the sanctum. "They're in the tower!"

All the guards on the wall looked up in time to see Bronwyn above them. They shouted and turned, lifting their weapons.

"Blow the gate!" Lara ordered, even though it was too soon.

"Already signaled," Athena replied. "Close your eyes and cover your ears."

A heartbeat later, the world exploded around them.

A REN INSTINCTIVELY CLAPPED his hands over his ears and closed his eyes, pressing his face against the parapet.

It did little good as the detonation shattered the air, the fierce glow of the burning chemicals searing through his eyelids, his ears ringing. He felt rather than saw Lara move next to him, and he opened his eyes to find her leaning over the parapet, reaching for Bronwyn who dangled below.

"You bitch," the tall brunette snarled as Lara dragged her upward. Her eyes were streaming with tears from the brightness of the explosion. "You couldn't have warned me? And don't bother arguing—I can't hear for shit."

Lara only dragged her around the top of the guard tower. Her other sisters were already climbing down the wall, taking advantage of the few moments the swarms of soldiers would be as deaf and blinded as Bronwyn.

Following suit, Aren watched two more sisters dressed in Maridrinian uniforms exit the interior of the guard tower. One motioned for the group to pull up their hoods and follow as she sprinted down the interior stairs and into the chaos. The air was full of smoke, the gate blown inward by the force of the explosion. Several soldiers were on their knees, clutching their bleeding ears.

But that wasn't the direction the women led him in. Instead, they entered the stables in the far corner, the horses inside spinning in their stalls in distress. Several of the animals were wearing saddles and bridles, and the women swiftly entered the stalls, then crouched low.

Lara dragged him into one stall, then pulled him down. "Won't be long," she muttered.

Sure enough, shouts cut through the stone walls. "It's them! They're outside the walls!"

Peering through the slats of wood, Aren watched soldiers storm into the stables, the men taking the horses in the first rows of stalls and swinging into their saddles before galloping out the doors in pursuit of what Aren assumed were decoys.

"Now." Lara rose, taking the reins of the horse in the stall and handing them to him.

He stared at the enormous animal. "I don't know how to ride a horse."

"Learn. And for the love of God, keep your hood up."

Wary of the horse's mouthful of teeth, Aren led the animal out of its stall, then eased the reins over its head. He stuck his foot in the stirrup, only his death grip on the saddle keeping him from falling as the animal lurched sideways.

"Hurry up!" Lara was already in the saddle of another animal, her hood pulled forward to hide her hair and face, baggy clothing giving bulk to her slender form. A bow was hooked over her shoulder, a stuffed quiver attached to the saddle. "I could use some more weapons," he growled.

"Focus on staying in the saddle."

Glowering, Aren sprawled over the horse's back, barely managing to get his other foot in the stirrup before Lara slapped his horse on the haunches. Then they were on the move.

The horses' hooves clattered loudly against the cobbles as they surged through the smoking gate, the uniforms and trappings on the animals convincing those manning the walls that they, too, were in pursuit of the decoys galloping into the city. Though if any of them were paying attention, they'd realize instantly Aren wasn't a Maridrinian soldier. Not with the way he clung to his mount's mane, bouncing wildly on its back, reins flopping uselessly in front of him.

The rioters in the streets dived out of their way as the group surged past. The women guided their horses expertly down the switchbacking streets. Aren's mount followed the other horses, which was a mercy, because he hadn't the slightest idea of how to direct it, his entire focus on not falling off.

"The harbor will be swarming with soldiers," he shouted. "They'll have the chain up. We'll never get a ship out."

"We aren't going to the harbor," Lara responded. "Trust that we have a plan, Aren, and focus on not falling off your horse."

As if I can ever trust you, he thought, but further conversation proved impossible as it began to rain. The cobbles grew slick, but the women maintained the pace despite the horses' struggle to keep their footing. Aren's mount slipped, nearly going down, and his heart lurched, sweat pouring down his back.

Behind them, the palace's drum tower hammered out a message. The women cocked their heads, listening, and Aren grimaced at not knowing the code, though he suspected the crux of it was that their ploy had been discovered.

"Right on time," Bronwyn shouted, and the group veered down a main boulevard, heading in the direction of the eastern gates, the horses galloping full out. In the distance, the sky burst brilliant as explosives detonated at the gate. Several of the horses shied, eyes wild, as the enormous boom split the air.

As the ringing in his ears cleared, Aren picked up the sound of clattering hooves and shouts. Soldiers converged on them from all directions, racing to intercept them before they reached the gates.

Drumbeats filled the air, and this message Aren recognized: *Eastern gate under attack.*

Ithicana. It had to be.

"Faster!" Lara called. "We need them to commit!"

The horses surged forward, the buildings on either side nothing but dark blurs, the rain now a blinding deluge. There were flames ahead, part of the gate on fire, the light illuminating dozens of soldiers lining the wall. And countless more soldiers below working to extinguish the blaze and secure the gates.

The drums tower at the gate rolled, repeating the same message. "They see us!" Bronwyn shouted. "They're calling for reinforcements!"

An arrow shot past Aren's face, another slicing across the haunches of Lara's horse, the animal squealing in pain. Three more clattered against the walls of the houses, the only thing keeping them from striking true the darkness and the rain.

"Almost there!" Lara shouted.

The drum signal repeated, then abruptly cut off in the middle of a pattern. Next to him, Lara ripped back her hood, eyes on the roofline. Aren followed her gaze, picking out a shadowy figure on a roof ahead. The figure lifted a brazier, illuminating her face. *Lia.*

His friend and bodyguard saluted him once as they thundered past, then Lara reached down and snatched hold of Aren's reins, hauling both animals to a halt. The other sisters did the same, the animals twisting and circling each other as the soldiers at the gate formed a line and their pursuers raced up behind.

Lia threw something to the street.

An explosion tore through the air, causing the horses to buck and plunge, Aren barely managing to hold on as another explosion split his ears a block farther on, hemming their group in on both sides and concealing them with smoke.

Three of the girls heeled their horses down an alley leading north. But his horse was heading in the opposite direction, Lara tugging on the reins and guiding him into an alley, Bronwyn leading the way, one of the other sisters holding up the rear.

They plunged through the near darkness of the alley, then careened onto a street, galloping back in the direction they'd come.

The streets were nearly empty now, the Maridrinians, believing Vencia under attack, taking shelter in their shuttered homes.

"Where the hell are we going?" Aren demanded.

"West." Lara's eyes were on the street behind them. "We've only got a few minutes before they get the drum tower signaling again, and we'll have the whole garrison after us." Then she swore. "Cresta! Bronwyn! We've got company!"

As soon as the warning exited her throat, Lara's horse stumbled and nearly fell, struggling to right itself. Its hindquarters were drenched in blood from where it had been shot with an arrow. The animal wouldn't be able to keep pace for long.

"Pick me up on the far side," she called to Bronwyn. "I'm going to buy us some time."

She reined the struggling horse close to the buildings before climbing onto its back, where she crouched, bow looped over one shoulder. Then she jumped.

Risking his balance for a backward glance, Aren saw her dangling from a balcony. Climbing. Then she had an arrow nocked and another two clenched between her teeth as she aimed at the soldiers in pursuit. One of them fell from his horse and another reached up to clutch his shoulder where an arrow protruded. The other soldiers caught sight of Lara, pointing and lifting their own weapons, but Aren's horse skidded around the street corner, killing his line of sight.

I need to go back. The thought tore through his mind, but Bronwyn drew knee-to-knee with him, shaking her head. "She knows what she's doing. Keep riding."

They climbed the steep street, the horses' labored breathing almost as loud as their hooves.

She could be dead, he thought. *She could be lying bleeding in the street.*

"If she is, she deserves it," he growled at himself. Yet despite his admonition, relief flooded him as a shadow appeared at the top of the buildings ahead. Lara leapt onto a balcony and then jumped to the street, where she dropped into a roll, back on her feet and running in the blink of an eye.

Bronwyn galloped toward her, Lara catching hold of her sister's stirrup at the last second. She leapt into the air, her leg arching over the back of the horse. Bronwyn gripped Lara's free hand to help her settle onto the animal's back.

The drums began to roll a new pattern, the sound like thunder as it chased them through the streets.

The west gate barely deserved the name, for it was nothing but a barred slit in the wall leading to a narrow path, which led to a vertical climb down to the shoreline. There was nowhere to moor a boat; the only way to reach a vessel would be to swim out to meet it. He could do it. Easily. But Lara and her two sisters . . .

They pressed up the hill via the twisting streets, the horses winded and near their limit. Then the gate came into sight, a narrow steel portcullis defended by six heavily armed soldiers.

"We don't have the codes." The other sister—Cresta—pulled up next to Aren, the group slowing to a trot and then to a walk. "Tell them the drum towers have been compromised, but that there have been reports of Ithicanian vessels outside the breakwater. We just need to get close enough to take them out."

"Halt and identify yourselves!" a soldier shouted.

Aren cleared his throat, fighting to regulate his voice enough to take on a Maridrinian accent. "Drum towers have been compromised," he called, sliding off the side of the horse, his legs aching.

"The codes," the man shouted, lifting his bow and leveling an arrow at Aren's chest.

"The codes have been compromised, you jackass," Aren shouted, improvising. "The Ithicanians have them. How the hell else do you suppose they broke in and out of the king's goddamned harem?"

The soldier's brow furrowed, but he didn't lower his weapon, and his fellows kept their hands on the hilts of their blades.

"There are reports of Ithicanian vessels outside the breakwater. Last reliable update was that the Ithicanian king was making for the south gate. If he circles around the city, he can get down the cliffs and reach the water without you bloody idiots any the wiser."

The man lowered his bow, but when Aren took a step his direction, the soldier shook his head. "Humor me, friend. What's tonight's co—"

The man broke off, a knife embedded in his throat.

Lara and her sisters attacked, a flurry of steel blades clashing together. Aren picked up the man's fallen sword and threw himself into the mix, cutting down one soldier and then shooting another in the back with the dead man's bow as he tried to flee down the length of the wall.

It was over in minutes, but from behind, horses were racing toward them. Reinforcements.

The sisters had the portcullis half-open by the time he turned around, the four of them rolling under the partially raised iron spikes, the chain jammed with a sword to slow down pursuit.

They moved cautiously along the dark trail until they reached the junction, one branch leading down to the inlet and the other up the steep slope. The sound of waves filled Aren's ears, the air heavy with the smell of brine. It had been months since he'd seen the sea. Heard it. Had the smell of it fill his noise without the stench of the city tainting it. In a few hours, he would be back in Ithicana.

But Lara was tugging him in the other direction. "This way."

He refused to budge.

"Aren, there are no ships. No boats," she hissed. "It was just a ruse. There are fresh horses waiting in the trees a short distance from here."

He didn't want to go with her. Didn't want to be anywhere near her, not just because of what she'd done, but because he didn't trust his instincts around her. "To take us where?"

"To the meeting point where we have supplies." She turned to look back down the pathway toward the city, betraying her nerves. "We have to hurry."

"I'm not going anywhere with you, Lara. I'm going back to Ithicana." Because he could do it alone. Could keep to the coast until he was able to steal a vessel, then make his way back home.

"Don't be a fool." There was anger in her voice now. "Weeks of preparation were put into this plan, and you intend to throw that all away."

"I don't trust you," he snapped. "Or your plans. I told you I never wanted to see your face again. That I'd kill you. You're lucky I don't toss you off this cliff."

"Just try it, you ungrateful prick," Bronwyn snarled, but Lara waved a calming hand in her direction.

"I don't blame you for not trusting me," she said. "But perhaps put your faith in your sister. In your grandmother. In Jor. In every Ithicanian who has invested everything in this plan. Trust them."

Indecision crept into his gut, and Aren glared at her. For all the good it would do in the dark.

"When I showed up at Eranahl, the *only* reason Ahnna allowed me to live was because she knew that I was Ithicana's best chance of getting you back. And she was very clear that once you were free and returned home, she'd kill me if I ever stepped foot in Ithicana again. For once, can you please show *some* of her pragmatism."

How in the hell had Lara made it to Eranahl? was the first thought that struck him, but he pushed it away. "Fine."

"Climb, you idiots," Cresta said from where she stood watching the path back to Vencia. "They're almost on us."

Gritting his teeth, Aren clambered up the cliffside, finding handholds by feel alone in the darkness. Below, boots hammered up the pathway, the soldiers in swift pursuit after having discovered their dead comrades.

Faster.

"They're climbing!"

The shout filtered upward, and a second later, bowstrings twanged, arrows bouncing off the cliffside.

Aren grimaced as one sank into the rocky ground inches from his hand, another glancing off the heel of his boot.

But they were almost there.

Then a cry of pain filled his ears.

"Bronwyn!" Lara gasped, and Aren looked past his feet to see a figure sliding down the cliff, catching herself perhaps fifteen feet below him.

"Go!" Bronwyn called. "Get him out of here!"

"I'm not leaving you!"

Aren heard Lara begin a downward climb, and he hesitated.

"No!" Bronwyn's voice was shrill. "If they catch or kill you and Aren, that means Father wins. It means he gets away with everything he did to us. Everything he made us do. *Please,* Lara. You need to keep fighting."

Lara stopped moving beneath him, and Aren could sense her making a decision. He knew in his heart what it was.

But he was through with people dying for him.

"Get to the top and cover me," he hissed to Cresta, then he started downward.

Lara reached for his arm as he passed, but he batted it aside. "Get your ass to the top and make every shot count."

It took him seconds to reach Bronwyn, her breath rasping with pain. "Where?"

"Right shoulder." Her voice was tight. "Go. Don't let them get another lucky shot."

Ignoring her, Aren slid his head and shoulder under her good arm. "Hold on."

She tightened her hold, wrapping her legs around his waist, a slight whimper escaping her lips as her injured shoulder was jostled.

From above, bows twanged as Lara and Cresta exchanged shots with the soldiers, shouts of pain from below suggesting that the women were having more luck hitting their targets. Aren ignored all of it and climbed, grinding his teeth against the extra weight, his balance precarious and his strength not what it once was. He could feel the heat of Bronwyn's blood soaking into his clothing, the scent of it thick on his nose, but her grip on him didn't falter.

An arrow bounced off a rock next to his face, and faintly he picked up the sound of the soldiers below climbing, but he didn't look down. Didn't look up to see how much farther there was to go.

"I've got you." Lara's voice. Then Bronwyn let go of him, her sisters dragging her upward.

Aren's hand found the edge of the cliff and he scrambled over, keeping low in case any of those below had held back any arrows.

Then they ran as fast as possible over the rough terrain, boulders and brush catching at their feet, Lara dragging Bronwyn.

"Run ahead and get the horses," Lara whispered to Cresta. "They'll be up the cliff in minutes, and there will be riders coming around from the south gate by now. We have to hurry."

Cresta disappeared into the darkness, and Aren pushed next to Lara and Bronwyn, pressing a hand against the latter's back. It was drenched with blood.

"Shit," he swore, then scooped her up into his arms. "Do you have any arrows left?"

"Three," Lara replied. "But I have other ways of killing them. Just leave me a horse."

Then she fell back.

T HINGS WERE *NOT* going according to plan.

Lara moved on silent feet back the way she'd come, bow held loosely as she listened for sounds of the soldiers pursuing them.

She heard the faint thud of boots, and she moved to the side of the path, counting the men as they ran past, swords in hand. *Six.* And there'd be more on the way soon enough.

Skirting up behind them, she shot arrows into the backs of three soldiers, then slid into the shadows as the remainder shouted in alarm, moving to find cover. Pulling out a knife, Lara crept around the rocks, taking her time to avoid detection, then paused to listen.

Nothing.

But a breeze brushed her cheek, and it carried with it the rank smell of sweat. Smiling, Lara crouched low, keeping her nose to the air as she took slow steps, stopping when she caught sight of a large rock that would provide good cover. She threw a stone in the distant bushes, marking the faint motion as the men turned their heads in that direction.

Tossing another stone, she took several quick steps and threw her knife.

A meaty *thunk*, rather than a scream, spoke to the trueness of her aim, and pulling her sword, Lara quit all pretense at stealth and attacked.

The soldiers lifted their blades, filling the night with clangs of steel as they engaged. She fought one of them in earnest, dodging the other's swings as he tried to stab her in the back, luring him closer until he lunged. Then she stepped sideways, removing his arm from his body a heartbeat after he stabbed his companion in the chest.

The soldier screamed, falling to the ground to clutch at the bleeding stump, but Lara whipped the tip of her blade across his throat, silencing him and then his dying comrade. She retrieved her knife from the third man, rising as the sound of hooves filtered over her.

The guards from the southern gate.

Swearing, she sprinted in the direction of the copse of trees where the horses were hidden. As promised, one remained, and she flung herself into the saddle, digging in her heels and riding in the direction of the coming soldiers.

With Bronwyn injured and Aren utterly incompetent on horseback, she needed to lure the pursuers off. Give them time to reach Sarhina, who had more supplies.

Pulling back her hood, she tore the tie loose from her hair so that it flowed down her back. Even in the dark, it should be enough to confirm her identity.

Flying down the road, she waited until the group was within sight, then hauled her horse up, wheeling the animal in a circle as though she were lost. Panicked. Then Lara laid the reins to the animal's shoulder and tore back down the road, smiling grimly as they gave chase.

The rain had stopped, but the road was muddy, filthy water splattering her mount and her legs as she led her father's soldiers away from Aren and her sisters, heading toward a small town in an inlet west of Vencia. The animal skidded and slid down the incline toward the stone houses lining the slope, lamplight glowing in the windows. Only a few people were out in the streets. They gaped and jumped out of the way as she galloped down to the small docks where the fishing vessels were moored.

"Wait!" She screamed loud enough that half the town would hear. "I'm coming—don't leave me behind! Aren, don't leave me behind!"

Reaching the dock, she flung herself off the side of the horse and unfastened the lines mooring the vessels, pushing them away from the dock until the harbor was in disarray. Then, hearing the soldiers had caught up, she swung under the dock, her body mostly submerged, fingers gripping a barnacle-crusted pier.

The waves pulled and dragged on her, and an old familiar fear rose in her chest. What if she lost her grip? What if the tide pulled her out to sea? What if there were sharks lurking below?

"Do you see her?" a soldier shouted. He and several of his companions ran over the dock above. "That was her horse!"

More soldiers raced onto the dock, boots making heavy thuds that covered her gasping breaths. They went to the far end, and she could imagine them peering out over the dark sea, searching for any signs of a vessel.

"There are witnesses saying she was shouting to someone down here, sir," a man said, striding above her, his shadowy form visible through the gaps in the planks. "For them to wait for her. She used the Ithicanian's name."

The commanding officer swore. "They're on the water. Get the signals lit for the ships patrolling. If the navy doesn't pick them up soon, they'll be lost. Get some of the fishermen down here to help with the hunt."

Lara waited for them to retreat back to shore, then moved slowly down the underside of the dock, slipping her fingers between the gaps, knowing she needed to hurry. Once daylight hit, trackers would swiftly determine that Aren and her sisters hadn't gone this way, and her father would suspect a ruse. They needed to be gone by then.

Reaching the rocky beach, Lara crawled in the knee-deep water, cringing every time a wave washed over her head. Her hands and knees were bleeding from the sharp rocks, but she couldn't risk climbing to her feet while still in sight of the group of soldiers.

And there were more arriving by the minute. They weren't fools.

They would search every boat and up and down the shoreline, and it wouldn't surprise her if they brought dogs to assist with the task.

Deeming herself out of eyesight, Lara emerged onto the beach, wincing at the way her boots squelched, the noise seeming to echo through the night. Skirting the edge of the town, she climbed the hill at a jog, then cut east, keeping a dozen paces back from the road until she reached a bridge over a small river, the rushing of water filling her ears. It began raining again, the occasional flash of lightning brightening the sky. She followed the river upstream and searched for the nearly indecipherable smear of glowing algae that would mark her path.

And only when she found it did she allow herself to wonder whether Bronwyn was still alive. Whether any of her other sisters had been harmed. Whether they'd been killed.

Guilt bit at her insides. They'd known what they were getting into when they agreed to help, but they were still in this position because of her. She'd saved their lives only to risk them again.

And Aren?

Thinking about him made her sick to her stomach. The way he'd looked at her, the hate in his voice. There'd been no reason to believe it would be different, but she'd still hoped.

Following the faint markings of algae and wiping them off as she passed, Lara climbed the hill, arms and legs feeling like they were made of lead, countless little injuries leeching away her strength.

Reaching the mouth of the small cave, she saw the horses tethered to one side. Saw the droplets of blood on the rock leading inward. *Please all still be alive,* she prayed. *Please still be here, Aren.* "Huntress." Her voice was raspy, and she swallowed before adding, "It's Lara."

Then she stepped inside, only to be greeted by a familiar, sour voice. "Well, the stars are truly *not* in our favor tonight, for here you are, still alive."

FTER TEN MINUTES of riding, they had to stop in order to tie Bronwyn to her horse.

"Take it out," she muttered to him. "It hurts."

"It's all that's keeping you from bleeding to death." But Aren was not unsympathetic, having been shot more than once himself. "We'll get it out as soon as we're somewhere safe."

If she made it that long.

Cresta held the reins of her sister's mount, Bronwyn slumped over the horse's neck, but even in the blackness, Aren marked the way Cresta kept looking back, occasionally stopping to check her pulse. Distracted.

"Where are we going?" he finally asked. "And who is meeting us there?"

"Up the river there's a small cave. Our sister Sarhina will be there with the supplies you and Lara need for the journey."

"Journey where, exactly?" He hated not knowing the plan. Hated being a follower when he'd spent his whole life a leader.

"Lara will explain when she meets up with us."

"Or not. She could be dead."

Cresta laughed softly. "I'm grateful not to be going with you two. There is nothing worse than being the third wheel in a lovers' quarrel."

"She's no longer my *lover*," he replied through clenched teeth.

Her only response was a sound of amusement, as though the conflict between him and Lara were nothing more than a disagreement over the décor in a room. "As you say, Your Grace. But don't think you'll get off so easily. Lara won't be killed by our father's soldiers. The woman is next to impossible to kill—that's why we call her the little cockroach—and the very fact that we haven't been caught suggests that everything is going exactly according to her plan."

Bronwyn took the opportunity to moan, and Aren thumped his heels against his horse, awkwardly pulling on the reins until it moved next to her, the river water splashing up to soak his legs. Reaching down, he pressed his fingers to her throat, the pulse beneath them weak, her skin cold. "We need to hurry."

But in the darkness, the horses could only move at a slow pace up the river, hooves slipping on the slick rocks. Aren would've been able to go at twice the speed on foot, but not while carrying Bronwyn. He was exhausted, his body unused to such strenuous activity, and he hated it. Hated feeling weak when all his life he'd been strong.

He caught sight of the familiar glow of algae before Cresta did, his chest tightening at the sight of it. A piece of Ithicana and proof that his people were involved in this step of the plan.

Another ten minutes of following the path through the trees brought them to a low cliff, a cave opening revealed by the glow of flickering firelight.

Dismounting hurriedly, Cresta tied up the horses while Aren untied Bronwyn. Easing her out of the saddle, he carried her toward the cave.

"Huntress," Cresta called out, and a moment later, a pregnant woman with long, dark hair appeared, a sword held in one hand and a knife in the other.

"Bronwyn got shot."

"Shit!" The pregnant woman, whom Aren assumed was the sister Sarhina, sheathed her weapons, striding toward him. Then she froze. "Where's Lara?"

"Luring them off," Cresta answered. "She'll be along soon enough."

"Get inside."

Aren carried Bronwyn into the cave, stopping in his tracks at the sight of a familiar face. "Nana?"

She was standing and holding her own weapons, but when she saw him, the machete dropped from her hand with a clatter.

For what seemed like an eternity, Nana didn't speak, and then she whispered, "You're alive. You're here. Thank merciful God . . ." Then tears began to pour down her face.

In all his life, he'd never seen his grandmother cry. Not even when his father—her own son—had been lost to the sea.

Then her eyes moved to Bronwyn, and she wiped the tears from her face, composed in an instant. "Bring her here."

"Arrow through the shoulder," he said, lowering the young woman to the ground. "She's lost a lot of blood."

Nana only grunted, pulling a knife to cut away Bronwyn's clothing.

"Oh, Bronwyn." The pregnant woman elbowed Aren in the side until he made space for her, lowering herself slowly and taking her sister's hand. "Why are you always the one who gets hurt?"

The arrow had punched clean through her shoulder, the broadhead glittering with blood in the firelight. Cresta had come around the other side, her face pale with concern. "Will she be all right?"

Nana didn't answer. "Aren, break this arrowhead off and then go outside and keep watch. You"—she shot a dark glare at Sarhina—"go with him."

"Cresta will go."

"Cresta will remain," Nana retorted. "I need an assistant, and unlike you, she follows instructions."

Ignoring the battle of wills going on between them, Aren reached down and snapped the head off the arrow, Bronwyn only moaning in response. Tossing it aside, he rose to his feet, when a hoarse voice called from outside: "Huntress," then "It's Lara."

Relief flooded through him as his errant wife stepped inside, shoulders rising and falling with her rapid, panting breath. She was drenched, her honey-colored hair hanging in lank tangles over her shoulders. There was a livid bruise on one cheek, and the knees of her trousers were torn through, the skin beneath bloody. Yet when she lifted her face to regard him, Aren's heart still skipped.

Nana's voice pulled him back into the moment. "Well, the stars are truly *not* in our favor tonight, for here you are, still alive."

"Sorry to disappoint." Lara's gaze went to Bronwyn, her lips thinning at the sight of her sister. "Is she . . . ?"

"Alive, but barely. Get your hands cleaned up and come help me. For once, you might actually be of use."

Without a word, Lara edged past him, and Aren practically threw himself at the opening to the cave. His chest felt too tight, his lungs not bringing in enough air, and it wasn't until he stood beneath the cloudy sky, warm rain washing the sweat from his upturned face, that his muscles relaxed enough to draw in a deep breath.

Cresta walked past. "I'm going to scout." As silent as any Ithicanian, she disappeared into the trees, a wraith in the night.

A sob of pain came from inside the cave, suggesting the arrow had been removed, and he walked farther down the slope, not wanting to listen. Not wanting to feel.

"So you're the King of Ithicana."

Aren jumped, startled. He turned to find Sarhina standing next to him, the rain soaking her dark hair. Despite looking like she was only weeks away from giving birth, she'd moved as silently as Cresta had. Twelve of them. Silas had made twelve of these weapons. And Aren suspected that only now was the man realizing just how dangerous they were. "I was."

She huffed out an exasperated breath. "Please don't turn all dreary on me. My sister might be dying inside, and I've no patience for unnecessary bellyaching."

"Unnecessary?" His voice was full of venom, but he didn't care to temper it.

"Ithicana hasn't fallen yet. Eranahl has held against every attempt to breach its defenses, and my understanding is that the majority of your civilians were able to reach the safety of the island ahead of my father's soldiers."

He knew that. Knew that most had arrived with little more than the clothes on their back, only Ithicana's career soldiers remaining on the other islands to combat the Maridrinian forces. For months, he'd lived out in the open with what remained of the Midwatch garrison, sleeping in the dirt and eating what they could hunt or forage for in the jungle, all the while fighting soldiers who were living in their homes and eating like kings off supplies coming through the bridge. "And just what do you suppose all those civilians are eating now?"

She leveled him with a steady stare, unfazed. "They are on rations, obviously. Which is why time is of the essence. Your sister is undertaking the first part of Lara's plan, and with you free, the second half can begin. You will sit on your throne again, mark my words. My father pissed off the wrong woman when he pissed off your wife."

"Don't call her that."

"Why not? It's the truth."

"Because she's a liar and a traitor who deserves to have her throat slit, that's why!"

Abruptly Aren found himself on his back, a knife pressed against his jugular. "Let me make myself abundantly clear, Your Grace," Sarhina hissed, the only thing visible in the darkness the white of her teeth. "You will never speak about my sister in that way or it will be you whose throat is slit. Understood?"

Glaring at her, he didn't answer.

The knife blade pressed harder, a droplet of blood trickling down his throat. "You mean nothing to me. You are nothing. The only reason that the rest of my sisters and I agreed to help you was because *Lara* loves you, and we love her. Never mind that we owe her our lives."

She eased up slightly, and Aren considered how he might get her off him without hurting the child.

But pregnant or not, Sarhina knew her business. He was at her mercy.

"You have no idea what she has endured," Sarhina continued.

"What we all endured at the hands of my father and Serin and the rest of them. *Fifteen* fucking years of being brainwashed to believe that our people were starving and dying because of Ithicana. They beat us and starved us and turned us into murderers, and through every bit of it they whispered that it was all to save Maridrina from *you*. That it was because of *you* that we needed to suffer. That you were a hateful demon who cared nothing for the innocents you harmed, only for the satisfaction of your own greed!"

There was fury in her voice, and reason told him that to provoke her was ill-advised. But Aren couldn't seem to stop himself from snapping, "She saw the truth within days of arriving in Ithicana. Over and over again she had reality shoved in her face, and she still chose to believe your father's lies and stab me in the back!"

"Chose?" The word came out between the woman's teeth. "Why are you so stupid that you can't understand that his lies were like poison? A poison we will *never* truly recover from. I know the truth. I have seen it with my own eyes, and yet more nights than not I wake up in frenzy, my hatred for Ithicana back like it had never left at all."

As abruptly as she'd attacked him, Sarhina rose to her feet, rubbing at her lower back. Eyeing her warily, Aren rose, touching his stinging throat.

"Lara made a mistake," she said wearily. "If she'd trusted you with the whole truth, none of this would've come to pass. But please understand that her coming to trust you at all is nothing short of miraculous. She's as much a victim of my father's machinations as you and Ithicana. Though unlike you, she isn't willing to let him win. Lara remains Queen of Ithicana even if you've given up on being its king."

Without another word, she strode inside, leaving him out in the rain. A few minutes later, Lara appeared in the entrance to the cave, where she paused. Then she walked toward him.

"How is Bronwyn?"

"We stopped the bleeding, but she's very weak. It will be another day or so before there can be any surety she'll recover, and even then, there's always risk of the wound fouling." She rubbed her temples, weariness and the toll of whatever she'd done to lose their pursuers palpable, and he curbed the urge to reach over to rub her neck where he knew it always knotted.

"She'll get through it," he said instead. "She's a fighter."

Lara dropped her hands from her face, looking up at him. "I'm surprised you care one way or another."

Of course I care—I'm not like you, he wanted to snap, but instead said, "I have no grievances with your sisters."

"Not even the one who just about cut your throat?"

She reached one hand up to his neck, but he swatted it away. "Do not touch me."

Hugging her arms around her body, she took a step back.

"Sarhina said you roped Ahnna into this plan of yours," he said. "Where is she? What is she doing? And where exactly do you presume that I'll be going with you?"

"Ahnna is on her way to Harendell," Lara answered. "She's gone to fulfill her half of the Fifteen Year Treaty and to plead for Harendell to assist Ithicana with taking Northwatch back under our control." She turned her head away. "Under *your* control, that is."

Aren's hands turned to ice. "You gave my sister away for a treaty that no longer exists? She has no power there. No allies. They can do anything they want to her." He turned away, mind racing as to how he could stop Ahnna before it was too late. "The only reason they would ever have been good to her was because it earned them favorable terms on the bridge. A bridge Ithicana no longer controls! In their eyes, she's worthless."

And Ithicana was worthless. If Harendell wished to wrest Northwatch from Maridrina's control, they probably could. But there'd be no reason they wouldn't keep it for themselves. "This plan is folly."

Lara was silent, then she said, "I disagree. After we parted ways, I spent months in Harendell. This is a venture they will gladly join, but only if you hold up the other end of the bargain."

"Which is?"

"It's one thing for Harendell to take Northwatch. Quite another for them to sail across the Tempest Seas to take Southwatch right from under Maridrina's nose. We need to secure another ally."

Aren's gut dropped because he *knew* what she was planning. Just like he knew that it was madness to even dream of it happening.

"Which is why," Lara continued, "you and I are going to ride south and mend Ithicana's relationship with the Empress of Valcotta."

I T WAS NEAR dawn, the sky having cleared overnight to allow a brilliant sunrise of pink and orange and gold, though the beauty of it was lost on Lara. She stood outside the cave's opening, nibbling on a heel of bread despite having no appetite.

She'd barely slept.

How could she when Bronwyn was on the brink of death, her injury the result of Lara dragging her into this mess. Every time she'd fallen asleep, Lara had jerked awake, certain her sister had stopped breathing. Certain that she'd lost her. That she'd killed her as surely as she had killed Marylyn.

It was made all the worse by Aren. After she'd told him the plan, he'd made every effort to keep as far from her as the cave would allow, refusing to meet her gaze, choosing instead to stare into the depths of the small fire for hours.

Guilt had been her constant companion since the night she'd been exiled from Ithicana, but it surged anew, making her stomach ache. She'd caused so much harm. Even if her plan worked, even if Ithicana secured alliances and took back the bridge, that harm would not be undone.

"You ready?"

Sarhina came up behind her, handing Lara a tin cup full of steaming liquid.

"He hates me." Despite herself, a hot tear burned down Lara's cheek, which she brushed away angrily. "I thought—" She broke off, shaking her head. "I don't know what I thought."

"That he'd forgive you because you rescued his ungrateful, albeit rather perfect, ass?"

Lara made a noise that was half-laugh, half-sob.

Casting a backward glance at the cave, Sarhina took her arm and led her down the embankment.

The light had grown enough that Lara could see her sister's face, the shadows under her eyes and the tightness around her mouth. Exhaustion and worry, none of it good for the baby.

"He might never forgive you, you know that, right? And you have no control over whether he does or doesn't."

Lara's neck clicked as she nodded, her muscles tight. "I know."

"Does that change anything?" Sarhina asked. "Do you want to walk away from this? Because you can. We can give that old bitch and His Grace horses and supplies, then the four of us can get out of here and leave them to do what they will."

"No." Lara couldn't walk away. She'd die before she walked away, regardless of how Aren felt about her. Because freeing Ithicana from her father's yoke was something she needed to do to live with herself. "Even if he does forgive me, the rest of Ithicana never will. And I won't make him choose between us. I'll see this through, and then I'll leave, and . . ."

Leave and then what?

Her plans were limited to freeing Aren then liberating Ithicana, and she'd not allowed herself to imagine what she'd do once she achieved those goals. Not allowed herself to dwell on the moment when she'd have to walk away from Aren and never look back. "I suspect I'll go after Father."

Sarhina exhaled. "Or maybe you put all of this behind you and come find me. Make a life for yourself somewhere that isn't burdened by politics and violence. Move on with someone who will put you first."

Lara's chest tightened, a sudden rush of anguish filling her, and she looked away. "It hurts to think about that." And as illogical as it was, what Sarhina described was *not* what she wanted. It was not *who* she was.

"It hurts now because the pain is fresh. It will get better with time." Sarhina pulled Lara close, pressing her lips to her forehead. "You do what you need to get to the other side of this, and then you come back to us. Promise?"

Before she could answer, footsteps thudded against the ground, and Lara turned away from her sister to see Aren standing at the mouth of the cave, arms crossed and his mouth drawn into a thin line.

It was the first chance she'd had to look at him in the light of day, and Lara found her eyes drifting over his tall form, shoulders broad and square, head held high. His hair was longer than he'd worn it in Ithicana, showing some of the curl that Ahnna's possessed, and his face was shadowed with stubble.

"Bronwyn's awake and asking for you," he said, his deep voice unreadable.

"Thank you for telling me." She tried to meet his gaze, but he looked away, saying, "I'm going to load the horses."

Sarhina snorted. "As if you know how. I'll help you."

"I'm going to say good-bye to Bronwyn and Cresta," Lara muttered. Going inside, she sucked in a breath as she saw Bronwyn sitting, her weight resting against Cresta as Nana spooned broth into her mouth. "It's good to see you awake."

"Reluctantly." Her sister smiled. "But I couldn't let you leave me unconscious next to another fire again, now could I."

Nana huffed out a breath and then spit into the corner as she abandoned them.

"God, but she's ornery," Bronwyn muttered, her still-pale face scrunching up. "How did you tolerate her for a year?"

"By keeping my contact with her minimal." Lara smirked. "I

needed to sneak out one night, so I dosed her with a laxative. I had hours of freedom while she was confined to the outhouse."

Both her sisters laughed, Bronwyn clutching at her shoulder. "Stop. Stop. That hurts."

Lara leaned in, pressing her forehead against her sister's. "You get better. I'll have it no other way."

"You've gotten very authoritative, Your Majesty," Bronwyn said before leaning into her.

Then Cresta pressed her head against theirs. Then another set of arms wrapped around them, and Sarhina's pregnant belly pushed its way into the hug.

Lara allowed herself a moment to breathe, before saying, "Stick with the plan. Get back to the mountains and stay safe." Such an easy statement to make, but Lara knew her sisters were still in grave danger. Those still in Vencia would remain in the city, laying low until storm season eased, then splitting up and taking ships north and south, while Sarhina, Bronwyn, and Cresta would meet up with a merchant caravan of Ensel's people, who'd provide them cover and get them back to Renhallow—hopefully before Sarhina's baby came.

"We'll leave immediately." Sarhina stood. "The wagon has a smuggler's compartment—we'll hide Bronwyn and Cresta inside in case we cross a patrol. No one is going to suspect an old woman and a pregnant girl. And no patrol is going to want to search a wagon full of dried cow dung for contraband."

"You plan for everything."

"You should try it sometime," her sister replied, then gave Lara a smile and a little shove toward the mouth of the cave.

Outside, Aren stood with the horses, deep in conversation with Nana, but they broke off the moment they caught sight of Lara. Striding up to her horse, Lara tightened the girth and checked that the saddlebags were well secured before mounting. She averted her eyes as Aren awkwardly climbed on his horse, though there was a certain petty part of her that enjoyed seeing him incompetent at something. Especially after all the mockery she'd endured over her seasickness.

"If anything happens to him—" Nana started to say, but Lara was tired of her threats.

"Yes, yes. You'll hunt me down and feed me to the sharks. I remember." Then she clicked her tongue at her horse to get it moving, riding down the trail to the river. A moment later, she heard the *thud thud* of Aren's horse trotting after her.

She waited until they'd crossed the river, heading south and east toward the low mountains before falling in next to him. "By now they'll have determined that my ploy last night was just a ruse and that we didn't escape by water. But they'll anticipate that's our intention, so I suspect the patrols along the coast will be intense. For that reason, we'll skirt the edge of the Red Desert until we reach Valcottan territory, then we can return to the highway and ride straight to Pyrinat." The capital city of Valcotta was the surest place to find the Empress.

Aren's eyes remained fixed on the path ahead of them, knuckles white from gripping the reins. "Assuming Keris got Zarrah free, all of this is unnecessary. She gave her word to supply Eranahl."

"Which buys time but doesn't solve the problem. And we have no way of knowing if she made it out, especially given my half brother is involved. You're too bloody trusting, Aren."

"Full brother."

Lara opened her mouth, then closed it again. After a moment, she asked, "Pardon?"

"You have the same mother, or so he claimed."

It was possible. Lara had left the compound when she was five, and while she remembered Keris, her memories were hazy and unspecific.

"And I don't trust Keris—not by a long shot," Aren said. "But I do have total confidence that he'll do what it takes to stay alive, and for that to happen, he needs to take the crown from your father. And for that to happen, he needs Eranahl to endure."

Lara listened silently as Aren explained Keris's plan, which was overly complicated, in her opinion. But instead of focusing on her *brother's* plot, the first question that came from her lips was, "My mother . . . Is she still alive?"

Aren was silent for a long moment, then he shook his head. "No."

Grief stabbed her in the stomach, the long years since she'd seen her mother doing nothing to temper the hurt. "Do you know how she died?"

"It's better if you don't know." Aren kicked the sides of his horse, moving ahead of her on the path.

A flash of anger seared through her veins, and Lara galloped past him, wheeling her horse around to block his path. "Don't be petty, Aren. Withholding this just to piss me off is a low blow."

"Big presumption that I care enough to piss you off."

He looked away as he said it, and she narrowed her eyes, knowing he was trying to redirect her. Exhaling slowly, she asked, "Please tell me the truth."

Silence stretched.

"What I know is what Keris told me." Aren met her gaze. "He said your mother tried to go after you to get you back and that your father strangled her as punishment. And as a warning to the other wives not to cross him." He hesitated, then added, "I'm sorry."

Lara couldn't breathe. The world spun in and out of focus, and she doubled over, hands clenching into fists around the reins. Between her teeth, she snarled, "I hate him!"

"So does Keris. So trust that, if you trust nothing else." He thumped his heels against his horse's sides, bouncing ahead like an oversized sack of potatoes, leaving her no choice but to follow.

The swift pace and the necessity of remaining alert served well to distract her from the ache that sat heavy in her stomach as they rode along the winding path leading through the hills and mountains bordering the Red Desert. They passed the occasional farmer or shepherd, but the people paid them little attention, as both of them were dressed as Maridrinian merchants, Lara's weapons all hidden.

They stopped near a stream at midday to eat and allow the horses to drink, but still Aren hadn't said a word. So Lara jumped when he said, "How did you do it?"

"Do what?" she asked, despite knowing what he referred to. This wasn't a conversation she wanted to have.

"How and *when* did you write your plan to infiltrate Ithicana on that letter I sent to your father? I wrote that just before we—" He broke off, turning to fuss with the saddle of his horse. "Never mind. It doesn't matter. I don't want to know."

"Aren—"

"I don't want to know." He clambered onto his horse. "Let's go."

Chest tight, Lara filled her waterskin in the stream, then mounted and rode after him. "I wrote it the night you were shot in the shoulder by those raiders." As she said the words, a vision of him kneeling on the muddy path, bleeding everywhere as he tried to explain his dream for a different Ithicana—one not burdened by constant war and violence—filled her mind. "I wrote the message on every single piece of stationary knowing you'd eventually write something to my father."

"I don't want to hear it." He kicked his horse but hauled on the reins at the same time, and the irritated animal only snorted and pranced on the spot. "Move, you stupid creature!"

"The night we were first together, before I came out to you in the courtyard, I was in your room destroying the paper. All that spilled ink you blamed on your cat was my doing. And I counted all the pages. The letter you'd started and the rest—they were all there. I don't know how one slipped past me, but please know that when I came to you that I believed I'd put an end to my plans."

Giving up on the horse, Aren slid off the side and strode up the path. "It doesn't matter, Lara! It still happened."

How could it not matter? How could it not matter to him that she'd tried to stop her plans from ever seeing the light of day? How could it not matter to him that she'd turned her back on her father and a lifetime of training? How could it not matter to him that the invasion had been as much a shock to her as it had been to him?

Snatching up the reins of his horse, she cantered after him. "Aren, listen! I know this is my fault, but please understand that I didn't intend for it to happen."

He wheeled around, reaching into his coat and removing a page creased and worn from constant folding and unfolding, and Lara recognized it as that goddamned letter.

"I've read this every day since your sister shoved it in my face. Every *fucking* day, I read your plans and I see how you manipulated me. How every moment together was just part of your strategy to lure me in and make me trust you. To find the information you needed to destroy everything I cared about."

Folly or not, that had been the reason she'd never told him she wrote it in the first place: because this was how she'd known he'd react.

"But that's not the worst of it," he shouted. "You had your reasons for doing what you did. What's my excuse? Every detail you learned, every opportunity you had to spy—those were my mistakes. Bringing you to Ithicana was my mistake. Trusting you was my mistake. Loving you was my mistake." Picking up a rock, he hurled it at a tree. "Ithicana fell because of me, and if you think it will rise again under my rule, you are sorely mistaken."

She understood then, in that moment, what fueled the anger in his eyes. Not her. Not what she'd done. It was himself whom Aren truly blamed.

And what could she say? To argue that he shouldn't blame himself for having gone into their marriage in good faith seemed hollow and foolish. Lara opened her mouth and closed it again, rejecting every word that rose to her lips. "Aren—"

She broke off, the sound of hooves filling her ears. Turning in her saddle, she looked back the way they'd come, but it was impossible to see anything through the trees. "There's someone coming."

"More than one." He came up next to her horse, head cocked as he listened. "Do you hear that?"

She picked up on the faint sounds of barking dogs. "They're tracking us. We need to ride hard. Now!"

For two days they wove through the hills and valleys, struggling to evade pursuers who seemed to never tire, always only a few steps behind no matter how many tricks Lara employed. She stole fresh mounts for them when they came across small villages and farms, leaving their exhausted animals behind in payment. But they weren't the quality of the mounts her father's soldiers rode, so with every passing hour the sound of barking dogs and galloping hooves drew closer.

"They know where we're trying to go," Aren said to her, shifting in his saddle as the horses drank from a tiny stream.

"I know." She capped the waterskin and handed it up before filling the other. "I expected Serin to figure out my plan, but not this quickly." She only prayed that it was because he knew her well and not because he'd captured one of her sisters.

"Your father will have soldiers riding hard up the main highway on the coast and then moving east to cut us off. We don't have any chance of outpacing them. Not on these nags."

"They aren't nags," she muttered, patting her sweating horse as she climbed back into the saddle. "They're just not built for speed."

"I apologize for offending them," Aren snapped. "But the fact of the matter is that speed is what we need right now."

Sleep was what they both needed. Neither of them had had more than a few hours, all of it in the saddle while the other led the horses. She was exhausted and sore, and Aren's constant vitriol was grinding at her nerves. "We'll move closer to the edge of the desert. Won't be much in the way of water, which is why they might not expect the move. Once we get around them, we can cut back to the coast and purchase faster horses."

If only she were half as confident as her words.

Digging in her heels, she led him up the narrow path, casting occasional glances backward. It was impossible to hide the route they took in the rough terrain, which was now devoid of trees, and she could see the glint of sunlight off a spyglass, the cloud of dust rising beneath hooves.

What she wouldn't give for rain at that exact moment, for clean cold water to fall from the sky and wash away the filth, to fill her mouth, drown the scent of their trail. But the only sort of storm they were likely to encounter now was the sort filled with dust.

With each passing hour, they rode farther east, the air growing drier and the wind holding the familiar scent of sand. Urging her horse up to the crest of a hill, Lara paused to look down at the red sands stretching out before her, endless and vast as the ocean. "We track south from here for as long as we can until the horses need water. Then we'll—"

She cut off, eyes going to the cloud of dust moving toward them. *Impossible.*

"Damn it!" Aren snarled the words, pointing behind them. Two more groups, moving in fast. Pinning them in from all sides.

All sides, that is, but one.

Wheeling her horse, Lara stared east, the red sands seeming to shift and move with the heat waves.

They weren't equipped for this. Didn't have enough water, especially considering the horses. But out there, at least they had a chance, whereas to remain meant death or capture.

Making a decision, Lara dug her heels into the sides of her sweating horse and led Aren and his mount into the Red Desert.

25
AREN

H<small>E'D NEVER KNOWN</small> heat like this.

For days they'd been riding deeper into the desert, the dust of their pursuers always visible on the horizon.

He'd exhausted the last of the water, his mouth now dry as bone, his skin burning beneath the ceaseless onslaught of the sun, lips cracking. Beneath him, his horse staggered, its sides heaving and hair crusted white from dried sweat. It let out a groan and fell to its knees, sending Aren tumbling into the sand.

"Get up!" he shouted at the animal, pulling on the reins, but it only lay on its side, nostrils flaring.

"Leave it." Lara pushed past him, unfastening the animal's saddlebags, handing them over before removing her own. Untacking both animals, she gave them several strokes on the neck before shouldering her bags.

"We're going to die out here," he said to her.

Instead of answering, Lara held up a hand to shield her eyes as she stared into the distance. "Not yet. Now walk."

Hours passed, every step an act of will, every breath painful. But Lara didn't falter, and he refused to be the first to break.

They climbed a dune that seemed to reach to the sky, a mountain of sand that slid and moved beneath Aren's feet, causing him to stumble. To fall. To climb back up again only to repeat the process.

He was so thirsty. Thirsty in a way that he hadn't known possible, the need for water so terrible that panic was creeping in, like being caught underwater and desperately needing to breathe. Except this torture seemed to go on forever.

Reaching the top of the dune, he stopped next to Lara, panting for breath, knowing he should look back to see how close their pursuers were but unable to summon the energy for it.

And then he lifted his head and saw what had caused Lara to pause in the first place.

The wall of sand had to be a thousand feet high, lightning crackling through it, the thunder echoing across the dunes moments later.

Lara didn't move, staring into the storm as if mesmerized, the wind sending her hair trailing out in a golden cloud. Tearing his gaze from her, Aren watched the eight men on camels in the distance, their arms flapping as they beat their mounts to greater speed.

"Lara!" His mouth was dry as bone. "Can the camels outrun the storm?"

She turned around to regard the rapidly approaching force. "That's what they're banking on. Catching or killing us, then racing toward the edge where they'll take cover in tents until it blows over."

"Then we fight them and take their animals."

And maybe, if they weren't both on the brink of dying of dehydration and exhaustion, it would be a plan. But they had no arrows left to whittle down the ranks, and even pulling his weapon from its sheath took almost all the strength Aren had. It wasn't a fight they'd win.

And from the grim expression on Lara's face, she knew it. "The storm needs to fight this battle for us." Breaking into a jog, she headed into the nightmare of wind and sand.

I T WAS THEIR only chance.

Most would have thought it a mirage or wishful thinking, but she'd seen the shiver of green in the distance, some sixth sense ingrained in her from a life lived in the desert. All they had to do was race the storm.

Her head pounded, a steady percussion that rivaled the growing volume of the thunder, but still she pushed onward, dragging Aren with her.

He stumbled and fell, but she helped him up, pulling his arm over her shoulder even though her knees were barely holding her own weight. A backward glance revealed riders coming ever closer.

What had her father offered them? What reward, what riches, were worth them riding toward potential death in order to claim two lives?

Or maybe it wasn't a reward.

Maybe it was fear of what her father would do to them if they failed to bring back her and Aren's heads.

The winds were rising, filling the air with sand, and Lara stopped to adjust her scarf so that it was tight over her mouth and ears and did the same to Aren, but with him, she covered his eyes. "Don't let go of me," she shouted, then led him onward.

Her eyes stung from sand and grit, her body incapable of making tears to flush them.

But she could smell it. Water. Salvation.

They were so close.

She heard the shouts of her father's men even as the sun disappeared from the sky, concealed by the rapid swirl of sand. Minutes. They had minutes until the storm was on them and all sight was lost.

They had to keep going.

The roar of the wind was deafening, the strength of it buffeting them from side to side, the sand scouring over her exposed flesh, her eyes pure agony as she gripped Aren's hand, dragging him forward step by step.

You can do this, she silently screamed at herself. *You will survive this.*

Darkness fell, and Lara shut her eyes, pulling the scarf up to completely conceal her face.

She had no sense of direction. Barely any sense of up and down.

There were heavier things than sand in the air now, and she cried out as a rock sliced across her shoulder.

Next to her, Aren was coughing violently, then he fell, hand jerking from hers.

"Aren!" she screamed, fumbling around in the sand, now coughing as well, tiny particles sneaking through her scarf to choke her lungs. "Aren!"

But she couldn't find him, and she was terrified to move lest she went the wrong way. "Aren!"

She reached as far as she could, turning in a circle on her knees. Pieces of rock hammered her, slicing through her clothes. Through her flesh. "Aren!"

Her fingers brushed fabric, and Lara lunged, finding his slumped form. She pressed her lips to where the fabric of his scarf covered his ear. "Get up!" They'd be buried if they stayed still for long. "Crawl!"

He stirred, dragging himself onto his hands and knees. She could feel him jerking with each cough, though she couldn't hear him over the wind. Over the loud crackle of thunder.

Through her eyelids, she saw a flash of lightning, her ears aching from the *boom* that followed. Then her nose filled with the smell of smoke.

The lightning had hit one of the oasis trees.

Barely able to breathe, she clutched tight to Aren's coat, following the elusive smell that swirled and danced around her.

Keep going, she chanted. *You will not let him die.*

Her fingers jammed against something hard. Coughing, Lara felt the object. Smooth stone. Blocks.

The wall of the training yard, now almost buried by sand.

She eagerly pressed onward, following the wall, which would eventually circle around to the building where weapons were stored. They could take cover inside until the storm blew over.

Aren collapsed.

"No!" she screamed. "No!" Then a fit of coughing made words impossible.

Catching hold of him under the arms, she dragged him, step by agonizing step. Falling and forcing herself back up again, checking constantly to ensure the wall was still next to her.

But he was so damned heavy. Twice her size, and she was spent. Was exhausted and choking, and if she could just lay down and rest . . .

"No!" The word forced itself out between choking breaths.

Step.

Step.

The wall disappeared from beneath her left hand. Trusting her memory, she moved forward until she collided with a building. Lowering Aren to the ground, she kept one hand on his as she felt for the door.

There.

It was open, and she dragged Aren inside, laying him down next to the back wall. She retreated to the door, shoveling handfuls of sand out of the way, then hauling on the wood until it shut, the heavy latch falling into place.

Her eyes burned, and with every third breath, she coughed, her mouth full of grit and too dry for her to spit. But Aren, she feared, was in a worse state.

He hadn't stirred from where she'd dropped him. He coughed almost continually, but it was the dehydration that concerned her most because it could kill him. *Would* kill him, if she didn't get him water soon.

But the storm could last for hours. Days. And the waterskins strapped to their sides were as dry as bone.

Leaving her scarf wrapped around her face, Lara crawled in the direction of his coughing, fumbling around until she got her fingers against his naked throat. His pulse was racing, and his skin was burning hot with fever. "Aren." She shook him. "Aren, you need to wake up."

He grumbled and stirred, pushing her away.

"Damn it," she snarled, panic rising in her chest. "Don't you dare die on me, you idiot."

She needed to retrieve water from the spring, and she needed to do it now, storm or no storm.

After pulling down the scarf covering his eyes so that he wouldn't wake up blindfolded, Lara felt her way back to the door. Making sure her scarf was secure, she pressed her shoulder against the door and pushed, her boots sliding on the stone floor as she fought against the wind.

Slowly, it opened a crack, and then the storm caught it, wrenching the wood from her hand and slamming it against the wall of the building.

Sand and wind swirled inside, her ears filling with a thunderous roar as she fought to get it closed again. She put herself between door and building and straightened her legs, pushing the door shut. She jammed her knife into a hinge to keep it from opening again, then she began to crawl.

The only sense left to her was touch, and Lara moved with painstaking slowness because if she lost her way, she wouldn't make it to the spring, much less back to Aren, before the storm killed her.

Her memory guided her, fingers trailing along the sides of buildings and digging deep to find the path of mosaic stone that had been buried by sand. The last time she'd come this way had been to that fateful dinner, about to fake her sisters' deaths in order to save their lives. Memory filled her head with the click of her heels, the smell of food on the air, the feel of silken skirts against her legs. The only thing this journey had in common with her last trek was her terror.

Inch by inch, she moved in the direction of the spring, coughs wracking her sides and her hands burning as the sand abraded them. The wind hit her from one direction, then the other, knocking her down and pummeling her body with stones and branches torn from the plants in the oasis, blood trickling down her skin in a dozen places.

Her head throbbed so badly she could barely think, disorientation making her question every motion she made, nearly freezing her in place.

Keep going, she silently screamed. *Only a dozen more paces.*

But what if she were wrong? What if she'd gotten turned around?

Lara froze, panic choking her as much as the sand, her breath coming in too-fast pants that gave her lungs nothing of what she needed. Dizziness washed over her. Her arms and legs cramped, her body curling in on itself until she was a tight ball in the sand.

Keep going. You are the goddamned Queen of Ithicana! You will not be defeated by sand!

With painful slowness, her limbs obeyed, and she crept forward.

Her memory told her that the footbridge over the spring was right ahead, but as the low stone walls lining the path ended, all that she felt ahead of her was sand. Keeping one foot pressed against the wall so she wouldn't get lost, Lara stretched out, leaning her weight on one hand as she reached around, feeling for something familiar.

Then the ground collapsed beneath her.

She toppled face-first into a mixture of sand and water. Flailing, she rolled, getting her knees underneath her and sitting up, waist-deep in the slop.

Cursing, she remembered the last time a sandstorm had hit the compound and how it had taken weeks to dredge the spring, and another month before it flowed normally. The water would be drinkable, but she'd need to filter it.

Unfastening one of the waterskins from her waist, Lara tore a piece of fabric from her clothes and wrapped it over the opening, making sure it was tight. Then she plunged it into the soupy mess, waiting until the waterskin was full before pushing aside her scarf and taking a mouthful. It was gritty and tasted terrible, but still the feel of the cool water in her mouth was nothing short of bliss, and she rinsed her mouth and spit before taking a long swallow.

Lara drank as much as she could without making herself sick. She refilled the waterskin as well as Aren's, ensuring they were fastened securely to her belt before moving back onto the path.

The water gave her strength, and she crawled swiftly back the way she'd come. "I'm coming," she muttered between coughs. "Hang on."

Reaching the weapons building, she muscled the door open, securing it behind her. Over the roar of the storm, she could make out Aren's coughing. Crawling blindly toward him, she lifted his head and shoulders so that he was resting against her, then unfastened the lid to one of the waterskins.

Waiting for a coughing fit to subside, she pried open his mouth and trickled some water inside before pushing his jaw shut until he swallowed, repeating the process. The fourth time, he choked and spluttered. Pulling out of her grip, he rolled onto his side.

"Aren?"

"More water," he croaked, and Lara pushed the waterskin into his grip, listening to him swallow until she deemed it enough, then snatched it back.

"More."

"Any more and you'll just puke it up," she told him, drinking from the waterskin herself. "And I'm not going back out there to get more until the storm eases."

Lara sat against the cool stone of the wall, taking another sip of water. Her eyes stung with maddening fierceness, and she prayed the damage wouldn't be permanent. They needed to be flushed, but for that, she required cleaner water than she had. She was soaked from having fallen into the spring, sand scratched in places where it really shouldn't, her guts ached, and all of her muscles were cramped. But worst of all, she was freezing, her wet clothing like ice against her skin as the desert's temperature dropped in the growing night.

"Where are we?" His voice was raspy. "What is this place?"

It was a secret place. A place she'd never intended to ever return.

"This," she whispered, unbuttoning her sodden dress and pulling it over her head, "is where it all began."

AREN WALKED DOWN the cool corridor, listening to the thunder of the typhoon outside, the air heavy with moisture and the charge of lightning. He had a hundred things to do. A thousand. But like iron to a lodestone, he was drawn from even the most important of tasks to find her.

Pausing on the landing of the stairs, he rested his elbows on the railing to look down into the foyer of the palace. Lara sat on the floor amidst a dozen children, who all watched her with rapt expressions. She was reading to them, as she often did during storms, her voice rising and falling dramatically, the children leaning forward with anticipation as the tale reached its climax. Sensing his presence, she looked up, a slow smile crossing her face.

Boom.

The palace shook with the intensity of the thunder, and several of the children jumped in alarm.

"Easy now," Lara whispered. "There is no danger here."

Lightning flashed, illuminating the vaulted room, and it struck Aren that for it to do so was strange, because there were no windows.

Boom.

All the lamps guttered out, plunging the palace into darkness. Screams filled the air, and Aren raced down the steps, tripping and stumbling in the darkness. "Lara!"

More screams.

"Lara!"

Lightning flashed again, and for a heartbeat, Aren could see. See the palace floors and walls splattered with crimson. Then once again he was cast into darkness.

Boom.

"Lara!" he shouted her name, feeling around in the darkness. "Where are you?"

More lightning, illuminating Lara on her knees, her father standing behind her with a knife to her throat. "Tell us how to break Eranahl."

Aren jerked awake.

All around him was blackness and noise, and he coughed violently, his mouth as dry as sawdust, tongue tasting like grit.

Panic raced through him, and he clawed away the scarf wrapping his face, his knuckles brushing against the soft texture of hair.

Lara.

Her shivering body pressed against his. One of his arms was beneath her neck, the other wrapped around her torso, their fingers linked. She coughed, then rolled to face him, still asleep. And though he knew he shouldn't, Aren tightened his arms around her, holding her close against the icy cold of the desert night.

The noise was incredible—as intense as that from any typhoon—the raging wind slamming sand and God knew what else against the sides of the small stone building. Thunder made the ground shake. Despite the closed door and the total lack of windows, dust and sand still hung in the air, forcing him to pull the scarf back over his nose and mouth, though he hated the suffocating feeling of it.

Lara had said little after revealing they were in the compound where she'd been raised, both of them so exhausted they'd fallen asleep next to one another, her wearing his shirt in lieu of her soaked dress. But it hadn't required any explanation for Aren to realize that she'd saved his life.

He last remembered being surrounded by gritty, choking blackness, and then nothing, until he'd woken to her pouring water into his mouth. Which meant she'd managed to both find this building and drag him inside, and then she'd gone back out to retrieve water. Seemingly impossible feats, though she'd proven them otherwise, and it elicited from him a grudging admiration.

Lara's capacity to endure hardship was nothing short of astonishing, and that surprised him and yet somehow . . . *didn't*. Even when she'd been hiding her true nature from him, she'd shown herself to be both adaptable and willing to push herself through the worst sort of circumstances. Part of it was training—what Serin and the rest had put her and her sisters through during their time in this place, but that wasn't the whole of it.

Willpower. That was what kept her going. Sheer force of will and a stubbornness to match.

But what did she hope to gain from helping him?

If it was him taking her back, she was wasting her time. It didn't matter if the letter reaching her father had been a mistake; the consequences were the same. And it was all the result of her lies, her deception, her manipulation. The woman he'd fallen in love with didn't exist—she was just a mask Lara had chosen to wear for a time. He didn't know her. Didn't want to.

Liar, a little voice whispered inside of his head. *Look at yourself! If you weren't both half dead, you'd probably be between her legs!*

Anger fired through him, and Aren pulled his arm out from under Lara's neck and sat up. Searching around in the darkness, he found her dress, which was dry, and rested it over her sleeping form. Then the winds abruptly died, the barrage of projectiles attacking their shelter ceasing their assault.

The door was outlined by faint light, and he eased it open, blinking at the brightness of the early morning sun, watching as the wall of sand and storm moved steadily west. Entirely different than the typhoons that battered Ithicana, but no less deadly.

Shutting the door behind him, he assessed the place where Lara had grown up.

There was red sand everywhere, piled high enough to cover parts of the stone buildings at the perimeter of the compound, but his gaze went immediately to the trees and foliage, which seemed so out of place in the wasteland of the desert.

As was the smell of water.

Aren walked between the buildings, which were soot-stained, some of the doors shattered or charred. But he didn't pause to investigate, his thirst driving him forward.

Reaching the trees—battered and leafless trunks thanks to the storm—he found the spring that fed the greenery, though it was nothing more than sandy soup. Scooping out sand until a pool of water formed, he drank from his cupped hands, gagging on the grit even as he relished the feel of the tepid liquid on his tongue. Only when his thirst was quenched did he proceed to the center of the oasis, where he found a large table surrounded by toppled chairs nearly buried by sand. Scattered silverware peeked out, glinting in the sun, and there were broken plates and pieces of glass strewn about.

Curious, Aren stepped closer, but his foot caught something in the sand and he tripped, nearly falling. Reaching down to untangle his boot, his hand froze as he realized what he had stepped on.

A desiccated corpse.

Swearing, he pulled his foot free of the bones and fabric, but as he lifted his head, he realized the body wasn't alone. Everywhere he looked, bones protruded from the sand, the scene no longer appearing like an abandoned party, but like a grave.

He searched the surrounding buildings, the contents smashed and burned, and found more bodies. Dozens of dead, the fire not hot enough to consume the evidence. Despite having seen more than his fair share of corpses, this place made his skin crawl.

"Aren!" Lara's voice reached his ears, and he stepped outside, blinking in the bright sun. "Aren, where are you?"

Let her panic, the angry part of his conscience whispered. *Let her think you left, that you don't need her.*

Then he saw her coming down the path wearing only his shirt and her boots. She was moving slowly, a blindfold still wrapped around her eyes. What was wrong with her?

"Aren!" Her arms were outstretched, reaching for the sides of buildings for guidance, but her boot caught on a rock and she tripped and fell. She was up again in a flash, but from the way she swayed he could tell she was disoriented. Lost. "Are you all right?"

The anguish and fear in her voice made his chest tighten. "I'm fine, Lara. Stay still. I'm coming."

Striding in her direction, Aren carefully removed her blindfold, grimacing at the sight. Her eyes were nearly swollen shut, the skin around them red with scratches, the tears streaking her face full of sand and blood. "Can you see at all?"

"Not well."

Memory of the storm flooded over him, of her covering his face, including his eyes. Of her leading him to safety while her own eyes suffered the price. "Let me have a look."

Not that he was entirely sure how to help her. Eyes were delicate things, and while he was handy enough with setting bones and stitching wounds, this wasn't something he knew much about. But at the least they needed to be flushed, and he could manage that. "I found the kitchen in my exploration. Should have what we need to clean you up."

Taking her hand, he led her through the pathways, trying not to notice the texture of her skin beneath his. No longer buffed and polished the way it had been when they were in Ithicana, but dry and calloused. Even so, the shape of her hand, the way it curled around his, was achingly familiar. He dropped it the moment they reached the kitchen.

"Stay here," he muttered. "I'm going to get some water."

The sand was beginning to settle in the spring, but the water was still murky. He filled a kettle and a pot, carrying them back. After a bit of thinking, he went to one of the buildings where he'd seen the remains of dresses and retrieved an armload of silk. With repeated attempts, he was able to filter the water through the fabric until it ran clear, then he boiled it on the stove, setting the kettle aside to cool. "You told me once that your father had everyone who knew of his plots killed. Is this where it happened?"

She turned her head away, wiping at her cheeks. "Yes."

"Did you help him kill them?"

"No." Her voice was toneless. "But neither did I do anything to save them."

Aren watched her, waiting, seeing the slight twitch of the muscles in her jaw. The faintest furrow in her brow that he now knew meant she was considering whether to tell the truth or to lie.

Lara sighed. "My father came with his cadre to retrieve the girl Serin had chosen to marry you, which was my sister, Marylyn."

The woman who'd tried to kill him on Midwatch—who *had* killed Eli as well as the boy's mother and aunt and God knew how many others. The sister *Lara* had killed with one snap of the neck.

"I was close with my master of arms. On the first night my father's party was here, he arranged so that I'd overhear their plans. I discovered that my father intended to kill me and the rest of my sisters the night Marylyn was officially announced as his choice, the costs associated with us remaining alive more than he wished to pay. Which meant I had a matter of days to figure out how to save all of our lives."

"Your father told me this story."

She frowned. "Why?"

"I don't know." A lie. There'd been comfort in his belief that Lara wasn't the sort of person to risk herself in a rescue attempt. Silas had taken that away. "Why didn't you tell your sisters and then escape? With your training, it would've been easy."

"Yes, but it also would've meant us spending our entire lives on the run unless we'd also killed my father and all of his cadre, which had obvious risks. Plus . . ." She trailed off, giving her head a slight shake. "At that point we all still believed what we'd been told of Ithicana's villainy and Maridrina's suffering. To leave would've meant abandoning what I believed was my country's only good chance of healing itself, and I couldn't accept that." Her face scrunched up. "It seems so stupid now to have believed that, but I suppose it's hard to imagine being blind when one can see."

That was why Silas had kept them hidden away. Not to protect them from assassination, but to keep his daughters from learning the truth. "Why you? You could've faked your and your sisters' deaths and let Marylyn carry on as your father's choice."

"There were some logistical reasons." She bit down on her bottom lip. "But mostly, it was because I didn't think she'd survive you." She gave a bitter laugh. "Little did I know I had it backward, and that it would've been you who wouldn't have survived her. If nothing else, at least I spared you from that." Her voice cracked on the last.

A pair of tears rolled down her swollen cheeks, and it was all he could do not to pull her into his arms. Instead, he rose, tested the water, and found that it had cooled. "Rest your head on the table," he said, rolling a silk dress into a pillow to place underneath her cheek. "This will hurt."

She clenched her teeth but said not a word as he carefully poured the water into her bloodshot eyes. Her face was marked with scrapes and bruises, but she was still beautiful.

Would he have fallen for any of the other sisters, if they had been the ones to come? Would he have made the same mistakes?

Maybe, but he didn't think so. There was something about *her.* Something that had spoken to his soul in a way no other woman he'd met ever had.

Ithicana will never forgive her, he silently chided himself. And to ask them to would be to spit in the faces of all his people who'd lost children and parents and sisters and brothers. He couldn't do it, no matter how he felt about her.

Yet that didn't mean he needed to continue wallowing in the pain of all the things that could not be undone. The past was the past, and his eyes needed to be on the future.

Reaching into his pocket, Aren pulled out the letter. He read the front and then the back, but for the first time since Marylyn had given it to him, the words failed to ignite his anger. He faced the stove, staring at the flames flickering beneath the kettle of water.

Lara shifted, lifting her head. "What's burning?"

"Nothing important," he answered, then continued to watch as the letter turned to ash.

T HE COMPOUND MIGHT have saved their lives, but it was not their salvation. Not when there was no food. And not when more of her father's soldiers would be on their way to ensure she and Aren were dead. Which meant the biggest challenge was ahead: how to get out of the Red Desert alive.

Her sisters had stripped the compound of supplies, and what remained was fouled with sand, broken, or burned. Worse, while her sisters had taken the shorter journey north to Maridrina, Lara and Aren needed to head south to Valcotta, which was twice the distance.

"Find whatever you can that will hold water," she'd told Aren. "And anything edible, though I doubt there will be much."

She'd been right on that count. Other than a handful of dates, a lone sack of flour, and a jar of pepper, Lara had found nothing to eat. There were several trees that produced fruit on the oasis, but the storm had stripped them bare. The gardens were buried with sand, and what she found beneath was nothing more than inedible pulp. Which meant they were looking at close to two weeks without food.

"Not much to be found." Aren dropped the supplies he'd gathered on the ground next to the spring, which Lara had been using a shovel to dredge, her dress soaked with sweat from the effort. It was cursedly hot, but they needed clean water more than she needed a wash, and it was a task she was able to do with her eyes closed. Which, given the way they still stung, was a blessing.

Fumbling around for a cup, she filled it and handed it to him. "Water is the most important."

"It's also heavy." She heard him drinking, then there was a splash, and he muttered, "God, that feels good. What I wouldn't give for a swim."

"Get out!" she shrieked, forcing her eyelids open, her horror at what he was doing worse than the pain. "It's forbidden!" Ignoring how he was staring at her as he climbed out, Lara held up a hand, lifting her fingers one by one as she said, "No animals are allowed to drink directly, lest they foul the waters. Only clean vessels are to be used, preferably of silver or gold. And no damned baths!"

"It's full of sand and there isn't anyone here but us."

She glared at him, the effect ruined by the flood of tears running down her face. "How about I don't want to drink the water that has soaked your sweaty feet."

He shrugged as though that were the only valid part of the argument. "We should cut back to the coast. It's closer."

"The coast will be heavily patrolled. My father's soldiers will be watching the desert in case we emerge."

Her eyes demanded to be closed, but Lara ignored the pain as Aren pulled off his shirt and tossed it to one side. Then he lifted a hand to shadow his face as he scanned the surrounding desert. He had a new scar running along his ribs and another just above the elbow, and she found herself examining him for more changes to the body she knew so well. He was leaner than he'd been, captivity having eroded some of his muscle mass, though it did nothing to detract from his appearance. Aren turned back, and she closed her eyes again before he caught her staring.

"There's no way those soldiers survived that storm," he said. "And when they don't return, your father will assume we're as dead as they are."

"Or that we killed them."

He huffed out a breath. "Maybe."

"And just because that group is dead doesn't mean more won't come," Lara said. "Serin will suspect that I'd try to make it here. He'll leave nothing to chance."

"We could ambush whoever he sends. Take their mounts and supplies."

Leaning on her shovel, Lara considered the idea. "He won't send a small group. And they'll come under the cover of darkness."

"We could hide and then ambush them from behind come daylight."

"That might work if we had any arrows, but my sisters took them all when they fled, and I don't relish the thought of going hand-to-hand with upward of two dozen trained soldiers."

Aren was silent for a moment. "What do you propose, then? That we sit here and slowly starve to death?"

A bead of sweat rolled into the scratches around her eye and Lara winced, curbing the urge to rub away the pain. "There is a caravan route east of here. I propose we ambush a merchant party and take what we need to reach Valcotta. They'll have guards, of course, but nothing the two of us shouldn't be able to handle."

Silence.

Lara returned to shoveling sand, refusing to open her eyes and look at him because she could already feel his judgment. Already knew the words that would come from his lips even as he inhaled the breath needed to form them. "You want us to kill innocent merchants to take their supplies? That seems somewhat ruthless."

She was a survivor, and to be one often necessitated ruthlessness. "Would you rather we die?"

"I'd rather we consider less extreme options. Why can't we ask the merchants for help? Or just steal what we need and leave them alive. Or better yet, use some of that gold I know you have to *buy* what we need."

It was strange to think she'd once believed him to be a cruel and merciless man, utterly devoid of compassion. That she'd spent nearly all of her life certain every Ithicanian was the same.

Pushing the shovel blade into a pile of sand, she turned to face him. "The merchants we'll encounter are those heading north on the heels of that storm, which means if we leave them alive, it will only be a matter of days until they reach the outskirts of the Red Desert. Where they will no doubt encounter my father's soldiers, who will question them extensively. Right now, we have the advantage that my father isn't certain whether we are alive, which we lose as soon as those merchants describe being accosted by a pair meeting our description."

"I'm aware of that." Aren's tone was cool. "But we'll have too much of a head start for them to catch us in the desert."

"But not enough of a head start that fast riders able to switch mounts every day won't be able to beat us to Valcotta and intercept us on the opposite side."

"You have an answer for everything, don't you?" There was a dull clang as he kicked her shovel, then a splash as it toppled into the spring. "And how shocking that your answer is killing."

Lara could feel her temper rising, the blood in her veins boiling as she fought to keep her composure. But it was a lost cause. "Do you think I want to kill people? That I enjoy it?" Opening her eyes, she stepped over the pile of sand and closed the distance between them, her hands balled into fists. "I'm not trying to save myself. I'm trying to save *you* because you are the only person capable of securing an alliance with Valcotta."

"Why does it need to be me?"

"Because!" she shouted. "Other than Ahnna, you are the only Ithicanian whose identity the Empress even knows! Do you think she's going to commit her navy to a costly battle because Jor asks her to? Because Lia asks her to? It has to be you because you're the only person she will believe can deliver on the promises you make."

He looked away.

"I know hard choices, Aren." Her voice shook. "I know what it feels like to sacrifice the lives of innocents in order to save the lives of those I care about." She gestured to the island, full of the bones of servants and musicians she'd done nothing to protect. "And it haunts me, but that doesn't mean I wouldn't do it again, because the alternative was the lives of my sisters. Just because a choice is hard doesn't mean you don't make it." She paused, then asked, "So what will it be: a handful of merchants or every goddamned soul in Eranahl? Choose!"

The only sounds were the trickle of the spring and the roar of blood in her ears.

"No." He shook his head. "I'm not killing innocent people to save my own skin. I refuse."

Frustration clawed at her like a wild thing, fueled by desperation, because while she could protect him from storms and soldiers and starvation, she could not protect Aren from himself. Lara opened her mouth to argue, but the sound of hooves striking stone filled her ears, and her heart lurched. "Hide!"

Grabbing his arm, she dragged him into the compound, ducking behind one of the dormitories. She pushed him against the wall, far too aware of the hard muscles of his bare chest against her palm, the familiar scent of him in her nose.

Focus, you fool!

The hilt of her sword clutched in one hand, Lara peered around the corner, listening.

"How many?" Aren whispered, his breath warm against her ear, his hand gripping her forearm.

She could hear only one, but that didn't mean there weren't more. Didn't mean that they weren't coming up from all sides, ready to attack.

Twisting, Lara pressed her back against the wall next to him, scanning their surroundings for any sign of motion while cursing her blurry vision.

But there was nothing. Nothing but the single individual whose camel was now drinking at the spring. An easy kill.

Or would be, if she weren't blinded by tears.

Lifting her weapon, Lara took a deep breath. "On three," she mouthed to Aren.

"One."

Aren raced around the corner. Swearing, Lara ran after him.

Only to collide with his back.

"What are you doing?" she snarled.

"Thanking Lady Luck," he answered, then stepped aside. "See for yourself."

T HE CAMEL HAD its head shoved into the spring, its throat
convulsing as it swallowed mouthful after mouthful of water,
though one eye shifted in his direction as Aren approached.

It still wore a bridle and saddle, the latter sitting upon trappings
in Maridrinian colors, but what interested Aren more was the dead
man dangling upside down next to the camel, foot tangled in part of
the saddle.

"I suppose no one explained the rules about the water to the
camel." He started toward the pair.

"Aren, it could be a ruse!" Lara leapt into his path, panning their
surroundings.

He sidestepped her. "I don't think so." Or at least, that was what
his gut—along with years of experience repelling raiders —was telling
him.

The camel sidled sideways when Aren reached for the dangling
reins, making an awful noise before snapping its yellow teeth at him.

"Don't bother it while it's drinking." Lara came up next to him, weapon still in hand. With a frown, she unhooked the dead soldier's foot, the man falling to the ground with a thud.

Aren dragged the corpse out of reach of the camel's hooves, then crouched to examine it. The soldier's body was battered from being dragged, skin scoured by sand and storm, but Aren judged that he'd been dead for less than a day. Which meant he was very likely one of their pursuers. And hopefully that meant the rest of them were dead.

Lara removed the animal's saddle and dropped it next to Aren, leaving him to unfasten the buckles on the saddlebags and extract the contents. Dried meat, fruit, and nuts. Not much, but it would be enough to sustain them for a few days. Possibly a week.

There was also canvas and ropes for a tent, the missing poles easily replaced. Two waterskins, which he added to the pile, and at the bottom of the saddlebag, a flask that was filled with whiskey.

"Seems sound." Lara released the camel's rear hoof, which she'd been inspecting, and gave the animal a pat on the rump. "Do the bags have what we need?"

"Enough to make do."

"Good." Lara dusted her hands on her skirts. "We'll let this boy drink his fill and then give him what fodder is left in the stables. Let's get some rest. We leave tonight."

INSTEAD OF HEEDING her own advice, Lara left Aren asleep on one of the beds, unable to resist further exploration of the place that had once been both prison and home.

Her legs carried her through the dormitories, moving from room to room until she reached the one she'd shared with Sarhina, which was largely untouched. Barely big enough for the two narrow cots it contained, it was devoid of any personal touches, for such things had always been forbidden to her and her sisters. The small chest of drawers was marked with soot, but opening it revealed the clothing she'd worn during her time here.

Pulling off her ruined dress, she inspected her injuries as best she could, her eyes still streaming tears. She pulled on clean undergarments, trousers, a linen shirt, and a coat, then braided her hair, feeling more human than she had since the night she'd rescued Aren.

Dropping to her knees, she lifted the loose stone beneath her bed, revealing the tiny hole where she'd hid her wooden box of childish treasures. She sat on the bed with the box in her lap and lifted out the contents one by one.

A bracelet Bronwyn had woven for her out of leather, which she slipped onto her wrist.

A shiny silver coin Sarhina had found and given her, the face worn beyond identification, which she tucked into her pocket.

Scraps of paper with notes complaining about their masters, which her sisters had written and passed among each other.

Those she flipped through, smiling at some, her heart breaking at others, for many of her masters had been cruel in their tutelage. Serin's name was notably absent, none of the girls brave enough to write anything critical about him. He'd always been too good at ferreting them out.

Setting the package aside, she reached back into the box and pushed aside a vial in favor of a silver necklace with a sapphire pendant dangling from it. It was sized for a child, too small to fit around her neck now, but she still held it to her throat, tears that had nothing to do with sand welling in her eyes at the feel of it.

Her mother had given it to her. Lara had only a few memories of the woman, but one of them had been of her fastening this necklace around Lara's neck. She'd been wearing it when her father's soldiers had taken her, and she'd hidden it all these years, her most cherished possession. Proof that at one point, she'd been loved.

And the mother who'd loved her had died for it.

A sob tore from her throat, and she doubled over, shoulders shaking.

"You all right?"

The cot across from her creaked, and she looked up to find Aren sitting on it, elbows resting on his knees as he regarded her.

"My mother gave it to me," she said, holding it up. "It's the only thing I have left of her."

"I'm glad you had the chance to retrieve it."

Rubbing her thumb across the stone, Lara nodded. "I was wearing your mother's necklace the night . . ." She trailed off, giving her head a shake. "It was how I got back. I traced the stones on a piece of paper and used it for a map."

"Clever."

"I assumed you'd want it back, so I left it in Eranahl."

He didn't answer, only stared at the ground between them. "When I looked for you, I found the room where Serin kept his . . . *implements.*"

She stiffened, knowing exactly what Aren meant. Serin considered torture an art form to be perfected, and courtesy of his *training,* she'd been on both the receiving and delivering end of the implements.

"Serin couldn't physically harm me, so he made me watch while he tortured the Ithicanians he caught. When he wasn't asking damnable questions about how to breach Eranahl's defenses, he'd talk about the things he'd done to you and your sisters. And the things he'd had you do to each other."

Lara felt the blood drain from her face, and she looked away. "We twelve weren't the only girls brought to the compound. There were twenty of us. Two died from illness. Four were killed in combat training, and one in an accident. But one . . . Her name was Alina, and she refused to play Serin's games. Refused over and over again. Then one night, she went missing." Lara swallowed hard. "I don't think she escaped."

Aren nodded slowly. "He especially liked to tell me what he intended to do to you, when you were caught. Would trick me into believing they had you. And I was terrified because I knew if they ever succeeded, I'd tell them anything they wanted to know."

A dull ache formed in Lara's stomach. For the pain Aren endured, and also because Serin had been able to use her against him. "He'll get what's coming to him one of these days, I promise you."

"I'm not sure that will change anything."

Needing to cut the tension, she asked, "What's my brother like?"

Aren huffed out a breath. "He's bloody awful. I can't stand him."

"I didn't ask for your opinion on him. I asked what he was like."

"He's a scheming smartass and quite taken with his own intelligence."

"Is he intelligent?"

Aren gave a grudging nod. "Yes. But he's . . . hard to pin down.

He claims he only wants the crown because the alternative is a grave next to his siblings, but I'm not convinced. Your father detests him for not fitting the mold he has in mind for an heir, but Keris provokes him rather than accommodating him." Frowning, he stared at the cracked stone floor beneath their feet. "He's willing to risk his life to stand by certain principles, but he speaks of himself as though he were a coward. He makes no sense to me."

"Don't trust him, Aren. He only helped you and the Valcottan woman escape because feeding Eranahl furthers his own ambitions."

"I think it's more complex than that," he answered, then reached into her treasure box and plucked out the last item. "What's this?"

"Poison."

"Most girls keep love letters in their treasure boxes, but you keep murder weapons."

The laugh that exited her throat was bitter. "It's what I used to fake my sisters' deaths—it's my own concoction. More than a few drops and you're dead, so mind you don't stick your feet in my drinking water again."

"Noted."

Rising to her feet, Lara shoved the bottle, along with the necklace, into the pocket of her coat. "Let's go. The sun's about to set, and we need to start walking."

*D*ON'T PUSH HIM *too hard.* For about the thousandth time, the thought circled Lara's head, and she cast a sideways glance to where Aren trudged through the sand, his shoulders bowed, face marked by the shadows of the lamp she carried.

They'd been walking for a week, and they still hadn't reached the nearest oasis in the outpost of Jerin.

She hadn't accounted for the toll captivity had taken upon him, mentally or physically. The Aren she knew in Ithicana was as fit as a man could be, able to push himself to extremes for days—weeks—at a time without faltering. But during imprisonment, he'd been shackled, never walking farther than the distance between his rooms and the palace courtyards, the sedentary life so at odds with who he was that it was a wonder he hadn't been driven to madness.

If they'd been able to stick with her plan and journey up the coast, he would've been fine, or near enough to it not to cause concern, but the Red Desert was an entirely different journey. An entirely different beast.

Aren knew heat, but not like this. And she doubted he'd ever gone more than a few hours without water. Why would he have to when the skies of Ithicana provided more than one could ever drink? Even true hunger was a stranger to him, for the islands were full of things to eat if one knew where to look—which is why his people were surviving even cut off from the bridge as they were.

The thought of the Ithicanians made Lara grind her teeth in frustration. She and Aren were behind schedule, which wasn't something they could afford. The calm season—what had once been War Tides—would soon begin, which meant they had little time to secure Valcotta's assistance to drive out Maridrina. Any further delays and they'd lose the opportunity, for an attack during storm season would be impossible. Even if her father lost the support of the Amaridian navy, it would still be next to impossible for those in Eranahl to survive another storm season without the bridge.

Aren chose that moment to stumble, nearly falling, and Lara's heart sank. Tugging on the camel's lead until it stopped, she said, "Get on and ride for a bit."

"Not a chance."

Aren did not get along with the camel, which she had christened Jack, both of them casting dark glares at each other when they thought the other wasn't looking. She'd convinced him to ride once before, but while Aren was still righting himself in the saddle, Jack had stood, sending Aren tumbling headfirst into the sand. To say that he'd taken the incident poorly would be an understatement.

Lara chewed on the insides of her cheeks. "The Jerin oasis is only a few hours from here. If we're going to get in and out without being caught, you need to be *not* stumbling over your own boots."

"We've got plenty of water left. We bypass it and keep walking."

They probably did have enough water to get through, but the small amount of food that had been in Jack's saddlebags was long gone. Lara didn't think Aren would make it through another week of these conditions on an empty stomach. Wasn't certain if she could.

"Jack has gone a week without drinking. He needs some water." A lie, given the animal could easily go another week without, even in this heat. But Aren didn't know that. "So unless you want to give up your share, we need to stop."

"I'm not killing innocent merchants."

Lara cast her eyes up at the stars, begging them for patience. "There are likely close to a hundred people in Jerin, so killing everyone to keep them silent isn't an option. Stealth is. But right now you couldn't sneak through a Harendellian tavern full of drunks."

She could all but hear his stubbornness warring with his practicality, but eventually the latter won over and he stopped walking. "Only for an hour."

"Fine." Urging the camel to lay down, she waited for Aren to climb on and then extracted some rope.

"What are you doing?"

"In case you fall asleep. I don't need you falling off and breaking your neck."

That he allowed her to tie him to the saddle was testament to his exhaustion, but Lara said nothing as she completed the work, nudging Jack back to his feet and leading him onward.

They walked through the night and, as she'd anticipated, the rolling stride of the animal slowly lulled Aren to sleep, his shoulders slumping lower and lower until his face rested against the camel's neck. It was at about that moment that a faint breeze rolled over them and Jack lifted his head in interest, his pace quickening.

"You smell the water, boy?" she asked, patting him on the neck. "Good. You keep walking in that direction."

Groaning, Jack pulled on the lead, trying to get her to move faster.

"I know," she murmured, "but I need you to buy me some time."

Stopping the animal, she hobbled him so that he could only move at a slow walk. Removing all the empty waterskins, she flipped them over her shoulder. "Take care of him for me," she said, stroking the camel's neck, then she broke into a slow run in the direction of the oasis.

It only took her an hour or so to reach the trading outpost encircling the small lake, bright lamplight causing the outpost to glow like the burning rim of an eclipsed sun.

Crouching behind the lip of a dune, Lara examined the buildings. They were stone, nearly windowless structures like those on the compound where she'd been raised. Chimes made of colored glass hung from the rooflines, filling the air with a gentle music, and in the well-lit grove between the buildings and the water, panels of colored silk hung from the branches. Valcottan influence, the border between the two nations as undefined here as it was along the coast, although far less contested. Neither nation much cared about a few miles of sand, or at least, not enough to march an army into the desert to fight over it. As such, Jerin was an outpost of both nations or none, depending on who you asked.

Moving closer, Lara eyed the people in the streets, the business of the outpost reflecting the nocturnal habits of those who traveled the caravan route. Many were her countrymen, recognizable in their close-fitting trousers and boots and coats, whereas the Valcottans favored voluminous garments that cinched at wrists, ankles, and waists, leather sandals strapped to their feet. The Valcottans also possessed significantly darker complexions, their curly brown hair either cut short or wrapped into tight knots on the tops of their heads.

They all moved about in groups, and Lara noticed that they gave each other a wide berth despite the unwritten rule of peace in the oasis. A sign, she thought, that the conflict between Maridrina and Valcotta was reaching a fevered pitch. Which would only work to Aren and Ithicana's favor.

Moving at a slow run toward the outpost, she stopped when two barking dogs burst from between buildings, heading straight toward her. Extracting the pepper that she'd found on the compound—and had brought with her for just this purpose—she tossed it in the animals' faces as they neared. The dogs immediately began to sneeze, pawing at their muzzles, allowing Lara to duck into the narrow space between two buildings unmolested.

And there she paused.

There was a scuffle of noise, and someone opened a door. "What's all that racket about, you cursed creatures? Get back here!"

Lara jumped onto a barrel and reached up for the lip of the roof. Pulling herself silently on top, she crawled along the flat surface until she reached the opposite side where she could survey the comings and goings.

Her weapons master, Erik, had described the oasis to her once, and that information, along with what she could see, were the limit of her knowledge. Many of the buildings were lodgings for travelers, though some were private residences of those who permanently made their home in the oasis. There were several establishments that purveyed food and drink and entertainment, a smithy, a series of stables, and a number of brightly lit buildings that seemed to provide necessary services to those who crossed back and forth across the desert.

There were primarily men moving through the narrow streets, but Lara caught sight of a few Valcottan women, heads held high and proud, the staffs they favored as weapons gripped in their hands. There were people of other nations as well, identifiable by their garments and complexions. None appeared to be Ithicanian, but that meant little because she knew how easily Aren's people adopted disguises.

The savory scent of cooking meat wafted past Lara's nose, her attention flicking a few buildings down to where a woman stood next to a grill, which was loaded with skewers. Her mouth watered even as her stomach growled. *Water first,* she decided, turning her focus to the darkness of the lake beyond. She'd have to cross three streets to reach the trees, all well-lit, and her being alone would draw immediate attention.

Which meant she needed a distraction.

Fire was the obvious choice, but as though he were sitting next to her, Lara felt Aren's judgment at the idea of destroying people's homes or livelihoods for the sake of a distraction. Frowning, Lara considered her options as she eyed a group of camels tethered at the edge of the town, their backs laden with goods and supplies, a single boy standing watch over them. But there was only open space around them, making it next to impossible to sneak up to the animals.

Below her, the dogs had finally recovered from the pepper, yipping as they ran up and down between the buildings.

Which gave Lara an idea.

She waited for an opportune moment, then rose and leapt the gap to the neighboring building. Then the next. Easing up to the front of the house, she listened to the woman humming as she went back and forth between tasks inside and rotating the grilling meat. Unsheathing her sword, Lara held the tip of the blade, waiting. When the woman went back inside, she leaned over the edge, hooking her sword hilt under one of the skewers, sliding it up until the meat was secured. Then she carefully lifted it and scuttled to the rear of the home.

Unable to resist, she pushed a piece into her mouth, not caring when the meat burned her tongue. Pulling the rest of the meat loose, she abandoned the skewer and lowered her hand between the houses, immediately catching the dogs' attention.

Wincing as they barked and jumped, Lara hurried to the opposite side of the house, the dogs following. Waiting until she knew they were watching her, she threw the meat onto the laden backs of the camels.

The dogs bolted after the prize, the camels jerking up their heads in alarm as the animals raced toward them, the air filling with their loud bellows.

As one, the camels surged, pulling their tether loose and galloping into the town, the dogs in hot pursuit. Their minder shouted, trying to catch at their leads, but it was a lost cause, and soon the streets were wild with men and women chasing after the camels, the air filled with shouts.

Making sure her scarf was secure over her hair, Lara leapt from the building and joined in the chaos, weaving her way through street after street before ducking into the shadows of the grove. Moving carefully through the foliage, she hurried toward the lake.

To keep the oasis clean and pure, stones had been carefully placed so that the water could be reached without stepping into it. Dropping to her knees, Lara reached down to fill a waterskin. One after another she filled them, then made her way back to the edge of the grove.

In the distance, she could make out angry shouts, the merchants whose camels she'd spooked berating the owner of the dogs. They were Maridrinian, judging from the accents, whereas the dogs' owner was Valcottan. More and more voices joined the fray, the incident tipping the fragile peace between the people of the two nations, and soon fists began to fly. More people came running from all directions, and Lara winced, realizing that fire might have caused less damage than the fight she'd instigated.

But there was nothing to do about it now.

Lara joined with those shouting and running toward the altercation, which was in the market. The camels had overturned several stalls, and there were more than a dozen brawling men adding to the chaos.

Weaving among the people, Lara snatched up a sack of dried apricots that had been knocked from a market stand and a handful of small buns from a tray on another, everyone too distracted by the fight to notice her theft. Grabbing a few more items of foodstuff, Lara stepped back between two stalls, creeping behind a row of them.

All she had to do now was get out of town, intercept Aren and Jack, and then—

Meaty hands reached through the back of the stall, closing on her forearms. And a deep voice said, "Here's our little thief."

AREN WOKE WITH a start, hands scrambling for purchase as he slid sideways. His fingers latched on the camel's neck, his head swimming with dizziness as he carefully righted himself in the saddle. To which he was tied.

He eyed the rising sun, then growled, "Why didn't you wake me?"

No answer.

Pivoting in the saddle, he scanned his surroundings, but Lara was nowhere in sight. Unease filled his chest. Had she collapsed? Was she back behind him somewhere, lying helpless in the sand?

Snatching up the reins of the camel, he yanked them, trying to force the animal to turn, but Jack ignored him, ears perked forward toward something Aren couldn't see in the dim light.

"You don't want to leave her behind," Aren said, hauling again on the reins. "She likes you. I don't."

But his efforts were fruitless.

Giving up, Aren dropped the reins and began to unfasten the knots tying his legs to the saddle, the only thing that had kept him from falling off entirely. Sliding to the ground, he dug in his heels, forcibly pulling the camel to a stop. It was only then that he noticed the hobbles around Jack's forelegs.

Had she tried to stop for the night and the camel had wandered off with Aren aboard? Even as the thought crossed his mind, he shook it away, his head aching with the motion. Lara's coat and all of their supplies were still attached to the saddle, and even if he'd spooked, Jack couldn't move fast enough in the hobbles to escape Lara's practiced hands.

A faint breeze brushed Aren's face, and the camel tugged insistently on the lead, showing more enthusiasm for speed than Aren had seen from him during their entire trek. And there could be only one reason for that: water. The camel was heading toward the oasis Lara had spoken of.

In an instant, Aren's sun-addled mind understood what Lara had done, and he swore, kicking at the sand. Jack took the opportunity to try to carry on, but Aren hauled him back. "We need to wait for *Her Majesty* to return lest we foil her precious plan."

The edge of the sun appeared in the east, rising higher and higher, but Lara didn't return. Aren drank deeply from one of the waterskins, wiping sweat from his brow as he scanned the horizon for movement.

Jack voiced his displeasure at the delay, the noise echoing over the empty dunes.

"I know," he replied to the camel. "She should be back by now."

Which meant something had gone wrong.

THEY PUT HER in a goddamned pillory.

In the middle of the market, the big man and his friends had forced Lara, kicking and screaming, to her knees while her head and hands were shoved into the wooden frame of the pillory, the top piece slamming down to hold her in place while she spat curses at them.

Not that it had done her any good.

Sweat rolled in rivers down her body, the rising sun baking her naked skin because of course they hadn't allowed her to keep her clothes. They'd taken everything from her, not even leaving enough to keep her decent.

And she knew exactly why.

"Drink, pretty one, drink."

A cup was held up to her lips and precious water poured into her mouth while she desperately tried to swallow as much as she could without choking. Then she rolled her eyes up to examine the giant man who'd captured her. He was a product of the desert, his face and complexion courtesy of ancestors from both Maridrina and Valcotta.

"An easy death is no punishment." He patted her cheek. "And I have money on you lasting through the end of the week. Long enough for the sun to cook the skin from your bones."

When a cup of water could mean life or death, theft was taken as seriously as murder in the Red Desert and punished accordingly. They'd found a piece of meat stuck in one of the camel's packs and determined she was the one who'd spooked them, and all the ire that had been directed against the dogs' owner had been turned on her. It was only this man who'd kept them from beating her to death, but it wasn't out of a sense of altruism. It had been his apricots she'd stolen, and he apparently appreciated a more prolonged demise.

"Kiss my ass," she growled, but he only laughed and slapped said ass, the skin, unused to exposure to the sun, already badly burned.

For that, she fully intended to gut him.

That delightful visual was circling Lara's thoughts when the sound of a man singing off-key reached her ears. It was a vulgar Harendellian tavern song about a man and a mule that she'd heard many a time during her weeks in the northern nation, but not once since.

Lifting her head, Lara squinted against the brilliant light, watching the lone camel approaching the town. The man riding him was swaying in the saddle, one hand holding the reins, the other holding a flask, the metal glinting in the sun. Riding into the market square, he hauled on the reins, the camel coming to a stop right as the man finished his song.

Aren awkwardly dismounted, his foot catching on the saddle and sending him sprawling, inspiring laughter from the few merchants who remained in the market.

"Damn you, cursed beast!" Aren shouted at Jack. "You moved!" Then he lifted the flask to his lips, apparently found it empty, and tossed it aside. "I need a drink! Someone sell me a drink!"

The merchant whose camels Lara had spooked wandered toward him, a bottle held loosely in one hand. "My friend, my friend, how is it that you have come to us alone and in such a state? What has happened to you?"

Lara watched as Aren rested his head in his hands, her jaw dropping as he abruptly wailed, "It's gone." When he lifted his head, tears streaked his face. "A storm like none I've seen before swept our camp, stealing away my companions and merchandise. All dead. All gone. My grandmother warned me not to risk my wealth to the sand, but my ambitions outweighed my good sense."

It was all Lara could do not to roll her eyes. Clearly Aren had noticed her in the pillory, the comment as much for her as the merchant.

"The desert is a fickle woman, my friend." The merchant patted Aren's shoulder. "How is it that you survived?"

Aren wiped his eyes. "Fortune clearly wished for me to live with my mistakes rather than to rest in ignorance in the endless sleep." Then his gaze latched on the bottle in the merchant's hands. "If you are a true friend, you'll help me drown my sorrows."

"Of course, of course." The man extracted a cup and poured a measure, handing it over to Aren, who downed it in one mouthful, holding it out for more. But the merchant clucked mournfully.

"Alas, friend, all things have a price in the desert."

"But I've lost everything!" he moaned. "Take pity on me."

That was a lie. Lara knew Aren had gold and silver in his pockets because she'd given it to him in case they were separated. It was more than enough to pay for lodging and supplies and for Jack to drink his fill. What was he up to?

"Perhaps you might have something you wish to sell?"

"I've nothing." Aren rested his head in the sand, masterfully playing the part of a spoiled merchant's son. Jack chose that moment to start walking toward the lake, Aren crawling after him, trying to reach for the reins. The merchant reached out and pulled Jack to a halt, his eyes running over both animal and trappings, calculating their value even as he measured the level of Aren's desperation.

"Perhaps we might come to an arrangement. That wretch"—the merchant jerked his chin in Lara's direction—"caused one of my animals to go lame, and I cannot spare the time for the beast to heal. If you'd be willing to part with yours, I'd pay you a fair price."

Lara's lips parted, the desire to scream, *Don't you dare sell him!* rising to her lips. They needed that camel if there was to be any chance of them getting out of the desert alive.

Except Aren was no fool. He knew they needed Jack, which meant he had a plan. It was only that her sunbaked mind was too sluggish to figure it out.

"But I need him," he whined. "How else am I to get to Valcotta?"

The merchant rubbed his chin. "Perhaps we can truly help one another, my friend. What say you to joining our party when we leave tonight? Your beast can bear a portion of my goods, and in exchange, we shall safely deliver you from the sands."

His face filled with disbelief, Aren blurted out, "You would do this?"

Yet even from a dozen yards away, Lara could see the glint in his eyes that suggested this was *exactly* the offer the King of Ithicana had planned to extract from the merchant. And Lara's blood ran cold. If he went with them, he wouldn't need her; the men were more than capable of delivering on their promise, and the camel was worth the price of their services and more.

He wouldn't leave her. He couldn't. But a voice inside her head whispered, *Why shouldn't he go? Helping you would be a risk, and he owes you nothing.*

"Fortune smiles on us a both! What is your name, friend? I'm called Timin."

"James. And I'm in your debt, Timin."

The merchant hauled Aren to his feet, leading him and Jack off in the direction of the stables. And Aren didn't so much as give her a sideways glance as he passed.

The ache in her chest surpassed the throb in her head for intensity, and Lara slumped in the pillory, her eyes burning, though she was too dehydrated for tears. She'd thought things had changed, that Aren had, if not forgiven her, at least let go of the hate that had been consuming him.

But maybe she'd only seen what she'd wanted to see. What she'd hoped for. Or maybe he'd only been pretending. Either way, it appeared as though Aren planned to leave her here to die.

Lara's chin trembled as she struggled not to sob, then she clamped her teeth down hard. She was a queen. A warrior. But more than that, she was the little cockroach.

And she had no intention of dying.

The hours stretched, the sun moving slowly across the sky, the only respite from its blistering heat the shadow cast by the pillory. Lara kept her head low, hair concealing her face, her hands curled as far under her wrists as possible in order to protect them from the sun. With her knees and toes, she slowly dug into the ground, covering her lower legs with sand while keeping her thighs beneath the shadow of her torso.

But there was nothing she could do to protect her back or her bottom, her exposed skin already burned to the point of blistering. More scars to add to her collection.

Like clockwork, the big man brought her water, which Lara drank greedily while contemplating how she'd kill him once she was freed. Never mind that she still had no notion of how to escape the pillory.

Not once did she see Aren.

He was resting, she supposed, taking advantage of the arrangement he'd made with the merchant to have a few hours of sleep in the cool confines of one of the buildings. But despite her own predicament, a flood of relief filled her chest when he returned to the market, flanked by the merchant and two of his companions. They walked toward the tavern and settled themselves at a table in the shade of the building.

Bottles of amber liquor and tiny glasses appeared, along with a plate of candied dates, and soon the men were drinking and laughing as though they were all old friends, none merrier than Aren. More men joined them, and soon it was a veritable gathering, Aren regaling them with a fabricated version of his survival of the sandstorm.

From time to time, one of the men would break away from the table to take a piss in the sand near the pillory. Lara flinched away from the disgusting splatter even as she imagined depriving each perpetrator of a certain body part. The stench around her was nearly unbearable in the heat.

The sun was low in the sky when Aren decided to take a turn.

"It's not looking good for you," he said, unfastening his belt. "These men take theft *very* seriously."

Grinding her teeth to keep her anger in check, Lara lifted her head. "Can you get me that bottle of poison? It's in my coat, which was attached to Jack's saddle."

He lifted both eyebrows. "This vial?"

The brown glass appeared in his hand, then disappeared just as quickly back into his pocket.

"Aren—"

"It's an interesting plan." Finishing, he buckled his belt. "But I wouldn't recommend it. They plan to feed your body to the dogs. You'd better come up with another idea."

Without another word, he turned back to his companions. "Excuse me for a moment, gentlemen. I'm going inside to chat with that pretty girl behind the bar."

He disappeared into the building and didn't emerge for a long time. And when he did, he appeared even drunker than before.

Aren wasn't going to help her, and whether it was because he didn't wish to jeopardize his escape or he thought she deserved this, it didn't much matter. Lara was on her own.

When the sun was little more than a glowing sliver of orange, Aren, the merchant, and the rest of their party rose, laughing and slapping their drinking companions on the shoulders as they said their farewells. Aren swayed unsteadily on his feet.

"Idiot," Lara muttered. "I hope you enjoy being on water rations with a hangover in tow."

"Talking to yourself, pretty girl?"

The big man was back. Crouching, he poured water into her mouth before carefully feeding a heel of bread to her piece by piece. "Eat! Eat!" he murmured, his breath stinking of alcohol. "I wish for the sun to cook your flesh from your bones, and that takes time."

Lara bared her teeth, but he only chuckled and straightened. As he did, he swayed drunkenly, catching his weight against the pillory. The wooden frame groaned and shifted, but he didn't seem to notice, more intent on adding to the puddles of piss around her.

Buckling his belt, he leaned against the pillory again, the sand beneath Lara's knees moving. "I'll see you later, pretty girl."

Lara waited until he'd rejoined his companions. And then she smiled. "You had better hope not."

34
AREN

H<small>OW LONG WILL THE</small> journey take?" Aren asked Timin, walking unsteadily down the path to the stables where their caravan was waiting. He wasn't precisely drunk. But neither was he precisely sober, his recent deprivations having given him no head for the strong drink these men preferred. If he were going to make this plan work, he needed a clearer mind.

"A week," Timin answered, clapping him on the back. "Perhaps ten days. Where will you go next, my friend?"

"The coast." One of the stable boys handed Jack's reins to Aren. The camel lifted one lip as though he might bite before deciding Aren wasn't worth the effort. "I've had enough of sand."

"Do you have friends there? Family who will surely be growing concerned for your welfare?"

It was all Aren could do not to roll his eyes at the obviousness of the man's ploy, but he answered, "My family is all in Harendell, thank God. I'll have time to think of a way to explain that I've lost all of their money." He belched loudly. "Might take my time, then use the storms as an excuse not to go back for a year."

Timin laughed before shouting at his men to start moving, the group striding out of the town and south toward Valcotta.

The air was swiftly turning cold, and Aren wondered how long that would be a blessing to Lara's burned skin before it turned into a curse. She'd looked miserable and deeply unwell. And every time one of the merchants had gone near her, it had been a struggle not to pull a weapon and go to her defense.

"So serious, James." Timin's voice broke into Aren's thoughts.

"Merely contemplating a week of walking."

"Ah, yes. Perhaps this will help ease your mind."

The merchant tried to pass Aren a bottle, but he held up his hands. "You've already been more than generous with the offer you have given for my camel. I couldn't possibly take more."

"Nonsense! The beast is of the best stock. It is I who am coming out ahead in our bargain."

Pretending to waver, Aren finally accepted the bottle and feigned drinking deeply. "You are a true friend."

They walked for close to an hour in the darkness, Timin singing the entire time while Aren pretended to drink, surreptitiously pouring the contents into the sand from time to time. He staggered frequently, colliding with the unamused Jack.

But he was stone-cold sober when he heard the blade being drawn behind him.

Turning, Aren regarded Timin, who held a long knife, his two partners flanking him. The younger one stood a distance back holding the camels' leads, his expression terrified.

"Drop your beast's lead," Timin said. "Then lay down in the sand."

"And here I thought we were friends." Aren dropped Jack's lead but remained on his feet.

The merchant lifted one shoulder. "What can I say? Business is business."

"This seems much more like theft."

The three men laughed and Timin said, "It is only theft if the individual suffering the loss is alive to report the crime."

It was Aren's turn to laugh. "I couldn't agree more."

Timin's brow furrowed in confusion, which turned to panic as Aren jerked his sword free from Jack's pack, attacking the men before they had a chance to react. He opened Timin's guts, then turned on the other pair, cutting them down mercilessly. In his periphery, he saw the boy drop the camel's leads and start to run, but Aren was after him in a flash.

Taller and stronger, he caught the boy easily, tackling him into the sand.

"Please," the boy wept. "Please, have mercy. I didn't know what they intended to do."

Likely a lie, but Aren wasn't in the practice of killing children. "I'm not going to kill you, but I'm afraid I need to keep you quiet until I'm well on my way."

Gagging the boy, then binding his wrists to his ankles, Aren left him near the camels, which he'd hobbled and staked to the ground. Then a groan of pain caught his attention.

With one arm cradling his innards, Timin was crawling toward the oasis. Following, Aren kicked him in the ribs, flipping him onto his back even as the man screamed for help.

"We're too far away for anyone to hear." Aren dropped on one knee next to the dying man. "But you knew that, didn't you?"

"Who are you?" Timin's words were strained. "What sort of demon are you?"

"The sort who's had his fill of backstabbing pricks," Aren replied before sliding his blade across the man's throat. "Now if you'll excuse me, I'm going to get my wife back."

35
LARA

L EAN FORWARD.
 Lean backward.
 Lean left.
Lean right.

Lara repeated the chant in her head, forcing her body to comply even though exhaustion and exposure were taking their toll. Her skin burned hot in the places the sun had scorched it, but the rest of her was freezing, her body wracked with shivers. She was thirsty, her stomach twisted with cramps, and her head throbbed. If she didn't escape tonight, the only escape would be death.

Lean forward.

Lean backward.

The pillory was set into the ground, but not deeply enough. The big man's weight had loosened it so that with hours of work on her part, it should've been easy to lift free. Except she'd discovered that she was too weak to do so. Her only option was to keep working to destabilize the damned thing, then try to tip it over, hopefully not breaking her neck in the process.

The market was busy with people going about the business of buying and selling goods, a large caravan having arrived from Maridrina shortly after sunset. Interest in her had fortunately diminished, though men and women both took the time to spit or throw sand at her as they passed. Lara didn't much care what they tossed at her as long as none of them noticed what she was up to.

The Maridrinian tavern was bustling, dozens of men sitting outside at the little tables, drinking and laughing, some with their heads bent close as they discussed business. It was loud, made louder still by a pair of musicians playing drums. A dancer who likely moonlighted as a prostitute swayed seductively on top of a platform that had been set up for her. For that reason, it took several moments for the crowd to notice her large captor slumping to the ground in front of the building, foam pouring from his mouth.

There were shouts of alarm, then two more men slumped off the sides of their chairs, exhibiting the same symptoms.

"Poison! They've been poisoned," someone shrieked, and the whole market turned into chaos, the patrons of the tavern shoving away glasses and bottles, eyes wide with horror.

This was her chance.

Getting her legs underneath her, Lara pushed, feet scrabbling in the sand. Her back screamed in agony, but slowly, the pillory toppled forward, pulling her with it. She tried to slow the fall of the frame, but it was wasted effort. Her body flipped upright, her ass in the air as the top of her head hit the sand hard enough that she saw stars. The opening encircling her neck slammed down against her chin, pressing hard against her throat. But she'd heard the latch flip open.

Digging the tips of her toes into the ground, she tried to push the top piece of the pillory loose to free herself. But it was wedged in the sand.

And she couldn't breathe.

Desperation filling her, she tried to pull the whole mess of wood backward and out of the sand, but she couldn't get the leverage.

If she didn't get out soon, she was going to pass out. And if no one noticed her, she'd be dead, strangled and crushed by her own faulty plan.

Catching a toe in one of the holes in the ground, Lara pulled, the bones in her wrists grinding against the wood, muscles trembling.

The frame shifted, and she felt the top piece loosen, freeing her wrists and neck.

She'd done it!

"That wasn't your most graceful maneuver," a familiar voice hissed, then hands were grasping her arms, pulling her upright. "You're lucky you didn't break your damned neck."

Aren.

"Let's go while they're still distracted."

He dragged her between two stalls, heading toward the lake. Moments later, she heard shouts of alarm as her captors realized she'd escaped.

"This way."

Aren guided her down to the water, but it wasn't until they were on the stones paving its banks that she realized what he intended. "It's forbidden!"

"I remember. And given most of these people are probably no better swimmers than you, they'll never think to look out here."

The water was warmer than the air around her, almost like a bath as Aren led her deeper into the lake, the depths rising to her hips and then her waist, but when it dropped off at the next step, she scrambled back.

"We're too close to the edge. Hold on to me."

There was no sense arguing given that bobbing lights were coming down to the water, a search for her underway. Wrapping her arms around Aren's shoulders, she tried to keep her breathing steady as he walked silently toward the center of the lake, where he paused, the water just beneath his chin.

They were searching the grove surrounding the lake, moving steadily around the perimeter, but not once did one of them look to the darkness of the waters. Farther away, she could hear sounds of the town being searched, the voices filled with fury. They'd leave no stone unturned.

Lara's head spun, the small sips of water she took doing nothing to quell her growing nausea. Her arms cramped, the effort of holding onto Aren almost beyond her capability. Her body shuddered, and she took deep breaths to calm her racing heart, but it did no good.

Then Aren's hand caught hold of her wrist, pulling her around in front of him, where he gripped her waist. Her burned skin screamed at his touch, and she bit down on a whimper.

"Use your legs."

Trembling, she wrapped her naked legs around his waist, the skin of her inner thighs mercifully unburned. Easing her arms around his neck, she rested her forehead against his cheek, feeling his breath brush her ear. His chest pressed against her breasts, and she wasn't certain if it was his racing heart she felt or her own.

"Easy," he murmured, his hands catching her under the arms for added support, careful not to touch where it would hurt. "You'll be okay."

"You came back for me."

"You thought I wouldn't?" Though his voice was nothing more than a whisper, she heard his incredulity.

Her jaw trembled, and she gave the slightest of nods.

"Lara . . ." His hand cupped her cheek and moved her face so that she was looking him in the eye, though it was too dark to see more than shadows. His breath was warm against her lips, and she heard it quicken as she tightened her legs around him, tangling her fingers in his hair.

God help her, but she loved him. Needed him like she needed air to breathe. Wanted him, despite her body feeling like it was on the brink of death.

Then his lips brushed hers, and it felt like everything fell away. Like there was nothing in all the world but the two of them. She trembled, pulling herself closer against him, until he whispered, "Lara, no matter where you are in the world, if you need me, I'll come for you. Please know that."

Reality slapped her in the face, and with it, pain that filled her core. *No matter where she* . . . Because she might be anywhere, but it wouldn't be with him. Couldn't be with him, she knew. And yet . . .

They remained silent, hiding in the water until the searchers moved away from the shore, then Aren started toward the low cliff where the tiny waterfall that filled the lake trickled. Reaching the edge, he held her steady until she had a grip on the rocks.

They climbed, then Aren paused to peer over the lip. "It's clear. Can you run?"

Lara felt like she could barely walk, but she nodded.

"Go."

Her bare feet thudded softly as she ran. Her wet hair slapped against her naked back, making her wince in pain. She stumbled, barely able to keep her footing, but it wasn't until they'd crossed over a dune and were down the other side that she finally collapsed.

"I've got you," Aren said in her ear as he picked her up. "You'll be all right."

Blood roared in her ears, the stars above spinning, then all the world fell into blackness.

H<small>E CARRIED HER</small> shivering body through the darkness, following the tracks in the sand. No easy task, given he needed to keep the lantern to a nearly imperceptible glow, lest he draw the attention of the searchers in the town.

The camels, boy, and corpses were where he'd left them. The boy's eyes widened as they landed on Lara, who remained unconscious.

"Look the other way," Aren growled at him before lowering his naked wife onto the sand. Turning up the glow of the lantern, he grimaced at the sight of her sunburned back and shoulders. She was feverishly hot to the touch, both her breathing and pulse far more rapid than they should be.

Digging through the packs on the camels, Aren found the boy's bag, which contained a spare set of clothing that would fit Lara. She whimpered as he pulled the garments onto her, trying to curl in on herself. The task took up more time than he cared to spare. After stripping Jack of the merchant's goods, he draped Lara over the camel's back, using lengths of fabric rather than coarse rope to bind her to the saddle. Then he turned on the boy.

"I'm going to let you go. Find yourself better travel companions."

Adjusting the boy's bindings so that it was possible to crawl, Aren pointed back to the oasis. "If you start now, you might make it before the sun comes up."

Checking that the animals were still secured to one another, Aren took up Jack's lead and then nudged him with the stick to get him and the others to stand. "Keep your teeth to yourself," he warned the animal. "I've got two replacements right behind you."

Jack gave him a reproachful glare but dutifully followed Aren as they headed south.

Lara was sick for days, barely able to keep food down, and too exhausted to do anything but slump in Jack's saddle. The skin on her back blistered, and where it didn't, it was a livid red. Her jaw locked with pain every time he applied the salve he'd found in one of the camel's packs. She was unconscious more often than not, mumbling and crying out in her sleep, though whether from old terrors or new, he couldn't have said. Yet Aren had no choice but to set a grueling pace across the red dunes, riding through the night and into the day until the heat became unbearable.

Only when they reached the edge of the desert and into the rolling hills of Valcotta, did she recover. And the sight of her striding next to him, sword belted at her waist, was more welcome than the gurgling streams of precious water that appeared. With the return of her health, his mind had the opportunity to turn to thoughts beyond survival.

"We can camp here until tomorrow morning," she announced, veering off the road toward a copse of trees. A brook ran through them, prior travelers having dammed it with stones to create a pool a few feet deep.

"Barely back on your feet and you're already telling me what to do. Makes me long for the days when you couldn't string together a coherent sentence."

Lara rolled her eyes, then set to caring for the camels, her voice soft as she slipped bags full of grain over their noses so they could eat. Wisps of her hair had come loose from her braid, and they blew in the gentle breeze, the afternoon sun gleaming off them. She started to unload the tent from a camel's back, but Aren caught hold of her wrist. "I'll do it."

She looked up at him, her azure eyes drawing him in. Drowning him, as they always had. "I'm fine, Aren."

"I know you are. And I know you can do it yourself. But let me do it for you anyway."

Color rose to her cheeks, and she looked away. "As you like."

They began making camp, and though his hands were kept busy setting up the tent, lighting a fire, and retrieving water from the stream, his mind was all for her.

And all for that kiss.

He shouldn't have done it, Aren knew that much. He told himself that it was because he'd been terrified she was dying in his arms. That it was nothing more than a chaste brush of the lips. That it meant nothing.

Except that it meant everything, for that one kiss had shattered the crumbling walls he'd built up against her in his heart, and he knew that if she wanted it, if she offered it, that what came next would be anything but chaste.

After setting a pot on to boil, he retrieved a sack of lentils and what remained of the dried fruit, and then sat across the fire from his wife.

"The pain was better." Lara lifted her shirt to scratch at her peeling back. "I've never been more goddamned itchy in my entire life."

"You've certainly never looked worse," he responded around the dried apricot he was chewing, then dodged sideways when she tossed a piece of dead skin his direction, a laugh tearing from his throat.

"Asshole." She pulled out a bar of soap from one of the packs. "I'm going to have a bath while you cook. You might consider doing the same at some point—you smell like camel."

"And yet you don't dote on me half as much as you do them."

Lara gave a low chuckle. "Keep watch, then. I'd rather not have to leap out of my bath and fight ruffians in the nude."

"Might work out to your advantage."

"I'm advantaged enough, thank you." She winked, plucked up a knife, and strode barefoot to the stream, her hips swaying in a way that made it impossible to look anywhere else. Then she called out, "I said keep an eye out for soldiers, Aren. Not keep an eye on my ass."

"The ass that's peeling like a ship's boy with a sack of potatoes?"

Whirling around, she slowly raised her middle finger, giving him a pointed glare before turning back to the water.

What are you doing? he silently asked himself. *Why are you acting like everything is right between you when it could not be more wrong?*

Ithicana would never accept her, much less forgive her, and he could not in good conscience ask them to do so. Even admitting that he'd forgiven her would be a mistake, for he knew that many would see that as its own form of betrayal. And given he still had his own atonement to consider, allowing himself any form of intimacy would be a mistake. Especially since they would part ways at some point.

He poured the lentils into the pot, then retrieved a spoon to stir them, trying to focus on the task at hand.

When?

When would she go? *Now* was probably an opportune time, given they were in Valcotta, which was a far more dangerous place for her than for him. He was going to meet with the Empress to beg forgiveness, and having the woman for whom he'd broken ties with Valcotta on his arm was far from a prudent course of action.

Despite his intentions not to, Aren turned, eyes drinking in the sight of his wife. She'd removed the boy's clothes she'd been wearing and was seated in only her undergarments on the edge of the stream. She'd washed her hair, the long honey locks reaching down to the small of her back, concealing the healing lesions from her sunburn. Scars on top of scars, but instead of diminishing her beauty, they only made her fiercer. Made him want her more.

She lifted one arm to wash it, revealing the side of one curved breast, her nipple peaked. His cock stiffened, desire coursing through him as he watched the water sluicing down her skin. She tilted her head back, her eyes closed as she squeezed more water from the cloth, her lips parting with pleasure.

Digging his fingernails into his palms, Aren fought the urge to go to her. To peel that last scrap of clothing from her thighs so that he could taste her. Make her lose control and scream his name, her body shuddering beneath him, her fingers tangling in his hair as he buried himself inside of her.

She was everything. Mind, body, and soul, she was everything he wanted. Everything he needed. The queen Ithicana needed.

But thanks to Silas and his greed, she was everything Aren couldn't have.

Aren twisted back to the lentils, hands balled into fists. He wanted to hit something. Wanted to rage. It wasn't fair. It wasn't goddamned fair.

She came up next to him, the clean smell of soap wafting ahead of her. "You all right?"

"I'm fine."

He felt her eyes on him, felt her considering what to do. What to say. And all he wanted was to plead for her to *break him.* Because it would only take one touch from her, one word, and his willpower would shatter.

Do it, he silently willed her. *Make the decision for me.*

But instead she said, "When I went back to Eranahl, the only reason they didn't kill me was that Ahnna wouldn't let them. And the only reason she didn't kill me herself was that she wanted to rescue you more than she wanted to see me dead."

Taking a deep breath, Aren turned. Lara stood with a length of fabric wrapped around her body, bar of soap in her hand.

"They cursed my name. Spit on me. Demanded my death in the worst sorts of ways. Because they hate me. And they are right to do so."

He opened his mouth to argue, but Lara held up one hand. "I will remain with you until we reach Pyrinat and find the Ithicanians who are supposed to meet us there. And then I'm going to leave."

It felt like someone was shoving something dull into his heart, crushing it slowly rather than slicing it cleanly. "Lara—"

"I love you, Aren." Her eyes were gleaming. "But it's over between us. It has to be, and we both know it. Pretending otherwise is only going to make it worse when I walk away."

She was right, and he knew it. But in his heart, he knew that even if he never saw her again for the rest of his life, it would never be over.

She would always be his queen.

THEY TRAVELED STRAIGHT to Pyrinat, the capital city of Valcotta, most of the journey on a riverboat after Aren demonstrated his Ithicanian negotiation skills and sold the camels for twice what they were worth.

They'd pretended to be Harendellian, though more than a few Valcottans had frowned at Lara, her coloring suggesting she was Maridrinian regardless of the high-necked Harendellian dresses she wore.

They were nearly a month behind schedule, the number of weeks Aren had to convince the Empress of Valcotta into an alliance reduced to a matter of days.

And that was if she could be convinced at all.

Yet for all the pressure the delays put upon them, Lara wasn't certain she'd give up any of the time spent with Aren. Not when there were moments when she could've closed her eyes and believed they were back in Eranahl, playing games and drinking wine and bantering with each other, always a heartbeat from falling into bed to make love.

But unlike in Eranahl, the latter never happened.

Despite the naked lust she saw in his eyes—lust that she willfully provoked in her weaker moments—Aren took her words to heart and never once came close to giving in to the heat between them. Heat that, despite what she'd said to him, seemed to burn hotter by the day.

It's over, she told herself time and again. *He's the King of Ithicana—he needs to put his people first.*

But in the darkest hours of the night, when she was curled around herself on the bed, her body aching with a twisted mix of desire and loneliness, logic meant little and hope everything.

It was only once the riverboat docked in Pyrinat that she finally abandoned those hopes, dedicating her mind wholly to the task at hand.

Taking Aren's arm to help her across onto the dock, Lara paused to marvel at the enormity of the city around them.

The river Pyr, nearly a mile wide at points, ran through the center of Pyrinat, branching in countless places to create canals that wove through the city like watery streets. The buildings that backed onto these canals had doors leading to small docks, and there were dozens of curved bridges with narrow sets of stairs leading down to the water. The buildings themselves were all made of sandstone blocks, most with large windows of the clearest glass in all the world, and banners of colored fabric hung from the balconies overlooking the streets.

The smell of the sea blew inland, mixing with the scents of spices and cooking food, the pristine city streets devoid of filth. Valcottans dressed in bright, voluminous clothing filled the streets, the air filled with the sound of their voices as they bartered with vendors in the teeming markets.

Musicians seemed to play on every corner—and unlike in Vencia, they were finely clothed, apparently more interested in entertaining the crowds that gathered to listen than in earning any coin. Singers often accompanied them, young men and women whose songs Lara had never heard before, their instruments unlike anything she'd seen.

Aren, familiar with the city from prior visits, led her through the fabled glass markets, the vendors displaying everything from vases to glasses to sculptures that climbed to the sky, the sunlight filtering through them casting a rainbow of color on sandstone pathways. She stopped in her tracks more than once to watch in amazement as men and women blew strands of glass into ornate shapes, to which they often added wires of gold and silver to create art worthy of the Empress herself.

"This way," Aren said, tugging at her arm. "What did you say the name of the place was again?"

"The Nastryan Hotel. The owner is apparently one of your spies." And at the reminder, Lara's awe of the glassworks faded, to be replaced by trepidation. There was supposed to be someone here to meet them with information about the state of Ithicana, but with the delay, what were the chances that the individual had remained? It wasn't that she and Aren couldn't manage themselves, but she'd hoped for updates. On Eranahl. And on her sisters. Not knowing if they'd all made it out safely was a burden she'd been trying not to acknowledge.

"Here."

Aren stopped before a three-story building, the main level open to the street and boasting a large coffeehouse. At least a dozen people sat on colorful cushions around low tables, sipping steaming brown liquid from glass cups. A tiled corridor led to a large wooden desk, behind which sat a Valcottan man, his skin gleaming in the light of the lamps set to either side of him.

Approaching, Lara smiled. "Good morning. We have a reservation."

The Valcottan's eyes widened fractionally, flicking to Aren and then back to her. Then he nodded. "You are somewhat overdue."

"Unforeseen circumstances delayed us." She hesitated, afraid to ask. "Are there any messages?"

The man gave a slight shake of his head, and Lara's stomach dropped. Had something happened? Had Ahnna failed in her attempt to secure Harendell's support? Had Eranahl fallen?

"No messages," the man repeated. "But perhaps the other member of your party might be able to give you the information you seek."

Then he gestured into the coffeehouse to a lone figure sitting at a table in a corner.

Lara smiled.

I T WAS A struggle to keep his composure. To keep from breaking into a run across the coffeehouse. To keep from breaking down entirely.

But Aren forced himself to walk slowly between the tables. To keep silent as he drew out a chair and sat down across from his countryman.

Eyes fixed on the cup in front of him, which was *not* filled with coffee, Jor growled, "I'm not interested in company."

"Not even that of an old friend?"

Jor stiffened, then with painful slowness, he lifted his face. The old soldier stared at Aren for a long moment, then whispered, "I'd almost given up hope. Weeks . . . weeks, I've been here waiting."

Then Jor was across the table, glass crashing to the floor as his arms tightened around Aren, the both of them nearly going backward. "You're alive."

Other than his brief meeting with Nana, it had been months since he'd spoken to anyone from Ithicana. Having Jor in front of him now was almost as good as being home.

"I thought you were dead." Jor's voice was choked, like he was trying to fight back tears, though Aren had never seen the man cry in all his life.

"It was a near thing more times than I care to count," Aren said, noting that all the other patrons were staring. Pushing Jor back into his seat, Aren righted the table and sat back down. "Believe me, if I never see the desert again, it will be too soon."

"The desert?" Jor's eyes widened, then he turned to look at Lara, who stood a few steps away, a faint smile still on her face. "That wasn't the plan, girl. You've got some explaining to do."

"Later. We've more important matters to discuss."

Jor's gaze darkened, and he nodded. "But not here." Rising, he called to one of the serving girls, "Put it on my tab, lass. The glass, too."

"You ever going to pay that tab, old man?" the girl responded, but there was affection in her voice. "I'll have food sent up to your room. Mind you eat it—you're withering away."

It was true. Aren picked out the differences in Jor as he followed him out of the coffeehouse toward a flight of stairs. His shoulders were stooped in a way they hadn't been before, his frame narrower, and his steps slower. Less certain. He was no longer a young man, but it wasn't time that had aged him in the months they'd been apart. Jor had watched over Aren since he was old enough to walk, sacrificing his own opportunity for a family in order to keep Ithicana's heir safe— to keep him alive. And Aren knew that Jor blamed himself for his capture, which meant he'd have blamed himself while believing Aren dead. "Thank you. For getting me out. And for waiting for me."

Jor looked over his shoulder, brown eyes meeting Aren's. But the only acknowledgment he gave was a short nod. Fishing a key out of his pocket, he opened the door to a room on the second floor, revealing a suite that overlooked the atrium at the center of the hotel.

"Fancy."

"Was meant for you. It's a good thing you showed when you did because I think our man downstairs was considering evicting me in favor of a paying customer. Only the fact that Silas's men are crawling all over the city gave us any hope that you were still alive."

Scowling, Aren tossed his meager bag of belongings in the corner. "Serin anticipated where we were going and cut us off. That's why we had to go through the desert. But never mind them. What of Eranahl? And Ahnna?"

"Eranahl still stands, as does your sister. She's there now."

The relief that rushed through Aren almost brought him to his knees. "Thank God."

"Don't go thanking anyone just yet. The city's surviving thanks to the supplies delivered by a mystery benefactor to some of the neighboring islands, but even if that individual is inclined to make another drop, there's no way to get it unless we get a bad storm. Eranahl is surrounded day and night by Amaridian ships. And the calm season this year has lived up to its name."

"So Zarrah was true to her word," Lara said.

"As was your brother."

Jor raised one eyebrow in confusion, so Aren added, "It was Zarrah Anaphora who arranged for the supplies. She agreed to it in exchange for me arranging her escape from Silas, though in reality, what I was arranging was a distraction so that Keris Veliant could free her."

"The *crown prince?*"

Aren nodded. "It turns out the philosopher prince is quite the political schemer. He wants to rid Maridrina of both his father and our bridge, so in him we have an ally."

"You shouldn't trust him."

"That's what *I* said," Lara muttered. "We are a means to an end with him, and if another opportunity to achieve what he wants presents itself, he'll throw us to the wolves without shedding a tear."

"Maybe." Aren had had a great deal of time to consider Keris's motivations—the long game, as the prince had put it, and he wasn't convinced that Keris was as self-motivated as he presented himself to be. Anyone with resources and coin could've arranged for a ship full of supplies to be dropped in Ithicana, which begged the question of why Keris felt Zarrah had needed to be freed in order to achieve that end. And Aren was fairly certain he knew the answer. "Is Zarrah here?"

"If she is, I've not heard word of it. Perhaps she's returned to her command of the Valcottan garrison in Nerastis? That's where Keris is, by the way. The chatter around Pyrinat is that he set sail from Vencia the day after your escape. He's resumed his own command of the Maridrinian forces on the border, and he's taken a much more active interest in his duties than he has in the past."

"Likely cover for the fact that he smuggled Zarrah out from beneath his father's nose."

"Do you have word about my sisters?" Lara's voice was steady as she asked the question, but Aren saw the way her hands clenched and unclenched, revealing her nerves.

"You're an aunt."

She gasped. "Sarhina?"

Jor smiled and slapped Lara on the shoulder, making her stagger. "Right as rain. Nana delivered her baby girl not half a day after you parted ways. Bronwyn was holding strong the last I heard before I departed, and the rest of your sisters in Vencia made it through relatively unscathed."

Lara gave a quick nod, wiping at her eyes.

"What of Coralyn?" Aren asked.

Jor gave a heavy sigh. "She's not been seen, I'm afraid. But neither could we confirm her death."

Aren could only hope that Keris had intervened on his aunt's behalf, because if Coralyn was alive, she might well be wishing she were dead. "You said Ahnna is back in Eranahl?"

"Aye. Apparently had to swim in under the cover of darkness when she came back from Harendell because she couldn't get a boat past the Amaridians."

Aren blanched. During the calm, the waters outside of the island fortress were teeming with sharks. "She shouldn't—"

"She had to," Jor interrupted. "Morale is bad. Lots of talk about abandoning the city. Abandoning Ithicana. She's holding everything together to buy you time, but . . ." He hesitated. "As soon as storm season drives off the fleet, there will be an exodus north to Harendell, which has offered safe haven."

And Ithicana would be no more. "Maybe that's for the best."

"If they thought it was for the best, they'd have all left last storm season," Lara snapped, then tossed her own bag next to his. "They plan to leave because there's no other choice, not because it's what they want. We need to give them another option. Jor, what did the Harendellian king say to Ahnna's proposal?"

Before he could answer, there was a knock at the door, and Jor went to it, taking a tray of steaming food and thanking the girl who'd delivered it. Pouring water from a pitcher, he handed Aren a glass. "The Harendellians are rightly sour about Maridrina holding the bridge, especially given the favoritism being shown to Amarid at Northwatch. Our friend King Edward was quick enough to agree. With conditions, of course."

"Which were?"

"Trade terms, mostly." Jor's mouth tightened. "And Ahnna's word that she'd return to Harendell once all is said and done. Apparently, it's about time Crown Prince William was wed."

Aren opened his mouth to argue that he wouldn't agree to that, but Jor cut him off. "She gave her word already, so save your breath. But all of it is predicated on you securing Valcotta's support; there is little point in King Edward coming to our party unless the Empress does, too."

"So it's all on me." Aren drained the water, wishing it were something stronger.

"On you, and you've only got a few days to do it. It takes time to organize a party with so many guests, and it has to be done before the storms hit. We're almost out of time."

"Then I suppose," Aren said, "that it's time the Empress and I had a conversation."

Jor snorted. "I'm not sure it's going to be much of a conversation. More like you groveling on your knees for forgiveness."

Going to retrieve his bag, Aren dug out his razor, rubbing sadly at the beard he'd been using as part of his disguise. "If I am to beg, then I'd better look my best."

"DO YOU HAVE A way to prove your identity?" Lara asked Aren, stepping over a puddle on the street, the colored glass beads on her sandals glinting in the sun. Jor had supplied them with appropriate Valcottan clothes. Lara had never seen Aren wear such bright colors, and she might have been amused by his discomfort if not for the gravity of their situation.

"There are details that only Ahnna or I would know," he answered, leading her out of the way of a donkey pulling a cart, the driver lifting a hand to them in thanks. "That's not the part that concerns me." He gave a sharp shake of his head. "Maridrina possessing the bridge is undesirable for Valcotta, and yet the Empress has done little about it other than stymie trade. Why?"

"Perhaps she's biding her time? She knows you're free—maybe she's waiting for an offer of alliance?"

Aren grunted softly. "An alliance with Ithicana was always a possibility, even with me imprisoned. There are others who could've brokered a deal, and she knew that, but chose not to."

"Do you believe she's still angry about Ithicana siding with

Maridrina and breaking the Southwatch blockade?"

Actions that were taken based on *her* advice. And it was advice Lara didn't regret giving. The months of Ithicana filling Maridrinian bellies had not only saved lives, it had also won Maridrinian hearts.

"I suppose we'll find out soon enough."

They approached the gates to the walled palace, and Aren muttered, "Let me do the talking for once. They won't be apt to listen to a Maridrinian, especially one with eyes like yours."

Heavily armed guards watched as they approached, one holding up a hand until they stopped a few paces from him. "Your identities and your purpose, if you please."

"King Aren of Ithicana," Aren said. "I'm here to see the Empress."

The soldier's jaw dropped in surprise that mirrored Lara's. *This* hadn't been part of the plan. By midday, the whole damn city was going to know they were here, and then her father's assassins would be after them. What the hell was Aren thinking?

"Your Grace." The soldier pressed his hand to his heart, the Valcottan way of showing respect. "We were not aware that you were in the city. Please forgive my rudeness."

Aren inclined his head. "No forgiveness necessary. For reasons I'm sure you're aware, announcing my presence would've posed an obvious risk."

"I understand, Your Grace." The soldier's brown eyes flicked to Lara, hardening. "Then this is . . ."

"Lara." Aren's tone was cool, effectively shutting down whatever comments the man might make about Lara's identity.

The soldier nodded, but Lara didn't fail to notice that he offered her none of the courtesy he had to Aren. Not that it mattered. They could hate her Maridrinian guts all they wanted as long as they forgave Aren and Ithicana. "This way, Your Grace."

The heavy doors swung inward, revealing an expansive courtyard with a large fountain at the center of it. Dispatching a young boy to deliver word of Aren's arrival, the guard led them across the open space, through a pair of bronze gates on the far side, and into the palace.

It was a building quite unlike anything she'd ever seen, mostly because it could barely be called a building at all. Above, iron was wrought into delicate curving shapes containing the colored glass for which Valcotta was famed, the light passing through it casting rainbows across the pathways of translucent glass tiles that wove through gardens filled with blooming flowers.

"This way, Your Grace," the soldier said, leading them to the left, following one of the paths to a gazebo. At the center of it was a low table surrounded by large pillows encased in jewel-colored silk, the tiered fountain to one side filling the air with a gentle music.

"The Empress is currently occupied. But if you'll wait here, refreshments will be brought." The soldier touched his hand to his heart, then backed away before turning to walk briskly down the path.

Two young boys appeared with glass bowls filled with water, towels dyed in Valcottan amethyst draped over their arms.

Lara carefully washed her hands and dried them on the towel, then seated herself on one of the cushions, smoothing the fabric of her wide trousers. A girl with coiled braids wrapped with gold offered her a long glass flute filled with sparkling liquid, and another brought a plate filled with chocolate truffles that smelled of mint.

Lara nibbled on a truffle. "They are taking no chances that you aren't who you say you are."

Aren drank deeply from his glass, then frowned at the contents and set it aside. "The Valcottans are a polite people, but they have no tolerance for dishonesty. If it's discovered I'm lying, they'll have me executed before the sun sets."

Eating one of the chocolates, Lara tilted her head skyward to admire the chandelier above her. Countless tiny basins hung on delicate chains, scented oil burning within them, the light reflected off the ceiling, which was plated with silver. Bushes with wide leaves framed the gazebo on three sides, giving a semblance of privacy, but through them, Lara could make out the figures of the guards who were watching them.

"Quit pacing," she murmured at Aren, who'd already crossed back and forth across the space a half dozen times. "It makes you look nervous."

He ignored her and kept pacing, not stopping until soft footsteps approached. A stunning young woman dressed in military attire appeared, a wide smile blossoming on her face at the sight of Aren. Lara immediately recognized her as the woman who'd joined them for part of their escape from her father's palace.

"Good to see you alive, Your Majesty," Zarrah said, touching her hand to her chest. "I heard you ran into some trouble after we parted ways outside the gates of Vencia."

Lara kept her face smooth at the woman's lie. Obviously she had told her people that Ithicana was solely responsible for her escape, keeping Keris's involvement a secret. It was, in Lara's opinion, a smart move, and one that could only work in Aren's favor.

Aren's eyes narrowed slightly, but he only said, "Likewise—I'm pleased to see you are well."

"I didn't have the opportunity to thank you, so allow me to do so now. Perhaps there will come a time when I might repay you."

"I think we're even."

Zarrah gave a slight shake of her head, eyes full of warning even as she smiled. Her delivery of supplies to Eranahl was clearly not something she wanted known, which meant she'd done it without the Empress's approval. Lara glanced at Aren to see if this revelation concerned him, but his face was unmoved.

Zarrah waved a hand at the guards beyond. "Stand down. His Grace is who he says he is." Then her head cocked sideways, dark eyes meeting Lara's. "As is she."

Silence stretched as they stared each other down, taking each other's measure. She was more beautiful than Lara had had the chance to appreciate during their escape, her short brown curls revealing high, rounded cheekbones, and large brown eyes that Lara might have described as doe-like on another woman. But Zarrah was no more prey than Lara was herself, her tall body possessing the strength and grace of a panther on the hunt, her fingers flexing around the staff she held. Then she said, "I enjoyed your dance very much, Your Majesty. Though not as much as I enjoyed watching you kick wine into your father's face."

Lara inclined her head. "I enjoyed that as well."

Zarrah's attention shifted back to Aren. "Come, come. My aunt wishes to know the face behind the name. I expect she's also looking forward to a chance to berate you for every choice you've made in your reign."

Zarrah led them down the path, Aren walking next to her, Lara trailing behind. "Silas has been spreading rumors of your death, Aren. Up and down the coast, though the story of how you died changes with every telling. We, of course, questioned the veracity of the claims. Silas is a braggart, and no Ithicanian heads adorn Vencia's gates."

Turning around, Zarrah added, "No women fitting the descriptions of those who assisted you, either. Were they truly all your sisters?"

Lara met her stare. "Yes."

The other woman's eyebrows rose. "Fascinating. I wonder if it's ever dawned on your father that Maridrina might win the war between our two nations if he set aside his foolish notions about a woman's role."

"That would require him admitting he was wrong in the first place," Lara replied. "Which seems unlikely."

"I'm inclined to agree." Zarrah lifted one shoulder. "Your homeland's misfortune has long been to Valcotta's benefit, so I cannot honestly admit that I'm sorry."

Lara didn't bother answering. Aren, she noticed, was listening intently, but he made no comment either.

They continued down the pathways in silence, Lara drinking in the beauty of the enormous garden, which was crisscrossed with streams, ornate footbridges or smooth stepping stones allowing people to cross the water. There were places where the water pooled, and children swam and played in its depths, reminding her of Eranahl's cavern harbor, where they'd done the same.

The towers that she'd seen from outside the walls were the only enclosed structures, rising several stories high, and it was to one such tower that Zarrah led them.

Armed guards swung open the doors, which were made of twisted metal inset with glass of a thousand different colors to create the image of a Valcottan woman with her hands held up to a blue sky. Inside, a curved staircase led upward, but Zarrah gestured past it to a windowed chamber filled with small tables and large cushions.

Against one wall stood an enormous soldier. Taller even than Aren, his bulging arms were thicker than Lara's legs. Despite his size, Lara's attention was drawn to the slender woman sitting upon one of the cushions, hands engaged with what appeared to be a small doll that she was creating with colored yarns.

"Aunt," Zarrah said, with a distinct lack of formality, "might I present His Royal Majesty, King Aren of Ithicana, Master of the Bridge—"

"Ah, but you're not its master anymore, are you, boy?" the Empress interrupted, attention still on the doll. "That honor belongs to the Maridrinian rat. I imagine that's why you're here, isn't it?"

Before Aren could answer, she continued. "And you, girl. I assume you're the rat's get? You'll be accorded no titles in this house. Be glad I don't have you dragged outside and your throat slit."

Lara tilted her head. "Why don't you?"

The woman's hands stilled. "Because as much as we might wish it otherwise, your life doesn't belong to Valcotta. Nor your death."

"Your honor is my salvation."

The Empress huffed out an annoyed breath. "Don't speak to me of honor."

Setting aside the doll, the woman rose to her feet. Taller than Lara, she was both lean and muscular, adding credence to the tale that she'd once been a formidable warrior in her own right. Beautiful, the only sign of age was a slight crinkling of the skin around her eyes and the gray of her hair, which stood out from her head in tight curls. Woven through it were wires of gold, on which dozens of amethysts sparkled. The wide-legged trousers and stomach-baring blouse she wore were golden silk, her belt heavy with embroidery and gemstones. Gold bracelets climbed both arms to her elbows, her ears were cuffed with gold and gems, and her throat was encased with an intricately carved gold necklace. It was amazing that she could stand beneath the weight of all that metal, but she bore it as though it were light as a feather.

"Your Imperial Majesty," Aren said, bowing his head low. "It is a privilege to meet you in person."

"A privilege or a necessity?" The Empress asked, circling Aren in measured strides, her bare feet making no sound on the tiled floor. The

Empress was, Lara thought, the most regal person that she'd ever met.

"Can't it be both?"

The Empress pursed her lips, making a noncommittal noise in response. "For the sake of your mother, who was our dearest of friends, we are pleased to see you alive. But for ourselves?" Her voice hardened. "We do not forget how you spit upon our friendship."

Lara stiffened, wishing desperately that she had a weapon. Bringing Aren here had always been a risk, but she'd believed the Empress too honorable to do him any harm beyond refusing to aid Ithicana. What if she were wrong? Could she get him out? Was escape even possible?

The giant soldier standing near the wall had seen her motion, and he moved closer, brown eyes watching her intently, judging her, correctly, as the threat. Aren wouldn't hurt the Empress, but Lara suffered no such compunctions.

Aren also showed no signs of concern. Rubbing his chin, he regarded the Empress thoughtfully. "You speak of my mother as your dearest friend, and yet it was her who proposed the Fifteen Year Treaty between Ithicana, Harendell, and Maridrina, including the marriage clause. My mother formed the alliance with your greatest enemy, and for it you held her no ill will. And yet when I followed through on her wishes, I lost favor in your eyes."

The Empress paused in front of Aren, expression smooth, dark brown eyes unreadable. "Your mother had little choice. Ithicana was starving. And the treaty as she wrote it cost Valcotta nothing. It was the terms you agreed to fifteen years later that were the slight." She leveled a finger at him. "My soldiers dying on steel supplied by Ithicana's bridge."

Lara knew that Aren had hated those terms. Had wanted to supply Maridrina with *anything* but weapons. Just as she knew her father hadn't given him any choice.

But instead of using the argument, Aren gave a slow shake of his head. "Steel supplied by *Harendell,* which Maridrina was already importing by ship. It cost them less, yes, but to say they were at any greater advantage against your soldiers is a fallacy. It also gave Valcotta the unique opportunity to prevent Silas from retrieving his precious import for the better part of a year, so one might argue that the terms worked in your favor."

It was true, though the thought had never occurred to Lara. Prior to the treaty, the steel had come on ships from Harendell or Amarid—ships which Valcotta could not attack without risking retaliation from those two nations. But after the treaty, all the steel went through the bridge to wait on Southwatch until Maridrinian vessels could retrieve it—Maridrinian vessels that Valcotta had no qualms against sinking.

"What benefit we saw faded swiftly when you turned your shipbreakers on my fleet," the Empress countered. "You chose your alliance with Maridrina over your friendship with Valcotta, and now you come weeping because you discovered your ally was a rat."

Aren shook his head. "You put Ithicana in a position where all paths led to war, and when I gave you a path to peace, you refused it."

"It was no choice." The Empress threw up her hands. "If we'd dropped the blockade, Maridrina would've gotten what it wanted without a fight. More steel to use against Valcotta. Besides, it was clear that the last thing Silas wanted was peace. Especially peace with Ithicana."

Lara held her breath, waiting for Aren to react to the revelation. Waiting for his anger to flare. But all he said was, "If you foresaw what was to come and said nothing, what friend are you?"

"Just because I see the clouds in the sky doesn't mean I can predict where the lightning will strike."

Aren only rested his chin on one hand, tapping his index finger against his lip thoughtfully.

The silence stretched, and to Lara's surprise, it was the Empress who broke it.

"We have more to discuss, but I believe it a discussion best done in private." She turned her cool gaze in Lara's direction. "You will wait here."

There wasn't a chance Lara was letting Aren out of her sight. "No."

The Empress's eyebrows rose, then she snapped her fingers at the soldier. "Welran, subdue her."

With a nod, the huge man charged across the room.

A REN STRUGGLED TO stand his ground as the massive Valcottan tackled Lara, twisting her arm behind her back, her face turning red from the effort of trying to breathe beneath his weight.

The Empress motioned for Aren and Zarrah to follow as she headed for the stairs.

Aren trailed after the women, but paused next to Lara and the guard, Welran. The last thing he needed was things escalating. Pressing a hand against the big man's shoulder, he said, "I can't in good conscience go without warning you."

The Valcottan's brown eyes darkened.

"She saw you coming from a mile away. Palmed your knife when you took her down. And all that wriggling she's doing? I'd bet my last coin that the blade is only about an inch from your balls."

Straightening, Aren started toward the stairs, the sound of Welran's booming laugh following him upward.

They climbed to the top, the staircase opening into a large room with stained glass windows featuring prior rulers of Valcotta, all with their hands reaching up to the sky. Zarrah stood next to the door, staff still in hand, but the Empress motioned for Aren to sit on one of the many pillows. A servant appeared with drinks and trays of desserts. Though he was not partial to sweets, Aren dutifully ate one of them, washing it down with the sticky wine the Valcottans preferred.

"Let us start first with a discussion of why you are here, Aren," the Empress said. "I have my own theories, of course, but I'd like to hear it from your lips."

He nodded. "I think you know that having the bridge under the control of Silas Veliant benefits no one, not even his own people."

She made a noise that was neither affirmation nor denial, so he continued. "I've received word that my sister, Princess Ahnna, has secured Harendell's support for retaking Northwatch. It is my hope that you'll see the merit in assisting me in securing Southwatch from Maridrina and reinstating Ithicana as a sovereign nation."

Picking up a glass, the Empress eyed the contents. "Southwatch isn't assailable. Or at least, not without an unpalatable loss of vessels and life."

"It is if you know how. Which I do."

"Giving up such a secret would make Northwatch and Southwatch forever vulnerable—would make *Ithicana* forever vulnerable."

As if he didn't know that. As if he had a choice. "Not if Harendell and Valcotta are true friends and allies."

She gave an amused laugh. "The friendships between nations and rulers are inconstant, Aren. You yourself have proven that."

"True," he said. "But not so the friendship between peoples."

"You're an idealist."

Aren shook his head. "A realist. Ithicana cannot continue as it has. To endure, we must change our ways."

Silence sat between them as the ruler of the mightiest nation in the known world ruminated on his request, her eyes distant. Behind him, Aren could hear Zarrah shifting her weight. Valcottan rulers chose their own heirs from their bloodline, and it was known that the Empress did not favor her own son. Was Zarrah to be her choice? Would she remain the Empress's choice if the woman knew what Aren knew?

"You look like your mother," the Empress said, tearing Aren from his thoughts. "Though your father was equally easy on the eyes."

Aren's brow furrowed. "How could you possibly know that?"

Amusement passed over the Empress's face—and pleasure at knowing something that he did not. "Surely you don't believe that I'd bestow friendship upon someone who only spoke to me from behind a mask?"

He'd never gotten a straight answer from his mother as to why her relationship with the Empress was so close, and now Aren was beginning to suspect why. "She visited Valcotta."

"Oh yes, many, *many* times. Delia was not one to be confined, and your father chased her up and down both continents trying to keep her safe. I was bested only once in Pyrinat's games, and imagine my shock to learn that the victor was an Ithicanian princess." The Empress smirked and rubbed a faded scar across the bridge of her nose. "She was fierce."

It was an incredible revelation, and his voice was strangled as he answered, "Yes."

"Is it true your father died trying to save her life?"

He nodded.

Sorrow passed over the woman's face, and she pressed her hand to her heart. "I will grieve her loss, and his, until the end of my days."

It was true grief, not merely words said out of politeness or obligation, and though it loathed him to do so, Aren had to capitalize upon it. "If you knew my mother so well, then you had to have known her dream for Ithicana and its people."

"Freedom? Yes, she told me." The Empress shook her head. "But I agreed with your father in that it wasn't possible. Ithicana's survival was always dependent on it being impenetrable, or at least, nearly so. To unleash thousands of people who knew all of Ithicana's secrets would see them secret no longer." Her gaze hardened. "And worse still to allow others a view from the inside. But then, you learned that lesson, didn't you?"

He had. A thousand times over.

"And yet not only do you allow Silas Veliant's weapon to live, you keep her close. Why is that?"

"She's not his weapon. Not anymore." Aren bit the insides of his cheeks, annoyed that he sounded so defensive. "She broke me free of Vencia, and after that, I needed her to survive the trek across the Red Desert."

"It could be another ruse, you know. Ithicana has not yet fallen—a fact that sorely grieves Silas. How better to take Eranahl than to deliver into it the woman who cracked the defenses of the bridge?"

Aren considered the Empress's suggestion that Lara's motivations were not as they appeared. That his rescue was part of a greater plan orchestrated by Silas or the Magpie in order to achieve what they had failed to take by force. Yet it seemed improbable given the risk both Lara and her sisters had taken—Bronwyn had nearly died. And Lara herself had nearly lost her life multiple times on the journey.

"It would be nothing for us to rid you of that particular problem," the Empress said. "She could disappear."

The thought of the Valcottans dragging Lara to some dark place and slitting her throat filled his mind, and Aren's hands went cold. "No."

"Your people will never accept her as queen. She's the traitor who cost them their homes and the lives of their loved ones."

"I am aware. The answer is still no."

Silence.

"And if I say that Valcotta's support is contingent on her death?"

Lara's life in exchange for the return of the bridge. Setting aside his own feelings, it seemed the obvious choice. The *right* choice to ensure his people endured. Except he *knew* that the Empress was not so petty as to make her assistance conditional on the life of one woman. "No."

The Empress shoved away her glass, rising to her feet in a flurry of motion. "Even now you put Maridrina first."

Aren rose as well. "I put the chance of peace before old grievances. Which is something you might consider."

The Empress whirled back around, eyes flashing in anger. "Peace with Maridrina? Son of my friend or not, in this you go too far. On my life, I'll not lay down my staff until Silas Veliant lays down his sword, and we both know that will never happen."

"It won't," Aren agreed. "But Silas won't rule forever." He cast a backward glance at Zarrah, who was staring at the floor. "And neither will you."

Inclining his head, Aren pressed a hand to his heart, praying that he wasn't making the biggest mistake of his life. "It was an honor to meet the friend of my mother, but now I must take my leave. Tonight, I sail to Ithicana."

Zarrah didn't try to stop him as he left the room, and no one interfered in his progress down the curving stairs. In the main room at the base of the tower, he found Lara sitting on the floor with Welran, the pair playing some sort of board game. She rose at the sight of him.

"I'm pleased to see you still intact," he said to the big man.

"A near thing, Your Grace." Welran pressed his hand to his chest. "You must sleep with one eye open and your hand on your dagger with such a woman in your bed."

"Perhaps one day you'll be so fortunate." Aren inclined his head to the Valcottan, then to Lara he said, "We need to go."

"**W**HAT DID SHE SAY?" Lara demanded the moment they were clear of the palace gates. "Will Valcotta help?"

"No." Aren glanced up at the sun, then shook his head. "She has no more interest in peace between Maridrina and Valcotta than your father does."

"That should be to our favor." Lara broke into a trot to keep up with his long stride. "Plucking Southwatch from my father's hands should have been an irresistible opportunity. Unless . . . does she want the bridge for Valcotta?"

"No." His tone was angry. Clipped. "That's not what she wants."

Lara considered the situation, realization dawning on her. "She made Valcotta's assistance dependent on my death. That's what she wanted, isn't it?"

He nodded.

"Why?" Though the real question she wanted answered was why he hadn't agreed.

"Because your death would ensure any chance of a future alliance between Ithicana and Maridrina would be well and truly dead."

She'd underestimated Aren. This entire time, she'd believed all he cared about was getting home and driving her father out of Ithicana, but it appeared he still had larger ambitions for the fate of his kingdom.

"You blew the doors to Ithicana wide open, Lara. There's no closing them again. No going back to the way things were before. Which means I need to find another way to keep my people safe."

"Peace with Maridrina?" Lara rubbed her temples. "God, Aren, that's impossible. You have to see that my father will never allow it to happen."

"No, but your brother might."

"Whatever sentiments Keris might hold for me hardly matter. Without Valcotta, we can't take back the bridge. Earning the Empress's favor must be your first priority."

"Allowing her to set the terms will only bring us full circle." Aren opened the door to the hotel. "And it's not Keris's sentiments for *you* that I'm banking my kingdom on."

Inside, Lara followed as he took the stairs two at a time, striding down the hall to the room where Jor waited.

"Well?"

Aren shook his head. "We proceed as though we are on our own. How quickly can we get home?"

"We can be on a ship tonight, though only Valcottan naval vessels are allowed past Nerastis. From there it's a matter of making our way north to the meeting point."

Panic flooded through Lara's veins. "Aren, we can't go without convincing the Empress to ally with us."

"I'm not willing to do what it will take to convince her."

"Then this is a lost cause," she shouted, her temper flaring out of her control, because she knew what needed to be done. "Not only is it impossible for us to take Southwatch without the Empress's navy, Harendell's assistance was predicated on the Valcottans' involvement. We *need* them."

"No."

"What does the Empress want?" Jor asked, looking back and forth between the two of them.

"Me dead."

Jor winced. "I see." But Lara had already rounded on Aren.

"Agree. Give her what she wants. It's not as though I'm going to be able to live with myself if we lose Ithicana because of this." Her heart was a riot in her chest, terror and sorrow twisting through her veins because she didn't want to die. But she would. For Ithicana. For Aren. For herself, she'd do this. "Let them kill me."

Aren lowered his head. "No."

"Then I'll do it myself," she snarled. Twisting out of reach of his hands, she dived toward the door, hauling it open.

Only to find Zarrah Anaphora standing in front of her.

The other woman pushed Lara back, glancing over her shoulder before stepping inside. "We don't have much time. There are soldiers on their way to escort you to the harbor and put you on a ship to Nerastis. My aunt wants you gone."

"Time for what?" Lara looked to Aren, who appeared entirely unsurprised at Zarrah's arrival.

"Time," he said, "for General Anaphora and I to negotiate an alliance between Ithicana and Valcotta."

"SHAME THAT WE COULDN'T have had this conversation before I had to endure the Red Desert." Aren motioned for Zarrah to take a seat. "Everything could be said and done by now."

"I didn't know you intended to ask my aunt for assistance until I heard word of trouble in Jerin oasis and realized your intentions. You really ought not to leave witnesses alive, Your Grace. I won't be the only one who's heard the tale."

He shrugged. "I don't murder children."

"Your principals would be commendable if the stakes were not so high." Zarrah rolled her shoulders. "But in this instance, it worked in my favor. I needed to get here ahead of you to ensure our stories remained aligned. My delivery of food to Eranahl was not precisely *sanctioned* by the Empress."

It wasn't the only thing she was keeping from the Empress, but Aren only nodded.

"As it is, we wouldn't be having this conversation at all if my return to Pyrinat had not made clear to me certain details about my aunt's plans for the future."

Lara was watching Zarrah with narrowed eyes. "I think you need to start from the beginning."

"I don't have time for that."

"Make time."

Exhaling a long breath, Zarrah began. "I've been stationed in Nerastis since I was seventeen. Which means for nearly five years I've been on the front lines of the war with Maridrina, watching as we fought and killed over the same pile of rubble, the same ten miles of coastline. Back and forth with no end in sight. And why should there be an end, when we've been fighting this same war for hundreds of years? No one even knows what it's like *not* to be at war."

How well Aren knew that feeling.

"Except my aunt does see an end." Zarrah hesitated, biting at her bottom lip. "She believes Silas has overcommitted himself in taking the bridge, and she's right. Maridrina is stretched too thin, and that makes it vulnerable. Valcotta has been blocking trade so that the bridge earns no money in tolls, knowing well that there will come a time when Silas won't be able to pay the Amaridian queen for the use of her navy. And when that day comes, what remains of the Ithicanian people will begin attacking the Maridrinian forces holding the bridge, which will mean that Silas will have to pull more soldiers from his war against us in order to hold it. That raiders and pirates will attack those men in the hunt for Ithicana's hidden fortunes, requiring even more of Maridrina's soldiers to bleed in its defense. Which means he'll have to pull all of his naval forces from the coast around Nerastis in order to combat them, because his pride will force him to do what it takes to keep the bridge."

"And in doing so, he'll be leaving Maridrina ripe for the picking," Aren said, his stomach twisting. "The Empress intends to watch and wait until Maridrina is weak, and then attack. That Ithicana won't survive long enough to see Maridrina lose the bridge doesn't matter to her."

Zarrah shook her head. "It matters. But she's deemed the loss worth sacking Vencia and eventually conquering all of Maridrina." Her eyes met Aren's. "The game is bigger than you realize, and infinitely more far-reaching."

The words echoed those Aren had once heard Keris speak. "What is Keris's opinion on the matter?"

"How should I know the thoughts of a Maridrinian prince?"

"I was under the impression that you two were rather close." Next to him, he felt Lara straighten, her surprise palpable. "Why else would he risk so much in breaking you free from his father?"

"Keris Veliant is my enemy." Zarrah's gaze met his, unblinking. "He offered me a deal: He would get me free of Vencia if I agreed to supply Eranahl. As we both delivered on our ends of the bargain, our arrangement is over. Even so, I'd rather the Empress never learned the arrangement existed at all."

Aren gave a slight shake of his head. "Anyone with money and means could've delivered a ship full of supplies into Ithicana, and Keris has both. If all he'd cared about was Eranahl enduring, he could have managed that without either of us. Which suggests to me that supplying my city was merely bait to entice me into achieving his greater goal."

"And which goal might that be, Your Grace?"

"Freeing you."

Zarrah rolled her eyes. "You're insane. Why would he want that?"

"Because you and Keris plan to end the war between Maridrina and Valcotta." Leaning back on his hands, he tried to keep the smug smile from his face. "That is Keris's long game, but it's not one that has a hope of being achieved if the Empress takes advantage of Silas's greed and invades Maridrina."

Zarrah was silent, then she finally said, "Keris and I are like-minded in our belief that the war between our nations needs to end."

More than like-minded, Aren thought, but he kept his suspicions about the nature of the relationship between Zarrah and Keris to himself. "Then why not just tell Keris the Empress's intentions? He could supply the information to his father, and Silas would have to withdraw from Ithicana to protect Maridrina and his throne. We could win this war without a fight."

Lara clicked her tongue against her teeth, shaking her head. "Ithicana would win its war with Maridrina, but what are currently border skirmishes and a few sunken ships will turn into a war between

Maridrina and Valcotta unlike any seen in generations."

Zarrah gave the slightest of nods.

"So what is your suggestion?" Aren asked. "Because I'm not allowing my people to be starved and stripped of their homes for the sake of preserving the peace between Maridrina and Valcotta." Jor and Lara nodded their agreement.

"I would not suggest that, Your Grace," she answered. "Ithicana must be liberated from Maridrina, but it must be done in a way where Valcotta is perceived not to be involved. Which is why I intend to sail with you back to Nerastis, crew the Maridrinian vessels we've captured with my soldiers, and then take back Southwatch for you." She smiled, and as much as the young woman might be fighting for peace, Aren could see she was also one who knew war, and knew it well. "The only witnesses to our involvement will be the dead we leave behind on your island."

It was overcomplicated, with too many players, but Aren didn't have any other options. "One problem," he said. "You'll be going directly against the Empress's orders. Sabotaging her plans to invade Maridrina. And as loyal as your soldiers might be, there is no way you can possibly keep something like this quiet, especially given that casualties are inevitable. You'll be charged with treason and executed."

Licking her lips, she hesitated before speaking. "My fleet witnessed the Maridrinians moving on Southwatch, and we knew they intended to attack. We had the opportunity to warn Ithicana but did not."

A warning that might have changed everything. "Your naval vessels had been warned to stay clear of Southwatch or our shipbreakers would be turned on them. I can't hold you—"

"With respect, Your Grace, do not attempt to absolve me. I could've warned you, but I did not. Kings and queens make decisions, but it is the common folk who pay the price." Her voice quivered ever so slightly, but she lifted her chin and stared him down. "There was no honor in what I did, Your Grace. I will not insult you by asking for your forgiveness, but please know that I will fight until my last breath to see Ithicana liberated."

He had his alliance. "I pray you won't breathe your last for many years, General."

Zarrah gave a slow nod, and in her eyes, he saw a dream fading away. Not just one for her country, but one for herself. "Some things are worth dying for." Rising to her feet, she said, "Pack your things. We sail for Nerastis tonight."

43
LARA

THE VALCOTTAN SOLDIERS arrived shortly after to escort them to the harbor, the Empress clearly having no interest in either Lara or Aren remaining in her country any longer.

Zarrah was already aboard the ship when they arrived, once again wearing the uniform of a Valcottan general. Soldiers and sailors scurried about the deck as they readied to make way, but as the young woman lifted her hand, every one of them stopped in their tracks.

"On the orders of the Empress, we are transporting the King and Queen of Ithicana to Nerastis," she said, her voice carrying over the ship. "They are to be accorded every respect. If I hear otherwise, the individual will answer to me, and ultimately, to the Empress herself. Now carry on."

"So much for avoiding detection," Jor muttered from where he stood at Lara's left. "Whole damn city is going to know that we were here and where we are headed."

"That is her intent," Lara murmured. "Serin anticipated we were coming to Valcotta, which means he knew what we were after. The city is crawling with his spies, which means word that the Empress declined to assist Ithicana will travel at pace with us back to Maridrina. Assuming Zarrah knows how to keep a secret, and I think she does, the Valcottan attack on Southwatch will come as a total surprise."

Nothing more could be said, as Zarrah had made her way over to them. "If it pleases you, Your Grace, follow me. We'll have dinner in the captain's quarters."

The room she took them to was large, with windows that overlooked the ship's wake as they headed out to sea. The paneled walls were painted in bright hues, and elaborate glass sconces glowed with burning oil. Gesturing to the low table, which was laden with food, Zarrah said, "Please. Take a seat."

Lara sat on one of the pillows, curling her heels under her as she took in the spread. Most of it was unfamiliar to her, but that was not what drove away her appetite. The ship was out of the harbor now, and the seas were far from smooth. A sour taste filled her mouth, and silently cursing the loss of her sea legs, Lara rose. "Please excuse me."

"Lass isn't good on the water," she heard Jor say as the door shut behind her.

Dashing back the way they'd come, she barely managed to make it to the railing before her stomach contents came rushing up. The watching sailors laughed quietly.

"I thought you'd gotten over this."

She lifted her head, seeing Aren had come to stand next to her at the rail. He handed her a cup full of water, then turned his attention to the waves, barely visible in the growing darkness of night. When she was through rinsing her mouth, he handed her a shiny candy. "It's ginger."

Slipping the candy into her mouth, Lara smiled at him. "Thank you."

"There was a whole bowl of them on the table. I took them all." Reaching into his pocket, he extracted a handful of the candies and tucked them into the pocket of her loose Valcottan trousers, his hand warm through the thin fabric covering her leg.

"You should go back," she said, knowing that plans needed to be made and that it was just as well she wasn't part of them.

"Soon enough. Zarrah won't talk business until after dinner is done, and Jor has a healthy appetite."

"That makes one of us." She crunched the candy between her teeth, replacing it with another as she considered whether the ambient noise was loud enough to conceal their conversation. "How did you know Zarrah would help us?"

"I wasn't certain until I realized that the Empress didn't want the war with Maridrina to end, at least, not peaceably. Which was why she set a term she knew I'd never agree to." He rested his elbows on the rail, then added, "Keris always spoke in riddles, but the longer I thought about the things he said, the clearer they became. What he wants is peace between Valcotta and Maridrina, and for that to be possible, Zarrah had to want the same. Ithicana is but a minor player in the game."

She tilted her head to look up at him. "You're quoting him?"

"More or less."

"The heirs to the greatest enemies in the world are allies," Lara mused. "I wonder how they met."

"I'm sure it's quite the story. And equally sure neither of them will tell us any of it."

They stood together in silence, the last vestiges of the sun's glow disappearing on the horizon, the cloudless sky above soon sparkling with stars. The wind grew cooler, and Lara shivered, her bare arms prickling with goose bumps. "How long will it take for us to get to Nerastis?"

"With these winds, three days. It's a fast ship."

Three days.

Her eyes burned, and knowing she needed to say it before she lost her nerve, Lara blurted out, "That's when I'm going to leave you and Jor. I've done everything I can for you, and for me to go to Ithicana with you would be a mistake."

He sighed. "I know."

She held her breath, waiting for him to argue with her. Waiting for him to tell her that leaving would be a mistake. But he only pulled her into his arms and said, "I wish things could be different."

Hot tears spilled onto her cheeks. "But they can't."

She felt him press his face against her hair. "I need you to know that I forgive you, Lara. That I—" He broke off, clearing his throat. "I should go back. They'll be wondering where I am."

She nodded, unable to speak. Unable to say a word as he let go of her and went back inside. But in her head, the same phrase repeated over and over again.

I love you.

EVERY DAY THAT passed made him one step closer to returning to Ithicana.

And one step closer to letting Lara go.

It was made easier in that he, Zarrah, and Jor closeted themselves away in the captain's quarters discussing strategy, specifically how to take Southwatch with the least amount of Valcottan losses, while Lara chose to remain on deck in the fresh air.

But he knew her reasons had nothing to do with seasickness and everything to do with her distancing herself from him.

It hurt. Hurt so badly that there were moments he felt like he could hardly breathe knowing that it was a matter of hours until she'd walk away from him and that he'd likely never see her again.

And on top of that hurt was fear because Aren knew where she intended to go. Just as he knew that he had no power to stop her.

"So this is Nerastis." Lara stood next to him at the rail, watching as the ship crept past the enormous city. "It looks pretty at night."

"Don't let all the lights fool you—it's a shithole," Zarrah answered. "Half of it is burned. Half of it is rubble. It's full of filthy drinking establishments, louse-ridden brothels, and dens of disrepute that cater to every possible desire or addiction. The only individuals you'll find within its wall are those being paid to fight over it and those who are too poor to leave."

And yet we can't stop fighting over it. Aren wondered if Lara heard Zarrah's unspoken words as clearly as he did.

"We'll get as close to the coast on the Maridrinian side as we can, and then I'll row you to shore," Zarrah said. "And then you're on your own."

The last was for the benefit of the sailors and soldiers around him, for the moment they parted ways was the moment things began.

"General," the captain called softly, wary of Maridrinian patrols. "We're lowering sails and readying the longboat. Are you still certain you wish to row them to shore yourself?"

"Quite."

No one on the ship spoke as they climbed into the small boat, which was lowered into the water, Jor taking the oars.

"Be wary," Zarrah said. "Word I was bringing you here might have raced ahead of us on good horses or faster sails. The Magpie might well be waiting for you."

Aren instinctively touched the weapons at his waist, keeping his eyes on the shore for any signs of motion in the moonlight.

But there was nothing.

"I'll remain here in Nerastis until the last possible hour so the Maridrinians don't suspect," Zarrah said. "Then I'll sail north and anchor my fleet off your coast, as we agreed. As soon as we receive your signal, we'll move on Southwatch Island."

"You're sure," he asked for the dozenth time, "that they'll follow your orders?"

Zarrah nodded. "I'm the Empress's chosen heir. None will believe I'd jeopardize my position by going against her wishes. They'll follow me unquestioningly."

"Beach," Jor muttered. "Stay quiet."

The surf pushed them up on shore, Jor and Aren hopping out to pull it farther from the water.

"I'll keep watch," Lara whispered, then pulled a knife and scampered up the beach into the darkness. Aren watched her go, afraid it would be the last time he saw her. That instead of saying good-bye, she'd slip away into the night.

Zarrah handed him a bag of supplies. "Good luck, Your Grace. I look forward to fighting alongside Ithicana."

He watched as Jor pushed the boat deeper into the water. Zarrah put her back into the oars, and the vessel faded into the darkness. Then they walked up the beach to the base of the steep, brush-covered hill.

Lara materialized out of the darkness, and the three of them stood together in the silence. Jor cleared his throat. "There's a village just north of here. I'll go scout it for a vessel that will serve our purposes."

Aren nodded, but before Jor could move, Lara reached out a hand, catching hold of the old soldier's arm. "Goodbye, Jor."

"Goodbye, Lara." Jor inclined his head. "Thank you for getting him back for us." Then he took off at a run down the beach.

They stood in silence, the only sound the roar of the surf and the wind rustling in the bushes. Finally, he asked, "Will you tell me where you plan to go?"

"Likely I'll lay low for a time. Stay close to the coast so I can be the first to hear how the battle goes. Hopefully I won't have cause to regret leaving you to your own devices."

Ignoring the jest, Aren closed the distance between them. "Don't lie to me. Not now."

She was quiet, the moonlight turning her hair and skin silver. "He needs to die."

"I know, but it doesn't need to be you who does it. Let Keris earn that crown he wants so badly—it's about time he got his hands dirty." Aren lifted a hand, cupping the side of her face. "I have enough to worry about without you attempting to assassinate Silas. It's bad enough that I have to—"

He broke off, leaving the last unsaid. *Bad enough that I have to let you go.*

"If I can kill my father, this might well end without a fight. If Keris is so keen on peace, he'll pull out of Ithicana and turn his head toward his grander ambitions with Zarrah and Valcotta."

"Or you might be captured and killed."

"It's worth the risk."

He shook his head. "I wouldn't use you as an assassin before, Lara. And I refuse to do it now. Promise me you'll let this go."

"No." She was adamant. And in that moment, he knew that there was no point in arguing: She'd never concede. It was what he loved about her.

And what he hated.

Kicking at the sand, he glared at the moonlight. Then something caught his eye. The flash of light against a weapon. Diving forward, he knocked Lara over, rolling with her behind a boulder. "Run!"

Staggering to their feet, they dived into the bushes, arrows shooting past them.

"You go, I'll cover you!" Lara shoved at Aren, but he caught hold of her wrist, yanking her along with him.

"Not a chance."

They crept through the underbrush, hiding under the cover of darkness as they circled around toward the village Jor was scouting for vessels, the Maridrinian soldiers crashing about as they searched.

"Call for reinforcements! Tell them we've got Valcottan raiders coming in from behind!" a man ordered, the voice familiar.

Because it was Keris's.

The soil was damp, and he and Lara were leaving a trail a blind man could follow. They had to hurry.

Progressing north toward the village, Aren moved with practiced silence through the trees, Lara so quiet that the only reason he knew she was there was the grip he had on her wrist.

"They went this way!" Shouts echoed from behind them, and up the slope, a horse galloped down the road in the direction of the village.

Giving up on stealth, Aren crashed through the underbrush. They were so close. They couldn't get caught now.

Then they were in the open, racing down a narrow beach. But so was the soldier on horseback.

The gray horse galloped in their direction, rider bent low over its neck, glittering blade held in one hand. Then the man leaned back, hauling on the reins, pulling back his hood to reveal his face.

"What the hell are you doing in Nerastis?" Keris demanded, then shook his head. "Never mind. You need to run. They're coming, and I'm not in any position to help you."

Maridrinian soldiers exploded out of the brush and onto the beach, racing in their direction. Keris's face twisted in frustration, then he shouted, "Catch the Valcottans! They're getting away!"

Still holding onto Lara's wrist, Aren raced toward the waterline, where Jor was pulling loose the rope anchoring a small fishing boat to the beach. Together, they pushed it toward the water, boots digging into the sand.

But the Maridrinians were already on them.

Swords clashed, and Aren turned to see Lara fighting them, her sword a blur of silver in the moonlight. But there were a dozen of them and only one of her. "Go!" she shouted. "Don't stop!"

"Come on, Aren," Jor snarled. "Push!"

Aren ignored him, letting go of the boat and racing in Lara's direction. Pulling his weapon, he carved into a soldier, barely hearing the man's scream as he dropped, because all that mattered was getting to her. He killed another man, then another, and then he and Lara were fighting together, holding them off.

But more Maridrinians swarmed onto the beach, reinforcements arriving.

This was where it was going to end.

And it was not, Aren thought, the worst way to go: with his queen fighting at his back.

"Retreat!" Keris's voice echoed across the chaos, the prince standing in his saddle. "Retreat!"

The Maridrinian soldiers raced to comply, and Aren twisted around in time to see the first Valcottan longboats hit the shore, dozens of soldiers spilling out. "For Valcotta!" Zarrah screamed, but as she ran past him, she said, "Get going, Ithicana."

Jor had the fishing boat in the water, and Aren and Lara splashed through the waves, pushing it farther out while Jor fought to get the sails up alone. Clambering in, Aren helped unravel lines, Lara holding onto the edge and kicking hard, pushing them into deeper water, the Valcottans already retreating.

"Get in," he shouted at her, the sail rising. "We need to go."

But Lara didn't answer.

Dread filled him, and Aren spun around. "Lara!"

She was still there. Still swimming. But she looked up, meeting his gaze. "Goodbye, Aren," she said, and let go of the boat, aiming toward shore.

Instinct took over.

Aren lunged, reaching down to catch hold of her belt and haul her out of the water. Her ankles caught on the edge and she fell backward, landing in his arms.

"What are you doing?" She twisted in his arms so that they were face-to-face, their legs tangled together in the bottom of the boat.

What was he doing?

Unsure of the answer, he said, "It's time we went home."

THERE HADN'T BEEN a chance of him leaving her behind.

Aren told himself it was because the beach had been swarming with soldiers, that he'd done it to keep her from being caught and killed. That he hadn't had a choice. But the real reason was that when the moment had come to let her go, he hadn't been able to do it.

"She would've been fine." Jor cast a glance over to where Lara slept, the slow rise and fall of her chest visible in the growing light of dawn. "The waves would've pushed her right back to shore."

"Into the arms of waiting soldiers."

"Better the arms of Maridrinian soldiers than ours. Keris could've manufactured an excuse to keep her alive long enough for her to escape. You think you're going to be able to manage the same?"

There was little response Aren could give to that because he knew that he'd pulled Lara out of the frying pan only to cast her into the fire. The plan was to sail directly to Ithicana to meet up with what remained of the Midwatch garrison. And there was a good chance his soldiers would try to kill Lara on sight.

And Aren wasn't certain what exactly he could do to stop them.

"We should return to Maridrina's coast tonight," Jor said. "We can drop her off and let her make her own way."

"We don't have time. The calm season is almost over, and we *need* to attack before the first storms hit." Aren dropped a net into their wake, his stomach grumbling with hunger, most of the supplies Zarrah had provided them abandoned on the beach. "And there's too much chance of being caught by a patrol. We'll stay in open water."

"Patrols are out in open water, too. And there isn't a chance of us outrunning them in this Maridrinian hunk of junk."

"I said no."

Jor spit into the water. "You're going to get her killed. You might get yourself killed as well just for bringing her back into Ithicana."

Fastening the net to the back of the boat, Aren turned to find Lara awake and watching him. "I'll figure it out."

She shook her head, but said nothing, only rolled onto her side, pulling a piece of sail canvas over her shoulders.

Yet for all his words, no ideas came to him as they sailed north, eventually reaching the outskirts of Ithicana. Once there, avoiding detection had required all his attention as they crept through secret— and dangerous—routes between islands, hiding beneath the cover of fog while trying to avoid being wrecked on the endless hazards lurking beneath the waves.

By the time they reached the island where Jor believed the Midwatch garrison was hiding, all three of them were salt-stained and weary, nerves and tempers stretched to the limit.

"Stupid Maridrinian piece of shit." Jor kicked at the fishing vessel. "I'm going to burn this the second I have a chance."

Aren didn't answer, only looked to Lara. "Put your hood up. I'd rather have an opportunity to talk to them before they recognize you."

The slight flex of her jaw was the only sign of her nerves as she pulled her hood up to conceal her hair and face, a knife appearing in her hands only to disappear again a heartbeat later. He drew his own hood up, not wanting his people to recognize him before he was ready, either.

Taking the paddle that Jor passed him, he added his strength to the effort of driving the boat into the narrow gap in the rock, the clifftops overhead concealed by mist. There were no sounds but the cries of birds and the splash of water against the rocks, but he knew his people were up there. Knew they were watching. And, given they were in a Maridrinian boat, that arrows were probably pointed at their heads.

They made their way deeper, the cliffs high enough now that no sunlight reached the water. But Aren still noticed the large finned shape swimming beneath them, tracking their progress. The shark rose, its head lifting out of the water so that it could look at them, and then it slipped back into the depths.

"Bad omen," Jor muttered, but Aren ignored him, easing the boat around a bend, the cliffs falling away to reveal a small lagoon with a dozen Ithicanian vessels pulled up on the tiny spit of beach.

Lifting his paddle from the water, Aren allowed them to drift toward shore, picking out movement in the trees a heartbeat before his soldiers appeared, weapons trained on the boat. His stomach clenched at the sight of their ragged appearance, clothes patched where they weren't torn, hair unkept, and many of the men sporting thick beards beneath the leather masks they wore.

But their weapons gleamed sharp and bright.

"Point those somewhere else." Jor climbed out of the boat. "You bastards all know who I am."

Not a single one of them lowered their weapons.

"Get out of the boat," one of the men said, his familiar voice making Aren cringe. "Slowly."

They obeyed, getting out and standing in the knee-deep water.

Jor stepped up onto the beach. "Who's in command? Hopefully someone with more sense than you brainless fools."

"I am," the other man responded, pulling off his mask. Though he'd recognized his voice, Aren still cursed the sight of Aster's face. Not only did the old man begrudge Aren for replacing him with Emra as commander of Kestark garrison, Aster had mistrusted Lara from the beginning and had never let the sentiment go.

"We haven't heard from you for weeks, then you arrive in a

Maridrinian boat," Aster said. "How are we to know this isn't a trap?"

"It's not a trap." Aren pushed back his hood, and gasps of surprise echoed from his soldiers, more of whom stepped out of the trees with their weapons lowered.

"Your Grace!" Aster's eyes widened. Then they narrowed again, his focus going past Aren's shoulder. "That better not be—"

Aren knew Lara had removed her hood because every weapon abruptly lifted. Moving quickly, he stepped between them and his wife. "You want to kill her, you'll have to kill me first."

"The bitch is a traitor," Aster snarled. "She deserves to die a thousand times over. You said so yourself before you were taken. I said so from the moment she stepped onto our shores."

"I know more now than I did then," Aren answered, seeing motion out the corner of his eye and knowing he was being surrounded. "She freed me from captivity. I owe her my life."

"And she's apparently been working her own brand of magic on you ever since." Aster made a vulgar gesture. "No other explanation for you bringing her back to Ithicana. The witch has a hold on you."

"What I brought back was a plan and the allies to see it through." Aren forced himself to remain calm despite the terror building in his gut. He'd known that it would be difficult to convince his soldiers to accept Lara's presence, but with Aster in command, it might be impossible. "Valcotta has agreed to help us retake the bridge and drive out the Maridrinians."

His soldiers shifted, weapons wavering, and he noted how thin they all were. Little more than skin and bone. It couldn't be much better for those in Eranahl.

"Ahnna has likewise secured the support of the King of Harendell. In conjunction with their navies, we'll conduct a coordinated strike against the garrisons. Then we'll hunker down and let the storms take care of the rest of them."

"As if that's so easy." Aster rocked on his heels, eyes flicking past Aren, then back again. "We spent months trying to retake those garrisons, and all it earned us were dead comrades."

"That's because before we were scattered," Aren said. "This time we'll be more strategic. This time we won't lose."

Aster shook his head, as did several of the others. Unconvinced, yes. But also afraid. This invasion had taken its toll.

"Perhaps you might consider what will happen if you *don't* fight. Eranahl is starving. If we don't retake the bridge, the city will have to be evacuated come storm season, and it won't be people returning to their homes. It will mean people fleeing to Harendell or Valcotta, or wherever the wind takes them. And without its people, Ithicana is no more."

"Maybe that's how it has to go."

Aren shook his head. "If *any* of you believed that, you would already be gone. And yet here you stand." Knowing he was taking a risk, he strode forward so that he stood among them. "We have one chance to take back what's ours. Hear me out, and then make your choice."

Picking up a stick, Aren began to trace shapes into the sand, slowly drawing Ithicana by memory. "This is what we're going to do."

The plan that had been building in his head poured from his lips, and weapons slowly lowered as he explained to his soldiers how they'd retake the bridge. How they'd retake their homes. How they'd retake their kingdom. By the time he was finished, the sky was beginning to grow dark, and his throat was dry and parched. "Well? What do you say?"

"It's a good plan," Aster admitted, scratching at his beard, but then his eyes went back to Lara, who stood silently next to Jor. "How does she factor in?"

Before Aren could answer, Lara spoke.

"You all have cause to hate me," she said. "I came to you as a spy for Maridrina. I deceived you. Manipulated you. Conspired to betray you."

The soldiers shifted, expressions grim, but they were listening.

"My father raised me on lies so that I'd hate Ithicana. So that I'd hate *you* enough to dedicate my life to your destruction. But when I came to understand his deception, I turned my back on my father's schemes. Except that means little because the damage was already done." She paused, then added, "I'm not here for forgiveness. I'm here to ask you to allow me to fight because I assure you, I hate my father more than any of you ever could."

Aster spit on the ground at her feet. "You deserve a traitor's death."

"I know. But allow me to avenge the harm done to Ithicana instead."

Aren kept quiet as his soldiers stepped back, heads together, and debated Lara's request. Cold sweat trickled down his spine because he knew that they had every right to ask for her death.

Why did you bring her here? he silently demanded of himself. *Why didn't you leave her on that beach?*

Aster stepped away from the group. "You still consider her your wife?"

Yes, Aren thought, but he shook his head. "No."

"Queen?"

"No."

"She leaves as soon as this is done?"

Aren didn't hesitate. He couldn't. Not if he wanted to get Lara out of this alive. "Yes."

Aster exchanged long looks with several of the other soldiers, and then he nodded and pulled a horn from his belt, tossing it to Aren. "I think you best tell Ithicana you're home, Your Grace."

Taking a deep breath, Aren raised the horn to his lips, then he called his kingdom to war.

IN TRUE ITHICANIAN fashion, there were no delays.

And for that, Lara was profoundly grateful. For three days and nights, Aren strategized with Jor and Aster, horns blaring constantly as the plan was conveyed the length of Ithicana, the soldiers scattered across all the tiny islands massing together, careful to conceal their movements with darkness or mist. The Midwatch garrison swelled to close to three hundred, and every time another boat arrived with more soldiers, Lara clenched her teeth, knowing what was to come.

Not threats.

Not attempts on her life.

Not further requests for Aren to execute her.

What they gave her was the truth, and that was a far worse thing. One after another, they'd sit down and tell her what they'd endured because of the Maridrinian invasion.

Because of her.

Aster had been the first. "My girl Raina was part of your

brother's *escort* through the bridge." His voice was flat. "Your people slaughtered her, then hung her corpse beneath the bridge to rot with her comrades."

Lara blanched, but Aster wasn't through.

"They killed my nephew. But not before they made him watch his wife die. I know it because their son witnessed it from where he was hidden in the jungle. We found the boy and a few of the other children half-starved, living off the scraps they could find in their burned-out village. Living with the corpses of their parents because none of them were big enough to move them."

Lara threw up, guts heaving even when her stomach had run dry. "I'm sorry."

He only looked at her with disgust. "My wife and other children are in Eranahl. Haven't seen them in almost a year. Don't even know if they're alive, only that if they are, they're hungry. Scared. And I can't get to them."

"I pray you'll see them again."

He only shook his head at her. "Likely not in this life."

A female soldier had been next. "My three boys are in Eranahl. It has always been a sanctuary. But now . . ." Her voice cracked. "I *left* them there."

"It was the right choice. They are safer there than they are here."

The woman shook her head slowly, eyes full of hate. "They shouldn't have been in danger at all."

A boy, sixteen if he's a day, had followed. "They've got my sister as a prisoner on Gamire Island." His hands balled into fists. "Do you know what your people do to prisoners?"

God, but she knew. "We'll try to get her back."

"You mean we'll get what's left of her back." He spit in her face. "Traitor."

She lost count of how many of them spoke to her, but she didn't forget any of the names, which marched through her thoughts every time she closed her eyes, sleep a near impossibility beneath the burden of her guilt.

If Aren was being subjected to the same, she couldn't have said, because she barely saw him. Partially it was because he spent every waking minute strategizing, but she knew the true reason was that he was avoiding her. And though she knew he hadn't had a choice, his conversation with Aster had haunted her.

Not his wife.

Not his queen.

Not his.

"You ready?"

Lara jumped, turning to find Aren standing behind her. He was back to wearing Ithicanian garb, but his hair was still long, dark locks brushing against his cheeks. A machete was belted at his waist and his bow was slung over his shoulder, along with a full quiver.

He handed over her sharp sword, the blade glinting. "It's time."

Lia, having recently rejoined them, stood in the boat. With the young woman were Jor, Aster, and three other Ithicanians, and beyond, another vessel filled with soldiers floated in the lagoon, waiting for them. Lara clambered inside, moving instinctively to where she'd be out of the way, Jor and Aster taking up the paddles to move them between the narrow cliffs.

A heavy mist hung over the calm water, reducing visibility to a few paces in either direction. No one spoke louder than a whisper as they meandered through the islands.

Aren knelt next to her, bow resting across his knees. His face was expressionless, but little signs betrayed his nerves to her. The way he bounced the bow against his knee. The way the muscles in his jaw tightened, then relaxed. The way his eyes jerked toward any sound.

Then his gaze came to rest on her, and Lara's heart skipped as he said, "We're going to take Gamire."

Gamire was Nana's island. "Why not Midwatch?"

"It's where they're keeping the prisoners. We'll free them and take control of the island, then move on to Midwatch tomorrow."

Midwatch was a strategically better target, but she understood why he'd made this choice.

Pulling a mask from his belt, he handed it to her. "For the fight. Once we're on top of the bridge, keep close. Follow my lead."

"Don't stab anyone in the back," Aster muttered. Neither she nor Aren reacted to his barb. Now was not the time.

The bridge appeared through the mist, a shadowy gray shape winding its way above them. The Ithicanians lowered the sails, the boats drifting toward one of the piers rising out of the ocean. Spikes jutted out from all angles, preventing the vessels from coming too close, and above those, the rock was so smooth that not even the best of climbers would be able to scale the slick surface.

But at the front of the boat, Lia was pulling off her boots, a length of slender cable looped around her neck and one shoulder.

"There's an opening below the surface," Aren murmured, his breath against Lara's ear sending a slight shiver down her body. "She'll swim up it, then climb the interior of the pier, where there's access to the bridge top. She'll drop the rope, and the rest of us will climb."

"Why climb? Why not swim down?"

Leaning over the edge, Aren pointed as a large shadow passed beneath their boat. And it wasn't alone. Fear prickled up Lara's spine as she watched the enormous sharks circle the pier.

But Lia showed no concern, one hand resting against the mast as she watched the water. The other boat was some distance away, and Lara watched as they pulled still-flopping fish from a sack, along with a bucket that she suspected was full of blood.

"Lia's fast," Aren said softly. "She'll only need a few seconds to get down and inside the pier." His eyes flicked to the woman in question. "Ready?"

Lia nodded, and Aren lifted his hand to signal the other boat. One of the soldiers tossed the blood into the water, then they began throwing the dying fish into the mix, the creatures making splats against the surface.

Lara's attention jerked to the depths below, the large shapes darting in the direction of the disturbance.

Lia bent her knees, ready to dive.

Then voices filtered down from above.

Lunging, Lara caught hold of Lia's hand and pulled her back, slapping a hand over her mouth when she started to protest. With the other, she pointed up and mouthed, "Patrol."

Everyone in the boat went still, Aren gesturing to the other crew for silence as they listened.

Lara could pick up male voices, though the bridge itself was too high above for her to hear what they were saying. Or for her to determine how many of them were there.

But Aren shook his head, his hands moving in silent signals telling the other boat to move away from the pier and out into open water.

Only when they were a distance away did he swear and slam his fist down on the edge of the boat. "Of all the places they could choose to have lunch, it had to be there."

"Is there another pier we can use?" Lara asked.

"None near Gamire," Jor answered. "And we're on a tight schedule."

"There's one." All heads turned in Aren's direction. "It's closer, so even with the delay, we'll keep to the timeline."

"No," Jor said flatly. "We'll find another way."

"We don't have another way," Aren snapped. "At least not one that keeps to the timeline. We need to come in from the bridge top and take out the Maridrinians manning Gamire's shipbreakers, or when our people attack, they'll be sitting ducks."

"We go farther south, then. There're a couple piers we can climb. If we move fast—"

"The Maridrinians aren't stupid. They're patrolling the bridge top. How many would we have to fight in order to get back to Gamire? What are the chances they wouldn't get a signal off that we're attacking? This is the only way."

Jor's face was red. "I said no. I'm too slow, and I'm not risking any of this crew to that sort of nonsense."

"It should be me anyway," Aren said. "I'm the fastest."

It was then that Lara realized just *how* Aren was suggesting they reach the bridge top.

Snake Island.

Right as Jor snarled, "Not a goddamned chance," Lara said, "I'll do it."

Both men stopped their argument to stare at her, as did the other Ithicanians in the boat.

"I'll do it," she repeated. "I'm fast, and I'm a good climber."

Lia whistled through her teeth in obvious approval, but Jor shot her a look that silenced any further outbursts. But he couldn't silence the way the Ithicanians were looking at her with interest.

Aren's jaw worked back and forth. "It's harder than it looks, Lara. And if one of the snakes gets its teeth into you, there is no way for us to help. You won't make the climb before the paralysis kicks in, and if the fall doesn't kill you, one of the bigger snakes will finish the job. And you need to do it all while carrying rope."

She shrugged, hoping the gesture hid the skitter of fear working its way up her spine. "No great loss to you if I die. And if they're busy trying to eat me, then it might give you a better chance of making the climb yourself."

"She's got a point," Jor said. "But it's your call."

Aren said nothing, but in his eyes, Lara could see him warring with the decision, knowing how it would look if he risked anyone else, including himself, in her place. Finally, he said, "Let's go."

Sweat poured down Lara's back by the time they reached the small island, the mist and cloud cover hiding them from Maridrinian patrols above and on the water. On the day that Aren had raced the snakes, it had been sunny. But today the hundreds of snakes that teemed beneath the ledges and among the rocks were hidden by the fog.

Which made what she was about to do all the worse.

"This isn't a bravery trial." Aren slung his bow over his shoulder and handed Jor a sack of still-moving fish before retrieving his own. "We'll keep baiting them off the path, and then we'll cover you as well as we can with arrows. But with this visibility . . ."

"It's fine," Lara said with a confidence she didn't feel. "Either I make it to the pier ahead of them or I don't. A handful of arrows aren't likely to make a difference."

Aster moved next to her, draping a thin length of rope over her shoulders, then securing it to her belt. It was heavier than she'd hoped. Heavy enough to slow her down.

"You don't have to do this. I—" Aren started to say, but Lara only hopped out of the boat and onto the submerged sandbar, making her way toward the island until she was only knee-deep. Interlocking her hands, she stretched her arms in front, her back cracking. "I'm ready."

She wasn't ready. Not even close. Over the sound of the surf, she could hear the snakes moving, their coils rasping against each other as they watched the intruders, the hisses of hundreds of tongues blending together into one monstrous voice.

The crews from both boats were in the water, and several of them took the sacks of fish and started splashing noisily in opposite directions, baiting the snakes away from the path. The rest lifted their bows, Aren included.

You can do this.

There was movement on the beach, sinuous figures disturbing the fog as they moved onto the sand.

"The path is relatively smooth," Aren said. "Trust your feet, and watch for the snakes."

As if she didn't know that.

"They can jump. You need to get at least a dozen feet up the pier before you're out of reach. At best, you'll only have a handful of seconds to make the climb."

Lara clenched her teeth, fighting the urge to nod. Any movement would draw the snakes' attention.

"On my mark!"

She couldn't do this.

"Go!"

Lara broke into a sprint, water splashing as she hit the beach, her legs pumping. She didn't look to see if they'd thrown the fish. Didn't look to see if the snakes had noticed her.

She just ran.

The deep sand shifted and sank beneath her feet, but she'd been raised in the Red Desert, and the sensation was as natural to her as breathing.

But the desert didn't have snakes like this.

Dimly, she heard the Ithicanians shouting, trying to hold the creatures' attention.

She knew it wasn't working. Could feel the creatures converging on her, an invader and a better prize than any fish.

The fog swirled as she hit the path, her gaze fixed just ahead of her feet, searching for movement.

There. A dark head flashed toward her, all teeth and scales. Lara dived, flying over the lunging serpent, rolling and then on her feet again in a flash.

But they were behind her. Gaining ground.

She ran faster.

Bits of rock cut into her bare feet, but Lara barely felt the pain as the bridge pier emerged out of the mist.

An arrow sliced past her, spearing the head of a snake that had appeared out of nowhere, its body slamming against her ankle as she passed, making her stumble.

Keep going.

She raced onward, sensing others converging in her periphery.

Faster!

"Run, Lara!" Aren's voice filled her ears, the desperate edge of it driving her to greater speed. She leapt over a rock, a gasp tearing from her lips as something knocked against her heel.

"Run!"

The pier was only a dozen paces away, but she could hear the heavy bodies of the snakes hitting the ground behind her as they lunged.

She was almost there. Gathering her strength, Lara flung herself at the rough stone.

Her body slammed against the pier, fingers scrabbling for a handhold, sliding, her fingernails tearing, the weight of the rope pulling her down.

"Lara!"

Sobbing, she clawed at the rock, fingers finally catching hold. She climbed, heart in her throat.

Then something struck the back of her knee and pain lanced up her leg.

Terror filled her, but she didn't dare stop to see if she'd been bitten when others were flinging themselves against the pier just beneath her feet.

"Climb higher!"

Her toe slipped, her weight making her arms scream, but she struggled on. Foot by foot, her whole body shaking.

Had it bitten her? Was she moments from falling to her death? Lara didn't know. Wasn't certain if she was feeling sweat or blood dripping down her legs as she climbed.

Higher and higher she rose, shifting around the side of the pier so that she could climb up the bridge itself.

Finally, she made it to the top. Rolling over the edge, she rested on her back, gasping for breath. Only for voices to fill her ears.

Voices that didn't belong to the Ithicanians below.

JOR AND ASTER had him by the arms, hauling him back, all three of them falling with a splash in the water.

"She's up! She's climbing!"

But he'd seen the snake hit her. Even a shallow bite was enough to be deadly. He had to get to her.

Shoving Jor away, Aren clambered through the water toward the beach, only to have his head pushed under the water, his face smacking against the sand.

Jor hauled him out by the hair. "Don't make me half drown you to make you see reason, boy. Look! She's already at the top."

He was right. Through the mist, Aren could faintly see Lara circling the pier, moving with a steady confidence as she climbed up the side of the bridge, disappearing on top. Exhaling, he lowered his head to find several snakes approaching the waterline, watching him with interest.

"Just try it," he hissed at them, but moved back toward the boat rather than tempting fate.

And it was then he heard voices.

"Shit," Jor muttered. "Patrol."

Aren could barely breathe, terror wrapping around his chest like a vise. Lara only had a belt knife, and she'd be exhausted from her race and subsequent climb. He needed to get up there. Needed to help her.

Except the beach was covered with snakes, and they'd used all the fish to bait them away from Lara. But he had to try. He had to—

Jor's hand latched onto his wrist, his other hand pointing.

Lara had climbed back over the side of the bridge and was hanging there, barely visible through the fog.

"Shouts were coming from over here." A Maridrinian's voice.

"I don't see nothing," another responded. "You're hearing things."

"It's the cursed fog," yet another said. "It's enough to drive one to madness, never being able to see."

At least three, but probably more.

"They can't see us," Jor said under his breath, then signaled Lia and the others to stay silent. "They'll move on soon enough."

Except the Maridrinian soldiers stopped right next to where Lara dangled by her fingertips, voices filtering down.

"The Ithicanians are up to something," the first one said. "I can feel it. All those horns blasting the other day, the same message over and over."

"So what if they are. It's wishful thinking. Can't be more than a few hundred of them left alive, and if they feel like throwing themselves against their own defenses, so much the better. The sooner they're all dead, the sooner I can return to my wine cup and women."

The Maridrinians laughed, the sound echoing through the mist.

Aren stiffened in anger, but Jor's grip tightened on his arm. "Save the fight for later."

But Lara, it appeared, had other plans.

Aren watched helplessly as she climbed silently onto the bridge top.

The air split with screams.

A shrieking soldier flew off the side, plunging down to land with a thud on the sand, the snakes on him in an instant. But Aren couldn't tear his gaze from the swirls of mist above, which was all he could see of the battle. Grunts and thuds filled his ears, and then another man fell, this time into the water.

Lia was on the dying soldier in a flash, slitting his throat before he could betray their presence.

Another scream, then running feet.

Then silence.

Aren couldn't breathe. Couldn't move. Couldn't do anything but stare up at the bridge, waiting.

Please be alive.

Then a whistle sounded, two quick tweets followed by a long trill, and he exhaled a heavy breath and retrieved his bow from where it floated in the water. A heartbeat later, Lara dropped the end of the rope.

Lia fastened the heavy knotted rope they used for climbing to the end of it, then Lara dragged it up, securing it to the bridge.

Another whistle.

"I'll go first," Lia said, but Aren ignored her, jumping up to catch the rope and then climbing, his shoulders burning by the time he reached the top.

Lara stood among the dead, her face and clothing splattered with blood, the only sign of injury a split lip.

"Are you hurt?"

"I'm fine." She swayed slightly, and fear crawled up Aren's spine. Dropping to his knees, he jerked up the leg of her loose trousers. There was a livid red mark from the force of the snake hitting her calf, but miraculously, the creature's fangs hadn't broken the skin.

"Aren, I'm fine." She tried to pull away, but he pushed his fingers through the twin holes in the fabric and met her gaze, noticing how she blanched. "What you are is lucky," he growled, anger chasing away his fear.

Not anger at her. But at himself.

Why had he brought her here? Why hadn't he left her on that beach?

Twisting away, he began pushing the bodies off the bridge in case another patrol came along. By the time he was finished, the rest of his team were on the bridge top. All of them eyed Lara with a new level of respect, even Aster.

"Let's go," Aren ordered. "We've only got three hours to bring down Gamire's defenses."

They encountered only one more Maridrinian patrol on their run to Gamire, the soldiers talking loudly enough that Aren heard them half a mile away. It was the way of it in the fog—those who weren't used to it didn't understand how it dampened sound, the way it distorted the direction any noise seemed to come from. But it was a weapon that Aren had used often. And a weapon he used well.

The men were dead before they could even reach for their weapons.

Still holding his blade, Aren silently released the trigger on the hatch the Maridrinians had been guarding, the springs pushing the slab of stone upward far enough for him and Jor to get their fingers under it. Aren listened for a heartbeat, then nodded once, and they pulled it open.

Slipping down into the bridge with Jor and Lia following, Aren breathed in the scent of mildew. He pressed his hand against the wall, the familiar texture of the bridge's interior easing the rapid patter of his heart as the others closed the hatch to drown out the sound of the sea.

Unlike the fog, the interior of the bridge amplified sound, making it seem like the chattering Maridrinians were only a dozen paces away rather than close to a mile.

Aren walked through the darkness for several minutes, then took the sack that Jor handed him. Inside, he retrieved a tin bowl, along with three canisters, the contents labeled by etched markings on the sides. He poured two of them into the bowl, then under his breath, he said, "Go. I'll be right behind you."

Lia and Jor retreated to the hatch, and once they were out, he carefully unstoppered the third canister. Sucking in a deep breath and holding it, he poured the contents into the bowl, hearing it fizz violently. Dropping the canister, he sprinted back toward the opening and jumped, not inhaling until Jor and Lia hauled him onto the bridge top.

"What did you do?" Lara asked quietly.

"Poisonous smoke," he replied. "The draft will push it toward the patrol."

She frowned. "They'll escape into the pier. Warn the rest of the garrison."

"Not if we get there first."

He moved at a near sprint down the bridge top until the island came into sight, then slowed so that his movements were silent. Crouching low, he peered down into the mist swirling around the bridge pier, listening. Jor was fastening a rope around Lia when Aren lifted his head. He held up two fingers, and she nodded. Then, weapons in hand, she dropped over the side.

Seconds later, there was a gurgle and a muffled thump.

It took a matter of minutes for Aren and the rest of them to descend, and he'd only just shoved a knife beneath the entrance to the pier to keep it from opening when muffled shouts filled his ears. Followed by the thunder of boots racing down the stairs and a thud as hands hit the door, desperately trying to open it.

The screaming lasted a few minutes, and then there was only silence.

Motioning the others back, Aren pulled his knife out from beneath the door, which popped open, spilling out smoke and corpses, the interior marked with scratches and blood. He glanced at Lara's face as he retreated a safe distance, but if the grisly death of her countrymen troubled her, she didn't show it.

They moved silently toward the edge of the island, pausing just before they reached it.

"How's the timing?" he murmured to Jor.

Licking his fingers, Jor held them to the air, then shrugged. "Twenty minutes, perhaps a bit less."

There was no way to know if the rest of his people were in position on the water. No way to signal without the Maridrinians suspecting an attack was imminent. All he could do was hope that they still trusted him enough to follow his plans. "Let's take out the breakers."

They broke into groups, Lara and Jor remaining with Aren as he led them through the tangle of trees and ferns and vines, the underbrush thick from eight weeks' respite from the storms. Lara moved as silently as any of his people, but Aren found himself glancing in her direction.

Scowling, he caught hold of her ankle, and when she turned, he gestured at the mask on his own face, knowing she had one tucked in her belt.

She mouthed the word *no,* giving a shake of her head.

But he didn't let go of her ankle. If any of the soldiers manning the breakers caught sight of her and shouted the alarm, all would be for naught.

Lara frowned, then shoved her hand into the mud, smearing it across her face, hiding the glow of her skin and making her seem wilder. Fiercer. Ocean-blue eyes met his, and Aren's heart thudded hard in his chest, a familiar aching need taking hold of his body. But he only nodded and started toward the roar of the ocean.

Four soldiers sat in the cover to either side of the shipbreaker, two of them panning the fog with the disinterest of those who'd been at a tedious task too long. The other two faced inland, but they were eating a lunch of bread and dried meat, glancing up only occasionally. Jor lifted his bow, silently nocking an arrow as a throwing knife appeared in Lara's hand.

But these men weren't alone. Patrols moved along the perimeter of the island, groups of men with their eyes on the seas, not nearly as distracted as Aren had hoped.

Holding still as a group of men joined the four, Aren clenched his teeth, fighting the urge to attack even though he knew they were grossly outnumbered.

Then the wind began to rise.

Aren heard it before he saw it, the rustle of leaves and branches as the breeze rolled across the island. It gusted again, gaining strength, the mist swirling violently.

An alarm bell sounded from the far side of the island, and Aren smiled.

"Attack! Attack! The Ithicanians are attacking!" The shouts raced across Gamire, along with orders to move to position, the Maridrinian soldiers pulling weapons and dropping low, several scanning the mist, which remained thick on this side of the island.

The wind rose higher, and on the far side of Gamire, it would already have dissipated the fog, revealing the dozen boats full of Ithicanians panicking as their cover was blown away. Or at least, pretending to panic.

Sure enough, the sound of shipbreakers being deployed filled the air with their familiar crack, the Maridrinians lobbing stones at vessels full of Ithicanians well aware of the weapons' range and exactly how quickly they could be reloaded. Already, they'd be moving inside the weapons' range, using all the tools in their disposal to make the Maridrinians believe it was a genuine attack.

Not the decoy that it was.

An explosion sounded, then another, followed by the call for reinforcements.

One of the Maridrinians guarding the breaker rose to his feet, then lifted a spyglass as though it could pierce the fog, shaking his head in agitation.

Go, Aren silently urged him, knowing it was a matter of minutes before the wind cleared the mist from this side of Gamire, revealing the true threat. *Go!*

"Shit!" One of the men in the patrol snarled the word in agitation, instinct warning him where his eyes failed him. But several more explosions and calls for assistance could not be ignored. "You four stay with the shipbreaker," he ordered. "Under no circumstances do you leave, understood?"

There was a crunch of underbrush as he and the rest of the Maridrinians raced across the island to join the defense.

And not a moment too soon.

The wind was blowing hard and steady now, and Aren's practiced eye caught movement on the water: Boats silently moving into position.

"What is that?" one of the soldiers manning the breaker said. "It looks like a—"

Aren lunged, the twang of Jor's bow filling his ears. One soldier clutched the arrow piercing his chest, another falling sideways, Lara's knife embedded in his spine. The other two soldiers spun around, Aren's blade taking off one's head. But before he could kill the other, Lara's booted foot crushed the man's throat.

The soldier stumbled back, eyes wide, mouth flapping as he gasped for air, but Lara only twisted and kicked out again, foot hitting him square in the chest and sending him flying off the cliff onto the rocks below.

Aren glared at her, annoyed that she had ignored his plan, but before he could say anything, the boats advanced toward the cliffs, his soldiers deftly leaping off to land on the rocks revealed by low tide. Jor was already removing the shipbreaker's spare ropes, knotting them to the weapon and then throwing them down to aid the climb.

In minutes, there were dozens of Ithicanians surrounding Aren, and if all had gone to plan, the same would be happening at the breakers the rest of his crew had secured.

"Show them the same mercy they showed us," he said, then led his army across the island.

ARREN HAD BEEN afraid that his people wouldn't follow him. That they wouldn't trust him to lead them into battle. To lead Ithicana back to freedom.

But Lara had never doubted him.

The Ithicanians moved across Gamire Island without hesitation, their king in the lead, confidence radiating from him with every stride as he deployed his army to attack the enemy from the rear.

Lara had been raised to fight. But she hadn't been raised to lead men and women into battle. Not the way Aren had. And it wasn't that his strategies and tactics were masterful—though they were. It was that every warrior following him knew that he'd fight for them. Die for them. They knew that Ithicana was everything to him.

And they tolerated her only because she'd brought him back.

Knife in one hand and sword in the other, Lara followed on Aren's heels across Gamire, moving in the direction of the battle. The Maridrinians had more in numbers, but despite recent history, they didn't expect to be attacked from the rear.

Fire burned from the explosives that the decoy forces had thrown on land, the haze of smoke drifting across the island on the wind. Every few minutes, one of the shipbreakers launched a projectile, the crack filling the air, but judging from the aggrieved shouts, they weren't having much success with their aim. Then a familiar voice filled Lara's ears, and her heart skipped even as Aren stopped in his tracks.

"I'm not helping you attack my own people, you Maridrinian prick." The woman snarled the words, and through the trees, Lara could just make out Aren's cousin.

Taryn wasn't dead.

Lara's body trembled, and if she hadn't already been on her hands and knees, she might have collapsed. Before exiling her from Ithicana, Aren had told her that the young woman had been killed by a shipbreaker as she'd tried to escape Midwatch with warning of the invasion, but somehow, her friend was alive. A flood of relief made Lara realize how deep the guilt she'd felt over Taryn's loss had been. Only to be replaced with the guilt that Taryn had been a prisoner in her own home all these long months.

"Make them work properly, or I'll slit your throat," one the Maridrinian soldiers shouted, lifting a knife.

Taryn only squared her shoulders, the ropes binding her wrists doing nothing to diminish her defiance. "They work fine. You lot just have shitty aim."

The soldier slapped her. Taryn stumbled, then lunged to spit in the man's face. And Lara knew what she was doing. Knew her friend was trying to get herself killed so there'd be no chance that she'd be used against her people.

But there wasn't a chance that Lara was going to let Taryn die without a fight.

Ignoring Aren's frantic hand motions to stay put, Lara moved forward in a crouch, picking up speed as she went.

The Maridrinian soldier lifted his sword, readying to swing when Lara burst from the tree line, her knife flying.

Taryn's eyes widened as the knife sank into the soldier's sword arm, but a lifetime of training had her catch the man's weapon as he dropped it.

"Attack!" Aren shouted from behind her, but Lara barely heard, losing herself to this one piece of the battle.

Raising her sword, she stabbed the man who'd slapped Taryn, then rotated to attack the other soldiers surrounding the shipbreaker.

She was outnumbered ten to one, but Lara had never let bad odds stop her before.

Two of them charged, and she ducked beneath one blade, then parried another, keeping between the men and Taryn, who was using the sword to free her bound wrists.

Then Aren was there.

He sliced open the guts of a soldier before twisting to punch another in the face. It was all she had the chance to see before the Maridrinians attacked.

She relied on speed rather than strength, anticipating strikes and moving out of the way only to dance back in for the kill. But she was handicapped by the need to protect Taryn, to keep them away until she was free and could fight.

One of the men punched Lara, and she stumbled, barely evading a strike to her knees. Rolling, she came up to her feet, her eyes latching onto one of the injured soldiers as he lifted his knife.

Holding his guts in with one hand, he stumbled toward Taryn, rage in his eyes.

"No!" Lara threw herself into the man's path.

Pain burned down the side of her leg, but she ignored it, raising her weapon to block any downward strike.

Only to see Taryn stab the soldier in the face.

The other woman pulled the weapon loose, watching dispassionately as the man fell. Then she met Lara's gaze, arm wavering as she lifted her sword. Ready to strike.

Lara didn't move.

But Taryn only said, "Killing you won't change anything," and without another word, she ran into the fray.

—— 49
AREN

GAMIRE WAS LIBERATED.

It was one island out of dozens, but the victory felt as sweet as any he'd ever had. The Ithicanian prisoners who had been kept on the island were, if not well, at least alive, and Aren had allowed them the satisfaction of executing their captors.

"We thought you were dead," he said to Taryn, filling her cup with wine, noticing how the hand that held it trembled. "Lia saw the stone hit your boat. You went under. Didn't come up. If we'd known you were alive—"

"I managed to swim to the cove." Her words were toneless. "They decided I had more worth as a prisoner than as a corpse."

And Maridrinians were notoriously hard on their prisoners. Aren knew that firsthand. "I'm sorry, I—"

"Why is she here, Aren? Why isn't she *dead?*"

"A lot has happened that you don't know about. Things have changed." He exhaled in frustration. "Lara saved your life, Taryn.

Despite everything she's done, can you at least be grateful for that?"

It was the wrong thing to say. A stupid thing to say. Aren knew it the moment the words exited his mouth, though Taryn confirmed it by tossing her wine in his face.

"She ruined my life!" she screamed. "It would've been better if she'd stabbed me in the heart!"

The soldiers nearby had paused in their celebrations, all of them watching the exchange.

"When the war is won, she'll leave. She's only here to fight."

Taryn's hands balled into fists, and she gave a shake of her head. "Be sure that she does." Then she stormed away through the village. Lia handed off her drink to chase after her.

"Lia will talk to her." Jor came up next to him. "She'll explain what's happened."

Except everyone around him *knew* that explanation, and it had changed nothing. Draining his cup, Aren turned, searching the soldiers for a sign of Lara. He'd seen her earlier helping to clear the island, but now, she was nowhere in sight. And God knew there were plenty of men and women on this island with cause to try to kill her.

He started through the village, his mind occupied only with finding the familiar gleam of blond hair. Those blue eyes. The face he saw in his dreams.

But all he saw were Ithicanians.

Unease bit in his stomach, and he turned toward Jor. "Where is Lara?"

I T HURT.

God, it was deep, and it hurt, and even with the bandage she'd wrapped tight, blood was running hot down her leg. It took all of her willpower not to limp as they searched the village for any Maridrinians who might have survived the attack. Aren issued orders, entirely in his element.

It was working. His plan was working, and assuming Valcotta and Harendell played their parts, tomorrow Northwatch and Southwatch would fall, and Ithicana would once again hold the bridge. Aren would once again be Ithicana's king.

But Lara would be in no position to fight if she couldn't get her bleeding to stop. Already, she could barely walk.

Clenching her teeth, Lara eyed Aren and the rest, most of whom were gathered around the large fire in the center of the town, the intent to make it appear as though the Maridrinians were still in control of the island. Fish smoked on the grill, and several flasks were being passed from hand to hand, while one of the healers tended to the injured.

Instead of joining them, Lara limped up the pathway toward Nana's home, sword held loosely in one hand, though she was too spent to use it. Reaching the building, she cautiously opened the door, holding the lantern to illuminate the interior.

The Maridrinian soldiers had been inside, probably searching for anything valuable, judging from the mess. The snake cages were gone, though whether Nana had released the creatures or brought them with her to Eranahl, Lara couldn't say.

Going to the toppled shelves, she searched through the mess of jars and broken glass until she found what she needed, then set her lantern on the table and began to unravel the blood-soaked bandage from her thigh.

A fresh flood poured down her leg, and Lara grimaced as she eased off her torn trousers to reveal the injury. A clean slice just below her hip, but nearly down to the bone.

"Shit." She fought the flash of nausea that passed over her, a mixture of fear and pain and blood loss threatening to crack her composure.

Mixing the herbs into a bowl with some rainwater, she cleaned the injury, breath coming in short little gasps from the sting of the solution. But she knew the worst was yet to come.

Her hands shook, and it took several attempts to thread the needle. Trembling, she eased on top of the table, angling the bleeding injury into the light.

"You can do this." She hated how breathy her voice was, the world around her pulsing in and out of focus. "Just get it done."

Clenching her teeth, Lara pushed the wound together, the injured muscle slippery beneath her fingers. Then she jabbed the needle through.

A sob tore from her lips, and she twisted to press her forehead against the table, fighting the dizziness before pulling the thread and knotting it. Taking a deep breath, she pressed the needle against her flesh again, but her hands were shaking so hard she lost her grip on the muscle.

Tears poured down her cheeks as she struggled to get it back into place, to get a grip on the needle with her blood-soaked fingers.

Then familiar hands closed on her wrists. Lifting her face, she met Aren's gaze, the lantern light flickering in his hazel eyes.

"Why didn't you ask for help?"

"Because I don't have the right to ask any of them for anything," she said between sobs, turning her face away. "It's fine. I can do it. I just need a minute."

But Aren didn't let go of her wrists and held them steady as he bent to examine her injury. "It's deep."

"Once I stitch it, it will be okay."

"By the time you finish stitching, you'll have bled to death." He released her wrists. "I'll do it."

"You don't—" She broke off, the look on his face silencing her protest.

Finding some soap, he washed his hands in a basin, and she took this moment of distraction to watch him. To memorize his face. This was the first time they'd been alone together since their trek to Valcotta. And for all she knew, it could be the last.

"You need to stop doing this."

"Doing what?" she asked, though she knew what he meant.

"Throwing yourself into harm's way." He scrubbed hard at his skin, washing away dirt and the blood of his enemies. "It won't change anything other than eventually getting you killed." His voice went hoarse as he said *killed,* and Lara's chest tightened.

"Taryn's alive. She's free. That's something."

"It doesn't negate the fact that you caused her to be taken prisoner in the first place." His hands stilled. "It doesn't change how everyone thinks of you."

As a liar. As a traitor. As the enemy. Pulling her gaze from Aren's hands, Lara stared at the blood welling up from the gash on her leg and fought to suppress the hiccups from her bout of tears. "I'm not trying to change the way everyone thinks of me. I know that will never happen."

"Why, then?" His voice was angry. "Trying to get yourself killed?"

"No." Her throat tightened. "Trying to find a way to live with myself."

She sensed rather than saw him lift his head. Felt his scrutiny as he asked, "Is it working?"

Closing her eyes, Lara focused on the pain in her leg, trying to drown out the pain in her heart. "Not yet."

Aren's boots made soft thuds as he circled the table, and a tremble tore through Lara's body as he took hold of her leg, his hands warm against her naked skin.

"Do you want something to bite down on?"

She shook her head, pressing her forehead against the table as he pulled the lantern closer. She clenched her hands into fists as he picked up the needle, the tug of the thread sending bites of pain lancing up her thigh. "Just do it."

Her words were nothing but bravado, a sob tearing from her lips as Aren delved into the wound, drawing her flesh together, her self-control fracturing with each pass of the needle. She clawed at the table, her body shuddering so hard the light from the lantern danced wildly.

At some point, she passed out, coming to and finding Aren's bloody hands resting on her leg. Sweat beaded on his brow and his eyes were red. "Worst is over," he muttered, then he rethreaded the needle, pulling her skin together for another layer of stitches. "Given the amount of grief you gave me for so much as flinching every time you stitched me up, you're handling this rather poorly."

She gasped out a laugh. "I hate stitches. I'd rather be stabbed than stitched up."

"You're being a baby. It's not that bad."

"Asshole." But their eyes met, and the look in his chased away her pain. This was hurting him as much as it was hurting her. "Thank you."

"Thank you for saving my cousin."

One victory in a sea of loss, but the tension in Lara's chest still eased.

He finished her stitches, wrapping a length of bandage around her leg and knotting it with a practiced hand. Sitting upright, Lara slid off the table onto her feet, but a wave of dizziness made her sway, and she reached out instinctively to catch hold of his shoulders.

She expected him to push her away, but instead his hands slipped around her waist, holding her steady. And though Lara knew she shouldn't, she rested her forehead against his chest, feeling the heat of him through his clothes.

"You've lost a lot of blood." His voice was low, breath warm against her ear. "You need to rest."

He was right, but she was afraid to show any weakness. Afraid that they'd leave her behind if she was no longer any use to them. That she'd lose her chance to atone. "I'll be fine."

"Lara—"

"I just need something to eat and drink." Her knees were wobbling, betraying her. "Please don't leave me behind. Please let me fight."

"You can barely stand."

"Please," she choked out. "I know I have no right to ask anything from you, but please don't take away my chance to see this through. I have to make him pay. I have to force him out of Ithicana. I have to. If I don't—"

Aren's fingers flexed slightly where they gripped her, as if he knew what she'd left unsaid. He understood her like no one else ever had. "We're not going anywhere until morning," he finally answered. "We'll see how you are then."

Exhaling a shuddering breath, Lara nodded into his chest, waiting for him to step away from her and go back to the others. But Aren didn't drop his hands. Didn't turn his back on her. Instead he pulled her closer, his fingers sliding under the hem of her ruined camisole, stroking the small of her back.

Lara's heart accelerated, the fog of blood loss and exhaustion receding, her focus sharpening as her breasts pressed against him. Her hips. She slid her arms around his neck, his hair brushing against her bare forearms and sending a shiver through her body even as fear reared its head. Fear that this was a trick or a delusion, and that if she moved, she'd shatter the dream and he'd be gone.

But she refused to allow fear to rule her, and so Lara looked up.

Aren's eyes were closed, but she could see the rapid flutter of the pulse in his throat. Could feel the raggedness of his breath against her cheek as he lowered his face, one hand sliding up her body to tangle in her hair.

His lips a hair's breadth from hers, he whispered, "Awake or asleep, all I see is your face. All I hear is your voice. All I feel is you in my arms. All I want is *you*."

Lara was trembling. Or he was. She couldn't tell. Not when it seemed the world was tilting, her body aching in a way that had nothing to do with the injury to her leg. "Aren—"

His lips silenced her, mouth closing over hers with a fierceness that made her knees buckle, only his arm around her waist keeping her upright as his tongue chased over hers, tearing a gasp from her throat. She clung to his neck as he devoured her, teeth scraping over her jaw, catching the lobe of her ear, biting at her throat.

In one swift motion, he pulled her camisole over her head and tossed it aside, his hands encircling her ribs, then rising to cup her breasts. He pushed her back against the table, eyes dark with desire as they raked over her nearly naked body.

Lara gripped the table for balance, watching as he tugged his tunic over his head, revealing the tanned skin and hard lines of his chest, his body somehow more perfect for the scars that marked it.

He unbuckled his belt, the weight of the weapons hanging from it pulling his trousers low. Dragging them down to reveal paler skin, then hipbones, then *all* of him, and the sight nearly undid her.

Lara started to slide to her knees, but he caught her by the hips, his thumbs hooking the waist of her undergarments, easing them over her bandage. He knelt, kissing her navel as his hands chased back up her legs, fingers teasing her thighs apart.

"You're perfect," he growled, and she could feel the heat of his breath against the slick wetness of her sex, dragging a whimper of anticipation from her lips as he spread her wide, fingers sliding inside her even as he lowered his face to consume her.

Lara sobbed as pleasure stole over her, need that had long been denied building in her core as his tongue teased over her sensitive flesh, his fingers stroking deeper, her body turning liquid beneath his touch. She ground against him, her fingers caught in his hair, the world spinning faster and faster until she was on the brink, and then in one swift motion, Aren was back on his feet.

"Not yet," he murmured, bending to kiss one of her breasts, his mouth hot as he sucked one nipple, then the other, her body shaking as his teeth scraped over them.

She wrapped one arm around his neck, kissing him. With the other, she caught hold of his cock, smiling as he groaned against her lips, his muscles flexing as she took hold of his length. She stroked it from tip to stem, stoking his desire as she pulled him toward the edge of breaking. Then she breathed into his ear, "I need you in me."

He turned her, his mouth tracing lines of fire down her neck, nipping at her shoulder. His fingers interlaced with hers as he bent her over the table, neither of them caring as their hands slid through the mess of blood, knocking her weapons to the floor with a clatter.

"There is no one in the world like you." His chest pressed against her back, and she could feel the thud of his heart. Could feel his cock between her thighs, turning her body to fire as she pushed back against him, needing him to fill her. Needing him to finish her. "You are my goddamned damnation, but there will never be anyone but you."

Then he drove into her.

A scream of pleasure ripped from Lara's throat as he thrust into her, over and over, the feel of him in her somehow both familiar and new, the sensation driving her to madness. Her shoulders shuddered, elbows giving way beneath his strength, the only thing keeping her from collapsing his arm around her torso, the other braced against the tabletop.

There was a wildness to it. A desperation, as if they'd both been deprived too long of water and needed to drink. Lara screamed as her pleasure built, then climaxed, every ounce of strength left in her used up by the intensity, even as it pulled Aren over the edge. He slammed into her, gasping her name, both of them collapsing against the table.

Spent past the point of endurance, Lara barely felt him as he lifted her and carried her to the bed. His arms wrapped around her as she slipped into oblivion.

When she woke hours later, she found herself curled around him, her face pressed against his chest, the steady *thud thud* of his heart beating in her ear. She inhaled, the familiar scent of him filling her nose, his hand pressed against the small of her back. It was the place she was meant to be—the place she hadn't dared hope to ever find herself in again. Yet instead of contentment, a sense of trepidation crawled through her veins.

Aren was awake; she could tell from the sound of his breathing. And yet he was entirely still, his hand stiff against her back rather than moving with the gentle strokes and caresses she was used to waking to.

Something wasn't right.

She lifted her face. Aren was staring at the ceiling, his expression barely visible from the light of the lantern across the room. But at her motion, he shifted, easing out from under her and swinging his legs over the side of the bed.

"Where are you going?" Her voice rasped and she coughed to clear her throat.

"I need to take a turn on patrol."

It was an excuse. She reached for his hand, needing him to stay. Needing to extend this moment that in her heart she'd known was too good to be true. "Let someone else do it."

But he was already across the room, pulling on his clothes, his back to her.

"Aren." She fell out of bed, her legs tangling in a sheet, dizziness forcing her to pause as she stood. "Don't go."

His hands stilled on his belt, then he finished buckling it and reached for his boots, dragging them on. "This was a mistake."

"It wasn't. Don't say that."

"It was. I promised my people we were done. What we did tonight is no better than me spitting in their faces."

It was like a vice clamped around her chest, tightening until it hurt to breathe.

"I can't be around you, Lara. I can't risk this happening again."

She knew he was right, but still she said, "I love you."

Aren only walked toward the door. He paused with his hand on the latch, before turning to look at her. "I'm sorry."

Then he disappeared into the night.

51
AREN

A REN STUMBLED HALF a dozen times walking down the path
to the village; it was a small miracle that he didn't step on
a snake or twist an ankle, his mind everywhere but on the
ground in front of him.

Her sob as he'd left had been worse than a knife to the gut, the
anguish in it a thousand times greater than when he'd stitched up her
leg. All he wanted was to go back. To scoop her up and lose himself
in her. To keep her safe until she was strong. To never be away from
her again.

Except every time he closed his eyes, he saw the expressions that
would cross his people's faces if they discovered what he'd done.
If they discovered that he, their king, had taken the woman who'd
betrayed them back into his bed.

Back into his heart.

He barely noticed the nods of his soldiers on watch as he made his
way toward the center of the village, to the faint glow of the fire and
the lone shadow sitting next to it.

"Took an awfully long time to stitch up that leg, even for you," Jor drawled, then stretched until his back cracked. "She all right?"

Lara wasn't anywhere close to all right, but Jor didn't need to know that. "Will be fine as long as it doesn't foul. As long as she keeps off of it."

"Not much chance of that." Jor held out a bottle. "*You* all right?"

Not even close. "I'm fine. Where's Taryn?"

"Lia's with her. Lass had a rough year, but she's strong. Put a weapon in her hand and she'll fight."

The last thing Taryn needed was more violence, but Aren only nodded, trusting Jor's judgment on the matter.

Sitting across the fire, he took a long mouthful from the bottle, staring at the flames. Trying to regain control of his emotions, but the wild twist of hurt and anger and guilt refused to let him be.

"You have to choose, you know." Jor took the bottle back, drinking deeply. "Between her and Ithicana. You can't have both."

"I don't want her." As if saying it could make it true.

"Could've fooled me with the sounds coming out of Nana's house."

Aren stiffened, then glared at the other man, but Jor only shrugged. "You don't honestly believe we aren't all keeping a close watch on you, do you, boy? We only just got you back, and we aren't keen to lose you again. Especially not to her."

"It was a mistake. It won't happen again."

"Right."

"I just needed to get her out of my system."

Jor handed him back the bottle. "You could bed that woman every night for the rest of your life and never get her out of your system, Aren. That's the trouble with love."

Aren clenched his teeth, wishing he could will away the ache in his chest.

"Ithicana is never going to accept a queen they can't trust. Especially not one who has already caused so much hurt and loss. And if you stay with her, it won't be long until they don't trust you either."

Part of Aren wondered how his people could trust him *now.*

Wondered why they still followed him after all the endless mistakes that he'd made. Continued to make. "I made my choice."

"Then you need to send her away now. Keep her around and *that*"—he gestured in the direction of Nana's house—"that will keep happening. It needs to be over. A clean break."

The thought of leaving Lara *now,* when she was at her weakest, made him want to vomit.

But Jor was right.

Taking one more mouthful, Aren stood. "Gather everyone and get the boats ready. We move on Midwatch tonight."

L ARA ROSE SLOWLY from the depths of sleep, her eyelashes sticking as she peeled open her eyes and blinked in the faint light filtering through the window. The throbbing ache of her leg was rivaled by that of her skull, and her mouth felt as dry as sand.

Pushing up onto her elbow, Lara eased her legs over the side and stood, wincing at the pain that lanced through her body as she limped over to the table where a pitcher of water sat next to a glass. Someone obviously brought it in the night. *Was it Aren?* She immediately rejected the thought. He'd meant what he'd said: Last night wasn't an error he'd repeat.

Her eyes stung, but she rubbed at them furiously, refusing to cry anymore. It was done. They were done. All that mattered now was liberating Ithicana and having her revenge on her father.

But the only way that was going to happen was if she could prove that she could keep up. That she could still fight.

Going to Nana's shelves, she searched the contents for pain suppressants as well as stimulants to compensate for exhaustion. Shoving them in a bag along with clean bandages for her injury, she started down the path to the village.

Her skin prickled with unease at the silence, the only sound the roar of the ocean in the distance and the faint breeze rustling the tree branches. The air smelled of damp earth and vegetation, but she caught no trace of woodsmoke or cooking food. Peering upward, she tried to pinpoint where the sun was through the clouds and the trees, but it was next to impossible to determine the hour. Given Aren had planned to leave in the morning to take Midwatch, it must still be early.

Then the clouds shifted, revealing a sliver of sunshine to the west.

Ignoring her pain, Lara broke into a run.

She reached the village in minutes, her stomach plummeting as she searched for signs of someone. For anyone. But the Ithicanians were gone.

Aren had left her.

A scream tore from her throat, and Lara dropped to the ground, hammering her fists into the dirt in a fruitless attempt to ease her anger. Her frustration. Her hurt.

What was the point? Why was she even trying? She wasn't wanted here—not by the Ithicanians and not by Aren. So why should she stay?

Because you promised. Because you said you wouldn't stop fighting until Ithicana was free.

Then the faint sound of a horn filled her ears, distant. It repeated, closer this time, then again farther off, the signal moving north. Passing the word.

Word that the Valcottans had been victorious at Southwatch.

It was over. Just like that, it was over.

Ithicana was free.

Pressing her face into the dirt, Lara wept.

H AULING THE DYING Maridrinian soldier's head back by his hair, Aren pulled his knife across the man's throat, then dropped him back into the mud, surveying the battleground around him.

The Maridrinians had been ready for them—not that it had done them any good. Aren and his forces had climbed the cliffs and taken the garrison from behind in a fevered hand-to-hand battle that he knew had cost him. Now, healers scrambled to aid the fallen.

How many had died in the fight to retake the bridge? Hundreds. Possibly more. Compounded on those lost when it had fallen, and in the year since. Catastrophic numbers.

It was enough to make him sick.

Then the sound of horns filled his ears. The message rippled past Midwatch, moving north, and he exhaled a ragged breath even as his soldiers began to cheer.

Valcotta had taken Southwatch. Zarrah had delivered on her word.

And if the battle proceeded as planned, it wouldn't be long until Northwatch conceded to Harendell, and Ithicana would be free.

Except the last thing Aren felt was victorious.

Wiping his knife on the dead man's uniform, Aren started up the path toward his home, stepping over corpses as he went, the sun already low in the west.

It didn't take him long to reach the clearing containing the Midwatch house—the home his father had built for his mother. The home he'd given to Lara back when he'd had ambitions and dreams for a better life for his people.

A fool's dreams.

The front door hung from broken hinges, and even before Aren stepped inside, he knew the Maridrinians had used the home hard, the smell coming from within nearly stopping him in his tracks. Of soldier and filth. Spilled wine and rotting food.

Of death.

But he forced himself to go inside, blade in hand in case one of the Maridrinians had escaped the slaughter. The floor was covered with dirt, the paneled walls cracked, artwork either missing or destroyed. The table in the entranceway was overturned, a dead Maridrinian on the ground next to it, his opened guts already buzzing with flies. Aren glanced into the dining room, eyes moving over the stacks of filthy dishes and shattered glass, the floor covered with broken wine bottles from what was likely now a looted wine cellar.

He kept on down the hallway, glancing into rooms as he passed until he reached the door to his own, which was ajar, a naked dead man in his bed. A whimper caught Aren's attention, and he turned to find a Maridrinian woman hiding in the corner. "Get out," he said, and she scuttled past him and into the hallway. Someone else could figure out what to do with her.

Aren surveyed the room, the dead soldier's belongings interspersed with his own, waiting for a reaction in himself. For some form of emotion. Sadness. Anger. Anything.

But all he felt was numb, so he walked out into the courtyard, striding to the center where he'd once stood in the eye of a storm and made the most catastrophic decision of his life.

More horns sounded, this time word coming from Northwatch that the Harendellians had the island under their control.

Aren stared at the waterfall. At the discarded wine bottle bobbing in the pool, steam rising around it.

He felt nothing. For anything. Not even this place.

Abandoning the courtyard, Aren went back inside, taking up an unlit lamp sitting on his desk and splashing the oil across the carpets. Across the bed. He went from room to room doing the same until he came across a glowing lamp. Picking it up, he held the flame to a splatter of oil, watching as it ignited. Fire crossed the room that had been Ahnna's, burning up carpets and linens and curtains. Smoke filled the air.

He retreated through the house, setting rooms aflame as he went, and only when he began to cough and choke on the smoke did he step outside. To find Jor standing in the clearing, waiting.

"It's done." The old soldier watched the house, the interior now an inferno, flames licking out of the broken windows of the dining room. "The Maridrinians are defeated."

"I heard."

"Wasn't much of a fight." Jor's voice was low.

"Tell that to the dead."

The other man exhaled a long breath, then shook his head. "You know what I mean. For months we fought tooth and nail trying to evict the bastards, and they pushed us back at every turn. Only to concede in a matter of days?"

"We didn't have Harendell and Valcotta as allies before."

Jor grimaced. "Even so. Doesn't feel right, which I expect is why you're here burning your house down rather than celebrating at the barracks."

Nothing felt right. Aren stared at the flames, wondering if Lara had finally awoken. If she was all right. How she had reacted when she realized that he'd left her.

Feel something! What is wrong *with you?*

Distantly, Aren heard the sound of horns, but he couldn't pick out the message over the roar of the flames.

"She'll be all right," Jor said. "We left her everything she needed. Likely, she's already on her way back to her sisters. They'll take care of her."

"I know."

"You made the right choice."

"I know."

"There will be other women. You'll find one you like—a good Ithicanian girl. Give the kingdom an heir to make everyone happy."

There'd never be another. Not like her.

But maybe that was for the best. Maybe it was better not to care so much because then his loyalties wouldn't be divided. He could focus on rebuilding Ithicana. On making his people strong again.

"Your Grace!" Aren turned, seeing one of his soldiers sprinting up the path toward them. He skidded to a halt, gasping for breath.

"What is it?" Jor shouted over the roar of the blaze. "Another attack?"

"Did you not hear the horns?"

"Obviously not. What did they say?"

The soldier wiped away the sweat dribbling down his face. "There was no battle at Southwatch."

Aren's stomach plummeted. "The signal was a false? Maridrina still holds the island?"

"No, Your Grace. When the Valcottans attacked, they found the island abandoned. And we're getting messages that our teams are finding most of the garrisons barely manned. No sign of the Maridrinian or Amaridian fleets anywhere."

Aren's skin prickled with unease. "What of Northwatch?"

"We've sent the query, but no response as yet."

As soon as the man said the words, Aren heard the blasts of horns in the distance, the message rippling through the signalmen and women strategically placed down the length of Ithicana.

Aren's eyes met Jor's. "They knew what we were planning."

"How? Even if they'd caught sight of the Valcottan fleet moving toward Southwatch, it wouldn't have been enough time for them to evacuate."

"Keris." Swearing, Aren kicked at the dirt. "He was on the beach when Zarrah and her crew came to shore to save our asses. He would have learned that the Empress had declined to help us, which meant that Zarrah was working on her own."

"But why tell Silas? Wouldn't it be better for Keris if his father lost the bridge?"

"To protect Zarrah. No battle. No losses. No treason. The Empress won't be happy with her, but she's unlikely to execute her. She might even keep her as heir, which is what Keris needs."

But something about the situation felt wrong. They'd retaken Southwatch without a fight, but it didn't feel like a victory. "It's not like Silas to retreat."

"Maybe Keris made him see reason."

"Unlikely." Aren *knew* the King of Maridrina. Knew the other man would never concede. And in that heartbeat, Aren knew exactly what Silas intended.

The bridge was not Ithicana. Its people were.

His stomach dropped.

Aren broke into a sprint up the hill, neither noticing nor caring if the others followed. All that mattered was getting to high ground.

The sun was little more than a glow in the west, casting long shadows as Aren skidded on the muddy path, his heart hammering in his chest.

Faster.

He hit the open ground at the top of the low mountain, racing toward the lookout tower. The steps were neglected, covered in debris, but he took them two at a time, hitting the top at the moment the sun set, casting Ithicana into darkness.

Aren snatched hold of the spyglass, but then his hand dropped to his side because he didn't need it.

In the distance, glowing in brilliant oranges and reds, was an enormous signal fire. A sight he'd never seen in all his life and had prayed he never would.

Jor shouted from across the clearing. "What is it?"

"Eranahl." The word came out strangled. "They're calling for aid."

S HE LIMPED ALONG the top of the bridge, heading south toward Maridrina.

Logically, Lara knew she should've stayed at Gamire Island until her injury had started to heal, or at least until she no longer felt the effects of all the blood she'd lost. There was food and shelter, along with all the medical supplies she might need.

But the thought of remaining in Ithicana without Aren was more than she could bear, so instead she'd packed what she needed and climbed the pier, not at all interested in being confined inside the bridge. Not when every breath was already a struggle.

She heard the horns relaying the message that Northwatch had been secured by the Harendellian navy, along with a series of others that she hadn't been able to make sense of.

And what did it matter, anyway? Ithicana was free, liberated from Maridrina and her father. It was what she'd wanted, what she'd been fighting for. What she'd believed would finally lift the burden of guilt that she'd been carrying for so long and allow her to carry on with life.

Except she felt the same. Felt worse, because at least before she'd had a goal. Something she'd been working toward.

Now she had nothing left but her need for revenge against her father. But thinking about that only left her cold.

So she walked, her direction determined by the path of the bridge and nothing else. The sun slowly set in the west, but she didn't stop. Didn't consider where she might spend the night. Didn't eat from her supplies or drink from the waterskin strapped to her waist.

Step.

Step.

Step.

Then a glow caught her attention, burning reds and oranges that made it seem as though the sun were reversing its course through the sky. Squinting, she peered at the glow, her pulse accelerating as she realized it was an enormous signal fire, visible only because it had been lit at the highest point in Ithicana.

And there was only one reason for the Ithicanians to light that flame.

Eranahl was under attack.

"**E**VERYONE WHO CAN FIGHT, into a boat!" Aren raced down to the beach where his soldiers were already moving vessels into the water.

"We've got dozens of injured." Jor was panting hard trying to keep up. "We can't just leave them."

"They'll manage." Aren climbed into the boat that Lia, Aster, and the rest of the crew had readied, their masks already in place. He pulled his own loose from his belt, the leather still splattered with blood from the fight to retake Midwatch. "If Eranahl falls, it will be slaughter."

"It could be a ruse." Jor climbed in after him. "A way to draw us out and fight us in the open."

"We've already fallen for the ruse. Silas knew we'd pull every soldier into retaking the bridge. He left only enough soldiers behind to ensure we took the bait. And now he's attacking Eranahl while our backs are turned."

Aren looked up at the stars, charting his route. All his life, he'd been told that to defeat Ithicana meant taking the bridge, but Maridrina had proven that false. Defeating Ithicana meant destroying its people. Without them, what did the bridge matter?

Silas, it seemed, had learned from his mistakes.

But the King of Maridrina was wrong if he believed he'd won, because Aren refused to let Eranahl fall without a fight.

S HE NEEDED A boat. Needed to get on the water and make her way
to Eranahl. What she could do once she got there, Lara didn't
know.

Didn't care.

A small jar of glowing algae in hand, she ran with reckless speed
down the length of the bridge, moving toward Snake Island where
they'd left the boats. Praying they were still there.

Her leg screamed, blood soaking into the bandage wrapped
around it, but instead of stopping, Lara shoved a pinch of one of the
medicines she'd taken from Nana's house into her mouth. It was only
a matter of minutes until she felt the stimulant take hold, driving away
exhaustion and pain and leaving behind nothing but the desire to fight.

She slowed only to peer at the mile markers stamped on the top of
the bridge, coming to a stop at the one she knew was near the island.
Below, the waves roared onto the beach, smashing against the piers,
but all her eyes revealed was blackness.

Lying on her stomach, she listened intently, finally picking up on the sound of water lapping against steel-plated hulls. The boats were still there.

But how to get down to them?

Descending the pier onto the island would be suicide with no way to bait the snakes away from the path. And the next closest pier was designed to deter climbers—she'd only fall and find herself impaled on one of the countless spikes.

The only choice she had was to jump and swim to the sandbar where the boats were moored.

Using algae to mark the side of the bridge above the moored boat, Lara set the empty jar down and started walking until she was over deeper water. The sweat running down her back turned cold as she found the approximate spot where Aren had once jumped, knowing if she misjudged that it would be a fatal leap. Too close to the island and she'd hit the shallows of the sandbar.

Too far out and she'd never make the long swim to the boat, especially if she got disoriented in the darkness.

Or if what prowled these waters came to investigate.

Lara's heart hammered a rapid beat against her chest, her breath coming in fast little gasps, her terror rising with every passing second. She lifted her gaze to regard the glowing signal flames coming from Eranahl and, taking a deep breath, she jumped.

Air rushed past, the darkness swallowing her as she fell. Then her feet hit the water and she was plunging down into the depths. Down and down, and panic raced like wildfire through her veins.

Swim! You will not die here tonight!

Kicking hard, she swam upward, her chest burning, but then her head broke the surface. Lara gasped in a desperate breath, awkwardly treading water as she rose and fell on the swells, searching for the algae she'd used to mark the bridge.

Paddling with her arms and kicking her legs, she slowly made her way in the direction of the sandbar. She was certain that at any second something would grab hold of her legs and tear her down into the depths, and she shrieked in surprise when her feet hit the bottom.

Standing, Lara splashed to the shallows, hands in front of her until she collided with a boat. Lifting the anchor, she waded out, the water rising to her waist, and then she clambered inside, moving by feel. It was bigger than the vessel she'd used to sail in and out of Ithicana, but she'd watched Aren and the rest of them handle these boats countless times. She could do it.

She had to.

Because she refused to let Eranahl fall without a fight.

"**G**OD HELP US," JOR muttered, rising to stand next to Aren, both of them staring at the chaos encircling the island.

There were over a hundred ships, but that wasn't what drew Aren's attention. It was the numerous fires burning on Eranahl's slopes. The shipbreakers, the island's primary line of defense, had been reduced to rubble and ash.

It was a gain, however, that had cost Silas badly.

Ships burned and listed, some sinking, the waves covered with debris. Yet dozens of crafts converged on Eranahl, sailors risking their lives against the towering cliffs as they tossed up grappling hooks.

Aren could make out the shadows of his people fighting to keep them from reaching the top, but archers on the ships were picking them off. The myriad blazes illuminated the sky like it was day.

The only gap in the fleet was near the entrance to the cave leading to Eranahl's underground harbor, and it was a result of the lone remaining shipbreaker still firing projectiles at any vessel that came close. But the soldiers on land were moving on that breaker. If it fell, the full force of Silas's fleet would converge on that cave, the portcullis the only thing that would hold them back.

"Harry them from the rear," he ordered, his words passing to the other vessels. "Keep them distracted."

"Distracted from what exactly?" Jor demanded.

"From us as we try to get inside." Retrieving a horn, Aren blew a series of notes, repeating it three times. His personal signal. He waited, his heart in his chest, then Eranahl answered the call. "Go!"

The sails pulled taut and the vessel flew across the waves, Lia guiding them between the ships, heading toward the mouth of the cave while the rest of his soldiers attacked the rear of the fleet, shooting arrows and deploying explosives in the way only they knew how.

But even with the distraction, it wasn't long until the enemy fleet caught sight of them.

Arrows whistled past his head, forcing them all to duck low, only Lia staying upright where she manned the rudder. Then she shrieked in pain, clutching at her arm. Pulling her down, Aren took hold of the rudder himself to guide them into the dark opening, the rattle of chains filling his ears.

"Hold on," he shouted. The speed they were sailing at verged on suicidal as they hurtled into the cavern, arrows thudding into wood and bouncing off rock.

The boat slammed against the side of the cavern wall, the outrigging smashing, and Aren nearly fell into the water, but the momentum was enough to keep them moving forward.

Beyond, he could see the lights from his people on the other side of the rising portcullis, weapons in hand and faces grim.

And for good reason. Behind him longboats were rowing in pursuit, all of them full to the brim with soldiers.

The mast caught on the half-raised portcullis. "Jump!" he shouted.

With Lia suspended between him and Jor, they all dived into the water, swimming beneath the already lowering portcullis toward the arms of friends waiting to haul them in.

The air filled with the splintering and cracking of the boat as the portcullis smashed into it, dragging it down into the depths, arrows from the encroaching longboats pinging off the heavy steel.

Ducking behind his people's shields, Aren crouched over Lia, examining the arrow wedged in her bicep. Her face was twisted with pain, but she said, "I've had worse. Find me a knife and I'll fight."

"Take her back," he ordered the soldiers in the boat, and without waiting for a response, he jumped into the neighboring vessel, sending both of them rocking wildly.

Half of those in the boat were shooting arrows at the enemy, the rest holding shields and wielding spears to ward off the Maridrinians just beyond the portcullis. An arrow whistled past his ear, and Aren ducked down between two soldiers.

"How kind of you to join us, Your Grace." Ahnna lowered her bow to give him a wild grin, then she dropped the weapon and flung her arms around him, fingers digging into his shoulders.

But this wasn't the time for reunions.

Letting his sister go, Aren peered between shields, seeing the chains and ropes grasped in the Maridrinians' hands, his stomach tightening. "We've only got one breaker still functioning on this side, but it's been damaged. They're starting to breach the cliffs, and we don't have the manpower out there to keep them off for long."

Ahnna's jaw tightened, then she loosed an arrow, taking a Maridrinian in the throat. "We're nearly spent on arrows." She reached in the water to pluck up two that floated past. "I don't know how much longer we can hold them off."

Fear bit at Aren's guts. The enemy outnumbered them, but worse than that, all of Ithicana's vulnerable were in Eranahl. Children. The elderly. Individuals who couldn't fight. And there was no escape.

"We have them in the storage caverns," Ahnna said, reading his thoughts. "Locked and barricaded from the inside."

Which would keep them safe for now, but it would be where they'd all starve if Aren couldn't keep control of the island.

"Last breaker is down!" A voice filtered through the cavern. "They're gaining the cliffs."

"Shit!" Ahnna slammed her fist down on the edge of the boat. But then her eyes turned on Aren. "What do we do?"

He felt the attention of all of his soldiers turning on him even as they fought to keep the enemy back, all of them waiting for him to offer a solution. To lead them toward victory. To be a king.

Crippling panic rose in his chest, but Aren forced it down. *You know how to fight. You know how to defend Ithicana. So do it!*

In the distance, thunder rolled, and a breeze that smelled like lightning and rain and *violence* swept through the cavern. And every one of his soldiers turned their faces into the wind, recognizing that scent.

The tempests that defended Ithicana weren't abandoning the kingdom when it needed them most. Aren only needed to hold out until they arrived.

"Leave me two boats and their crews and take everyone else to defend the cliffs," he ordered his sister. Then to Taryn, who was methodically shooting Maridrinians, a feral expression on her face, he said, "Get that breaker working again."

The boats shifted and rocked as soldiers shifted between them, the men and women who'd grown up with him, who'd fought beside him, who'd followed him all of his life, moving to his side.

Jor settled down on one knee next to him. "If they want this gate, they're going to have to bleed for it!" he shouted, and the cavern echoed with voices repeating him.

Aren stared through the shields, meeting the gazes of the enemy staring back. With one hand, he pulled off his mask and dropped it into the water, smiling as he saw recognition in their eyes.

"For Ithicana!" he shouted, then lifted his blade.

THE ISLAND WAS on fire.

Lara stared in horror, her hands growing slack on the ropes she'd only moments ago gripped so fiercely.

She was too late.

Even with the masses of ships between her vessel and the island, she could make out the swarms of enemy soldiers climbing the cliffs, the riot of fighting between Maridrinians and Ithicanians on the volcano slopes, the shipbreakers little more than smoldering shapes. Half a dozen ships crowded around the opening to the cavern, longboats full of soldiers lowering to the water and then rowing into the darkness. If the gate hadn't been breached yet, it soon would.

Eranahl was falling.

Pain struck her in the stomach, and Lara doubled over, gripping the sides of the boat, tears running down her face. All night she'd fought with the vessel, slowly working her way between islands toward the glow of Eranahl's signal fires, desperate to reach her home in time to make a difference.

But it had all been for nothing.

Anger abruptly chased away her grief, and Lara slammed her hands down hard. This wasn't how things were meant to turn out. Ithicana was supposed to be free, her father defeated, and now, despite everything she and Aren had done, despite how hard they'd fought, it was over.

Thunder rolled, and Lara lifted her head to watch the lightning in the distance. It had to be near dawn, but black clouds dominated the east, obscuring any hint of the sun. A violent wind rushed over her, her boat already rising and falling on growing swells.

The storms were meant to be the defenders of Ithicana, but even they were too late.

Turning her head back to the island, Lara watched the soldiers clambering up ropes dangling between boats and clifftops. The surf threw itself against the rocks, full of shattered boats and debris and corpses, but still they kept coming.

And the Ithicanians kept fighting.

Lara knew they'd never stop. They'd never surrender, not when everything that mattered to them was within that city. And those were *her* people. People who were struggling and dying while she *watched.*

Straightening, Lara narrowed her eyes at the ships surrounding the island. Then she dug into her pocket for the last of the simulant, not even tasting the concoction of herbs as she chewed and swallowed. Pulling the line in her hand taut, she watched the sail tighten against the wind, carrying her into the battle.

It was dark enough that the ships didn't notice her. As she grew closer, where the fires on the slopes of Eranahl illuminated the water, the soldiers still on the decks shouted and pointed in her direction. Arrows whistled past, hitting the water and striking the boat, and Lara crouched low, keeping her eyes on the cliffs. Searching for gaps in the chaos of longboats and wreckage at the base.

"You'll only get one chance at this," she muttered, picking her spot. "And if you fail, you're dead."

Her blood raced through her veins, urged on by adrenaline and stimulant, pain and fear falling away as she dropped the ropes. As she bent her knees, the surf caught hold of her boat and flung it against the cliff walls.

At the last possible moment, she jumped, reaching for handholds even as her boat slammed against the cliff walls, wood shattering.

Pain ricocheted through her as she hit the cliff, her fingernails tearing as she scrabbled at the slick rocks. One hand slipped, and she screamed.

But the other held true.

She dangled for a heartbeat, but the water roared toward her once more, so she shoved her free hand into a crack and pulled.

Water sprayed her, tugging at her ankles. Lara ignored it and climbed. Up and up, her fingers slicing open on the sharp edges, leaving behind smears of blood in her wake.

She barely felt it.

Higher and higher, the noise of the surf replaced by the shouts of Maridrinian soldiers as they rallied at the top, waiting until they had enough numbers to push up the slope.

Then she heard a rumble.

At first Lara thought it was thunder, but then she felt the rock beneath her tremble and realized what the Ithicanians had done.

Panic racing through her, Lara scrambled sideways beneath a tiny overhang, then pressed herself against the wall even as screams filled the air.

Clenching her teeth, Lara shut her eyes as the soldiers above threw themselves off the cliffs into the water below.

It wasn't enough to save them.

An avalanche of rock and debris exploded off the side of the cliff, raining down on the boats and soldiers in the water below. Crushing them or drowning them.

Bits of rock clipped her shoulders, slicing through fabric and flesh, but Lara hugged the cliff, arms and legs trembling with the effort of holding the position.

When the noise ceased, Lara relaxed long enough to look down. The surf was filled with blood and broken bodies, all mixed in among the shattered remains of longboats.

Climb.

But her strength was spent, her body shaking, her nails scraping along rock as she fought to keep her grip.

"Climb!" she shouted to herself.

Reaching up, Lara caught hold of a rock, only for it to come loose. A scream tore from her lips, and then she was falling.

THEY WERE OUT of arrows.

They fought hand to hand, both forces jabbing weapons through the metal bars in an attempt to drive each other back, and on both sides, bodies bobbed thick in the water. But where Aren was down to a dozen soldiers, the Maridrinians just kept coming.

The rising waves were not helping their cause, the surf making it nearly impossible to keep the boats close enough to the portcullis to fight. The Maridrinians slashed at their hands and arms when they tried to hold on to the bars.

Reaching through the portcullis, Aren stabbed a man in the face, but as the soldier slipped into the water, Aren saw what they had in their boat.

A chain, the links as thick as his wrist.

Just then a wave surged, flinging his vessel backward. The Maridrinian longboat slammed against the portcullis, spilling men into the water, but two kept their feet. And as Aren watched in horror, they looped the chain through the bars.

While his soldiers desperately tried to maneuver back to the portcullis, Aren saw the men passing the chain back through the boats packing the tunnel, the ends disappearing from sight.

His boat finally reached the bars, and Aren grabbed hold of the chain, pulling hard, though he knew it was hopeless.

The Maridrinian longboats retreated out of the tunnel, and a heartbeat later, the chain snapped taut.

S HE WAS FALLING.

Then her body jerked to a stop, a strong hand gripping her wrist.

Looking upward, Lara saw Ahnna's face. The princess smirked. "We just can't get rid of you, can we?"

With a violent heave, Ahnna pulled Lara upward, another Ithicanian helping to haul her over the edge, where Lara lay gasping for breath on her back before slowly climbing to her feet.

Ahnna stood with several Ithicanians, all of whom Lara recognized. They were bloody, shoulders bent with exhaustion. But their eyes still gleamed with defiance that said they had no intention of conceding this battle.

"Should we send someone to tell the king?" one of them asked.

"Aren's here?" Lara blurted out.

Ahnna gave the slightest shake of her head at the soldier, then turned to Lara. "He left you behind for a reason, Lara. You aren't wanted here. Tell me why I shouldn't toss you into the water with the rest of your people."

"I'm here to fight for Ithicana." She was here to fight for herself.

Ahnna looked her up and down. "You can barely stand."

Straightening her shoulders, Lara met the taller woman's gaze. "Care to test that theory?"

Before Ahnna could answer, a loud screech of metal split the air.

"What the hell was that?" one of the Ithicanians demanded, but Ahnna only blanched, then took off at a run.

Lara sprinted after her, leaping over debris from the rockslide as they rounded the island. The sun was up now, but in the distance, a wall of storm was racing toward Eranahl, the black clouds dancing with bolts of lightning, the wind howling.

They reached the edge of the rockslide, finding themselves in the thick of the fighting, Ithicanians going hand to hand against Maridrinians and Amaridians, the slope littered with bodies.

Lara threw her knife into one soldier's spine, then sliced her sword across the back of another's knees, not stopping to finish him off as she raced after the princess. The stitches in her leg were giving and tearing, blood running in hot rivulets down her leg, but she ignored the pain.

Ahnna didn't stop to fight, only cut down those who got in the way of her wild race around the volcano. And at the cliff's edge, more and more of the enemy were climbing over, then diving into the fight.

"Ahnna! We need to push them back!"

But the woman ignored her, pressing onward, a flurry of fists and steel that left corpses in her wake. Then the princess skidded to a halt.

"No!" Ahnna shrieked, and Lara tracked her gaze, her stomach dropping as she caught sight of the ship with its sails full of storm winds, ropes stretched out behind it and disappearing into the harbor cavern.

They were pulling out the portcullis.

Another grinding screech pierced Lara's ears, metal dragging along rock, twisting and warping under the strain. And the moment the Maridrinians got it free, the cavern would be flooded by the countless longboats filled with soldiers.

Ahnna abruptly threw herself into the fray, hacking and attacking anyone that stepped into her path. Lara kept on her heels, guarding the woman's back as they pushed toward a large group of Ithicanians defending the cliffside over the entrance to the cave.

"Taryn!" Ahnna shouted her cousin's name, the ranks parting to reveal the young woman working on a shipbreaker, the wood charred, its ropes frayed and blackened. "You need to get that breaker working!"

Taryn shook her head. "I need time, Ahnna. I need to replace the ropes."

"We don't have time! If they pull the gate clear, Aren will be overrun. We have to take out that ship!"

Aren was down there.

Stepping away from the argument, Lara raced to the edge of the cliff and looked down. There were hundreds of soldiers in the boats, all armed to the teeth. If they made it inside the volcano crater, the battle was over.

Wind whipped at Lara's hair, tugging it this way and that, her ears filling with the crash of thunder. The overfilled longboats rose and fell on growing swells, water spilling over the edges. And beneath, shapes moved, large fins cutting through the waves. Even fifty feet above them, Lara saw the fear on the soldiers' faces. Yet none of the boats turned back.

"The Amaridians are retreating!"

The words were repeated over and over, and Lara looked up to see vessels flying the Amaridian flag lifting their sails, abandoning those in longboats and those already on land, fleeing ahead of the coming storm.

Ship after ship abandoned the ring around the island, but the Maridrinians remained, pressing in toward the cavern entrance as the ropes strained, another screech of metal filling the air.

It was a race against the storm. A race for her father's fleet to gain control of the cavern and unload enough of their soldiers to hold the island while the ships fled ahead of the violent winds and rain that would see them all on the bottom of the sea.

Lara knelt frozen in place, knowing she couldn't make it to the cavern entrance in time to do any good.

A wave swamped one of the longboats, the men swimming to

cling to the edges of the other boats, all of which were in danger of sinking.

One by one the swimming men were jerked under the water, blossoms of red rising in the dark seas as Ithicana's sharks feasted on their enemies. And yet the longboats didn't turn back.

What made them want this island so badly that they'd risk death? Was it glory? Wealth?

Fear?

What could be worse than this storm? Worse than the sharks tearing apart their comrades before their very eyes?

A sudden certainty filled Lara's chest, and rising, she snatched a spyglass from one of the Ithicanians' hands. Lifting it to her face, she panned over the ship pulling the portcullis loose, freezing as a familiar man came into her line of sight.

Her father stood on the deck of the ship, arms crossed and eyes fixed on his target, no fear showing on his face.

He was what the soldiers feared. He was what kept the fleet from fleeing ahead of the storm. He was what drove the men onto those deadly waters.

Lowering the spyglass, Lara caught Ahnna by the arm, tugging her toward the cliff's edge. She pointed out over the water. "I need you to get me on that ship."

"**S**WITCHING SIDES AGAIN?" AHNNA'S face darkened, her weapon rising.

Lara shook her head, refusing to be provoked. "My father's on that ship. If you get me down there and I kill him, the fleet will retreat. He's the only thing keeping them in this fight."

Grimacing, Ahnna turned away to bark orders, sending a dozen Ithicanians running up the slopes, then her attention moved back to Lara. "It's impossible. We can't get a vessel out, and even if you could swim worth a damn, you wouldn't last a minute in those waters."

"Lower me onto the rope they're using to pull out the portcullis. I'll climb to the ship."

"They'll shoot you before you get anywhere near the ship. Aren will kill me if he finds out I agreed to it."

Lara balled her hands into fists, feeling the first droplets of rain smack against her forehead. Hearing the screech of metal as the portcullis was pulled from the cavern, inch by inch. "He won't be alive to care if we don't do something."

Jaw working back and forth, Ahnna stared at the ship rising and falling on the violent swells. "There might be a way." Grabbing two of her soldiers, Ahnna muttered something at them. The men nodded and retreated into the chaos. Moments later, one of them returned with a familiar weapon in his hands, giving it over to the princess.

"We won't be able to tie it off," Ahnna explained. "Not with the way the ship is bobbing and moving. We'll hold the line, but if the ship moves too far, we'll have to let go or risk being dragged off the cliff. So you'll need to be fast."

Lara turned to eye the drop. The rough seas. The fins cutting through the water. "I'll be fast."

Someone handed Ahnna a slender length of rope tied to the end of a large bolt, the princess cranking the weapon with a practiced hand. Then she paused and met Lara's gaze. "We won't be able to get you back."

Swallowing hard, Lara nodded and accepted a hook from the same soldier. "It's time for me to leave anyway."

Kneeling, Ahnna lifted the weapon, and Aster, along with several other Ithicanians, held the end of the rope, their faces grim. Training it on the bobbing ship, the princess aimed, and, without hesitation, loosed the bolt.

Lara stuck a knife between her teeth, watching as the rope trailed over the gap between cliff and ship, bolt embedding deep into the deck.

The Ithicanians pulled the line taut, then Ahnna shouted, "Now."

Lara didn't hesitate.

Flipping the hook over the rope, she jumped.

Wind and rain lashed against her face as she slid downward, the sea rising up to meet her with threatening speed. The line tightened and slackened as the ship rose and fell on the swells, causing Lara to bounce violently, her shoulders screaming with each jerk, her hands clenching the hook's handle.

On the ship, soldiers were pulling on the bolt, several of them pointing at her. *Not yet,* she silently pleaded, terror racing through her veins. *Only a few more seconds.*

Then one of them gave up on trying to pull the bolt loose. Lifting his blade, he sliced the line.

Lara dropped.

She screamed, then her heels hit the deck, her injured leg giving out. Instinctively she rolled, coming up on her feet, knife in hand.

All around, soldiers and sailors were staring at her in shock, several of them muttering, "It's the goddamned princess. The king's daughter."

"I'd like a word with my father."

The soldiers parted, and her father, the King of Maridrina, strolled down the deck toward her. His silver hair was soaked with rain, his clothing equally sodden, and he had a livid bruise across one cheek. None of which made him any less regal as he stopped a dozen paces away to eye her. "Lara, darling. How good of you to join us."

"I'm not here for conversation," she retorted. "You need to set sail. That storm's going to rip this fleet apart, and thousands of your soldiers will drown."

Someone yelled, "The gate's coming loose! Get ready to attack."

Her father lifted one eyebrow. "It seems I'll have my victory *before* the storm arrives."

Lara risked a glance toward the cavern, but the chain was still taut, the gate still holding.

"Why are you doing this?" she demanded. "What do you have to gain? Taking Eranahl and slaughtering innocents won't change the fact that the bridge will never be yours. Even if you kill every last Ithicanian, Harendell and Valcotta will never let you have control. You've *lost*."

Her father laughed. "Harendell is soon to be too occupied with their own troubles to wage war with us, and as for Valcotta . . . Let's just say your brother has finally proven his worth." He smiled, and it was all teeth. "Ithicana has lost, and so, Daughter, have you."

He turned away, gesturing to his soldiers. "Kill her."

"I challenge you. Here and now. You choose the weapon."

Her father froze, then he looked her up and down. "You're hardly fit for a duel, Lara. From where I stand, you've already almost bled to death. It would be no fight."

"Then you have no reason to fear accepting."

He snorted. "I'm not in the practice of fighting women."

"Just murdering them." A wave of dizziness passed over her, but Lara shoved it away. "Like you murdered my mother. Like you tried to murder my sisters. Like you'll do to me." She laughed. "Or, like you'll have your soldiers do to me, because apparently you haven't the balls to do it yourself."

The soldiers all shifted, interest chasing away their fear of the coming storm. If her father didn't accept, he'd be labeled a coward, and a mutiny would follow suit. And if he did and lost . . .

Her father saw the way they were looking at him. Knew that if he didn't fight her, he was done.

"As you like." He unsheathed his sword. "Have it your way. Maybe if you're lucky, you'll live long enough to watch your kingdom fall."

Lara pulled her sword free from its scabbard, then gestured with her knife for him to step forward. "Enough chatter, old man. Let's do this."

The soldiers pulled back to make space, and Lara held her ground as she watched her father circle.

Her words were bluster, and both of them knew it. He was a skilled swordsman, with years of experience, and while Lara was likely a match for him in skill, her body was failing her. The stitches on her thigh had completely torn open, blood running down to pool in her boot, her leg barely holding her weight. Dizziness and exhaustion rolled over her in waves, and even keeping her balance on the rocking deck was pushing Lara to her limits.

But she had to keep going. For the sake of everyone in Eranahl, she had to keep fighting.

He lunged, lightning flashing off his blade, but Lara anticipated the attack. She parried, her arm shuddering from the impact as he attacked again and again, driving her backward across the deck, attempting to wear her down.

"There's no sport in this," her father snapped, then spun away as she counter-attacked, her motion slow and sluggish.

"Then finish it."

His foot snaked out, hooking her ankle. Lara leaned back on her injured leg, crying out as it buckled beneath her.

Desperate, she rolled, pulling her sword up in time to block a downstroke that would have sliced her in two.

Their weapons locked, her father leaning his weight downward before recoiling as she swiped at him with a knife, her boot heel grazing his knee and causing him to stumble.

Crawling to her feet, Lara pressed the attack, slicing and stabbing and searching for an opening. The ship pitched sideways, both of them falling, sailors scrambling for handholds until the ship righted herself.

"It's loose! It's loose!"

It felt like a fist closed around Lara's heart as her father's face filled with triumph. "Attack!"

But his soldiers hesitated, weighing the chances of survival between trying to capture the cavern or staying aboard the ship.

"We need to set sail, Your Grace!" the captain shouted from where he clung to a rail. "The storm is going to tear us apart. We need to leave now!"

"No!" Her father dodged as Lara regained her feet and swung at his neck. "Any man who flees will be labeled a coward. A traitor! Any man who leaves will find his head spiked on Vencia's gates!"

But from the corner of her eye, Lara could see ships were retreating. Raising their sails and flying ahead of the storm that was about to descend with wicked vengeance. Yet that didn't mean Eranahl was safe. Not when the hundreds of men in longboats would now be fighting their way into the cavern, knowing that her father would never allow them to retreat to the ship.

She needed to give them another option, and she needed to give it to them now.

There had never been a chance of her surviving this anyway.

Catching her balance against the railing, Lara attacked, raining blow after blow upon her father.

She pretended to stumble. Saw the triumph in his eyes as his sword sliced along her ribs.

And the shock that blossomed on his face as she sank her knife into his chest.

The ship rocked, and they fell away from each other. Lara landed hard on her back while her father sank to his knees, fingers tugging futilely at the hilt of her knife.

"You are a traitor," he hissed. "To your family. And to your people."

"No, Father," she whispered. "That's what they'll say about you."

He glared at her with inhuman fury, then the light faded from his azure eyes, and he slumped to the deck.

Her father was dead.

Lara stared at the corpse of the man who'd made her what she was, barely noticing as the soldiers called for retreat, the longboats coming alongside only to be abandoned as men climbed up ladders and ropes, the deck around her filling with them.

"Full sail!" the captain ordered. "Anyone not aboard gets left behind!"

Sailors ran to obey, but as sails caught the wind, the ship shuddered and jerked. The masts groaned, and the sharp shriek of metal against rock filled Lara's ears.

"Cut the ropes, you idiots!" the captain screamed. "Cut us loose."

Whether anyone complied, Lara couldn't have said, because members of her father's cadre were approaching, murder in their eyes.

Fighting back pain, Lara climbed to her feet, blood gushing down her side to soak her shirt with each breath she took. Leaning against the rail, she stared them down, these men who'd supported and protected her father through all his villainy. If she'd had the strength, she'd have killed them all.

They lifted their weapons.

Lara leaned backward.

She somersaulted over the railing, plunging downward. Icy water closed over her head and she struggled upward, kicking hard.

Her head broke the surface only for a wave to wash over it. Choking and gasping for breath, Lara caught hold of some debris, clinging to it as she rose and fell on the violent swells.

The shipbreaker made a resounding crack, a rock crashing into a longboat. Then another into the wake of the ship. Then another into another longboat. Then it went silent.

Because the battle was over.

Everywhere Lara looked, ships were flying across the whitecaps, sails full with wind as they tried to outrun the storm that had fallen upon them with wicked fury. There were still sailors in the water, men screaming for the ships to turn back, for their comrades to save them, but one by one they were jerked down.

And around Lara, fins circled.

Her breath came in panicked little gasps as the sharks moved closer, a sob tearing from her throat as something thudded against her ankle.

"Swim, Lara! Swim!"

The sound of her name pulled her eyes from the fins to the Ithicanians standing on the cliffs above, the wind tearing at their clothes. Dozens of them. Hundreds of them. And Ahnna and Taryn were shouting at her, gesturing to the cavern below. "Swim!"

There was no chance that she'd make it. No chance that one of the sharks wouldn't take her down or that she wouldn't bleed to death.

But Lara started kicking.

Clinging to the wooden debris, she churned her legs, ignoring the pain and keeping her eyes fixed on the cavern opening. The screams of the abandoned soldiers fought with the storm for supremacy, lightning bolts crisscrossing the sky in violent succession. Fins circled her, enormous sleek shapes darting in only to veer away at the last minute.

They came closer, tails knocking into her legs as they thrashed away, and each time she waited for teeth to slice into her flesh. Waited to be pulled down and torn apart or drowned.

But she kept swimming.

Waves exploded against the cliffs, but the screaming had ceased, Lara the last person alive in the sea. Her arms trembled with the effort of holding onto the debris, her legs hanging uselessly as the waves flung her into the mouth of the cavern.

All around her was blackness filled with a deafening roar of wind and sea, and Lara felt herself falter. Losing her grip, she went under, only to struggle upward long enough to gasp for breath.

Keep fighting, she ordered herself. *You will not give up. You are too close to give up.*

Ahead, she caught sight of the faint glow of light, then the sea surged again, and Lara screamed as she was thrown into a web of twisted metal.

AREN

I T WAS HARD to see.

But he didn't need to see to know that the enemy was clambering over the gap between the top of the twisted portcullis and the cavern ceiling. He could hear their muttered voices. The grunts of effort. The splash when they landed on the other side and began to swim.

Only to find Ithicana waiting.

Aren slashed at any sign of movement, his arms numb from exhaustion, his motions weak and clumsy.

But he didn't stop. Couldn't stop when they kept coming, the water thick with bodies and swimming men. They swamped the boats, hands reaching up to grab at his clothing, pulling him overboard and down into the depths.

Part of him wondered if he was already dead, if this was some form of hell.

A slice of pain across his forearm snapped him back into the moment, and Aren fought to the surface of the water, bodies bumping into him on all sides.

"Retreat! Retreat!"

"No!" Aren choked out the word. "We will not retreat! I will not retreat!"

And then he realized the voices shouting the words were Maridrinian. He felt the *shift* as the enemy tried to pull back. Tried to climb through that small gap above the twisted steel.

Torchlight flared behind him, flickering off the water and illuminating the sea of corpses and men.

"Got you!" Hands hauled him back into a boat, Jor's face appearing above him. "They're retreating. Looks like the storm chased them off."

"I heard." Aren closed his eyes, trying to catch his breath.

Then a deafening screech filled the air, and he jerked upright, watching as the portcullis was dragged a dozen feet forward only to catch where the tunnel narrowed. Then the chains slackened and slipped into the sea.

There was no longer a way into Eranahl.

Which also meant there was no longer a way out, and dozens of enemy soldiers still swam on this side of the twisted metal gate. They pressed against the portcullis, fighting to pull it free, but to no avail. And almost as one, they turned to face Aren and the rest of his soldiers.

Instinct demanded he cut them down. Demanded he kill these men who'd been intent on slaughtering his people and destroying his home.

But in their eyes gleamed fear and desperation. "Care to surrender?"

There were swift nods of assent, and Aren inclined his head once in acknowledgment. "Drop your weapons, then come one by one. You cause trouble, you get your throat slit. Understood?"

More nods, and Aren said to his soldiers, "Tie them up. We'll deal with them later."

Boats approached from the underground harbor, voices shouting the news that the fleet had abandoned the attack, that the enemy soldiers still on the island were surrendering, and what were Aren's orders for how they should be dealt with?

"Accept their surrender. We've had enough bloodshed today to last Ithicana a lifetime. We'll keep them prisoner until Maridrina has fully withdrawn from Ithicana, and then I'll—" He broke off, uncertain of exactly what he'd do with these men. The last time he'd allowed an outsider into Eranahl, it had not gone well for him.

But Ithicana had to change. He had to change. "I'll negotiate their return to Maridrina."

"Yes, Your Grace."

The soldiers swam forward one by one, his people taking them into boats and binding them before retreating into the harbor. Aren climbed a ledge on the cave wall, resting his knees on his elbows. Breathing. Just breathing.

"Aren!"

He turned at the sound of Lia's voice, and through the dim light, he saw the boat carrying his bodyguard fighting its way closer against the force of the surging sea.

"You need to open the portcullis!"

Glancing at the twisted metal wedged in the cave, he gave a shake of his head. "That's impossible. We're going to have to cut it out."

"Then cut it!" Her voice was shrill. Desperate.

"Why?"

The boat reached him, and Lia leapt onto the ledge next to him, her arm wrapped with a bandage. "Because Lara's out there."

His skin turned to ice. "That's impossible. We left her on Gamire without even a boat."

"Well, she found a way." Lia held out a torch, illuminating the water surging into the cave, then retreating with equally violent force. "She challenged her father. Killed him. It's why they retreated when they did. She saved us, and now we need to save her."

The sea and storm reduced to a dull noise, and the torch light was suddenly too bright. "Get the tools to cut the metal!"

One of the soldiers holding a paddle said, "But Your Grace, the storm is almost upon us! We need to get out of the tunnel before the surge becomes even worse!"

"Get the goddamned tools!" Aren screamed the words in the man's face. "If we get it down fast, we might be able to catch the ship." And do what once he'd caught it, he didn't know. All that mattered was that he do everything he could to save her.

Lia gripped his arm, her fingers digging into his skin. "Lara's not on the ship, Aren. She's in the water."

As she said the words the sea surged, froth and water storming through the cave, carrying with it a slender form.

"Lara," he screamed, right before her body slammed against the steel of the portcullis.

THIS IS WHAT it feels like to die.

Pain shattered through her body as the sea slammed her against steel, then pulled her back, only to throw her forward again.

This is it. My battle is over.

Darkness filled her vision, then she felt a hand close around hers, fighting the sea as it tried to draw her back. Her shoulder screamed as she was pulled upward, then her face broke the surface, and Lara gasped in a breath of air.

Only to have the water close over her head again, pummeling her body.

But that one breath was enough.

Whoever it was gripping her arms helped her climb, the barnacle-crusted steel cutting into her feet as she eased upward. The waves were no longer washing over her head. Coughing and sucking in air, she opened her eyes.

And found herself face-to-face with Aren.

"I've got you." He tugged her higher until their heads were just beneath the ceiling of the cave. "I won't let you go."

Vaguely she was aware that there were others behind him, but all she saw was him. And all she felt was the most profound sense of gratitude to God or fate or luck for allowing her to see him one last time before the Tempest Seas took her.

"You need to hold on!" As he spoke, the water surged again, only Aren's strength keeping it from pulling her from her perch. "They're getting tools. We'll cut the bars. You just need to hold on until then."

She nodded, but it was a lie. Because there was no hope of her surviving this. With every surge, the water went higher, and once the storm hit with all its ferocity, not even Aren would be able to keep it from taking her. And it would be a miracle if he wasn't drowned himself.

"You need to let me go." She was so exhausted. So tired of fighting. "You need to get somewhere safe."

"No! I'm not leaving you." He slid an arm through the bars, wrapping it around her waist. She flinched as fingers pressed against the wound on her side, saw the way his face tightened as he realized how deep it was. Turning his head, he shouted, "Where the hell are those tools?"

But Lara knew they'd never make it in time.

Reaching through the bars, she caught hold of his face. "Look at me. Listen to me."

He resisted. Like he knew what she was going to say. But then he met her gaze.

"I'm sorry." A wave hammered her in the back, forcing her to pause while she fought the current. "I'm so sorry for all the hurt that I caused you. All the hurt I caused Ithicana. And I need you to know that I'd die a thousand times over if there were a way to undo it."

"Lara—"

She shook her head violently, because she didn't want his forgiveness. She didn't deserve it. "My father is dead. He's dead, and he can't hurt you or Ithicana anymore. Keris will be king, and there will be a chance for Maridrina and Ithicana to be allies in truth. For the first time, Ithicana has a chance at a better future. But it needs *you* to make it happen. Don't sacrifice that for me."

"But I need you." He pulled her tight against the metal, his forehead pressing against hers through the bars. "I love you, and I've never stopped. Not once, not even when I should have."

He kissed her then, his mouth hot against her chilled skin, his tongue tasting of the sea. And she leaned into him, the tears running down her face washed away as the waves hammered them.

"Since the day we met, there has never been anyone but you. And there never will be anyone but you. You are my queen, and I need you."

She wept. Even if she made it through this, there was no future for them. Not with Aren as king. And she refused to make him choose between her and Ithicana. "Aren—"

"I'm not letting you die." His eyes were searching the ceiling of the cave, and she watched as he let go of her long enough to brace his feet against the wall, muscles straining as he tried to heave the portcullis backward.

But it was stuck, wedged into place by the strength of a ship and sails.

Giving up, he pressed close to her again. "Do not let go. Promise me you won't let go."

He stared into her eyes until she nodded, wrapping her arms through the bars and holding tight as the water surged.

And Aren dived down into its depths.

She couldn't see him through the foam and the darkness, and fear overwhelmed the haze of blood loss and pain when he didn't emerge. "No. No. No," she sobbed. "You don't get to have him."

The Ithicanians in the boats tried to move closer, but the waves kept pushing them back. Farther and farther until the only one who remained was Lia, perched on a narrow ledge. The other woman started to set down her torch, clearly meaning to dive in.

Then Aren broke the surface.

He caught hold of the metal, climbing swiftly until he was face-to-face with Lara, blood running down his cheek from a cut on his brow.

"There's a space at the bottom," he said between gasps. "It's too small for me to fit through, but your shoulders are narrow. I'll be able to pull you through, you just need to hold your breath."

But to reach it she'd have to go down.

Down into the darkness and the depths of the water, and a familiar terror rose in her chest, tearing through her veins. "I can't."

"You can." He kissed her hard. "I've never once seen fear make a decision for you."

Lara shook her head. This was too much.

"I need you." His breath was hot against her lips. "And I need you to keep fighting."

Closing her eyes, Lara struggled against her terror of the water—the terror that had haunted her steps from the moment she'd stepped foot in Ithicana. *You are a princess,* she told herself. *A queen.*

But above all, she was the little cockroach.

Lara nodded once, sucking in a deep breath.

And then Aren pulled her down beneath the surface.

She could not see. Had no sense of up or down as the ocean ripped at her body, only Aren's grip on her keeping the water from tearing her out to sea.

Deeper. She knew he must be taking her deeper, because the pressure in her ears grew, and it took all of her strength to catch hold of the bars and drag herself down when instinct demanded she go *up*. Back to the surface and to air.

Down and down.

Panic raced through her veins, the need to breathe growing with each passing second, the only thing keeping her sane the knowledge that Aren was with her. That to save him, she needed to save herself.

Then her hands hit rock.

They were at the bottom of the cave.

Holding tight to her wrists, Aren pulled her sideways, and she felt the opening where the bars had been forced apart.

But the gap was small. So terribly small.

Her chest spasmed with the need to take a breath, but she didn't fight as he tugged on her arms, twisting her shoulders until she slid through.

Only to feel her belt snag.

Aren pulled, his feet braced against the bottom, but it wouldn't give. Desperately, Lara tore her hand from his grip, trying to reach between her body and the rocky floor to unfasten the buckle, but there was no space.

And she needed to breathe.

Needed to breathe.

Needed to breathe.

Lara inhaled.

BUBBLES RUSHED PAST him and Lara's arm went limp in his grasp. *No!* A silent scream tore through his head, and Aren pulled himself toward her, feeling in the darkness where she'd been caught by the steel.

Her belt.

His chest ached with the need to breathe, a lifetime spent in the water only buying him a few more moments.

After fumbling for his knife, he sawed on the leather until it split. Dropping the knife, he caught hold of Lara's arms and heaved with all the strength he possessed.

She slipped through the opening.

Holding her tight, he swam upward, the surging water pushing them farther into the cave as he rose, kicking hard.

I'm not going to let you die.

He broke the surface and sucked in a gasp, waves slamming him against the rocky walls, but then they pulled him back. Back toward the portcullis. And he needed to get her out of the water. Needed to save her.

Arms jerked him upward, and Aren landed on his back in the boat, Lara's limp body on top of him.

"Lara!" He rolled her, pushing people out of his way.

The torchlight illuminated her face, her eyes open and unseeing. Gone.

"No!" he screamed, slamming his hands down against her chest. Over and over.

"Get a healer!" someone shouted, but it didn't matter, because Lara was gone. His wife, his queen, was gone.

"Aren, enough." Jor tried to pull him back, but Aren shoved him away, hands back on Lara's chest. Willing her to breathe.

"Aren, she's not coming back. You need to let her go."

"No!"

The boat hit the foot of the harbor's rocky steps, and Aren scooped Lara into his arms, carrying her up the steps at a run to set her on the landing where he resumed compressions on her chest, his arms shaking with the effort.

"I love you." He could feel his people gathering around, feel the rain pouring from above. "I need you. Please come back."

She seemed so small. So unlike the indomitable warrior he knew her to be.

"Lara!" He screamed her name. "Fight!"

65
LARA

IT WAS A slow climb out of the murky darkness. The longest climb she'd ever made. Through blackness and sadness and terror, chased by all the villains who had haunted her life, none the least the villain inside herself. Grasping and reaching and struggling. But then she heard his voice. Her name. Heard the only command he'd ever given her.

Lara opened her eyes.

THE FIRST THING she noticed was the scent of Ithicana in the air. Of sea and storm and jungle.

The second was pain.

Wincing, she pried open her eyelids, the brightness causing her to blink back tears. She was in the bedroom she and Aren once shared in Eranahl, the water filling the bathing pool making a soft tinkling sound, the jars of glowing algae casting soft shadows on the wall.

And Aren, his head resting on one arm, was sleeping in the chair next to the bed.

Lara ran her gaze over his face, noticing the shadows beneath his eyes and the stitches holding together a wound on his temple. His knuckles were scraped and scabbed, his bare forearm marked with purple bruises. But he was alive.

And so was she.

Shifting, Lara failed to stifle a groan as pain lanced through her, and Aren jerked upright. "You're awake."

"How long was I asleep?" Her tongue felt as dry as sand, and she eagerly accepted the cup of water he held to her lips, not caring as it spilled down her chin while she drank.

"Three days." He set the cup aside, leaning over her, his eyes searching. "They tell me it's a bloody miracle you're alive given your injuries and—" He broke off, his face tightening.

"And the fact that I drowned?"

"Yes." His hazel eyes gleamed with unspent tears as they met hers. "You were dead. Dead in my arms, and I . . . I . . ." He rubbed a hand across his face, shaking his head.

"I heard you call my name," she whispered. "I heard you order me to fight."

"First damned time you ever listened."

She smiled, but sadness swelled in her chest. "Don't get used to it."

All of it was hazy. The battle. The moments in the tunnel with the portcullis between them. But she remembered. Remembered him telling her that he loved her. That he needed her. That he wouldn't let her go.

But those had been words spoken in the heat of the moment, when they'd both thought death was upon them. When anything seemed possible as long as they survived.

Now they both had to face reality.

She was the traitor queen. The reason Ithicana had lost the bridge. The reason hundreds, if not thousands, of Ithicanians had perished. That she'd been integral to their liberation meant little—some things were unforgivable.

"Is the war over?" she asked. "Do you have the bridge?"

Aren nodded. "The storm only lasted half a day, but it drove off both the Amaridian and Maridrinian fleets. With your father dead, they appear to have chosen to return to their respective ports. The soldiers remaining on our shores have been for the most part surrendering, and we'll allow them to depart at Southwatch. We'll do the same for the prisoners here once we're able to transport them."

"Aren't you concerned?" she asked, feeling trepidation bite at her core. "You're handing Maridrina back its army before you've fully regained control."

"Despite his betrayal, Keris is not your father. And we both know his mind is all for the conflict with Valcotta. And for Zarrah. With the calm over, the storms will do their duty and keep Ithicana safe while we get our feet beneath us. Already the people are clamoring to get home. To rebuild. Once we're sure the islands are clear, we'll start moving them back."

Lara's chest tightened, but she might as well get it over with. "As soon as I'm well enough to walk, I'll leave." Although where she'd go, she wasn't certain. First to find Sarhina. And then . . .

Her future was open and limitless, but it only felt empty.

Aren was silent for a moment. "If that's your decision, I won't stop you."

"Decision implies a choice, Aren. And in this there is no choice. I'm not wanted here."

He hesitated, his Adam's apple moving as he swallowed once. Twice. "I want you here, if you're willing to stay. If you *want* to stay."

Closing her eyes, Lara took a deep breath, wincing against the ache in her ribs.

It would've been easier if he'd told her to go. But now she'd have to do it knowing he still cared. She'd have to leave knowing that there was still a chance for them, if she was selfish enough to take it. "Ithicana needs you, Aren. It needs its king."

"And its queen." Leaning back in his chair, he pulled something from his pocket, and she recognized it as his mother's necklace. Gold and emeralds and black diamonds mapping Ithicana. She'd left it here for safekeeping, never expecting to wear it again. "Do you know how we try traitors in Ithicana?" he asked, interrupting her thoughts.

"You feed them to the sharks."

A faint smile grew on his face. "There's more to it than that. We suspend the accused traitor in the sea, then chum the waters.

If the sharks kill the person, it means the charges were deserved, as was the punishment. But if the sharks leave the person be, that means the person isn't a traitor—that they are true to Ithicana." His gaze sharpened, focusing on her. "I've never seen the sharks do anything but feast. Never heard of it. Until now."

Lara's heart skipped.

"Ahnna saw. Taryn saw. Aster, God bless his superstitious soul, saw you jump off that ship and then swim, bleeding and thrashing, through shark-infested waters, and not one of them touched you."

"Luck," she breathed, but Aren shook his head.

"There were hundreds of them. And Ahnna said the biggest swam right up next to you, looked, then swam away. Over and over again. They killed every single soldier in the water, but not *you.* And *no one* is calling you the traitor queen any longer."

A hot tear trickled down Lara's face, because she *was* true to Ithicana. She loved this kingdom and she loved its people, but . . . "It will take more than myths and legends for the people to grant me their forgiveness, Aren."

"True. But those myths and legends mean they'll give you the opportunity to *earn* their forgiveness. If you're willing to try."

She was crying now, gasping sobs of relief. That was what she wanted more than anything else. The opportunity to atone. The opportunity to be better. The opportunity to love.

"Will you stay?"

"Yes." She smiled as he helped her sit, and she wrapped her arms around his neck. Breathing him in. "I'll stay."

There was a knock at the door then, and Ahnna came in. The Princess of Ithicana's eyes were cool, but she inclined her head respectfully to both of them. "Everyone is assembled, Your Grace. They're waiting to hear you speak."

Aren rose. "I'm going to tell them my plans. You stay here.

Rest. I'll be back."

But Lara shook her head. Biting down on the pain, she rose to her feet, accepting Aren's arm for balance. Taking the clothing Ahnna passed to her, she carefully pulled it on, feeling the strain of stitched wounds and the ache of cracked ribs, and yet she'd never felt stronger. Never felt more alive.

Aren shook his head. "You don't need to prove anything to me, Lara. I know better than anyone how strong you are."

Buckling her belt, she looked up at him. "I swore to fight by your side, to defend you to my dying breath, to cherish your body and none other, and to be loyal to you as long as I live." Picking up her knives, she slid them into their sheaths with twin *thunks*. "And that means where you go, I go, too."

His eyes were full of heat. Of desire for her. Of respect for her. "As you say, Your Grace." Offering his arm, Aren bent low, his breath warm against her ear. "There's no one in the world like you, you know."

"No, there isn't." Lara squared her shoulders as the doors to the balcony were flung wide open, revealing a crowd of their people waiting below. "Because there is only one Queen of Ithicana. Just as there is only one King. And if any of our enemies dare come for our kingdom, we will bring them to their knees."

The story continues in book three of
The Bridge Kingdom Series

On the war torn streets of Nerastis, General Zarrah Anaphora finds common ground—and fiery passion—with a stranger, unaware that he is the heir to the crown of her country's mortal enemy.

Add book 3 to your Goodreads reading list today!

https://www.goodreads.com/book/show/52131393-untitled

Want to make sure you never miss a giveaway, cover reveal, or release day?

Sign up for Danielle L. Jensen's mailing list on her website:

https://danielleljensen.com/

While waiting for the next book in The Bridge Kingdom Series, enjoy Danielle L. Jensen's other work...

Start reading book one now: https://danielleljensen.com/dark-shores/

"Richly-woven, evocative, and absolutely impossible to put down—I was hooked from the first lines! *Dark Shores* has everything I look for in a fantasy novel: fresh, unique settings, a cast of complex and diverse characters, and an unflinching boldness with the nuanced world-building. I loved every word."—Sarah J. Maas, #1 *New York Times* bestselling author

"The book grabs readers from the beginning with its stellar worldbuilding and multidimensional characters, and the mythical elements are truly believable within the constructs of the story. The perspective shifts between the viewpoints of Teriana and Marcus from chapter to chapter, offering readers greater insights into each. ...A gripping introduction to a new series."—*Kirkus Reviews* (starred)

"The plot's twists and turns and fantastical elements add to the allure of this thrilling story. VERDICT Exhilarating fantasy-adventure romance for fans of Tricia Levenseller's *Daughter of the Pirate King*, Alexandra Christo's *To Kill a Kingdom*, or Natalie C. Parker's *Seafire*. Readers will eagerly await the next book in the series."—*School Library Journal*

"This is a lush, imaginative world, and as the focus shifts between Teriana and Marcus, it becomes clear that the readers are only getting a glimpse of its complicated history and mythology. ...Their secrets don't, of course, stop Teriana and Marcus from embarking on a steamy romance, and fans of Rutkoski's sighworthy *The Winner's Kiss* and the high-stakes sea adventure of Levenseller's *Daughter of the Pirate King* will want to know where Marcus and Teriana journey to next." —*Bulletin of the Center for Children's Books*

Enjoy Lara and Aren's story?
Fans of The Bridge Kingdom Series also enjoy...

THE MALEDICTION NOVELS

About book one, STOLEN SONGBIRD...

A USA Today bestseller and finalist in the 2014 Goodreads Choice Awards for Best Debut Author.

For five centuries, a witch's curse has bound the trolls to their city beneath the mountain. When Cécile de Troyes is kidnapped and taken beneath the mountain, she realises that the trolls are relying on her to break the curse.

Cécile has only one thing on her mind: escape. But the trolls are clever, fast, and inhumanly strong. She will have to bide her time...

But the more time she spends with the trolls, the more she understands their plight. There is a rebellion brewing. And she just might be the one the trolls were looking for...

Get book one: https://danielleljensen.com/books-2/stolen-songbird/

ABOUT THE AUTHOR

Danielle L. Jensen is the *USA Today* bestselling author of The Malediction Novels: *Stolen Songbird*, *Hidden Huntress*, *Warrior Witch*, and *The Broken Ones*, as well as the Dark Shores Series. She lives with her family in Calgary, Alberta.

Follow her on the web at:

https://danielleljensen.com/
Twitter: https://twitter.com/dljensen_
Facebook: https://www.facebook.com/authordanielleljensen/
Instagram: https://www.instagram.com/danielleljensen/

CPSIA information can be obtained
at www.ICGtesting.com
Printed in the USA
LVHW030114280621
691300LV00003B/18

9 781733 090360